PRAISE FOR
THE CALENDAR GIRL SERIES

"This book, and Mia's encounters, are hot enough to make your panties damp, make you squirm, and make you want to climb men like trees."
~ Give Me Books

"The author does a fantastic job of making each month and each man totally different and unique. Loving this series."
~ Harps Romance Book Review Blog

"Audrey Carlan takes you on a journey of self-discovery that is as riveting as it is hot!"
~ The Book Reading Gals

CALENDAR GIRL
VOLUME TWO

AUDREY CARLAN

WATERHOUSE
PRESS

DEDICATIONS

April

Anita Scott Shofner

Mia's journey in Boston is for you my sweet.
Like Mia, you recently started over.
I'm proud of you…for choosing you.
I think every person in this world
needs to choose themselves once and awhile.
Not only for being an incredible beta, which you are,
but also for being a lovely and supportive friend.
I cannot begin to thank you,
Namaste my friend.

May

Kris Ward

You cheer, you root, you love.
Everything about you is angelic.
Those around you crave that beautiful sense of self.
You remind me of my mother who has passed.
So Mama Kris, Mia's journey to Hawaii is for you.
May the sun always shine bright over you.
May the gift of true friendship stay yours always.
May the joy you give, come back to you tenfold.
May love surround you and complete your soul.
With love always.

June

Lisa Colgrove Roth

June is dedicated to you angel, because it's an
instrumental part of Mia's journey,
the same way you are in mine.
When you joined my street team,
I had no idea I'd be receiving such a blessing.
Your endless promotion, support, and friendship
has helped me a million times over.
With love and gratitude for all that you are.

TABLE OF CONTENTS

April

CALENDAR GIRL

WATERHOUSE
PRESS

CHAPTER ONE

"Well, hey there, sweet *thang*," were the first words out of his sexy-assed mouth. Too bad the words, along with the way his eyes traced over me, sent my temperature rising...and not in a good way. Mason Murphy leaned against a limo. He had aviator sunglasses, coppery brown hair, and a smirk that probably melted the panties of all his baseball fans. Fortunately for me, I'd been around several hotter-than-hot men the last few months and wasn't impressed.

I held out my hand.

He pursed his lips and pushed his glasses on top of his head, gracing me with stunning green eyes. They were as dark as emeralds and just as pretty. "What, no kiss?"

I narrowed my eyes, cocked a hip, and crossed my arms over one another. "Seriously? You're going with that?"

His head shot back, pulled his glasses off his head, and dangled the end of one side in his mouth. Again, he looked me up and down. "Feisty. I like a girl that's a bit of a challenge."

I closed my eyes and blinked several times to see if I was still asleep from the Benadryl I'd taken on the plane. Flying always made me jittery. Nothing like what I was feeling right now, though. "You're a real piece of work, aren't you?"

His eyes opened wide, and a huge grin slipped across his distractingly well-sculpted face. High cheekbones, a little dent at the chin, and those sparkling eyes looked wicked.

He moved close to me, hung an arm around my neck, and

kissed my temple. It took everything I had not to turn and plant one on him—a punch to the face, that is.

"You're going to remove your arm from me and back away. Have you no manners?"

Mason planted his feet in front of me and leaned close, as if to whisper. "I know what you are, and I'm totally okay with it. Very, *very* okay with it. We're going to have some fun together."

I pushed his chest enough to get him out of my face. "Look, Mr. Murphy..."

"Mr. Murphy," he said mockingly. "Ooh, I like that."

Sucking in a breath, I clenched down on my teeth. If I bit my tongue, I might have bitten it straight in half with how much this guy irritated me. "What I was trying to say before you interrupted me was that you've got the wrong idea about me. I'm an escort. Meaning, I escort you to things. Provide you with companionship in a friendly manner."

Again he got close, grabbed my hips, and slammed them against his. "I can't wait to get more *friendly* with you." He rubbed his pelvis against mine. I could just barely feel the outline of something coming to life.

I sighed. Letting it go, I pushed him away again. "Just take my bags."

He whistled at the driver. Yes, whistled at him. Like a fucking dog. He may as well have said, "Come here, boy. Good driver."

I cringed and removed myself from his grasp.

"Don't worry, baby. You'll get into the swing of things." He mock swung a baseball bat. I, on the other hand, rolled my eyes and opened the limo door, crawling in. He maneuvered his long body into the spacious vehicle and clapped his hands. "Want a drink?"

I'm pretty sure I looked at him as if he'd grown a tail. "It's not even noon."

He shrugged. "It is somewhere in the world," he said with a saucy wink.

Mason pulled out a bottle of champagne. His tongue came out and wet his full bottom lip. The space between my legs took notice instantly, twingeing delightfully. I shook my head and crossed my legs. He was a bastard, yet I couldn't help but notice that he was a good-looking one. Mason Murphy was tall, probably six feet or so, had a body that could grace magazines—and did, often. The muscles in his biceps bulged delectably, and his quads flexed as he shoved the bottle between his legs and twisted the top off with a plop. No foam. Pretty good, I'd give him that.

"Now, sweetness, let's get a couple things straight."

I opened my eyes wide, my eyebrows going straight into my hairline. He handed me a glass of champagne. Even though it was barely ten in the morning, I took the glass, figuring I'd need something to take the edge off my annoyance.

"You were sent here to be my girlfriend. That means, in order to have my fans, prospective sponsors, and the media at large believe it, you and I are going to have to get *friendly*, very quickly. And looking at you..." He licked his lips again as his eyes traced my form, from my booted feet up my jean-clad legs and stopped directly at my bosom. Pig. "I'm going to enjoy every fucking second of it."

This guy was going to be challenging. He was...smug, sexy as hell, irritating, sexy as hell, downright crass, sexy as hell, and immature. Did I forget anything? Oh yeah, sexy as hell.

He leaned back, displaying his body for me against the opposite seat. He smirked and downed the champagne in one go. I wasn't about to let this schmuck best me, so I lifted the glass to my lips and swallowed the entire lot back. His eyebrows lifted, and his eyes sparkled in appreciation.

"Woman after my own heart." He clutched at his chest in mock chivalry.

I leaned over, grabbed the bottle, filled my glass, and then gestured with a chin lift for his. He presented it, and I filled it too.

"Okay, look, we need to firm up a few things."

His face made a gesture that indicated that he was about to crack a joke, but I cut his words with a pair of green daggers in his direction. He leaned back and lifted his chin. I smiled, knowing I'd won that round. "I may have been hired to be your girlfriend for the month, but I'm not your whore." His eyebrows drew together. "Having sex with a client is optional on my part and not part of my contract. You should have read the fine print, buddy, because you're about to find out what a month of celibacy looks like."

His mouth dropped open, shock the prevailing response. "You're fucking kidding?" He smirked.

I shook my head. "'Fraid not. So you might want to get used to that there hand, because you're going to be using it a lot. If the press sees you outside, trolling along with any harlot you can get to give you a second glance, they'll know this—" I pointed a finger between the two of us "—is a sham, and the effort and the hundred thousand you've paid me will be wasted."

Mason ruffled a hand through his hair.

"It also wouldn't look so good to your prospective sponsors that you can't even hold on to your pretty new girlfriend for longer than a day. Remember, my fee is non-refundable."

At that point, I leaned back, crossed my legs over one another, and sipped my champagne, letting the bitter bubbles dance along my tongue, awakening my senses once more.

Mason looked at me, an unidentifiable expression on his handsome face. "Then what do you propose we do, sweetness?" He grinned, his eyes glancing along my legs and up over my chest to finally land on my face. The words were nice but lacked sincerity.

"First, you stop calling me sweetness."

He jumped in before I could continue. "Shouldn't a man have a nickname for his girl?"

I pinched my lips together to think about it. I supposed he was right. "Perhaps, if the way you said it didn't sound so douchey."

Mason tipped his head back and laughed. The sound reverberated through the car and lightened the mood. If I could hear that laugh every day, maybe this month wouldn't suck. He licked his lips, and again, that sensitive space between my thighs that still hadn't forgotten how good it was to have a man's perfect pout all over the tender flesh, thrummed in response. Down, girl! I wanted to chastise my libido. Ever since my fuck-fest with Wes two weeks ago, I've been needy, horny as hell, with no hope for relief. And now that my current client is definitely off the list of prospective bedmates, it looked like I'd be attempting celibacy right alongside him. Fun... *Not.*

"Look, I guess it's fine. I think the next step would be to learn a little more about one another. Tell me about yourself?"

He curled a hand around one of his big, jean-clad knees and looked out the window. "Not much to tell. Came from an Irish family. Dad works as a garbage man, even though I told him he could quit working for the rest of his life. He won't. Too proud."

"Sounds like a good man." Unlike my own father. Well, technically that's not true. He tried. Under the circumstances, after handling the blow of my mom leaving, he lost his way. I'm not sure anyone truly knows how to handle losing the love of their life.

Mason smiled, revealing white, mostly straight teeth. His eyetooth crooked in just enough to give his smile character. "My dad's the best, still a hard-ass. Works too hard though. Always did, providing for me and my brothers."

"How many brothers do you have?" I asked, actually finding this line of conversation interesting.

He held up three fingers as he sipped his champagne this time. "My brothers are all crazy bastards, but I love 'em," he said, his Bostonian accent popping to the surface. Sexy fucking accents. Damn, it would be hard to keep my hands off him if he was going to turn nice.

His eyes narrowed on me, the green turning dark. "They'll fuckin' love that I'm shacking up with such a hot piece of ass." And then the douchecanoe comes to life once again.

I shook my head and took a slow, deep breath. "Okay, three brothers. Younger, older?"

"All younger. Brayden is twenty-one, Conner is nineteen, and my baby brother Shaun is seventeen and still in high school."

I leaned forward and set my empty glass into the holder. "Wow, four boys."

Mason nodded. "Yeah, Brayden bartends and goes to community college during the day. Got a chick knocked up right out of high school."

I cringed.

"Bitch left the kid with him and ran off."

My mouth dropped open, and I gasped. How could a woman abandon her own flesh and blood? Then again, Mom did the same thing. Still, hearing it happened to some other child boiled my blood.

"So Bray lives with Dad and his daughter Eleanor."

Eleanor. "That's an old-fashioned name," I offered.

He smiled and looked out the window wistfully. "Yeah, it was after our mom."

"Are your parents separated?"

He shook his head. "Nah, Mom died ten years back. Breast cancer took her young. So it's just been us guys for a long time."

I leaned forward and placed my hand on his knee. "I'm sorry. I shouldn't have pried."

With a flick of his hand, he brushed off the gesture. "It was a long time ago. No matter. Connor is attending Boston U, and Shaun has his hands in teenage snatch all day."

Scowling, I groaned.

"What?"

"Nothing." I left out the part about any grown man referring to a woman's privates as a "snatch" in the company of a female lacked maturity, since that was a losing battle. "So what ads and sponsors are you up for?"

★ ★ ★ ★

When we arrived at his "pad," as he called it, I was surprised to be met by a pretty, waiflike blonde. I was not a small woman, more average for early twenties, but this chick was model thin. Only she looked like Corporate Barbie, all golden-blonde hair pulled back in a twist, sparkling sky-blue eyes, a perfectly pink pout, tall, and rocking a suit that fit her thin frame to perfection. It spoke of money and professionalism, both of which went against the way she looked at Mason.

"Um, Mr. Murphy." The woman pointed a finger up as he brushed past her and into the building. Her lips turned into an instant pout when he passed by her without so much as a glance.

I stopped on the step in front of the woman. When she finally stopped watching Mason's ass as he rummaged around in the entryway, her eyes flashed to mine. I grinned. "Hey, rudeness. The pretty blonde in a suit was trying to get your attention," I called to Mason while keeping my eyes on her. "And you forgot to get my bags." I shook my head and mumbled asshole under my breath.

"Excuse me?" She dipped her ear toward me.

I shook my head and held out my hand. "Mia Saunders. I'm Mason's girlfriend."

The blonde woman closed her eyes and took a breath, seeming to steal herself against something. "I know who you are, Mia. We suggested he hire you. I'm Rachel Denton, his public-relations representative. I've been assigned to work with the two of you on fooling the public. Usually, his publicist would work with him, but I offered to help." She bit her lip and looked away.

"Well, then, we'll get through this together, I assume. He's a real a character." I smiled just as Mason showed up at the door.

"Get lost, hot stuff?" His eyes were laughing, but his words grated.

I rolled my eyes and grabbed Rachel's shoulder and brought her to my side.

Mason seemed to notice her for the first time, and when I say notice her, I mean he looked her up and down...twice. "Rachel, what are you doing here? I thought Val would be working this job?"

She shook her head and blushed. Interesting. "No, Val's really busy securing the sponsors and ad lineups for you to interview with. I offered." She preened as he continued to eye-fuck her.

"Can't say that I'm going to miss Val," he said in a way that actually didn't sound condescending or skeevy. Also interesting.

Rachel giggled—yes, giggled. His eyes seemed to soften when he looked at Rachel's face. He then opened the door wide for the both of us to enter.

"Um, slacker, the bags?" I nodded to the car.

"Oh right." He stopped, looked at Rachel, backed up, knocked into the door that hadn't latched properly, and grinned. "I'll just, uh, get the bags."

I stared as the overconfident, womanizing douchecanoe fumbled over himself while in the presence of his PR chick, who wasn't doing much better hiding her own interest. Rachel's cheeks were a rosy red, and her teeth were permanently biting into her bottom lip.

I flicked a thumb over my shoulder. "You into him?" I asked.

She nodded mutely, and then her eyes widened suddenly. "No! What? Um, you have the wrong impression. I merely have a professional relationship with Mr. Murphy." She ended her verbal diatribe with a firm crossing of her arms and mighty pursing of her lips.

Snorting, failing at hiding my laughter under my breath, I

moved into the house. "Whatever you say." I'd have to dig into that a bit more later, just for the hell of it. If I wasn't going to be getting any on this trip, the least I could do was have a little fun.

Mason dumped the bags in the foyer and ushered us into the living quarters. The room was a long rectangle, as would make sense for a standard brownstone in Boston, with multiple levels going up and possibly one going down. I looked forward to having the grand tour.

In the center of the living room was a black leather sectional. Opposite the sectional was at least a sixty-plus-inch flat screen television hanging on the wall. There was baseball paraphernalia here and there. Some framed jerseys and a line of signed baseballs sat over the mantle. Each was within its own protective glass square or plastic case. Proved he took care of the things he cherished. Maybe there were two sides to Mason Murphy. If I had to spend a month pretending to be his girlfriend, I sure as hell hoped there was.

"So what brings you here, Rach?" he asked, his body turned completely toward her, even though it didn't need to be. Rach. Her name was shortened. When people shortened other's name, it connoted familiarity or a small intimacy.

She crossed her legs, her skirt riding up her thigh. Mason zeroed in on the movement, his eyes following the small slip of fabric. I snickered, but neither one heard me or was paying attention to the fact that I was even in the room. "I just wanted to make sure that you both were briefed for tomorrow. It will be your first public appearance as a..." She cleared her throat and pushed a long strand of blonde hair behind her ear. It didn't stay, slipping delicately down her jawline once more. Again, Mason's eyes were riveted to her, to that piece of hair as if he wanted to touch it, be the one to push it back, caress her skin. His hands gripped into the meat of his thighs. "As, uh, a couple," she finished. "You'll need to make it look realistic. Hand holding when outside of the stands, small touches, smiling...erm—" she cleared her throat and winced as if it pained her to finish "—kissing, that kind of thing. Do you have any problems with that, Ms. Saunders?" she asked.

I looked at her with widened eyes. "Do you have a problem with it?" I asked, honest to God not believing I was watching these two. It was obvious to me, and I'd seen them together for a total of ten minutes, that they wanted each other. What the hell was keeping them from moving on it?

Rachel's head slammed back as if punched. "Excuse me?" She clutched her chest and gasped. "Why would I have a problem with it?"

"Really?" I shook my head.

"What Mia is probably trying to ask is whether or not us having public displays of affection will be a problem with the sponsors or the agency?"

No, that is not at all what Mia was suggesting. What planet had I landed on when I got off that plane? Were these two for real? I sighed and decided it was best to play along until I figured out what was going on. "Yeah, what he said."

Rachel's lips twitched, and the tension seemed to ebb out of her shoulders. It was like watching a morning glory close up for the evening. Slowly relaxing, curling its petals inward to rest until the morning sun brought it back up again, or in this case, a nosey escort originally from Vegas with very little filter. "The team has spent long hours planning this. We understand it's an unconventional approach, but Mr. Murphy has not presented the public with an idol people look up to. Along with some other things, he'll need to change the frequent bar brawls, excessive drinking... Even the occasional cigarette is a no-go. The team believes that the horde of women he's paraded around all last season, never being seen with the same woman twice, did very little to help his image. We're committed to turning that around, and you're step one."

Finally, I chanced a glance at Mason. His elbows were on his knees, and his head was in his hands. A defeated posture if I'd ever seen one. I got up and sat right next to him, placing a hand on his back and rubbing up and down. He turned his head toward me. "Man, I've fucked up."

"We all fuck up. At least you've hired Rachel, and your publicist thinks you're worthy of turning it all around." I continued to smooth a hand up and down his strong back until he lifted his head.

He adjusted his shoulders, pushing them back, leading with his chest. "Okay, so you want PDA?" he asked Rachel, and she nodded.

"You got it." He turned to me with a fierce expression and a laser focus to his gaze. "Let's do this." Then his hands were clasping the side of my head and his lips were on mine.

I gasped, opening my mouth by accident. Instead, he took it as an invitation. Initially, it wasn't one, but then the taste of champagne still lingered on his tongue as he flicked over mine, and I hadn't been kissed in what felt like forever but was really only two weeks. Couple that with the yummy cologne that wafted over his body, and I was gone. Lost to his kiss. His tongue dipped in, demanding yet playful. I licked back, leaned forward, clasped the front of his shirt, and held him in place while slanting my head for more. More of his kiss, more of him. Fuck. This was not part of the plan.

When we finally pulled away, both of us were panting,

gasping for breath.

"How was that?" Mason turned around to where Rachel was sitting, but she was gone. I could hear her heels clicking on the tile. "Rachel?" he called out.

"See you tomorrow. Great job!" she called out through the house two seconds before the door slammed shut.

Mason slumped against the back of the couch. "Fuck me."

I shook my head and leaned back. "Not gonna happen."

He chuckled.

"What was that?"

"That was me kissing a seriously hot escort." His eyes glinted with a hint of lust, but I knew better. It was body mechanics. Sure, he was drop-dead gorgeous, and I can't say that kissing him didn't get my juices flowing, but attraction and genuine interest are two totally different things.

"You like her," I said, offering him an olive branch.

His lips pinched together, and he closed his eyes. "Of course I do. She's nice, and I pay them well. We're all happy. What's not to like?"

"That not what I mean, and you know it."

"Look, I don't know about you, but I'm hungry, and you need to get settled. There's a bunch of shit, in bags, that Rachel or Val purchased as part of the deal. I didn't put it away. I just set it on the bed. Pizza okay?" He stood quickly and started to walk away and then must have thought better of it. He turned and offered his hand. "Thanks for taking the job," he said as he pulled me to my feet. "Your room is the first door on the right, unless you want to share mine." He waggled his eyebrows and thrust his hips.

I blew out a fast breath and shook my head. As I started walking, he smacked me hard on the ass.

"That's a mighty fine ass ya got there, Mia."

I stopped, cocked a hip, and put my hand on it. "If you want to keep that hand, you'll keep it off my ass."

He backed away with two hands up. "Okay, okay, just getting a little practice in for tomorrow's game. No harm, no foul, right?"

"Save it for the game. You're going to need it." I sauntered to the stairs, thinking I'd gotten the last word, when I heard him respond just as I got to the top of the stairs.

"Honey, don't you know I always play to win?"

Oh brother.

CHAPTER TWO

The moment a girl like me finds bliss in clothing, it should be treated like a national holiday, highlighted, and circled on the calendar with a giant red Sharpie pen. Tugging on a sleek new pair of True Religion jeans, followed by a tight, Red Sox T-shirt, had me wanting to bow down to Aunt Millie for scoring me this gig. I was spending a month with a famous baseball pitcher. Sure, he was rough around the edges, immature, and needed a spanking...and not the good kind, but you couldn't beat a job where you got to rock jeans and T-shirts. I slipped on a pair of red Converse and just about melted.

I looked at myself in the mirror, sliding a hand over my rounded ass. Yep, still looking pretty tight. I hadn't put on any weight since this started. I was still a good size eight but felt tight where I needed and soft where I wanted. The overall picture seemed to be booking me gigs, and I was getting closer and closer to paying off Blaine. Four payments down, six to go. If I booked every month, I could leave this life before the holidays. Though, who was I kidding? I was making a hundred grand a month, sometimes with an additional twenty thousand. Why give it up?

As I pulled my long black waves into cute pigtails—another thing I found out men like Mason dig on—and placed a baseball cap on my head, my thoughts trailed to Wes. Out of anyone, he's the one thing I'd like to pursue. When we're together, it's everything. Apart, I find it too easy to come up with reasons that we're not meant to be or that our connection isn't as strong as I wanted to think it was. Basically, I figured out that I was really good at protecting my heart, but I missed him. It had been a couple of weeks. Wouldn't hurt to reach out...

I pulled out my phone and dialed his number. It rang a few times before a female voice I didn't recognize answered. "Hello," she said with a giggle.

"Um, hi. I think I may have gotten the wrong number."

She laughed, and I could hear feet slapping noisily against wood floors. Booming laughter rang out, which I knew for a fact belonged to Wes.

"Are you calling for Weston?" she cooed, and that sultry sound of her voice tinged the recesses of my memory. I knew that voice. Closing my eyes, I took a deep breath. Gina DeLuca, one of the most beautiful, sought-after, Hollywood starlets alive. The woman was currently playing the lead in Wes's movie *Honor Code*.

More rustling came through the line. "Gina...girl, you are so going to get it!" Weston's voice was rough yet playful. "Come here, sexy," he said breathily, obviously chasing after her.

"Sorry to cut you off, but Wes will have to call you back. He's very busy," she squealed.

"Gotcha!" I heard Wes say and then the unmistakable sound of kissing noises followed by a female throaty moan. "Get off the phone," he growled, and she mewled, obviously not paying attention to the phone. A jagged-edged knife dug deep into my heart, but even with the fiery pain, I couldn't hang up. I was glued to the spot, an onlooker staring in awe at the site of a car accident, only by phone. I had absolutely no right to be hurt, none at all, but it didn't change the facts. I felt gutted listening to Wes carry on with another woman. Is this what he felt, knowing I was going to a new man every month? Probably not anymore, if the noises of wet lips meeting flesh were any indication.

"It's your phone! Not mine. Some chick. Here." I heard her say, and then time stopped. My heart beat like a heavy drum almost counting the mere seconds before he realized who'd called and what I'd heard.

"Fuck," I heard him curse as the phone probably changed hands.

"What's the matter, baby? Okay, you win. Come back to bed." Her voice was distant, as if she was getting farther away, and riddled in apology.

A groan split the space between us. "Mia." His voice was a pained rumble in my ear. "I'm sorry. That, uh, that shouldn't have happened."

I shook my head, but he couldn't see me. Tears pooled at the surface, but there was no way I was going to allow them to fall. If I did, I'd be a pile of mush on the bed and incapable of pulling off the happy, pretend girlfriend to hot-shot Red Sox pitcher Mason Murphy. "Hey, no, it's okay. I just, uh, called to say hi. So, hi."

"Hi," he responded sadly. "Fuck, Mia. It's not...um, technically, it's just. Jesus Christ!" I could hear a door shut in the background and birds chirping in the distance. He was probably looking out over Malibu as far as the eye could see. If I were there, I'd be holding him around the waist and doing the same. Not now. No, now he's got Gina to do that for him. "This doesn't change anything," he choked out.

I snorted. "Really? It changes everything."

His voice was a growl when he responded, "How so?

We're still friends."

"That's true. We are friends."

"And this thing with Gina, it's totally casual—you know, we're letting off some steam. She knows I'm not the relationship type. Well, at least not for her."

"So you are for me?"

He let out a slow breath. "If I answer that honestly, are you going to do something about it? I've given you that chance more than once. You've not taken it. We both agreed to take this year. Are you reneging on that now?"

A traitorous tear slipped down my cheek. Fucking hormones. "No, I'm not, Wes. I just..." I let out a breath. "I guess I just didn't expect you to move on."

"What makes you think I have? Fucking Gina? Tell me you and Frenchie didn't spend a month fucking after you left me?"

"Wes," I warned, and he cut me off.

"It's true. This is no different. We're not together officially, but you know I'd drop anything and anyone to be with you, but as cliché as it sounds...a man has needs too. I think it's best we not discuss those."

I bit down on my lip and sat on the bed. "No, you're right. It's incredibly unfair for me to have any claim over you when I'm not willing to give the same, but, Wes..." My voice broke, and I couldn't finish.

"Sweetheart, tell me... Please, fuck, Mia. I'll do anything to stay in your heart. Nothing has changed."

He said that, but it wasn't true. It's like starting over again, my heart locked up tight in Pandora's little box. "Just, I don't want to lose you."

"Mia, you're always going to be on my mind, and when

you're ready for more and this thing between us gets a real chance...we'll deal with it. You and me."

"Yeah, okay. Just one thing, Wes."

"Anything, sweetheart."

"Remember me," I said and hung up and powered down my phone. There was absolutely no way I could talk to him for one more second. I had a job to do and needed to put all my baggage in its case in the closet so that I could focus.

Mason Murphy, you'd better watch out. You're about to get one helluva show.

★ ★ ★ ★

Instantly, I was assaulted by the scents of hotdogs, popcorn, beer, and the ball field. For a girl like me, this was as close to Heaven as I'd ever been. Mason held my hand and led me through the underground tunnels of the ballpark. It was almost impossible to play the cool-card when he walked me through the locker room. Yes, the fucking locker room. Half-naked and some completely naked drool-worthy men were standing around shooting the shit, preparing for the game. If I was a different girl, I'd have covered my eyes or at the very least tried to play modest. Nope. Not this girl. I ogled like a pervy pubescent teen watching the older sexy neighbor girl changing clothes with a pair of binoculars through a set of blinds.

"Hey, Junior, I want you to meet my girlfriend," Mason said to Junior Gonzalez, the starting catcher for the Boston Red Sox. I had a small fan-girl moment, squeezing Mason's rock-hard bicep like I was wringing water out of a towel trying to keep my cool. He placed his hand over mine and patted it, looked down at me, and gave me a wink. "Buddy, I think you've got a fan."

The Hispanic man was big and muscular. The pants he was wearing stretched over tree-trunk-sized thighs, sending a wild flutter to the sensitive space between my legs. Junior's hair was thick, black, and cropped short on top. His eyes were a chocolate brown, a stark contrast to the white of his smiling grin and mocha-colored skin. "Hey, mama, what's shakin'?"

He waggled his eyebrows, and I swooned. Straight up leaned into Mason's side and sighed. They both laughed, but I just stared in perfect silence at the magnificence that was Junior Gonzalez. Best catcher known to baseball and one beefcake piece of perfection I call man.

"You're amazing," I finally stuttered. He looked me up and down and then glanced over at his friend.

"You're not so bad yourself. You want to skip right on over this schmuck and hang with a real man, sweetheart?" he joked. I knew he was teasing, because he didn't make a move or gesture to bring me closer to him. Mason laughed. I shook my head but wanted to do the opposite. Junior Gonzalez would be a nice distraction from my conversation and feelings over a certain blond-haired movie-making surfer who was currently fucking a goddess with a body that men would fall onto a sword for.

"Mace tells me you're, uh, with us for the month?" His voice dropped, and he tilted his head, those chocolate eyes sharing the knowledge of my true reason for being here.

"Yep, all month long." I smacked Mason's chest and then rubbed it, pretending to be playful but really was anything but.

He winced and rubbed at the spot. "Easy there, tiger. I swear, the hottest chick they had at the escort service, as luck would have it, isn't an easy lay."

I wanted to hit him again at hearing those words.

Junior closed his eyes, dropped his head, and shook it from left to right. "Man, when are you ever going to learn you can't treat a lady like a piece of ass? Girl"—he emphasized the word—"I hope you teach this boy a lesson."

I winked and pushed Mason to move on. "I plan to."

"Shee-it." Junior snickered and turned away. "Good luck. You're going to need it."

"Lady Luck has never worked for me in the past. I can't imagine she will magically start now," I threw over my shoulder.

Mason scoffed. "Who needs luck when she's got me?"

"Come on, honey. Show me to my seat." I said this saccharine sweet while rubbing along his side.

He looped an arm across my shoulder and kissed my temple.

★ ★ ★ ★

There is an interesting thing about baseball most of the general public doesn't know about. A secret elite clique called the WAGs, which stands for "Wives and Girlfriends." Since we were running a tad behind, Mason dropped me off at the WAG section and bailed, putting a wad of twenties in my hand. Nothing says whore like dropping a handful of Jacksons in her palm. Just for that, he wasn't getting a penny back. I planned on burning all two hundred bucks on beer, brats, and trinkets.

I found my seat and sat down carefully, not wanting to bump into the gaggle of geese that were chatting a mile a minute. Even so, they made no bones about looking me over. Each chick was around my age, some a few years older or younger, but no more than a five to seven-year gap between us.

"Hey." I waved to the line. Four heads swung to me. "I'm Mia." I tried the friendly approach.

One girl, who I assumed to be the ringleader, leaned forward. "You Mace's girl for the night?"

My eyebrows narrowed. "Um, no I'll be with him all month. I flew in from Vegas. We're old friends but working on more. This month will let us know whether we can go long-term or not."

A blonde sitting two seats over choked back a laugh. "Long-term?"

The brunette ringleader twisted her lips. "We've never seen Mace in a relationship before. You know, he's been the type to go the route of the three Fs." She picked at her fingernail and then looked my way, bored. "You know, finger 'em, fuck 'em, and flick 'em off."

"Wow. Well, that's gotta suck for the bitches he's fucked in the past," I said nonchalantly, not letting her jab win.

A sweet-looking strawberry blonde with her hair in an adorable ponytail put her hand on my knee. "Don't listen to her. She doesn't know Mace. I know him pretty well, and I have faith he can be committed to the right girl. I'm sure you're probably her." Her smile and voice reminded me of an angel. Kind, pretty brown eyes.

I held out my hand. "I'm Mia Saunders."

She took my hand and shook it. "Kristine, but you can call me Kris. I'm with Junior." Her cheeks instantly turned a rosy pink. "We've only been dating for three months, but I'm head over heels for him." She clasped her hands together on her lap and smiled shyly. "That's why I know Mace. They're like brothers. Well, except for Mace's other brothers and Junior's clan."

I laughed. "Junior has a lot of family?"

"A lot doesn't begin to describe it. Junior is one of nine siblings."

"Wow," I offered, and then saw a food vendor coming our way. "Hey, over here. I'm starved. Brat and a beer?" I asked.

Kris's entire face lit up as if the sun had just shined directly on her. I could see the appeal for Junior. She was angelic and sweet. "Sure, thank you. That's so nice. See, guys? Mia's not a hoochie. She's cool," she noted to the other girls in our section.

"Jury's still out," the brunette said to the two women on her left.

I shrugged. "Whatever. I'm not here for them. I'm here to see my man kick some ass on the ball field. Between him pitching and Junior catching...we got this. Am I right?" I said to Kris, holding out my hand.

She smacked it and whooped.

"Hey, my guy kills it on first!" said one of the women. "I'm Chrissy, by the way," the sexy redhead added.

"Good to meet ya, Chrissy."

"And I'm Morgan!" a lovely light-brown-haired gal added. The brunette grumbled but obviously saw she was in a losing battle. I was winning over the WAGs. "This is Sarah." Morgan hooked a thumb to her side. "She's pissy because she and her guy, Brett, had a tiff over a groupie last night. He plays second base."

I nodded. "Yeah, your guy, he's hot. I could see how groupies would want to be all over him."

Her bravado slipped away, and her shoulders slumped. "This stupid skank had the nerve to come over and sit in his lap when I left to go to the bathroom. He didn't do anything... well, much. He played around like it was all fun and games and held her hips and everything!" She scowled and then let out a screechy sound like an animal dying.

Apparently, connecting with a woman was easier than I'd thought. I only had Gin and Maddy, but my chick arsenal was growing. I now added Jennifer back in Malibu, who was happily pregnant, and of course Tony's sister, Angie, who was also happily pregnant, but this type of experience was new. Seems, if you talked shit about your man, you were all of a sudden in the clique. Hmmm. I took note of this strange behavior. Let her complain, bitch, and then cry about how much of an asshole her guy was. By the end of the first inning, I was her new best friend. I plied them all with beers and brats with my free two hundred bucks and purchased myself a big red foam finger! It was an awesome finger. I was taking this sucker with me wherever I went. I loved it.

On the first strikeout of the second inning, I jumped up and shouted at the top of my lungs with my foam finger. "Mason, you go, *baby*! That's my man over there. Mason Murphy, striking 'em out left and right," I roared. And that's when I heard the clicking. Several photographers had their big black cameras pointing in my direction. Show time. I blew kisses to Mason, and at one point, he took off his cap, put it over his heart, and then put it back on and struck out the next player. Had to admit, we were already good at this. During the seventh-inning stretch, Mason went back to the dugout only a few rows down from where I sat. The WAGs had damn good seats. I clomped my way down to where the dugout was just out of reach. Mason rose up on one of the wooden sides and leaned over the railing. He clasped me around the neck and looked over at the cameras. He grinned and crushed his lips over mine. Again, he was a damn good kisser. We made it look good for the photographers, but in all honesty, there was no excitement, no twinge of heat, no wetting of the panties, just a nice kiss to a hot guy.

When I pulled away, his eyebrows narrowed. "This is doing fucking nothing for you, huh? Way to wound a man, sweetness," he purred into my ear and then pulled back, his green eyes focused on mine. They weren't the green eyes I wanted to be drowning in right now.

I smiled wide, draped my hands over his broad shoulders, and clung to his neck. Then he flipped my hat backward, and I leaned against his forehead. "I'm sorry. It's just I keep thinking about Rachel." Which wasn't altogether true. I was sad for the shy blonde who obviously lusted after Mason, and there was definitely something between the two of them, but mostly I was heartbroken over Wes.

Mason cupped the nape of my neck, kissed my forehead, and pulled back. With a wink and smirk, he said, "Don't think about her. I don't." His tone was full of bravado and lacked sincerity. "Later, sweetness."

I watched him go, pretending to pine after my hot baseball star, and usually, I would. But I wasn't feeling like myself. Ever since hearing Gina DeLuca's voice on the other end of Wes's phone, I'd lost a piece of myself. The drive I usually had bustling under the surface had fizzled to a dull ping, pushing me through the motions of my job.

It was unfair, completely ridiculous, to assume he'd wait for me, especially while I was fucking whomever I wanted to. For me, though, when he came to Chicago on that whim, something had changed, and I thought perhaps I could wait for *him*. Sex was sex. I liked sex—every red-blooded American woman did. Sex with Wes, though, was more than an experience. It was life changing. Alec was amazing in bed. It was fun, sensual, exotic, and great at the time. I enjoyed my time with him immensely, but my emotions weren't involved the way they were with Wes, and I feared that even though he said things with Gina were causal that she'd learn quickly what a catch he was, and ultimately, I'd come out the loser. I guess it was in my cards. Doing what I had to do for my family had to take priority.

In the meantime, I'd focus on the job and maybe make someone else's life better. Starting with Mason. He wasn't a lost cause. I could see a gentleman hiding under all that swagger. Life had taught him to live in the present, and the money being thrown at him hadn't taught him a thing about how to respect the people in his life. I wondered if he was truly happy. He couldn't be if he had to hire an escort to pretend to be his steady girlfriend. I mean, there was a horde of women screaming his name, begging for his attention. I needed to find out more about young Mason. What made him tick, what made him the womanizer he'd been or, perhaps, pretended to be? Either way, I was here for the better part of a month, and I wasn't going to squander that time away crying in my beer. No, I'd spend it slugging that beer back with a hot baseball player and his sexy-as-hell baseball friends. Game on!

CHAPTER THREE

Week one of pretending to be Mason "Mace" Murphy's girlfriend had ended up being a blast. I felt like I was on vacation all week. I went to four home games, three of which they won, and I gotta admit that being the girlfriend of a winning baseball player was awesome! We partied like it was 1999, only this time, all the reports of Mason showed him hanging all over the same girl, namely me, never smoking, and keeping his drinking under control. No sloppy drunkard pictures for the press this time. He was on his best behavior, and it showed with all the smut rags promoting the good news, yet still speculating when he was going to fall off his pedestal and be the bad boy they knew him to be. Well, they could just keep waiting, because it wasn't going to happen on my watch.

Over the past week, I'd also had some time to reflect on my feelings over Wes and Gina, which I lovingly now refer to as "Wesina," just to keep the fire in my belly burning. It wasn't fair, but I'd been avoiding Wes's calls and texts. I'd received one call and one text per day since last week when I found out he was banging perfect Hollywood hottie Gina DeLuca. I knew if I wanted to stay close with Wes, even as friends, I needed to respond. That's why when a text buzzed through from him, I didn't immediately ignore it or delete it.

To: Mia Saunders
From: Wes Channing

Was thinking about you while on location. This reminded me of you. It always will. Please talk to me.

Under his text was a picture of a beautiful ocean. In the sand was a single surfboard. Man, I missed surfing. By the time I got back to California, I would be so out of practice that he'd need to re-teach me. That thought made me snicker.

Without thinking too much about it, I shot off a text.

To: Wes Channing
From: Mia Saunders
That view looks like Heaven. Catch a few waves for me, will ya? I miss surfing with you.

Before I could put my phone in my purse, it dinged with an incoming message.

To: Mia Saunders
From: Wes Channing
She lives! Damn, sweetheart. You had me worried you'd never talk to me again. Glad that's not the case. How are you?

To: Wes Channing
From: Mia Saunders
Baseball, beer, brats, Boston...couldn't be better.

To: Mia Saunders
From: Wes Channing
Sounds like a dream come true for you. What about all the other letters of the alphabet?

I rolled my eyes and began typing furiously. It had been too long and the tension too high between Wes and me. We needed to find something that could work for us both. The truth was, we both cared deeply for one another, but we weren't in a position to be together. That didn't mean we couldn't care. And it didn't mean we shouldn't find a way to get over the fact that both of us were going to have relations with the opposite sex. I couldn't expect him to be celibate when I wasn't offering the same.

To: Wes Channing
From: Mia Saunders
Who needs the other letters when I'm enjoying the Bs?

Of course, he'd have to take me off-kilter and bring the serious back into play just as I was enjoying our causal banter.

To: Mia Saunders
From: Wes Channing
The letter C is pretty nice, too. California, Cuddling, Caring, Commitment, Channing...Cock.

I laughed out loud. Leave it to him to sandwich the serious shit in with a joke.

To: Wes Channing
From: Mia Saunders
If my memory serves, I've already had Channing Cock, and it was pretty fucking fantastic.

I knew I'd responded a bit boldly, but I was determined to

bring things back to the light, fun nature of our relationship. If I was going to hold on to him in any way, we had to keep that above all else. Yes, knowing he was fucking Gina hit me hard, but I'd had a week to think about it, and as much as I wanted to drop everything, head to California on the first flight out, and claim my man, that just wasn't in the cards for me. I had to hope Wes would keep things casual with Gina, and if he didn't, there was no other option but to be okay with that decision. I'd made it clear that our time wasn't now. I stood by that decision, as much as it gutted me.

To: Mia Saunders
From: Wes Channing
It will be waiting the second you want another go-round, sweetheart.

To: Wes Channing
From: Mia Saunders
Crazy man! Go surf. Don't let those waves pass you by. We'll chat more in a couple days. Duty calls.

To: Mia Saunders
From: Wes Channing
Crazy for you.

That was the last thing he texted before radio silence. Crazy for me. I was crazy about him, too, but I wasn't about to put things back on a serious tone. We needed time—lots of it— to get past the blow. He knew I was fucking other men. I knew he was fucking Gina. That was reality.

"What's got your face lit up, sweetness?" Mace asked,

entering my side of the hotel suite in a stunning three-piece suit. Damn, the man looked good in his uniform and in a pair of raggy jeans with a hole in the knee, but in a suit, he exuded a powerful air that I liked...a lot. Mason smiled, waggled his eyebrows, and slowly turned around, giving me the entire view. "You like?"

I nodded. "You know I do. I can't wait until Rachel sees you. She's been hiding out all week."

Mason's lips turned down into a scowl at the mention of her name. "You've got the wrong idea 'bout Rach and me. You need to get that outta your head."

This time I shook my head. "No way. I saw the way you two looked at each other last week. She's into you, but I don't know why she's hiding out."

"She's not. She'll be here to drive us over to Power Up."

That's when we both heard a knock on the door. I smiled wide and rushed to the door as quickly as my stilettos would take me. I swung open the door, and there she was in another smart suit, only in gray. A soft-pink blouse highlighted the pink in her cheeks and glow to her skin. This time, her blonde hair was pulled back into a tight ponytail at the nape of her neck. She had it done in this cool way where the rubber band was covered with her own hair, so it looked like it was magically holding itself back. I should find out how she did that. It would be a neat trick to learn, something I could teach Gin and Maddy, too.

"Hey, Rachel. How are you?" I swung the door open wide.

She looked me up and down. I was wearing a leather pencil skirt and a flowing white blouse. This skirt hugged my ass, and the billowy blouse gave a dose of cleavage that I found alluring. Definitely something a pro ball player's hot young girlfriend would rock.

She cringed. "That outfit is overtly sexy. That skirt was supposed to go with a button-up." Her lips pursed prettily but were still accusatory, and for the first time, I felt lacking.

"Um, okay, I didn't bring any of the button-up shirts because I thought they went with the trousers."

That's when Mace made his appearance. Just him entering the room stole her breath. I heard her take an audible breath and hold it. Her eyes widened, and her teeth sank sexily into her bottom lip. The girl was gonzo over the guy. Why the hell did he not see it? I turned and watched as Mason made a slow circle, showing off for the second time this morning, only really making a big deal about it for Rachel's benefit.

His grin was wide when he made it all the way around. "Does this say responsible spokesperson for Power Up sports drink and Quick Runners?"

Rachel nodded mutely.

"Apparently you're perfect and I look like a sexy ho," I mumbled but grabbed my purse.

Mason's eyes narrowed, and he swung an arm around my waist and brought me close to him. I slammed into his chest, and he looked down at me, eyes showing his concern. I glanced at Rachel and she instantly looked away.

"Hey, you look perfect. Sexy as hell. The media has seen you in jeans and T-shirts all week. Now it's time to see you looking posh and young. Exactly how I like my women. Besides, do you think the big wigs would think I'd be with some stuck-up professional with a stick up her ass?"

At that comment, I saw Rachel's shoulders slump. In her mind, she was the very definition of a stuck=up professional, and right now, I could see her squeezing those cheeks so tight she could shit diamonds. This did not bode well for my plan "Operation Hook Rachel and Mason Up." New tactics would have to be drafted and carried out if I had any hope of succeeding.

I kissed Mason's cheek and wiped away the lipstick left on his clean-shaven jaw. "Speaking of sexy... Doesn't Rachel look hot in her suit?" I gestured with a head tilt in Rachel's direction.

Mason's lip curled up at each corner, showing those drop-dead sexy dimples. "I'd do her," were the stupid words that came out of his mouth. You could take the player out of Boston, but you couldn't take the player out of the man. At this, I punched his arm.

"How many conversations have we had about you being a jackass?" I put up both hands and marked off each finger.

He rubbed his shoulder. "Sorry, Rach, but I'd totally fuck you."

I punched him again.

"Ouch! Stop fucking hitting me."

"Stop being a dick!"

That's when Rachel waded in. "Both of you, stop! Mia, it's fine. I'm used to Mason's crass behavior by now."

Cringing, I put a hand to my hip. "Doesn't change the fact that it's immature and tasteless."

Rachel laughed, and it sounded like bells jingling. Even her laugh was sweet. "True, but thank you for the compliment, Mr. Murphy."

An intense heat hit me like a wall of flames. Mason practically growled a response to her. "How many times do I have to tell you to call me Mason or Mace, Rachel? We've known each other for two years. We're beyond the professional.

At least, I'd like to think we are."

Her eyes jumped up to meet his, and she clasped her hands together and knotted her fingers. "Yes, uh, you're right. We are. I apologize. Old habits and all that. Shall we go?"

"Should I change?" I said dryly, really needing to know. I was here to make his image better. I thought I was rocking a kick-ass outfit, but apparently I needed to be schooled.

Rachel looked at me once more. "You do look really beautiful, Mia. You always do. I'm sorry. I didn't respond well. Everything's fine. Let's not keep our prospective sponsors waiting." She opened the door, and the three of us stepped through.

★ ★ ★ ★

The Power Up team was surprisingly boring. For a company that owned a sports drink geared toward young athletes, you couldn't have found a duller group. The offices were all white and black, with pictures of the drink standing on a white backdrop lining their walls. There weren't any fun pics of men doing wicked sports activities—like rock climbing, swimming, motor sports—while holding up a Power Up bottle as I would have expected. If you asked me—and they didn't, of course, so I stayed quiet—they needed Mace more than Mace needed them. If they had any hope of going against the big guys like Gatorade, they needed their own image change.

Rachel, however, spoke her mind and made it very clear why she could afford perfectly tailored suits and whatever fee Mason was paying her. She worked that room and had a room full of men eating out of her hand. She promised the Power Up executives that not only would Mason be in the media a whole lot more, his baseball record was proof positive that he was in the majors to stay. Young people loved a bad boy turned good guy. She even spun different ways the team could work with Mason to improve their own image and how her firm would be happy to work with their marketing team to come up with the best possible campaigns to successfully launch both companies to a new plane. And then his agent spoke money.

Apparently, being a spokesperson for a sports drink company was worth millions. When they started throwing around figures that were in the tens of millions, I almost lost my breakfast. I couldn't imagine that a few commercials, some photo shoots, and some meet and greets were worth that kind of money. Then again, I was being paid a hundred Gs to sit here and look pretty. People were bat-shit crazy everywhere. This was just how the other half lived, and now that I was the arm candy, I got to see it live and in living color.

Once we were done with Power Up, who said they would consider all that was discussed and make a decision within the next week, we took a limo over to the folks at Quick Runners. They were in line to be the next Reebok or Nike and just needed that extra bit of pizzazz to push them over the edge. Mason Murphy, the best pitcher in baseball today, was their ace in the hole. Rachel made sure the team knew that to be true. This office was the exact opposite of Power Up. Where that team was all staunch businessmen in suits, this office seemed to be filled with just-out-of-college grads wearing jeans, polos, and tennis shoes. We left that office with a verbal commitment for another bucket-o-millions, and as long as Mason kept his image squeaky clean, they would remain on board.

When we got into the elevator, the team waved and high-fived one another as the doors were closing. The second they closed, Mason turned to Rachel, grabbed her cheeks, and said, "You. Are. An. Amazing. Fucking. Woman!" And then he pulled her into his body and laid a fat kiss on her. I stood in the corner, hands to my chest, trying not to squeal with glee. When he pulled away, she looked dazed and loopy. He pulled away and grabbed me by the waist and hugged me to him. That's when I did squeal and jump up and down in his arms. "Did you see that? See our girl working those rooms? Holy shit. What a ride!"

Mason gripped Rachel's shoulders and yanked her to his side. He had each of us cuddled in one arm. "Ladies, today was a huge win for Team Murphy."

I snickered. "Team Murphy?"

He nodded vigorously. "Yep, Team Murphy. You"—he shook me by the shoulder—"And our queen, Rachel"—he shook her—"and, of course...the pretty face: moi."

Both Rachel and I sighed. "You're so full of yourself."

"Yes. Yes, I am. And now, it's time to celebrate and be full of something else: booze!"

Rachel's eyes got big. "Mason, we can't go gallivanting around. You've got eyes on you and a game tomorrow night."

"True. So we invite a coupla the guys and their chicks to the suite, order up some pies and some beers. Fun night in? You in?"

Beers, boys, pizza...um yeah. "Hell yeah!" I said. "Come on, Rach. You gotta celebrate. Let your hair down."

Mason's eyes went to Rachel's golden hair. "Now that's something I've never seen." His hand came up to her ponytail and spun it around his hand into a fist and let it go. "Would love to see this fuckin' gold down, curled around your face. So pretty." He leaned close to her ear, and this time my eyes went wide. She looked positively ready to drop to the floor either in surprise or fear. Could be a little of both. Mason sniffed against the space near her ear. "Christ, you smell good. That's the fuckin' almond smell I can't place. It's you. It's always been you. Smells so good I could eat it." He growled into her neck and inhaled loudly before pulling away. He looked at Rachel like a hungry lion before a juicy steak.

Then the doors of the elevator dinged, and the spell was broken. Rachel moved as fast as her stilettos would take her out the doors and into the New York evening. "Time to head back, get those pizzas and beer. You want to make some calls to your friends, Mason?" She pulled out her phone and ignored the forlorn look on his face.

He closed his eyes, took a breath, and climbed into the limo. "Yeah, Rach, I'll make the calls."

I slid in next to him and placed a comforting hand on his knee.

"See, told you so," he said, and put his phone to his ear.

Our suite was filled with Red Sox and, oddly enough, some Yankees ball players. We'd ordered in a couple kegs of beer and at least two dozen pizzas that were getting demolished at lightning speed. Women outnumbered the men in attendance, which I found downright strange. It made sense if there was a one to one ratio, but apparently, some of the single men offered up the pizza party to some of the groupies, and they told other groupies, and so on. Now we had women who were dressed normally in jeans and cute tops, and then there were the hos looking to get a piece of pro-ball-player dick in 'em to mark their bedpost.

Eventually, the party got a bit wild. So much so that I ended up in my room, sitting on the bed getting snockered with Rachel, passing a bottle of Jamison back and forth.

"You know, if you wanted Mason, you could have him," I told her blatantly, the liquor loosening my tongue.

She made a face and a noise with her mouth that sounded like air escaping out of a tire. Rachel pointed to her disheveled outfit. "You think he wants a piece of this?" She still wore her smart gray pencil skirt, but her pink blouse had been unbuttoned and was now wrinkled and half tucked in her skirt. Her hair was cocked to the side and her mascara smudged. I didn't even want to know what I looked like. I'd since lost the expensive blouse and replaced it with a tank top, though I kept the leather skirt on because I thought it was "tits" as my girl Ginelle back home would say. We'd made it up back in the day. If we liked something a lot, we'd say "tits," because very few things were as desired or coveted as a nice pair of boobs.

Getting up on my knees, I got behind her and pulled out her ponytail. Her long golden locks framed around her face perfectly, adding to her beauty. "Wow. You're fucking hot!" I said, and leaned over, took a sip of the whiskey, and passed it back to her. Then I got a tissue, licked it, and rubbed the smudged mascara off her face. "There. Now you're super hot! But you need to loosen up a bit. You're so worried about everything," I slurred and flopped back to the pillows.

Rachel pursed her lips in a way I'd gotten used to seeing with her. It said she was really giving what you said some thought before commenting. I liked that about her. "Yeah, you're right. I need to be more like you. Free, young, and ready to take on the world!" She put a hand into the air in a fist pump, but it lacked finesse, so she looked more like she was pretending to be the Statue of Liberty holding up her torch.

Without being able to stop, I chuckled, and then giggled, and then out and out laughed so hard I piggy snorted.

She pointed a finger at my face and then busted up laughing herself.

Finally, when I got it under control, I clasped her hand. "You should go for him. Tonight!" I held her cheeks, and her eyes widened to the size of half dollars.

"What!" I was squishing her cheeks together so it came out sounding like a bird squawking, which made me laugh again, but I was quicker on getting it in check.

"For realz! You should go up to Mace and tell him you like him!"

Rachel held her mouth open and shook her head. "You think I should tell him I like him? As in like him, like him?"

Why did this sound familiar? My brain was swishing from side to side, floating on a lake of Jamison Irish Whiskey, so I couldn't put two and two together, but my idea felt solid. "I'll help you!" I pulled her off the bed and stood her up. Then I plucked at the buttons of her shirt, opening two of them until I got to a nice expanse of rounded cleavage.

She smacked at my hands. "What are you doing?"

I groaned. "Duh! There are four things men like. The first being tits! You've got some. We need to show them."

She nodded and pressed her chest out in offering.

"Good, that's good. Do that when you see Mace! Okay, next, men like hair." I fluffed her hair and made sure it looked soft and sexy. "Nice." I pinched my lips between two fingers and swayed on my feet. "Ass!" I pointed at her, turned her around, and checked out her ass. The skirt hem was tiny, so I crouched down and ripped the hem up the middle so her ass and legs were showing more. Then I smacked her tiny ass. "Excellent!"

"I don't know about this," Rachel said in a tiny voice.

"No. No. No. This is gonna be so awesome!" Then I pressed my fingers into my temple. "I can't remember what number I was on, but mouths." I scampered over on my bare feet to my makeup bag, pulled out a lip gloss, and spread it over Rachel's sweet pout. "Men love to see shiny lips. Makes them think about you sucking their dick. Would you like to suck Mason's dick?" I asked drunkenly.

Her cheeks turned cherry red, but in a breathy whisper she said, "Yeah."

"Okay, then. That will be phase two. One is getting him to notice you and you telling him you like him, like him." I grabbed the bottle of Jamison and took a healthy swig, letting it burn a path down my belly before I handed it to her. "Your turn."

She followed suit, and then we were both headed back out into the party. I had a mission, and even though it was a stupid one, I was convinced it would work.

Boy, was I wrong.

CHAPTER FOUR

Remember that old saying, "The road to Hell was paved in good intentions?" Man, whoever said that shit was spot on. I had no idea what would happen when we left the sanctuary of our private girl party, but the atmosphere of our little pizza and beer soiree had changed considerably. There were people everywhere! Smoke billowed, and not just the kind you get from the cigarette store. No, the kind you get from a guy named "Bud" who says he can take you to an alternate reality just by one toke. This was not good.

Bodies were smashed together all around us. I had to sink my claws into Rachel to make sure I didn't lose her in the crush. What the fuck had happened, and how long had we been in that room? From the fact that I couldn't walk straight, it must have been a while. I didn't recognize anyone around us, until finally, I made it to Mason's suite.

I was not prepared for what I was about to see, but Rachel—sweet, innocent, in-love-with-Mason-Murphy little Rachel—was definitely unprepared. The room was dark, and music blared so loud I couldn't hear or see anything. Tugging on Rachel's hand, I pulled her into Mason's room, thinking he'd probably gone to bed. What a better way to surprise him than with a hot, supple woman he had a thing for! Of course, this was not what happened. Eventually, I found the light switch and flicked it on.

Mason was lying on the bed, only he wasn't alone.

And when I say not alone, he wasn't just with a woman. There were two of the scantily dressed groupies there with him. I watched in shock, horrified and turned way the fuck on, while I watched Mason getting his cock sucked by a brunette who I, in my drink-filled brain, thought had some seriously great dick-sucking technique. She was able to easily take him right down her throat, and that was a skill. Then, of course, there was a curvy blonde who was facing the back wall, her legs caging Mason's head, her pert ass glistening as she gyrated her hips. Mason's tongue was visibly pushing in and out of her pussy. He was eating her like a pro, gorging on her flesh as she rocked into him like she was riding a stallion. It was the most erotic thing I'd ever seen. So while I wanted to sit back and watch the show, maybe rub one out for good measure, I finally heard a sob through the symphony of moans.

Tears sluiced down Rachel's face, and a delicate hand came up to her mouth. Just as I was going to get her out of there, we both heard the blonde scream out, "I'm coming!" I looked back and watched as Mason gripped her ass, and he growled into her cunt while she screamed. Then his hips skyrocketed up into the air, and the brunette shoved a hand to her pussy, rubbed, and started bucking over his cock. His release shot into her mouth and dribbled out the sides as she came along with him. Fuck. I'd never seen anything so blatantly hot in my life. When I turned to Rachel, she was gone. The door was open about a foot where she must have slipped out. I was too drunk to chase after her and console her.

"Shit." I blew out a breath of air.

"Who the fuck are you?" The brunette sat up and wiped the cum off her lip with the back of her hand.

I crossed my arms over my chest.

Mason shoved the blonde off his face and looked up at me. "Mia, sweetness. This here is uh..." He looked left and then looked right. "Tasty Pussy and Super Sucker." He laughed, and the girls smiled.

"Seriously! And I fucking brought you a present," I snarled, put a hand to my hip, and stomped my foot.

His glazed eyes and red cheeks proved not only was he happily sated but drunk and possibly high. Both were bad for his image. Thank God we were in our private suite, or he'd risk losing his new sponsor and prospective sponsor. "Please tell me it's hiding under those clothes. I'll shoo these fucking bitches off quick to get a taste of your sweet cunt."

I sucked in a breath. "*You douche!* Stop thinking with your fucking dick!"

At that moment, said dick was hard and ready for round two. I gave it a gander. It was a really nice-looking cock, too. Long, thick, hard. Brunette wrapped a hand around it and rubbed it up and down. He groaned but kept his eyes on me. "Sure you don't want some? I'm offering..."

I shook my head. "I brought Rachel in here. She was going to tell you that she liked you, liked you! Then she saw you fucking these sluts and ran off."

That did it. He flung the brunette hobag off and then pushed off the bed, removing himself from hobag two. "Rachel was here." He pointed to the floor. "In here?"

I nodded.

"She saw me fucking these bitches?"

Pushing my lips together in a grim line, I looked at him like the stupid idiot he was.

"Fuck me!"

"Okay, baby, we will. Just come back. It's my turn to suck

on you," said blonde hobag.

He scowled and then sat on the bed. "Get out of my room," he growled.

Brunette hobag did not get the hint. She put her arms around him and rubbed her fake tits into his back.

"Come on, baby. We'll make you feel better, just like before."

"Leave now!" he roared, and then stood up and went into his ensuite.

"You deaf?" I opened the door.

"You just want him for yourself."

"Well, since I'm the girlfriend...I'm going to go with yes. Now get out!"

I'd just gotten the girls out of the room when Mason came out in a pair of jeans and was digging through his suitcase for a T-shirt. "I have to go find her."

Rubbing a hand over my face, I grabbed his hand. "And tell her what? Sorry you caught me fucking two floozies? I don't think that's going to work."

He pushed his hands through his hair and then flopped back down on the bed. "I can't just leave it like this."

"Technically, you don't owe her anything. Besides, it was my fault."

He blew out a tortured breath. "No, you were just trying to help, but as usual, I started thinking with my dick."

"What happened?" I tried. When I'd left him, he was hanging out with the guys, eating pizza.

Mason shook his head. "One minute I was chatting it up with my bros. The next minute I noticed you and Rachel were gone. The two groupies were all over me, and the more I drank, the more I didn't care. I just wanted to feel...something.

You know? I looked for you, looked for Rachel, but they kept on me, and I got weak." His shoulders slumped. "Do you hate me?"

I put an arm around his shoulders. "No, I don't. What I saw was fucking hot."

He chuckled softly. Man, he really was beautiful when he gave a genuine smile.

"I just don't think your girl, the one you really want, thought it was as hot as I did. She was really sad. Crying and everything."

His head shot up. "She was crying? Honestly, Mia, I knew she might be sweet on me, but it's never been like that between us. She's always been untouchable. Perfect, professional, pretty, the whole package. A girl like her would never be with a guy like me. We're in totally different leagues." He rubbed his chin, and the sound of hair grating along calloused palms sent chills racing up my spine. Reminded me of another time and another guy I adored.

"I get it. There's this guy I like, too. Way out of my league, but I'd like to think when the time is right, we'll be in the same league at the same time. I think you can do that, too."

"You like a guy?"

I grinned. Of course, that's what he'd zero in on. "I do, but the timing isn't right. When it's right, if it is ever right, it will just be. And it will work out. I have to believe that. But you can do something now."

Mason looked off into the distance and then brought those green eyes to me. They were soft, almost beseeching, as if my own held the answers to every question he'd ever want to know in them.

"Show her what type of man you can be. What type of

man you are in here." I pointed to his chest where his heart was. "Live like the man you want to be. She'll come around."

"You think?"

I smiled wide and hugged him into my chest. He smelled of sex and cheap perfume. "I know."

"Thanks, Mia. You're pretty all right, you know that?"

I laughed into his neck. "You're pretty all right yourself, but you smell like a whorehouse. Do the world a favor and shower. I'll work on Rachel. You work on you."

He stood up and helped me up. "I'll work on me."

"While you're working on you, can you work on getting these people out of our room? I can't sleep with people fucking on the couch, pot being smoked, bodies everywhere, and music blaring."

He opened the door from his room to the living area and took in the party. "Fucking hell. We're never getting smashed again."

I choked on a laugh. "Never say never."

The rest of our visit in New York City went by in a flash. The team had three games in NYC—lost one, won two. So far, their rank was looking really good. Quick Runners booked Mason as their official year-long spokesperson for the new performance all-around sports shoe. It was good for running, walking, playing ball, and all other varieties of sports. We still hadn't heard from Power Up. Apparently their people had heard about Mason booking with Quick Runners and wanted to make sure that having the same spokesperson was a good thing for their image and the way they wanted to run their campaign. This, however, was not bad for Mason, because another couple of opportunities came out of the woodwork for baseball gear and energy bars. Word got out fast. Now we just waited, and Mason played hard and stayed off the radar. Part of that was going home. Which was where we were driving to now. I was finally meeting Mason's family.

When we got to the small home outside of Boston proper, Mason walked right in without knocking.

"Back here, boy!" a loud voice yelled and was coupled with the squealing sound of a small child.

Mason held my hand and took me through the quaint home. Stuffed animals and dolls littered the floor where a child at play must have up and abandoned them for something else. The rooms were dark, lived-in, and homey. You could tell by the pictures on the wall that a woman had once lived here, but by the layer of dust on them and the lack of girlie adornments, it had been a while. In the center of one wall was a wedding photo. A redheaded, pale, beautiful woman stood in a very old-fashioned wedding gown and had her arms locked around a large man with dark-brown hair and kind eyes. A man who could be the spitting image of Mason. That apple did not fall far from the tree.

We made it through the home to the kitchen, where I was instantly assaulted with the smell of cooked meat. My mouth watered at the smell of sage and rosemary, along with whatever was brewing on the stovetop. A large roast sat on top of the counter, and a man with his back to us was carving it into slices and placing them on a platter.

A small redheaded girl with giant blue eyes clocked me the second I entered. She stood up and clapped her hands. She couldn't be more than four years old. "You're here!" she squealed in that way only small children were capable of, with their whole bodies and full of joy.

I smiled wide, and the man turned around, and boy was I not wrong. He looked exactly like Mason or what Mason would look like in twenty-five years.

"Hey, Dad. This is Mia. She's my, uh..."

The man smiled wide and laid out a hand. "You're the woman everyone says is my son's girlfriend."

I wasn't sure how Mason wanted to play this, so I stayed quiet about the girlfriend part. "It's good to meet you, Mr. Murphy."

"Call me Mick. Everyone does, 'cept my boys, because I'll tan their hide if they disrespect their elders."

At that I nudged Mason. "Your dad is awesome."

"Yeah, unfortunately when he's around, my cool factor goes down about fifty notches."

"And don't you forget it, boy! Now set the table, will ya?"

Mason proceeded to set the table while I introduced myself to Eleanor, who liked to be called Ellie. She walked me through the house and showed me every single one of her toys, and then her room, where she had everything princess and was very proud of it. I scanned the room. I'd never had anything like this as a child. A room devoted to the things I loved as a kid. Maddy and I had always shared a room, and neither one of us had a theme or anything much we could call our own. Made me sad for what I'd missed out on and happy that even though men were raising Ellie without a woman's hand, they were still doing right by her.

My heart ached when Ellie placed a crown on my head and one on her own. "You can be the queen, and I'll be the princess," she offered.

I nodded and hugged her little body. She held me tight before another look-a-like of the Murphy family interrupted us. Made me wonder if any of them looked like their mother.

"You must be Mia?"

I nodded and stood up from the floor.

Ellie clasped my hand tight. "Daddy, this Queen Mia, and I'm Princess Ellie. Do you want to be the king or the prince?" she asked, her eyes serious as she stared at her father.

"I want Princess Ellie to wash her hands for dinner and let Queen Mia get back to her king," he said, playing along.

Ellie looked up at me with her huge blue eyes that she must have gotten from her mother, because her dad had the same green eyes that both the other Murphy men had. "Will you save me a spot next to you at dinner, Queen Mia?" she asked in her too-cute little voice.

"Of course I will, Princess Ellie. I'd be honored." I bowed for effect, and she clapped her hands, spun on a toe, and was off running down the hall.

The big man with coppery hair and green eyes held out a hand. "Sorry about that. Ellie doesn't get much female time. I'm Brayden."

I shook his hand and held it. "Totally okay. I had fun. I can't remember the last time I spent playing with a child." And I couldn't. There weren't any children in my family that I knew of, none of my friends had kids—well technically, a couple of my new friends were going to have babies—and Tony and Hector's other family, the ones with children, didn't hang around us when I was there. So this was the first time in several years that I'd spent one-on-one time with a child. It was fun. I'd rather enjoyed it.

Brayden led me back to the table, where I sat down

and chatted up his brother and father. When the food was completely set on the table, a whirlwind crashed through the back door, skidded to a stop, and dropped his backpack on the floor behind him. "Shit, Mace. Your girlfriend is fucking hot!" a gangly, tall, ginger-haired boy with the same green eyes as the rest of the Murphy men shouted.

"Mouth!" Mick chastised with a fork pointing in the boy's direction.

"Sorry, Dad, but dang... Sweet girl you got Mace." The boy looked me up and down. "I'm Shaun. How are you, sweetness?"

Oh no, he didn't. He'd just called me sweetness. "Well, I can see who's rubbed off on this young impressionable mind." I glared at Mason, and he actually looked chagrinned. "Shaun, don't call chicks sweetness. They don't like it."

"Sure they do. I had my tongue in this sweet chick today."

My eyes widened, and Brayden pressed his hands over Ellie's ears. "Boy, I swear I'm going to take two inches off your height if you don't choose your words more wisely around my daughter. And stop disrespecting women. You're teaching her bad shit!" His teeth were clenched, and poor little Ellie was slapping at her father's hands.

"Daddyyyy, stop. I can't hear when you do that!" She scrunched up her little nose and looked at me. "Does Uncle Mace ever do that to you?"

The men at the table laughed.

I smiled and tapped her nose, giving the precious girl my full attention. "No, because I'm an adult, but your daddy is protecting you from hearing things that are not appropriate for you. He's a very good daddy."

She nodded and shoved a giant forkful of mashed potatoes into her mouth. Her cheeks pushed out like a chubby bunny.

I shook my head and looked up at Shaun. "If you want to keep a woman in the future, you'll learn to call her things that actually make her feel special, not like one of many. Remember that."

His eyes looked me over in a way that a teenaged boy who only has sex on the brain would. Extremely skeevy. "If it secures me a hot babe like you, I'll do whatever you say, sweetness."

Mason's forehead hit the table. Brayden shook his head, and I bit back a seriously profane comment. The patriarch, on the other hand, had no problem laying into Shaun, which he did after he pulled him by the ear into another room. When they came back, Mason and Brayden both had shit-eating grins on their faces. Ellie just happily ate more potatoes and asked for more.

"Sorry for being rude, Mia. I'll try to be more respectful," Shaun grumbled through a sour expression.

"Thank you, Shaun. That was kind of you. Now tell me embarrassing stories about Mason," I said, changing the subject, and every man besides Mason smiled and started sharing.

By the time dinner was done, my belly hurt so bad I could hardly breathe, let alone put any cheesecake into it. The stories were detailed and plenty. The guys spent hours telling me about crazy Mason. In his younger years, he was a class clown, thought he was the world's greatest inventor, and had absolutely no luck with the ladies. The last part I found unbelievable, looking at how he'd filled out. The whole package was nice, once you got past the douchey ways, but we were working on those, and he was making some serious progress. Not enough for Rachel to come around, but I had hope that I could work some magic there. The men cleaned up, another thing I found incredibly cool—guests of the Murphy household never did dishes, even if you were a woman. I guess they just got used to doing all the domestic duties themselves. It was enlightening but sad. So while they cleaned up, I looked at all the pictures. There were many of Eleanor the mother around the house. Pictures with each boy, with the boys all together, and happy ones with her husband, Mick. They looked really happy, a solid family. Here was a woman who fought cancer and probably would have given anything to just stay with her family, whereas my healthy mother had a happy family she left for her own selfish desires. To this day, I wasn't even sure where she was, and as much as I pretended not to care, I did. So much that it pissed me off.

Mason came up behind me, placed a hand on my shoulder, but didn't say anything.

"Your mother was really beautiful."

"Yes, she was. She was the perfect mom, too. Really cared about us. The cancer, when she got it, ravaged her, sweeping through so fast there was little we could do. Dad beats himself up that she didn't get tested early. Dad's only forty-five. Mom was gone shortly after she turned thirty-five. They had seventeen perfect years together if you ask Dad. Then she was just gone. She always said she'd get tested when she was forty like the rest of the world. That was too long for her." His tone was sad and filled with the longing of a man who missed his mother. I understood that all too well.

I thought about the beautiful Eleanor, who was lost to the world at such a young age with four boys and a husband who needed her. They carried on and had one another. They were still a family.

"We should do something for your mom."

Mason's eyebrows narrowed. "What do you mean?"

As I thought more about it, the idea swirled within my mind and took flight. It would be perfect. "I mean about breast cancer. Get involved in the cause. You're a big professional ball player. We should do a fundraiser or something—donate it to the local breast-cancer-awareness group in Boston. We could get pink bracelets that you and I could wear, shirts for me and the WAGs. If the team wants to get involved, they can. Not only would it help your mom's memory, the women fighting now, and those with family history who should get prescreened earlier than forty, but it would look good for your image."

Mason smiled, his tiny crooked tooth shining against his pearly whites. "We could help women like my mom," he said in total awe, like it was the best idea since major league baseball. "I love it! You're a frickin' genius!" He picked me up and twirled me around. "So what do you think we do first?"

For the next hour, we sat down with Eleanor's favorite cheesecake Mick had made in her honor, and we talked about how we could help get the word out using Mason's celebrity status as a pushing-off point.

CHAPTER FIVE

Think Pink was the campaign name we came up with. Once back in Boston, Mason and I got to work. We ordered special Think Pink silicone bracelets to pass out at games and special shirts for the WAGs that we rush ordered and paid an ungodly amount to ship overnight once the items were ready. My shirt I ordered personally and paid for without Mason knowing about it. The back and front had Mason's jersey number, and on top, it said "For Eleanor." It was super cute, and I knew it would mean a lot to Mason.

While he was practicing, I stayed back at his pad and wrote out a plan for a fundraiser. Rachel was all over the idea and thought it was great and offered to help make it something that would actually raise a lot of money for the cause as well as help Mason's image. We hadn't talked about last week's nightmare, and she didn't seem in the mood to. Each time she was present, she was all business, all the time. Somehow, I had to find a way to get back into her good graces to promote Mason as a prospective boyfriend, though I was at a loss, at the moment, for ideas on how to best do that. The orgy Rachel had witnessed definitely did some serious damage to her belief that he would be into her and probably made him seem less desirable. For me, he became more desirable, but that's because I needed to get laid. Just thinking back to watching that woman suck on Mace and him going to town on that blonde was enough to fill a couple of masturbatory sessions in the shower this past week, but I needed the real thing. Only...Mason wasn't on my mind. Unfortunately, a tanned blond from California, currently on location with the chick he was fucking, was.

I sighed and continued typing out my plan, and then figured I needed reinforcements. I pulled out my phone and dialed.

"What up, skank?" Ginelle's voice rang through the line. Just hearing her familiar voice made me happy. It also had the downside of making me homesick.

"Planning a fundraiser."

Gum-smacking and a full-bellied Gin laugh broke through my concentration on the list I was typing. "Uh, isn't the idea to raise the money you need to save Pops already happening? You know, lying on your back!" She laughed manically at her own joke.

"Not for me!" I sighed. "For Mason."

A strangled noise slipped through the line. "The rich baseball player needs money? Why?"

I groaned. "Just listen, bitch. We're improving his image by supporting the local breast-cancer-awareness group here in Boston. His mom died young from the disease, and he wants to do something to give back. Since he's playing ball and practicing, I'm working on an event where we could raise some money and help his image. Make sense?"

More gum smacking. Truth be told, I liked hearing the sound of that way more than the sound of her inhaling one of her cancer sticks.

"So what are you thinking?" she asked. My best friend, Gin was nothing if not creative. She'd come up with some good ideas.

I ran through the gist of the event. We were going to hold

it at some posh hotel downtown. Most of the starting team agreed to participate. Several friends of Mason's would be there, a famous DJ agreed to play the event free, and another restaurateur friend of his PR firm agreed to offer their services and food free of charge.

"Oh, and we're going to have a silent auction filled with baseball paraphernalia and other donated items from friends of the players. But I don't know... I need something that will really draw some high dollars. Got anything in mind?"

Ginelle paused so long I wasn't sure she was still there.

"Well?"

"I'm thinking. Don't get your panties in a twist...if you're even wearing any, that is," she accused, and she'd be right. I wasn't wearing any, because I had on tight leggings that would show lines, and no one needed to see that.

"Shut up!" I warned.

Gin laughed, and it sounded like home. My heart filled with love and joy as I waited patiently and did random Google searches for other charity events to see what they'd done.

"Okay, so you've got a bunch of really hot baseball players going to this thing, right? Like at least twenty?"

"Yeah," I said, not knowing where she was going with this.

"So instead of just doing a silent auction, why don't you auction them? Get an auctioneer guy—you know the ones that talk really, really fast—make sure the guys wear really hot outfits like tuxes, or maybe have them strip off their shirts. Rich women love that shit!"

She was not wrong. I could see women plied with champagne falling all over themselves to get at a shirtless baseball player.

"Gin, that is fucking brilliant."

She huffed, and I could imagine her twirling a lock of hair and gloating prettily. "I know. I'm good like that."

"Yes, you are. Have I told you lately that I got nuthin' but love for you, baby?"

"Whatcha got?" she sang back, bringing us both back to the old-school jam we liked to listen to on the radio back home. It played all kinds of throwback songs from the 90s. We were too young to know the songs then, but in our twenties we both appreciated the silly rap/pop songs from that era.

I thought about how this would work. I'd get the guys to agree to a date with the woman who bought them. She had to pay, but they had to do what the woman wanted for a four-hour period. Even the married ones would do it for the cause. "Gin, honestly, I think this could raise a lot of money."

"Well duh. The men are hot. What rich bitch wouldn't want a piece of that eye candy on her arm for a night?"

Again, not wrong. "I'm going to draw up the plan. Thank you, thank you, thank you."

"Eh, you can pay me back with pictures of hot dudes stripped to the waist. And I'm not kidding. You have this event and you do not send me pictures of half-naked men, I will find really evil ways to embarrass you in the future. And don't think I don't have pictures to prove some of the shit you did in the past."

"Whore!" I shot back, remembering she did in fact have an entire box full of trouble we'd gotten into over the years to pull from and use against me. "You wouldn't!"

She clucked her tongue. "I so would! Half-naked men pictures, sent to my phone, individually...and do not forget Mason. I want one of that sexy bastard."

I laughed hard as Rachel entered the kitchen, where I was

set up. I waved, and she went to the coffee pot and pulled down a mug and filled it.

"All right, you blackmailing dirty slutbag,"

Rachel's eyes were wide, and she almost dropped her coffee cup. I didn't have a chance to explain but tried to shake my head and wave in a gesture that meant everything was okay.

"You'll get your pictures. But you drive a hard bargain."

"Always do, and hey, Mads is doing great. That boy she's seeing is totally nice. I double-checked. Still a virgin, but girl, I'm not thinking for long. He's really cute, likes her a lot, and she falls all over herself to please him. It's actually really sweet. So far, though, he seems like a good guy. She could do a lot worse for her first time."

I groaned and put my head in my hand. "You think she's going to give up her v-card to him? For real?"

"Yeah, she can't stay pure forever, Mia. She's a grown woman. She's nineteen, for crying out loud. Shit, I'm not even sure I can remember how old I was when I gave up the card. It's been so long. I honestly can't remember a time where I wasn't getting hot cock."

This time I moaned. "Gin, don't talk about cock and my sister in the same sentence. You're going to make me break out in hives. And you better not be encouraging her to give it up to him either, or I'll hunt you down, pin you to a wall, cut off all your hair, put honey on your nipples, and leave you for the ants!"

"Jesus Christ on a cross. That's fucked up. You'd do that to your best friend? I need to make new friends. Mine's a goddamned psycho!" she roared, and then laughed hard. I followed suit, imagining her stuck to a wall with honey on her tits and her hair cut in chunks all over the place.

Controlling the laugher, I took a deep breath. "You're right. I wouldn't do that, but please, next time you see her, have her call me, okay?"

"Will do. I've got to go practice the new routine. Let me know how the event goes, and don't forget my reward!"

I shook my head. "Hey, skank, I love you, and I'm proud of you for laying off the cancer sticks. Want to keep you in my life so that we can grow old and get a bunch of cats and a beach house together."

"I've always loved cats," Gin said wistfully, her voice petering off.

She'd totally set me up for it. "That's because you love pussy!" I howled and then hung up on her before she could get in a retort. "Ah, all is right in the world." I opened my eyes and came face to face with a stricken Rachel.

"Are you being blackmailed?" Her eyes were as wide as milk saucers.

I laughed out loud and shook my head. "No, that was Gin, my best friend. We're always like that."

"You always threaten each other and call each other foul names?" Her voice was screeching, and I didn't understand why.

"Uh...yeah? Don't you with your best friend?"

She shook her head numbly. "No. No, I do not. We say very nice things to each other, do lunch, and shop together."

I cringed. They shopped together. Yikes. That is not something Gin and I did together. Drink beer, check out hot guys, gamble a little, play cards, go to concerts, yes. Shopping... er no. "Sucks to be you," I said, meaning every word of it.

"Somehow I doubt that," she said flippantly, and I grinned. So she had a little fire in her yet. That was good. Mason would light a fire under her so bright, she'd get burned if she didn't have a little of her own to battle it.

★ ★ ★ ★

Rachel was not excited about the auctioning men idea, but Mason thought it was brilliant. He called each guy on his team and came back with commitments from over twenty players who were available this weekend and willing to be auctioned off to the highest bidder and take their clothes off—well, their shirts—for charity. I found pink suspenders for each guy to wear and asked them all to wear a nice suit. The plan was to have the men remove their jackets, shirts, and be left with the suspenders. I was also planning on painting a pink breast-cancer ribbon over each man's chest, directly above his heart, to keep with the theme.

Once Mason got home, he sat down at the table with Rachel and me and brainstormed other ideas while he grilled steaks on the balcony, and I made the side fixings. Together, we came up with tons of ideas to get the word out in such short notice, along with ways to get his dad and brothers involved, too, since this was ultimately a way for them to honor their mother's memory. I told him to have his dad get a picture of his wife that he loved blown up and framed for use on one of the tables. The other players who had family members they'd lost to the disease would also share images of their loved ones so the donors in attendance would know the real reason behind the event.

We made certain the chapter president of the local breast-cancer-awareness group would be there and could say a few words.

"Mia, Rachel, I gotta hand it to you ladies. You're the bomb at planning a last-minute event." Mason grinned, hugged my shoulder, and then kissed my cheek. He went over to Rachel, who stiffened the moment he moved close.

Mason's voice got low, but I could still hear him. "I'm sorry about what you saw last week. It shouldn't have happened. That's not the kind of guy I want to be." He looked deeply into her big blue eyes, and she nodded but didn't respond. He moved close, inhaled against her hairline, and then kissed her cheek. "Thank you for your help with this. You didn't have to pull all those strings."

Rachel lifted her head and blinked, staring prettily into Mason's gaze. Could it be any more obvious how into one another these two were? I needed to up my game and get things moving in the right direction. "Mason, I'd help you with anything," she said in an equally low tone.

His fingers tunneled into the hair at the nape of her neck, his big hand cupped her jaw, and his thumb swept across her bottom lip. She gasped, and I watched with rapt attention, hoping he'd make the move and kiss her. "What you're doing to help my mom, it means a lot. I won't forget it. You need me, Rach, I'm there. Just call, anytime, anywhere. Got it?" he said, and leaned forward and kissed her forehead, as if she was something precious.

Right then, it dawned on me. To Mason, she was just that... Precious. For him, Rachel wasn't like all the other girls. He felt he needed to treat her with kid gloves, touch her as though she were spun glass or a fragile artifact. Wow. Once those two hooked up, that was going to be it for him. He might have been a player, but I think he saw a future in her eyes, one he desperately wanted but didn't know how to capture. Good thing I was here for another two weeks to make sure he got the girl.

"I do, Mace," she said, and smiled as he pulled back and went to the balcony to tend to the steaks.

I put my head in my hand and waited until he was gone. Rachel watched his every move as he left. "So... Smitten much?" I said, waggling my eyebrows.

Her head shot back to mine, and she narrowed her gaze. "I have no idea what you mean. Last week I was drunk and out of line. I may have given you the wrong impression about my feelings toward my client." She stressed the word client, but I wasn't sure if it was for my benefit or hers.

I tilted my head to the side and took a long sip of beer. "You aren't fooling me, and you definitely are not fooling Mace. He's on to you, honey. And soon, he'll be on you." I snickered at my own joke.

Rachel groaned and shook her head. "You need to stop, Mia. If you haven't forgotten, you are his girlfriend."

"Pretend girlfriend, and honey, let's not forget that. I'm doing a job. The fans love him. We're working on a fundraiser that will only do good for Mason's image professionally but more so it's good for him to do personally. Giving back in honor of his mom. He really loved her and misses her a lot. All the Murphy men do. You helping the way you are proves that you care, and not just about Mason's image. You have more than a little crush. Admit it." I dug the last shot in and sat back.

Rachel licked her lips and bit down into the bottom one. She leaned her head forward and nodded. "Fine. I admit it. I've cared for Mason for a long time. Heck, I think I fell in love with him the moment we met two years ago. But that hasn't changed the fact that I've watched him parade around with women, drink like a fish, and spent a lot of my own time picking up those pieces. Doing that changes your opinion of someone."

"It can. It does," I agreed with her. "But obviously it hasn't changed the way you feel, or you wouldn't be doing what you're doing. You wouldn't have volunteered to help him clean up his act. You genuinely care about him, and you're breaking at the seams trying to hide it. I've seen the way you look at him, how you light up when he enters a room. You're not fooling me. You may have been fooling him the last two years, honey, but his blinders are off. He sees you, and he likes what he sees."

Her delicate hands came up to her face, and she ran them over her features. "How can you be sure? I don't want to be the next up in a long line of throwaway women. I'd rather not have him at all and get to be in his life always than have a taste of him and lose him forever when he wakes up and realizes I'm not the type of girl he likes. If you look at his track record, you'd know I'm not." She pointed at me, my curves, and made a circular gesture. "No offense. Women like you are his type. Buxom, beautiful, sexy, all the things a man like him can get time and time again." She sighed and dropped her head into her hand with finality.

"Sweetheart, I'm not the type of girl you marry. I'm the type of girl you flirt with and fuck. Mason doesn't want to settle for a girl like me. He wants to have what his dad had. A wife, a home, children, the whole enchilada. You'd give him that and more. You're the whole package. Not an escort who's talented at waiting tables, can act, and rocks a man's world in the bedroom. That last one I'm pretty proud of, but it isn't going to secure me Mr. Right, just Mr. Right Now. I think you need to be open to more with Mason, especially since I'll be out of your hair in two weeks."

This time when she responded, she pursed her lips and leaned into the table. "If you were me, how would you go about making a move? Especially after last weekend's attempt was a complete and utter fail."

"Last week did suck a box of rocks." I nodded.

"It wasn't the only thing that was sucked," she quipped.

My mouth dropped open in shock. "You made a sex joke!" I laughed.

Her own eyes widened, and her cheeks pinked up. "I did!"

"There's hope for you yet!" I exclaimed, and we both giggled. "Seriously, though, Mason's pretty easy."

"Isn't that the truth?" Her retort came right on the heels of the last one and blew me away.

I shook my head and covered my mouth. "Two in one night. Bust out the calendar, girl. We need to mark this night off as the night Ms. Professional lost her poise and busted out her inner vixen!"

She looked over at the balcony and then calmed down. "I want to know, though. I don't have a lot of experience with approaching men when I want to, you know..." She trailed off.

"Fuck?" I guessed.

"God! No. Well, yeah, but date is what I meant. Jeez, you're just like him. So crass."

Holy hell. Was she right? Was I just like Mason? Nah, she was just overly prim and proper. At least, that's what I told myself to get past the potential truth in her statement.

Pushing my hair back into a twist and clipping it up with the claw I had dangling from the hem of my tank top, I cinched it into the bulk of the locks. "This is what you're going to do. At the charity event this weekend, you'll have a couple glasses of champagne to loosen up. You'll flirt a little with him all night.

Nothing impressive. You know, little touches here." I slid my hand from the ball of her shoulder down to her elbow and then pulled back. "Maybe some hand clutching." I clasped my hand with hers and proceeded to tug her to standing and walked around the living room. I'd stop, cock a hip, and bat my eyelashes at her, and then look away suddenly. "Make sure you give him some glances at your assets."

At the word "assets," Rachel's lips pinched tight. "I don't really have any assets," she mumbled.

I looked at her as if she'd grown a second head. "Girl, every woman has part of herself that attracts the opposite sex." I looked her up and down. "You've got a serious set of legs. Wear something short. Get a nice push-up bra and lift those girls, and make sure a good glimpse of them is available in the dress you choose." She nodded, so I continued. "Oh, and hair down. Remember how he mentioned he would like to see your hair down? Have it styled soft and in big curls to cascade down your back. If the dress has an open back, even better." I waggled my eyebrows for emphasis.

"Why?" she asked, and I wanted to groan and smack her upside the head. Could she possibly be that naïve when it came to men? The woman was in her early twenties, for crying out loud. She had to have some idea how a man thought.

Instead of telling her all this, I just answered, "Because when men see open bare skin, they think of sex. Thinking of sex and you in the same thought is a good thing when you want to ultimately bed Mace."

"I want to be with Mason, not just um, go to bed with him."

This time, I couldn't control the exasperated breath of air that left my lungs. "Men relate good sex with good times they could have with a good woman. Having a great sex life and being someone Mason wants to spend time with outside of the bedroom works in your favor. Though usually men think of the sex first. It's just an animal instinct. So you got it all? You're going to seduce Mason at the party this weekend?" I asked, giddy beyond reason.

"I'll think about it," she said.

I scowled but understood there was no moving this girl any faster. She had a way about her, and I think after a few days of thinking about it and building up her courage, she'd make the right choice. "Promise?" I encouraged.

She smiled wide, and it was true... Her smile could light a dark room. "Promise."

Mason entered the room then and shut the balcony door with one long limb and a push of his foot. "Are the two most beautiful women in all the world hungry or what?"

I shook my head. "Always a player," I laughed, and this time, Rachel did, too. I would have expected a sour expression, not a chuckle.

Progress was good.

CHAPTER SIX

Entering the swanky hotel venue for tonight's Think Pink event had both Mason and me stunned. Pink balloons covered the entire ceiling, lighting reflected pink breast-cancer ribbons, and our new tagline, "Think Pink," was splayed all over the pitch-black walls. A disco ball swirled around shooting specks of white light in every direction. Soon, the guys would show and the doors would open. Waiters were receiving their instructions off in the corner. All of them were wearing a pink T-shirt with our theme, and the girls were wearing a tank top that said "Save the Ta-Tas" over their breasts. It was crass, it was fun, and it was a ball player's type of event.

Mason and I, however, were dressed to the nines. He was in a pristine black suit and a pink button-up, the pink suspenders I'd asked every player to wear, and a tie that had breast-cancer ribbons all over it, which made him look like the professional he needed to be. His coppery brown hair was slicked back, and his green eyes were dancing all over the place, taking in the venue. High-top tables were covered in black cloths. Each one was adorned with pink roses bunched into the center accentuated by tea lights, setting the perfect mood. It was beautiful, classy, young, and yet still hip.

"Mia..." His voice trailed off. He was clearly taking it all in and loving everything he saw. I beamed with pride. My first charity event looked amazing. Of course, it had a lot to do with the striking blonde who was walking our way. I'd thought

I looked good in a hot-pink cocktail gown, sequins catching the light and twinkling like the ball above our heads. Not even close. Rachel made her way from the back of the room. She wore a soft-pink satin strapless number that came down to her knee but had a slit up to the hip, giving the ultimate sex appeal with a sweetheart neckline that showed off her breasts. Her hair was down in the old Hollywood fashion style they wore back in the day. A shock of bright-red lipstick topped her full lips. A fine line of black coal liner gave the perfect cat-eye to her baby blues. I did not expect her to look the way she did. She was a pin-up girl slash classy dame.

Mason stood in silence, watching her approach. His jaw was clenched, and his eyes were blazing hot. He'd never looked at me like that before. That steamy gaze was all for the tall blonde who made me feel positively whoreish in my flashy attire compared to her elegance.

"You guys look fantastic," she cooed when she made it to us.

Mason looked her up and down, grabbed her by the waist, cupped her cheeks, and looked deeply into her eyes. She didn't say a word, just allowed him to manhandle her, and I knew why. Because it was alpha, it was smokin' hot, and when a man like Mace grabbed you and handled you that way, you just took it and thanked the mighty Heavens that it was happening.

"You look fucking beautiful," he said, his eyes searching hers. "Every man here is going to want you."

"There's only one man I want," she responded with full confidence.

If I wasn't trying to shrink into the dark room and away from the duo, I would have high-fived her for that line. It was forward and pure sex. I'd give her props later.

"Is that right? Anyone I know?" He traced her face with his nose. She physically trembled in his arms. I almost felt the movement in my own body. It was like watching a steamy foreign film live. Only I knew what the characters were saying.

She licked her lips, and Mason's eyes traced the movement. She so had him hook, line, and sinker. The man was a goner! "Maybe. I guess we'll have to see how tonight goes," she whispered so close to his mouth, he had to feel her breath against his own lips.

"Well, save a dance for me, eh?"

Rachel smiled a secret smile only for Mason. "I'll have to check my dance card. Make sure it's not already full."

"There's room for me. I'll make room." He smirked, and she leaned into him and then pushed away slowly. He allowed it, but I wasn't sure if the room got hotter or if it was just the heat these two were pushing off one another.

A bunch of the players arrived wearing much the same thing that Mason had on—suits, button-ups, and pink galore. It was awesome. I couldn't wait to find out how the auction would go. Thinking of auctions, I grabbed Rachel's hand and led her over to the table where a wide variety of things were set out for silent bidding. Really expensive bottles of wine, memberships to clubs, trips, cruises, vacation rentals... You name it, it was on the silent auction table.

"So you invited the who's who right?"

Rachel picked up a clipboard and nodded. "Yep, we have four hundred people confirmed RSVPs for tonight's event, all who make seven figures a year."

"Damn, I didn't think there were that many rich people in the world."

"Well, we're dealing with celebrities, sports figures, team

owners, sponsors, and the like. We've got a lot of organizations coming just to get the face time, so they'll make a donation to look good and keep their in with the players and other investors involved. It's a vicious circle when it comes to people, business, and their money. They like to show it off under the disguise of giving it back."

"I don't care much how they do it or why, just as long as we leave here tonight donating a lot to the cause. Do you think we'll make at least fifty to a hundred thousand?"

At that comment, Rachel tipped her head back and laughed. Laughed so hard she had to put the tips of her fingers to her tear ducts to staunch the flow and not mess up her makeup. "Mia, if we don't make a million tonight, I'd be shocked."

One million dollars. In a night. I was working every day as an escort to rich dudes to make a million to pay back my father's debt to his loan shark, and we might make that much in an evening. "Unbelievable," I gasped.

Her hand came up to my shoulder and squeezed. "Different type of lifestyle. Don't worry. They can afford it."

"I guess so. At least it's all going to a really good cause. Mason will be pleased if we make that much for the charity."

"Come on. Let's get this party started. People are starting to arrive."

★ ★ ★ ★

The next three hours flew by in a whirlwind of meeting people, hob-knobbing, drinking champagne, dancing to the DJ's beats, and laughing with all the baseball wives. Everyone was having a blast, and the last I checked, the auction table had hundreds of thousands of dollars' worth of bids for the items being auctioned. Even if the player auction flopped, the charity would still get around half a million, which absolutely made me giddy with delight.

I shimmied on the dance floor sipping my pink champagne. All the drinks were pink tonight and flowing freely. The crowd was having a blast, and everyone was in a very giving mood.

Rachel came up to me and grabbed my hand, leading me off the dance floor.

I pouted.

"Hey, don't look at me like that. It's time for the Men of the Night Auction! Wanted to make sure you had perfect seats for the show."

Good looking out, I thought to myself. Oh yeah! Sexy baseball players stripping off their clothes. I pulled my cell phone out of the side of my boobs.

Rachel looked at me and shook her head. "I can't believe you can fit a cell phone in your bra. Men must love your chest."

I looked down at my plump ta-tas and grinned. "Never had a complaint," I offered, and she giggled.

The auctioneer we'd hired came up to a long stage and stood off to the side by a podium. "Tonight, we have a special treat for the ladies out there. Seeing as this is a charity for women, we're going to give the women something to bid on. Men, come on oooooouuuuuuut!" he said, drawing the word out.

All twenty-five baseball players came out onto the stage and lined up. It was a thing of beauty. Veritable eye candy no matter where you looked.

"We've got for your bidding pleasure...a date with a Red Sox baseball player! They take you out for no less than four hours for the date of your choice"—his voice tipped down—"within reason, ladies."

The DJ started playing a saucy stripper-type number, and the third baseman walked out.

"Oh my God, it's Jacob Moore!" one woman screamed and threw up her pink paddle before the announcer even got the chance to ask for a bid.

"Well, looks like we've got some excited bidders. How about you take that jacket off and show the ladies what you've got hiding under there, Jake!"

Jacob played along. His blond hair and blue eyes shined in the light.

"How about we start the bid off at one thousand dollars!"

Holy fuckballs! A thousand dollars as the starting bid! I couldn't believe it.

Needless to say, it wasn't enough. Jacob strutted around the stage, and the moment he unbuttoned his shirt, his bid upped to forty grand.

"There are some seriously rich, horny chicks here," I said to Rachel while clicking a pic of Jake and forwarding it to Gin.

Instantly, I got a response.

To: Mia Saunders
From: Skank-a-lot-a-Puss
I fucking hate you. Keep 'em coming...which is what I'd like to do to that piece of hot male action.

I laughed and showed Rachel what Gin said. She shook her head. "I can't believe you have your best friend in your phone as 'Skank-a-lot-a-Puss.'"

"Why not? It's funny."

She shrugged. "If you say so."

We watched an outfielder go for another twenty thousand. Next up, left field. There was a woman standing by the stage literally drooling over his chocolate skin. He matched the color of dark chocolate perfectly. He went for fifty. That woman was not about to let him go for anything less. She'd started her bid at twenty-five.

I nudged Rachel in the shoulder, clicked a pic, and sent the dark beauty to Gin.

To: Mia Saunders
From: Skank-a-lot-a-Puss
Fuck me. I'd take such a giant bite out of that chocolate ass. I wonder if he'd melt in my mouth and not in my hand.

With that and my easily tipsy state, I cracked up, full guffaws that were unladylike and made me miss one of the players being auctioned. I didn't tell Gin. That would just piss her off.

"So, Rach, we should mess with these bidders. Force 'em to go higher, right?"

"We could... They're doing a pretty good job on their own though. By my count, we're eight guys in and have already made three hundred thousand. The last two both went for fifty."

I watched the next guy come out. It was Junior. Kris, his pretty girlfriend, ran up to me, bouncing. "Junior is allowing me to buy him!" she squealed in utter and complete glee.

This ought to be good. Most women wanted a piece of Junior Gonzalez. He was perfectly edible. Tonight was no different.

"Sorry, Kris." I held up the camera, and when all the

mocha hotness came into view, his eight pack abs shining, the pink ribbon painted on his chest, I about swallowed my tongue.

Kris cried out, screaming, "Me, me, I want to buy him! He can catch me any day!" she roared, and I snapped a picture of Junior's male beauty. Okay, if I was honest, I snapped several. Face front, side view, and a definitely tight-ass pic where he squeezed those gluts and had all the ladies hollering out. I sent the array of pics to Ginelle, and my phone pinged with the ladies' screams.

To Mia Saunders
From: Skank-a-lot-a-Puss
OMG Junior! I love you Junior! Tell him I love him.

I couldn't even put my phone down before it pinged again.

To Mia Saunders
From: Skank-a-lot-a-Puss
That ASS! Have mercy on my slutty soul. I'd let him catch me, throw me, bat me, tag me, as long as he did it naked and fucked me stupid.

The bidding went wild for Junior, and at each bid, Kris would pout. Then the tiny firecracker got downright pissed off, waving her paddle around, yelling at the auctioneer, and shooting evil eyes at the women bidding.

Finally, she screamed, "One hundred thousand dollars!"

I almost fell back. Rachel caught me and tipped me back on my feet.

"Kristine! Are you allowed to spend that much money?" I asked, concerned that she was about to get in some serious shit with Junior.

She nodded vigorously, still waving her paddle and giving attitude. It was funny as all hell. Then she responded to me. "He wanted to donate to the cause anyway. This way, no one gets my man, and he gets his wish to donate the money in Mace's mom's honor. He said he always wanted to show his respect, and Mace is a brother from another mother. That's what he says."

She beamed and then danced around when the announcer cried, "Sold to the petite blonde for one hundred thousand dollars!"

Instead of walking back to his spot, Junior jumped down from the stage, eyes on his prize, picked up his girl, and crushed his mouth to hers. "You did so good, baby!" he said, swinging her around like a rag doll. She preened and kissed him all over. Those two were made for one another. I know... Usually a religious, old-fashioned Hispanic male would normally go for a Latina, but somehow he was making it work. It would be interesting to see how that all works out when he takes her home to his mother. I visibly shook thinking about it. With how much they loved each other, you could tell he did not give a crap about old-school rules. He had his pixie, and he liked it.

Man after man was auctioned off. Bids in the high tens of thousands all the way up to one hundred and fifty had already been called tonight before it was Mace's turn. The last man standing.

"All right, everyone, the man you've all been waiting for. Mason 'Mace' Murphy! He can throw a ball at one hundred miles an hour, he's been on sexiest-man-alive lists all over the globe, and now he's here for your bidding pleasure. Let's start tonight's bid at fifty thousand dollars!" the announcer called.

Paddles flew up across the room. A veritable sea of pink.

"All right, not high enough for you high rollers. Let's go to one hundred thousand!" Still at least ten paddles stayed up.

Finally, when it got to two hundred and fifty, only one paddle was up. "Do I hear two hundred and fifty thousand dollars? Going once, twice, and sold to the lady in the pink satin dress!"

I turned my eyes to my left and saw Rachel's paddle up in the air.

Mason winked at the crowd and jumped down. He stormed over to Rachel and pulled her into his arms. "Did you just buy me for a quarter of a million dollars?" he asked in awe.

I was right there with him. I couldn't believe it either.

"The company told me how much I could give. You're about to sign several spokesperson deals, advertisements, and product sponsorships. Overall, that's really a drop in the bucket on what we'll secure off our commission. Want to keep the client happy," she purred. Her lips glistened off the lights, making them look delectable.

A quarter of a million dollars was a drop in the bucket.

Fuck me. I was in the wrong career.

"I don't know what to say." Mason's eyes were soft and took in every inch of her face.

"Thank you would be a good start." Her eyebrow quirked, and for the first time, I watched sweet, innocent Rachel smirk. It was lovely.

He held her face, but photographers were already taking pictures. This did not look good. Instead, he hugged her close, said thank you into her ear, and moved to my side and nuzzled my hair. The cameras went off like crazy.

"Rachel, this isn't over. I want alone time with you after

the event. Don't run from me. I want you in my room when this is over so we can talk. Swear you will come," he pleaded under his breath.

"I will," she promised.

Then he kissed my cheek and went off to shake the hands of the donors who had given during the auction.

★ ★ ★ ★

The crowd continued to dance and participate in the festivities as the rest of the night wore on. Finally, Mason's voice broke through the loudspeaker and the lights turned up, signaling the night was just about over. It was after midnight, and my feet were killing me. I needed a hot bath, which I knew I could have back in my hotel suite. Mason had booked us another double-suited room so we wouldn't have to drive or take a taxi back the thirty minutes to his place. Instead, we were in one of the penthouse suites in the luxury hotel, as were most the players and their WAGs.

Mason cleared his throat, which sounded inordinately loud through the PA. "Can I get everyone's attention?" he asked the crowd, and slowly everyone made their way to stand around the stage. The spotlight went onto Mace's beautiful face. "I just wanted to thank everyone for coming tonight, for supporting breast-cancer awareness and the local Boston chapter. Ten years ago, my dad lost his wife and my three brothers and I lost our mom. She was only thirty-five years old. There isn't a day that goes by that we don't miss her. The cancer hit quickly and took her fast. She never even had a mammogram, because she wasn't forty. Even with a family history, she thought it wouldn't happen to her. Well, it did. Let's not lose any more of the women we adore to this devastating disease."

The crowd's applause was deafening. Mason put his hand out and shushed the crowd with a gesture.

"Though tonight was in honor of my mother, Eleanor Murphy, it's more for the women who have yet to be saved. That's why it is my extreme pleasure to welcome up the president of the Boston Breast-Cancer Awareness Group to accept a check for tonight's donations." Mason looked down at the check, and his eyes turned watery, and before he could man up, a tear slipped down his cheek. He rubbed his eyes. "Think I got something in my eye."

The crowd laughed, and so did I.

Mason shook his head, and his hand trembled. Seeing a big, confident man hit with some serious emotion made the entire crowd respond. It was like a tidal wave of happiness and sorrow mixed into one. Mick Murphy jumped up on stage and clapped a hand onto his son's shoulder and squeezed several times. Being there for his son, helping him stand proud during a very powerful moment, was something I wished I'd had from my own dad.

"It is with extreme pleasure and gratitude for everyone here that I present you with a check for one million, two hundred seventy thousand dollars." Mason held out the check, and the entire crowd screamed so loud it almost brought the house down. Chills raced up and down my arms, and gooseflesh rose across every inch of my skin. We had raised close to one point three million dollars in a single night. The man from the charity took the check, tears rushing down his face. He didn't try to hide them.

Through the mic that was held at Mason's cheek, you could hear the man say, "Son, I lost my wife a few years ago.

She would have been proud to see this. My daughter is alive because of the work we do and the prescreening she underwent at twenty. I can't thank you enough for bringing such attention to the cause in our own hometown but also spreading the word through your good name." He pulled back and finished. "And the entire Red Sox team. Thank you all. Everyone who's here tonight and contributed, we will put this money to good use right away!" He wiped tears from his eyes.

There's something about seeing grown men cry that turns a woman into a sniveling idiot. All the women around were weeping and blotting their eyes with pocket squares and handkerchiefs, myself included.

It was the best night I'd had in a long time.

★ ★ ★ ★

Back at the room, I sleepily pulled myself out of the tepid bath water. I'd long since lost the bubbles, drunk all the rest of my champagne, eaten my weight in chocolate-covered strawberries, and was now about to hit the sheets. I pulled on the comfy robe, wanting to go out and say good night to Mason. He had been so busy with his brothers. I'd told him I'd see him up in the room or in the morning first thing for some breakfast. He'd kissed me sweetly on the lips for the cameras that were anxiously waiting, held my hands, and thanked me for everything. One of the WAGs and I took to our rooms and left the men to finish up their male bonding for the night. Overall, I was really impressed with how things worked out. A crazy amount of money was raised, the entire event looked great for Mason and the Red Sox team as a whole, and a bunch of rich people got fat tax write-offs. Most importantly, Mason's mom was honored and more women than I could count on my fingers and toes would get the prescreening they needed and hopefully save lives.

I felt like a modern day Mother Teresa in fuck-me pumps, a tight skirt, and a leather jacket. I snickered to myself and stepped drunkenly into the open living room. It was empty, but Mason's suit coat was thrown over the back of the couch, so I knew he was back. I tiptoed to his room and saw a soft light shining through the two inches the door was open.

As I got closer, I heard some noises. My brain couldn't quite seem to come up with the appropriate response to what I was hearing until it was right in front of me. Through the crack in the door, there were two bodies. Mason was clearly on top of a woman, powering into her from behind.

"Fuck yeah, so tight," he said.

I watched, unable to look away as he slid a hand up the woman's spine and into her blonde hair. He pushed it aside, and that's when I saw who was on her hands and knees. Rachel. Sweet, professional Rachel was pressing her perfect little ass back into Mason while he plowed into her over and over. He curled a hand around her shoulder, and thrust hard.

"Mine. You're mine now, Rach. I'm going to take this sweet pussy every day for the rest of my fucking life," he roared.

Rachel screamed, "Yes, God yes. Mace, so good. I'm gonna, I'm gonna... Oh my God."

"That's it, baby," Mason said before he lifted her up to wrap a hand around her breasts and tweak both her nipples. She had small breasts, but they were the perfect handful, and he seemed to enjoy them without complaint. I knew I should go, that I shouldn't stay and watch, but they were so beautiful. Unlike the erotic kinky show I saw the last time I caught

Mason, this was something completely different. It was like watching art, truly capturing the act of love.

Mason tweaked Rachel's small nipples into tight little points. I bit my lip and squeezed my legs together. The space between my own legs was aching, wet, and desperate for attention. But I wouldn't do it. I wouldn't get myself off while watching them. That would be going too far.

Just as I started to back up and give them some privacy, Mason's hand flew between her legs where the blonde hair was trimmed into a neat little line. He moved two fingers around and around, and she arched back just as he hammered his way home. Both of them cried out in combined release. It was exotic, sensual, and something I wanted for myself more than anything. I just didn't know who or when I'd find it. For a brief time this year, I'd thought I had it, but now, I was back to square one and I was a free agent. I could be with whomever I wanted, and so could Wes.

Wes. God, even the thought of his name sent a fresh pool of desire to moisten the flesh between my thighs.

Quickly running back to my room, I shut the door and flung myself into bed. I didn't want to do what I did next, but I couldn't help it. I pulled out my phone, brought up the pictures I'd taken of Wes and Alec, and scrolled through their naked beauty. And then I touched myself. It took no more than thirty seconds, and I was crying out, muffling my cries against my forearm and sinking my teeth into the robe and meat of my arm as the tremors washed over me.

It felt good while it lasted, but then lying there in the quiet of the room, the overwhelming feeling that hummed just under the surface was an unbelievable sense of loneliness. For the first time in my life, I was by myself, truly and utterly alone.

CHAPTER SEVEN

Sponsors for Mason came out of the woodwork after our big charity event. Turns out that when a young pro ball player goes philanthropist, every major sports-related organization wants a piece of him. Rachel was fielding requests for interviews, ad campaigns, commercials, and the like all week. Me, I played the part of pretty, devoted girlfriend while gorging on beer and baseball. It. Was. Awesome. Three weeks in, and I was already bemoaning the fact that soon I was going to be leaving Mason and the easy life. Sure, I'd be sent to another rich guy who needed me for something else, and the amenities would be great, but they wouldn't be something I could wrap my arms around. Living with Mason, once we got past all his douche-bag ways, was really easy. He was funny, smart, and loved living life. I felt young for the first time in a long time. There was nothing for me to do except be me. Mason liked me for me. As a matter of fact, we got along like friends who had a long history, even though it had only been three weeks. We clicked.

The good news was that Rachel had been coming over more often. They were so unbelievably cute together. She was still shy, and he made a point of bending over backward to please her. Made me wonder how this was all going to work out when I left. I mean, the fans and the public had seen me for the last three weeks as the doting girlfriend, committed Red Sox fan, and the woman who helped her guy put on a huge charity event.

"Hey, Mace, do you think we need to plan some type of public breakup?" I asked while pushing eggs around the frying pan. It was my turn to make breakfast, and Mason ate a ridiculous amount of protein, so I was cooking a dozen eggs for just the two of us, ten of which he'd gobble up, bacon, and I'd cut up some fruit.

Mason stole a piece of bacon from the plate I had sitting next to the stove and munched on it thoughtfully. "I don't know. We should ask Rach. My guess would be that Rachel and I would keep our relationship under wraps for a few weeks so the public doesn't see me hopping from one girl to another, you know?"

I nodded, grabbed the shredded cheese, sprinkled some over the scrambled eggs, and added some salt and pepper. "Makes sense. How is it going between the two of you anyway?" Not that I couldn't hear the sexcapades from another state away. They could work to keep it down. I'd been in a permanent state of arousal all week just from hearing them through the walls.

He stole another slice of bacon and leaned next to the stove while I plated the food. Two eggs and two slices of bacon for me, ten eggs and four slices of bacon for Mason. I set the plates onto the bar top, where we preferred to eat. The dining room seemed too formal for either of us.

"It's going good." He grinned. "Never knew such a wildcat was under all those suits, but damn if I'm not the happiest fucker around."

I snorted and choked on my eggs. He slapped my back until it passed. "Wildcat? Seriously?"

He nodded, smiling so wide I could see every tooth. "Best lay I ever had."

That earned him a punch to the arm. He rubbed it. "True though. She's sweet and proper in her suits, but the second I get her out of them... Man, Mia, that little blonde rocks my fuckin' world."

This time I grinned. "I'm so glad, Mace. Do you think it will turn into something?" I asked, keeping my own hope in check, trying not to show how excited I was for them.

He tipped his chin and nudged me with his arm. "It's serious. I can't imagine any other man putting his hands on her." He shivered and groaned. "Makes me crazy just thinking about it. I figure, if thinking about her with another man makes me want to punch my fist through a wall, it's gotta mean something. Right?"

"Right," I agreed instantly.

"So, I gather I'll talk to her about it tomorrow night when we're in Seattle."

Seattle. We were headed to Seattle. Someone I cared a great deal about lived in that very city. "Seattle, really?"

"Yep, plane leaves first thing tomorrow morning. We'll be there for a couple days. Quick three-gamer. Get your shit together, sweetness." He cleared his plate so fast it was as if the eggs and bacon had been vacuumed up instead of eaten.

I licked my lips, and the possibility of burning off some of the loneliness I'd felt this past week sparked in my mind like flicking on a light switch. "Hey, I, uh, have a friend in Seattle. While you and Rachel are you know, doing your thing, would it be okay if I had a friend over?"

Mason's eyes widened, and he grinned. "You've got a friend?"

I narrowed my gaze at him. "Yeah, doesn't everyone have friends?"

"What kind of friend?" he hedged with a hint of mirth to his tone. "A male friend?"

"Does it matter?" I shot back, throwing some serious attitude. It wasn't really any of his business, and I didn't plan on sharing.

He shook his head. "Nope, just teasing. I don't care who you fuck, as long as the press doesn't catch wind that my fake girlfriend is cheating on me, we're good."

That's when I smiled and waggled my eyebrows. "I can be discreet."

Mason licked his lips and smirked. "I'll bet you can."

★ ★ ★ ★

Rain delay. Nothing but buckets were coming down when we landed and got to the field. The umps were holding the game and had been for the last hour. The fans, however, did not care one bit. The Mariners were diehards for their team and probably used to rain. Gave me time to text a certain sexy Frenchman I'd been missing.

To: Alec Dubois
From: Mia Saunders
Hey, Frenchie... I'm in town for a couple days. You free to meet up tonight?

I could not believe I was doing this. I hadn't spoken to Alec since I'd left almost two months ago. An hour later, I finally got a reply.

To: Mia Saunders

From: Alec Dubois
Ma Jolie, I will meet you anywhere, any place. Am I to assume this is what you Americans say a booty call?

Uncontrollable giggles left me at imagining Alec saying "booty call" with his French accent. I hugged the phone, already feeling lighter and no longer alone.

To: Alec Dubois
From: Mia Saunders
Are you interested?

To: Mia Saunders
From: Alec Dubois
Need you even ask? Wear very little. I want to see ta peau parfaite the moment you open the door.

Perfect skin. He wanted to see my perfect skin. He always had a way of showing me how much he adored my body. I thought back to his fingertips caressing my naked hip up my waist and between my breasts. He would whisper beautiful French words into my ear as he touched me. Alec made me believe I was beautiful. In every way.

Immediately, I became heated, desire swirling thick in my veins as the anticipation of seeing Alec spiraled through every pore and tickled along each hair, caressing me with the essence of need.

Tonight, I would see my Frenchman. I could not wait!

★ ★ ★ ★

I opened the door, and there he was. Alec Dubois, my Frenchie. Before I could say hello, he grabbed me around the waist, pulled me into his chest, and lifted me off my feet. His lips were on mine and my legs wrapped around his trim waist. He turned, slammed the door shut, and pressed me into it, deepening the kiss. The hardest part of him rubbed against the very space I wanted him most. I moaned, opening my mouth farther. He took the invitation and swept his tongue inside to swirl against my own.

Until that moment, I'd forgotten how much I missed kissing Alec. When he kissed, he did it with everything he had to give—passion, desire, and grace. So much grace and beauty I could hardly breathe. He ripped his mouth away and set his forehead against mine.

"*Ma jolie*, I have missed your love," he whispered against my lips.

Tears prickled against my eyes, and I caught his gaze. His eyes were golden yellow set with brown flecks that seemed to glow in this light.

I nipped his lips and nuzzled into his neck. "I've missed you, too, Alec. I had no idea how much until you were standing in front of me."

He curled his fingers into the nape of my neck, and his thumbs swept across my chin and lips.

His eyes seemed to catalogue every facet of my face the way only an artist who's extremely focused on details could. "You have been sad, *chérie*. Why?"

I shook my head, not wanting to get into it. "Later. For now, are you hungry? Can I get you anything?"

Alec pressed his length firmly into my center. Beads of excitement roared from the middle out and through my limbs. I tightened my legs, bringing him closer. His eyes flashed with an intensity I'd missed. It was the look of a man who is desperate, desperate to have his woman. "I have only the hunger to taste your sweet sex, *ma jolie*." And there was my filthy Frenchman.

Without further ado, he led me to my suite and kicked the door shut. He placed a knee to the bed and then folded over, letting me down as if I was as precious as one of his paintings.

"Undress for me," Alec said and stood. "I want to watch you expose your light."

The way he spoke, the fire in his gaze, sent me spinning with lust. With absolutely no finesse, I lifted up to my knees and pulled the tiny dress I wore over my head. I wore nothing underneath, remembering his preference for little clothing and the lack of barriers.

"*Vous êtes devenue plus belle.*" Alec spoke in French, and the words slid along the surface of my skin as if he'd touched me, light as a feather but just as tantalizing. Even with my rusty French and lacking experience, I knew what he'd said. He'd told me I'd gotten more beautiful.

I shook my head. "Only through your eyes."

He cupped my cheek. "You do not see yourself the same way the world sees you."

I laughed. "*You* are not the world, Frenchie."

Alec tapped my lip, and I sucked his thumb into my mouth and swirled my tongue around the digit. His eyes darkened, the light no longer showing the golden tone of his amber gaze.

"Oh, *chérie*, have you forgotten what you learned during our time?" he whispered, stripping off his T-shirt, exposing the square pecs I loved to sink my teeth into and the washboard abs that my fingers itched to trace.

"I haven't forgotten how much I love your body," I

retorted, fisting my hands at my sides, my breasts heaving, becoming heavy and needy. Both his hands came out and lifted the twin globes, squeezing and molding them as if he was reacquainting himself with my body. A cry spilled from my lips when he swiped both thumbs across the turgid peaks. He inhaled deeply when close to my neck, as if breathing in my scent.

Closing my eyes, I moaned and tipped my head back in offering. I could feel the edges of my hair trailing along the exposed skin of my bum. "I love your touch."

A wet sensation covered my right breast, and then I felt the nip of his teeth pinching the skin. A fresh bout of desire leapt from where he plucked and sucked straight down the length of my torso to settle hotly between my thighs. My clit throbbed and ached, primed for the moment he'd touch me *there*. And I knew he would. If I knew anything about Alec Dubois, I knew he loved the taste of me on his tongue. For long minutes, Alec feasted on my breasts, sucking, plucking, massaging, and biting down on the tips until they were ripe, red little strawberries ready to be eaten. My hips rotated in the air, searching for something, anything to relieve the ache.

"Alec," I pleaded, and he grinned against my nipple, sucked hard, and then pulled away. When I opened my eyes, I knew what he must have seen. A woman who was ready to be fucked. Only, Alec didn't fuck. He made love and told me so repeatedly.

His hands went to his jeans, where he unbuttoned and pushed them down his toned thighs. The thick knob of his cock was weeping at the tip when it sprang free of its denim confinement. I leaned forward and licked the pearly drop, groaning at the remembered taste.

"*Oui, mon amour,* take the edge off so I can gorge on you."

I was on my hands and knees when he tunneled his fingers into my hair and thrust into my mouth. I took him deep, so deep he slipped down my throat the way he liked. *"Si bon."* So good, he'd said. And he wasn't wrong. It was unbelievably good to be servicing Alec. His taste, his scent, reminded me of amazing times, of great sex, and a lot of laughter, love, and friendship. All of the things I needed in my life now. With Alec, I wasn't alone.

I doubled my effort, taking long laps of his length and worshiping the tip, sucking every drop of precum like a kitty with tiny little flicks to a saucer of cream. He watched me take his length over and over. When I looked up from my position, his nostrils were flared, his eyes intense half-lidded slits, his mouth a firm slash, twisting into ecstasy as he powered into my mouth. I took what he gave and loved every second of it. Then, with no warning—he never did warn before—he pressed deep and filled my mouth to the brim with his essence. Hot bursts of his seed rushed down my throat. I swallowed reverently, milking him for every drop until his hand turned into a fist at the roots of my hair and pulled me off his cock.

"Oh, *ma jolie,* I'm going to show you again how to love yourself, and others, by loving you this night. That, my beautiful Mia, was a perfect start."

★ ★ ★ ★

We'd just exited the shower after two rounds of serious fucking. "Thank you for coming tonight." I cuddled into his bare chest. His fingertips traced along my arm and the ball of my shoulder in patterns I couldn't place. Didn't try to.

Alec rubbed his jaw along the crown of my head. "Why are you so alone when you are paid to be with someone?" he asked. The tone was inquisitive, not accusatory.

Snuggling in, I licked his nipple and kissed it sweetly. "I don't sleep with all my clients, Alec."

His arms tightened around me. *"Vraiment?"* Really? he'd asked.

That brought out a chuckle. "Really," I answered.

"I do not understand this. Why, if they are paying you to be with them, are you not *with them* in the most beautiful way possible?"

Again I giggled into his warm skin. Of course he would lack understanding. "You know I didn't have to have sex with you."

His eyes narrowed, and I could tell he was trying to work something out. *"Chérie,* you and I were meant to love one another. It was never a question, *oui?"*

"Oui, but that isn't the case with everyone, Alec. I'm not paid to fuck."

"I do not fuck," he reiterated strongly, his voice a growl and something I knew very well.

I lifted my head up, placed my hands on his chest, and set my chin on top of them. "I know. And I adore that about you." His hands trailed up and down my back, as if he were painting something. For all I knew, he could have been. He was an artist. "You taught me to love the one you're with, but that doesn't always mean you have sex with them."

His eyes narrowed, and he looked positively affronted. "Why not? Everyone needs to release tensions, connect physically, and making love is the best way to do that."

Of course my Frenchie would see it that way. "Well, the

client after you was gay." I shrugged.

"So then you could have made love to both of them." He pulled me completely on top of him, slid his hands down to my ass, and separated my legs so I was straddling him. He was hardening under me. Alec was, by far, the most virile man I'd ever met. When he said he would make love to me all night, I had no doubt that I'd pass out from needing sleep before he stopped loving me.

Licking a trail from one nipple to the next, I sucked on the neglected flat disc until it hardened. "That would have been an experience, but it wasn't like that."

"I'll never understand that. Continue."

Tilting my head to the side, I used one finger and traced his mustache and beard. His long russet locks had dried and were wavy and sexy in a way that was intensely masculine. "This guy I'm with now, the baseball player. At first I thought I might want to share a bed with him, but he's in love with someone else."

"Ah, and the other woman does not share. Then why did he need you?" he asked thoughtfully, but it was hard to pay attention because at that moment, he decided to press a finger deep into my sex from behind. He leisurely fucked me with one finger until I was wet enough that he could fit another. "You were saying," Alec said with a grin, knowing exactly what he was doing to me. Sexy bastard.

"Uh, yeah. Well, he was kind of an ass when we met, and then I helped, oh God, fuck..." I dropped my head and pushed back, letting his fingers hit just the right spot. "Uh, get the girl he wanted."

He clucked his tongue. "Pity. More for me," he uttered, and pushed high into me with those two thick fingers. I pressed back against them, moaning and gasping, the sensation splintering all around me. Then I put my mouth on his chest and licked and nipped while he got me off with his fingers. When I was crying out, he rolled me over and kissed a path down my body. "Want your cream on my tongue, *ma jolie*. Need to remember your taste. Going to eat you now. Are you done telling stories?" Telling him stories. He thought talking was telling stories. Damn, the man was cute and fucking talented. Then I pressed into my heels and pushed up into his face. He growled and stuck his tongue as far inside me as it would go. His hands held my lower lips apart, and he rubbed his lips, mustache, and beard all over my sex. "Want your scent all over me while I sleep. Then I'll have beautiful dreams of my sweet-tasting, beautiful Mia. *Oui, ma jolie*?"

"Fuck yes," I groaned and cried out when he sucked extra hard on my O-trigger, sending me to the very top of the crest.

Alec took his time between my legs. He sucked, fucked me with his finger, nipped at me with his teeth, and even gave me a rosy quarter-sized hickey on my inner thigh. Over and over he brought me to the very pinnacle of release and then backed off until I was so exhausted and out of my mind with need I begged and pleaded for him to finish me off. My sex was so wet I could feel the slippery juices sliding between the crack of my ass. Alec didn't let it fly. He swooped down with the flat of his tongue and teased the tiny rosette I knew he loved, laid his mouth wide over my opening, and drank. His cheeks hollowed out, my back arched, and then he grated his teeth along my clit, and I shot into the stratosphere, bucking like a wild woman. While I was coming, he slipped on a condom and speared his thick cock deep into me and rode me hard, harder than he ever had before. We were wild, out of control, and fucking like we would never get another chance. At one point, he pulled my legs up high, cutting my body in half, and powered into me.

"Love your body."

"Love your sex."

"Love your heart."

"Love your soul."

"Love you, Mia."

Except Alec said all of those things in French.

What we did that evening was scalding hot, it was devoted, and it was one of the most passionate sexual experiences of my life. He brought us both to release again, and when the last vestiges of his essence poured into me, he collapsed against my body. Together, we passed out, still connected physically, emotionally, and mentally.

CHAPTER EIGHT

I woke in the middle of an orgasm. My legs were clamped around Alec's head as he took me there. Then without even a word, a good morning, he rolled on a condom. I'd lost count of how many we'd used the night before. He inched his way into overused, swollen tissue. Still, it felt divine. My poor hoo-hah tensed and pulsed like it had been through a battle and won. This time he made slow, careful love to me. We both knew it would be the last time, but I wouldn't say forever. I'd learned not to think that way. Between seeing Wes again and now Alec, never was not a word I'd keep in my vocabulary when it came to the men I cared for.

Once we were done, he methodically put on his clothes. "I enjoyed this night with you, *ma jolie*. When you are in town again or are in need of a reminder that you are loved, you will call, *oui*?"

I nodded, got up, and threw on a silk robe I had hanging over the door while he pulled his hair into a messy man bun. God, I loved the man bun. I leaned up on my toes and kissed him. He wrapped his arms around my body and held me close while we kissed for long moments.

He pulled back and kissed my nose. "I have much work to do, or I would feast on your flesh all day." He cupped my cheeks and focused his yellow gaze all over my face. "Sadness does not become you. This reason you are sad, is it a man?"

I pinched my lips together and thought back to that phone

call. God, how I wished I'd never made that call. I could have just texted him, and then we'd both blissfully go on, knowing that the other still felt it deep. And here I was now, doing the same thing he was doing. Losing myself in another man's body, in sex. Really good sex, toe-curling, mind-blowing sex, but it still wasn't with the one I wanted it to be with.

"Yeah, it was a man, but you know, having you here, helping Mason get his girl, I realize that it's all part of the process. My journey this year is long, and if at the end, I'm meant to be with a certain man, I will be." Alec nodded, and I smiled, the thought taking wings.

Alec pushed back my unruly hair and caressed the side of my face. "*Ma jolie*, you are very young. Give yourself time to enjoy life and all its offerings." He pressed his forehead to mine. "Including the pleasures of the flesh, *oui*?"

I knew what he was saying, and it reinstated my belief that this year was about me. Not about me and someone else. It was about me saving my dad and finding myself. Wherever that took me is wherever it took me. He was right. I was young and not in a committed relationship, and neither was Wes. I couldn't fault the man for wanting to find a connection to someone, to not be alone even for a short time he shared his body with someone else. I'd done that, too. And you know what, it felt amazing. I felt amazing. Refreshed, ready to take on whatever life was going to throw my way.

"You know, you're pretty amazing, Frenchie."

Alec grinned that drop-dead sexy smile, and I swear I felt it in my clit.

"This I know, *chérie*." He leaned forward and kissed me softly. "Only you, you need to remember you too are a gift to this world."

Alec always had a way with words. Words that could soothe, entice, and always worked their magic on my psyche.

I led him by the hand into the living-room portion of the suite. It was far too much to hope that Mason and Rachel would already be out for the day. Then again, I should have just looked out the window. Rain. Heaps of rain smattered against the sliding door. That meant practice would be delayed or canceled.

Rachel and Mason were both completely dressed and sitting at the dining area having what looked to be lunch, not breakfast. Fuck, what time was it?

Mason's eyes caught sight of Alec and then me in my robe, hair a mess, cheeks probably rosy from the recent orgasm—basically my entire look screaming I-was-just- fucked. Mason grinned. "Hey, sweetness. Sleep well?"

That's when Alec jumped in. "I wouldn't call what we did sleep." He waggled his brows seductively. My Frenchman was incorrigible. Rachel didn't say a word. Her mouth was wide open, her fork held midair close to her face with a strawberry sitting on the tines waiting to be eaten.

"Uh, this is Alec. That's Mason and his girlfriend, Rachel."

Rachel's hand came down, and the fork clattered against the plate. "Uh, hi?" she said. That was definitely the first time I'd seen the professional, put-together woman totally at a loss for words that didn't involve a large, sexy-as-sin baseball player.

Mason gave a chin lift. I turned Alec around and led him to the door. We weren't completely out of sight, but he never cared about what people thought. Instead of walking out the door, he pulled me against his body, placed one hand on my ass and one at my nape, crushing me to his lengthy form before he devoured my mouth. Tongue, lips, and teeth parried and danced the most delectable of good-bye kisses.

Finally, when we both couldn't breathe, he let me go. "*Je t'aime*, Mia," Alec said, his tone filled with the love I knew he had for me. I held a place in his heart, and I always would. That was enough for me.

"I love you too, Alec."

I watched him until he entered the elevator.

"Until next time, *ma jolie*," he said as the doors closed behind him.

Then I turned and went back to the table. When I got there, Mason handed me half of his club sandwich. I sat down and took a bite, suddenly ravenous.

Neither of them spoke until Mason turned his entire body to me, elbow to the table. "So you love this guy?" He hooked a thumb behind him.

I nodded. "Yeah, but not in the way you're thinking. I'm not *in love* with him. We just have something. When we're together, we're together. It's just us. But most of the time, we're not."

Rachel closed her eyes and then pursed her lips. "I don't get it. We heard him say he loved you. And in French. Oh my God, that was sexy." She gasped when Mason's burning gaze shot her way. "Sorry." She shoved a piece of fruit into her mouth and looked down at her plate.

Pushing a piece of hair back and pulling my leg onto the chair, I focused on my two new friends and decided I had nothing hide. I needed to be me, warts and all. If they were my friends, they'd accept me for who I was, not who they thought I was. "Alec was a client. We went there." I made a hand gesture that both of them understood. "Enjoyed the hell out of it. He taught me a lot about people, about loving myself and others. So yeah, I love him. Just not in the 'I'm going to marry him, want to have his babies, or be his girlfriend' type way. More like..." I thought about it for a moment while looking at the rain pelting the balcony. "More like 'I really love it when he fucks me into next week and I care about him and love him like a friend.' Does that make sense?"

Both Mason and Rachel shook their heads, and I groaned. "I can't explain it. Just...don't worry about it."

"From the sound of it, the fuck you into next week part sure as hell happened. Damn girl, I rolled over and fucked Rach so many times last night I think my dick might have been sprained listening to you take it over and over again," Mason joked boldly. Rachel and I both simultaneously socked him in the arm. "Ouch!" He rubbed his arms. "You enjoyed it." He pointed at Rachel, and her cheeks turned a mighty shade of red.

I polished off the sandwich and got up. "Need to shower."

"Smell you later...sex fiend," Mason said when I started walking away.

"Takes one to know one, fuck face!" I hollered back. Maybe Mason would be my boy version of Ginelle back home. That could be nice.

"You both are like children," was the last thing I heard Rachel say as I closed the door to my room.

★ ★ ★ ★

Over the next couple of days, Mason and the Red Sox won their games. Everyone was in the best of moods, and it showed. When we got back to Boston, we stepped off the plane, into a cab, and over to the Black Rose Pub, where his brother Brayden worked the bar. It was time to celebrate, and the team was ready. A truckload of guys poured out of cabs and town cars. The second we entered, Brayden whistled over the bar. A pretty waitress went over to something that looked like a stereo and hit a button.

"We Are the Champions" by Queen filled the bar. It was still early, and on top of that a weeknight, so the bar was practically dead at four in the afternoon, but that didn't stop the team. They were ready to slug back some beers and let off some steam. They'd been playing like rock stars on the field, and they had a few days' break to enjoy. Today was time to celebrate. The WAGs found their place cuddling next to or in the lap of their chosen player, and the drinking started. Several hours into the night, and I was feeling mighty fine.

"Mace, I'm going to head home," Rachel said, leaning close but not too close to cause suspicion. The team didn't know that he was bangin' Rachel and not me. All but Junior believed the sham.

"Baby, no. Meet me at my place?" Mason suggested with a pair of his best puppy-dog eyes. I had to give it to a woman who could deny a man what he wanted with that look.

Rachel shook her head. "Got to work tomorrow. I need to do laundry and be fresh for the day. I'll come by the house for an early lunch?"

Mason nodded and put his hand at her neck. Her eyes widened, and so did mine as I glanced around to see if anyone was watching. They weren't. Most the crew were already three sheets to the wind anyway.

"Mace," I warned, nervous he was going to break character. Instead, he just squeezed her neck and then patted her on the shoulder.

"Miss you, baby. See you tomorrow."

Rachel smiled sweetly at Mace and then hugged me. "Take care of him, will ya?"

I looked at her with mock seriousness, put my hand at my brow, and saluted her. "Yes, ma'am!"

"Children. I swear being around you two is like hanging out with twenty-year-old children." She shook her head and walked off. Mason watched her ass the entire time. Rachel had a nice ass. Small, but she worked it.

"Fine fucking ass, that woman. Damn, I'd like to take a bite out of it right now." He growled and then slugged back the rest of his brew. "Let's get shitfaced and take a cab back?"

Brayden came over to our side of the bar. "How you two doin'?" he said, his coppery hair glinting red off the neon-pink bar lights behind him.

"We're ready to get serious. Shots and beer chasers. Mia, we're about to play a game!"

I shimmied on my seat. "Love games. What's it called? Maybe I've heard of it."

"Called Bullshit."

"Bring it on, ball boy. My girlfriend Gin and I wrote the book on this fucking game. Never lost!"

Mason grinned a mocking evil little smirk. "Line 'em up, bro," he said to his brother.

Since Mace was throwing down the gauntlet, I unzipped my Red Sox hoodie and put it around my chair, leaving me in a tight tank. My girls were on display in a big way. He glanced down at my tits and groaned.

"That is not playing fair. What are you doing? Trying to distract me?" he accused, and I laughed.

"Well, we're going to need some more players."

Junior and Kris were sitting close. We brought them into the game, and Mason explained the rules. Then the drinking commenced.

★ ★ ★ ★

"Once upon a time, I was walking through the woods, and I stepped in some bear shit!" Mason said. Usually the stories were more involved, really creative, but we'd been at the game awhile, and we were all losing pretty regularly.

I was Bear Shit. So when he said bear shit, I had to respond with, "Bullshit!" I yelled, slapping my hand on the bar.

"Who shit?" Mace's head slammed back as if punched.

"Baby shit!" I snickered and pointed to Kris.

The way the game worked was, you started with a story, blamed "shit" on one of the player's fake names, and then they claimed "Bullshit" and the accuser would respond with "Who shit?" or some version of the same. The person accused would blame someone else. Then the new accused would claim "bullshit." And so on and so on. I was a master at this game, having played endless rounds with Ginelle growing up, but that didn't stop me from drinking the entire game, right along with the people who messed up.

"Uh, uh...shit, I forgot what I was supposed to say!" Kris pouted.

"Drink!" both Mason and I roared and pointed. We all did a shot because it was more fun to drink together than one at a time, and then we continued with the game.

By last call, Mason and I were blotto, barely holding one another up. We'd not had dinner but had munched on some fries and nachos throughout the game. I tried to slam back water every time Brayden put a glass in front of me, but I was certain for every glass of water I drank, I'd had three beers and a couple of shots to boot.

Brayden got us both into a cab, paid the driver from Mason's wallet, patted us both on the heads, and told the driver where to take us.

We weren't really sure how we got home, but there was a lot of singing baseball tunes, cussing, and hollering.

Eventually, we made it back to Mason's house. We stumbled up the walk.

"How the fuck do we get in," he slurred and leaned heavily against the door.

I swayed on my feet and looked around. The street was really pretty. Blurry swaths of color streamed past my vision. The wind blew my hair and kissed my skin, making the hairs on my arms prickle enticingly.

"I love your street. It's like art, all colorful and halos of light." I moved to step down, but Mason caught my arm before I tumbled down the stairs. He pushed me back against the door.

"Keys!" he said as if he'd won the lottery. He pushed a hand into his pocket and pulled out a set of keys, showing the prize. "Yes!" He pumped a fist in the air, and I tried to high-five him, but it didn't really work. It ended up being more a slap of his curled fist.

Together, we struggled to get the door open and then essentially tumbled into the foyer drunkenly. With effort, we leaned on one another and made our way up the stairs.

"Shhh, you might wake up Rachel," Mason said, bumping into the wall and taking me with him.

I concentrated hard and pushed him forward. "She's not here!" I reminded him.

His entire face went sad. "Oh man, that sucks so bad. I wanted to fuck her. Man." He slid a hand over his face.

"Aww, it's okay. You can totally fuck her tomorrow!" I offered, stumbling forward.

He pressed me into the wall, his chest crushing mine. "You fucking smell so good, Mia. Did I ever tell you that?"

I shook my head and blinked several time. "No, but that's super nice. You should be nice more often. I like you. Like you're awesome likable when you're not a douchebag."

He put his hands to my hips and held me close. "I miss Rachel," he said, leaning into my chest, his head on the soft pillows of my breasts.

Bringing up my arms, I patted his back and ran my nails through his silky hair. "It's okay. She'll be here soon. She's gonna make us lunch probably. She's really nice like that," I said but didn't have any idea what I was saying. If I'd known what I sounded like, basically an uneducated idiot, I might have tried hard to think straight, but the liquor was taking its toll. It dawned on me that technically I was a junior-college dropout, but whatever. That shit didn't matter anyway. I was making a hundred Gs a year. A month. Whatever it was. A lot of fucking money.

While I was thinking about my station in life, Mason had moved his hands up and was squeezing both my breasts, looking down at them in complete awe. "You've got the best fucking tits. Rach has small tits, but I like 'em. Yours are world-class, fuck-me titties. Can I fuck your titties? That would be awesome!" he screamed happily, and I pushed him away. He hit the other wall and barely stayed standing.

"No, stupid. You cannot fuck my tits. And thank you." I smiled wide and held my own boobs, appreciating their size and weight. "They are some good tits. Men like 'em a lot. It's one of my best features."

Mason shook his head vigorously and so many times that, in my drunken state, I worried it would break off.

"No, no, no. You've got great tits and ass for sure. But your hair and eyes could make men worship at your feet. Your eyes are like green diamonds." He came close and held my face up into the hall light. "Yep, like fucking jewels. You have jewel eyes!" he exclaimed and then rubbed his jaw into my neck. His body seemed then to slump against me. "I'm tired."

When he said it, I thought about it. My limbs became really heavy, as if I was carrying around a box of rocks in each hand and had a two-ton weight on my chest. The weight was Mason, who was leaning his entire body against mine, practically sleeping. I could tell by the tiny puffs of air that he was going to fall asleep standing up.

"No, we have to get you in the bed." I pulled against him, and we both maneuvered sloppily to his giant bed. "Now get ready," I told him.

He lifted his chin and pulled off his shirt. Fuck me. His chest was golden and muscled to perfection. I thought back to my Frenchie. He had a really hot body, just like Mason.

"Your turn."

For some reason, this request, in my current state, did not sound odd. I pulled off my tank, and then together, we unbuttoned our jeans and slid them down. I was in my bra and panties, and he was in his boxer briefs.

"Are we gonna fuck?" he asked, swaying on his feet.

I glanced down at his equipment. Nothing was happening.

"No! Stupid ass." I pulled back the covers. "Besides, you have whiskey dick." I giggled and cuddled into the covers. The second my head hit the pillow, I was falling asleep.

Mason rummaged around, pulled back the covers, and climbed in. "I do not have disky wick," he claimed, and I laughed hard, snuggling deeper into my cave of blankets. "I mean dick whiskey," he slurred, grabbed me by the waist, and plopped me on his chest. "Night, Rach," he said, holding me close.

"Not Rach. I'm Mia." I rubbed into his warm chest, enjoying the heat.

"Mmm, 'kay. Night, Mia," he said, and we both feel into a sleep of the dead, or, more distinctly, the sleep of the drunk.

★ ★ ★ ★

Vaguely, I could hear noises downstairs. I figured maybe Mason was making breakfast. My head was pounding like an entire marching band was playing a John Phillips Souza tune in my head. Instead of opening my eyes, I snuggled deeper into the warmth that surrounded me.

"Oh man, fucking hell, my head," I heard Mace say. Only it wasn't from downstairs or across the room or next to my bedside. It was a deep rumble against my ear, adding to the music in my own head.

I blinked several times and opened my eyes. At the same time I started to pull away from the body I was in bed with, the comforter fell to my hips and left me half naked in my bra.

"What the..." I said looking down at a bare-chested Mason, who was slowly opening his own eyes.

Of course, none of this made a lick of sense. My head roared, and I pressed my palms to my temples, desperately trying to relieve the pressure while trying to remember what happened.

That's when the door opened and a chipper, suit-clad Rachel entered, saying, "Wake up, sleepyhead..." Then she saw me, and Mace sat up, the blanket revealing his bare chest. "Oh my God." Tears instantly pricked at her eyes, and a delicate hand covered the horror wanting to spew from her lips. "No..." she uttered, and her entire body trembled.

Mason looked at me in confusion, and then Rachel, and jumped out of the bed as if a match had been struck under his ass. And then it got worse because he was wearing only his underwear. Rachel made a gurgling choked sound, and I shook my head.

"No, Rach. No, please. It's not what it looks like," I said, getting out of the bed stupidly clad only in a white lace wisp of fabric that could hardly be called panties and didn't at all cover my ass, as well as the demi-cup matching bra that my breasts almost fell out of. If I leaned forward, I'm sure I'd have a nip slip. I yanked at the comforter and pulled it against my body.

Rachel pointed at me. "It looks like you had sex with my boyfriend. Which I guess I should have assumed would happen, seeing as you're a whore for hire!" she screamed her hateful words, and they hit my heart and soul exactly as intended. Like a fucking knife shredding through me bit by bit, slice by slice.

"Rachel, nothing happened!" Mason walked over to her, and she held a hand out in a stopping motion in front of her form.

"I cannot believe I trusted you. A player. I thought you'd changed. You didn't change. You just hid your true self really well." She groaned, and tears slipped down her face. "I was in love with you, Mason! I was going to tell you when Mia left and it was just us!" she screamed and sobbed at the same time. Then she turned on her heel and ran out of the room. "You deserve each other!" she screamed behind her.

All we could hear was her heels hitting each step and then the door slamming shut.

CHAPTER NINE

Mason ran his fingers through his hair and pulled at the roots. "Fuck me, fuck me, fuck me. I can't believe we slept together. Shit!" He paced the room.

I reached for my tank on the floor, pulled it over my head, and then grabbed for my pants. When he was turned away, I slid them up and over my hips. "Mason, we did not sleep together."

He stopped and looked at me as if I'd said something supremely stupid and then pointed to the bed. "Um, hello?"

I blew out a tortured, annoyed breath. I needed coffee and a handful of Ibuprofen and quickly. The tiny men doing construction, drilling into my brain with their tiny little tools, while laughing at me for drinking so much last night needed to go away so I could think straight. "No. We slept together, but we didn't have sex. We were drunk as skunks. Believe me, I'd know if I'd gotten laid, and I'm a hundred percent positive I didn't."

He looked at me from tip to toe. "Yeah, you would." He grinned, and I cringed. "Sorry. Fuck!" he said again, obviously feeling like a jerk. "How the hell am I going to get her to believe me? She knows my history, Mia. This is just like the fucked-up shit I'd do before her." He slumped and sat down on the bed.

I sat down next to him. "Okay, this is what we're going to do. We're going to shower, get some food, coffee, and drugs into us."

His eyebrows rose.

"Ibuprofen or Tylenol, dumbass. And then we're going to call her up. You're going to grovel and explain that we were just drunk, didn't fuck, and though it looked really bad, nothing happened but sleeping next to one another."

He pushed his thumbs into his temples, his big hand spreading wide. "I remember fondling your tits and asking to fuck them." He groaned and looked at me guiltily.

"Well, don't tell her *that* part. That was just stupid drunk behavior, and no one else saw it. Harmless."

"Yeah, harmless," he grumbled. His shoulders slumped over. He put his head in his hands and elbows on his knees. He was the perfect vision of a man who'd lost his way, who thought the world was over.

I slid my hand up and down his warm bare back. "Do you love her?" I asked.

His head shot up, and his gaze focused intently on mine. He closed his eyes and nodded solemnly.

"You have to tell her, Mace. It might be the only way to get yourself out of this bind."

He blew air out his mouth, his cheeks puffing out with the effort. "She won't believe me. I know Rach. She'll think I'm saying it to save face. I should have told her the moment it hit me. Then she might have believed it."

Mason loved Rachel. Will wonders never cease? The chauvinistic, womanizing player had come a long way since the day I arrived almost a month ago. "When did you know?"

He stood, started pacing, and then went over to the window and observed the street below. "That first night we made love. It was...it just was, you know. It's like I knew then that she was the only woman I really wanted to be with forever. And I fucked it up. Christ!" He pulled back and slammed a flat hand to the wall. Thank God he hadn't punched it, or he'd be off the mound for the foreseeable future.

I walked over to Mace and set my forehead to his back. "We're going to fix this. You'll see. It will all be okay in the end."

He shook his head. "Why do you believe that?"

"Because there is simply no other option. If she's it for you, we have to find a way to make her see that. We'll figure it out. Together, we'll get your girl back. You've got to take chances in life. Go the way of the unknown."

"Thanks, Mia. You're a good friend."

"I know," I said, and bumped his hip with my own. "So first step: showers, meds, food with tons of water, in that order." I held out my hand for him to shake.

He smirked at my outstretched limb, probably thinking my antics were silly.

"Deal?"

He grabbed my hand and shook it. "Deal."

★ ★ ★ ★

Getting access to Rachel was a lot harder than I'd thought it would be. I was leaving in two days, and Mason had yet to talk to the elusive blonde. Every call I made to her went straight to voice mail, where I repeatedly begged for her to call me back, to call Mason back, to listen to one of us. Nothing but crickets. The woman had a resolve of steel. I was starting to believe that she really wouldn't give Mason another chance, and that broke my heart.

Even though Rachel had said some pretty hurtful things to me, I could understand why she'd said them. When you're faced with losing everything you've ever wanted, you lash out.

It's normal, and the brunette in bed with your boyfriend is a pretty good target. I deserved whatever and more of what she had to say. Though I didn't like that she believed I was a whore. It was something I, too, struggled with as an escort. One who'd had sex with her first two clients. Of course, I hadn't with the last two, but she thought differently.

My cell phone rang, and I picked it up. "Hello?"

"Hey, dollface. Are you ready to move on to your next client?" Aunt Millie's voice soothed over some seriously grated nerves like a calming lotion. The last couple of days, I'd felt like crap, knowing that Mason and Rachel were hurting, trying to accept my part in it, and doing what I could to fix it but not knowing how.

I sighed. "Actually, yeah, the sooner the better," I said for the first time. I'd never wanted to move on as badly as I did right now. Escaping the problem seemed like a good idea at the time.

"What's the matter, honey? The baseball hot shot not treating you well?"

I shook my head, but she couldn't see it. "No, he's cool. Once we got past all his scumbag ways and he learned a thing or two about how to treat a woman, he's been a lot of fun."

Aunt Millie's voice turned sultry. "Oh, yeah, then I guess I should expect that additional payout to be sent any day now, eh?"

"Aunt Millie! Jeez, do you think I fuck every one of my clients?"

"Honey, you're young, gorgeous, and an escort for incredibly rich, good-looking men. Yes, of course, I think you're going to get some of that. If I were in your shoes, I most certainly would. In the past, I definitely had my share of beautiful rich men."

That's when I sat down and worried my thumbnail. "You were an escort?"

"Dollface, how do you think I know so much about this business, what to charge, and who to send my girls to? Of course I had to be one in order to run the most successful escort service in the nation. I've done it all, sweetie, including having my share of clients, though back then, they didn't pay extra. It was an expected part of the service. Now, as you know, I don't run a brothel. I run a stand-up business and pay Uncle Sam what he's owed. Have my books audited regularly and keep a tight ship. If my girls want to go that extra step, it is expected that the men will accommodate such a gift by giving one of their own. You see? Easy."

"I see. I guess I just thought you ran a business."

"I do. But twenty years ago, that shoe you're wearing was on my foot. Only, I wasn't so smart."

At this, I paid very close attention to what she was saying.

"Back then, I met and fell in love with one of my clients, and he screwed me over."

One could say that history was definitely repeating itself with her niece, only I wouldn't quite agree to having fallen in love with Wes...yet.

Aunt Millie continued. "Now I treat men the same way they treat women. As something to enjoy while they're there. Nothing more, nothing less. No expectations for more, just a good time and a lot of pleasure."

This thought had merit. It's what I'd been trying to do myself and failing at because my heart was too tangled in the particulars. With Wes, I was knee-deep in emotional turmoil. With Alec, it was fun, pleasurable, and something I didn't feel as though I had left behind or lost because it was never mine to begin with. When Alec and I were together, we enjoyed it immensely. Outside of our time together, we moved on to the next thing that gave us joy, with absolutely no guilt or concern for the other because we didn't have that type of relationship.

I wished I was able to do that with Wes. And right then and there, I promised myself I would put that wall back up and make it so. When it was Wes and me, it was amazing— incredible, even. Best I'd ever had in terms of spending time with someone I cared for. Alec, he was a close second. Though with Alec, we both just knew it was for a short time, which made it wildly passionate and something to hold on to as a beautiful memory. When it was Wes, it felt fraught with meaning, complex with feelings and emotions neither one of us should have placed on one another. That's where we went wrong. Because Wes and I together were automatically more. Somehow, some way, a delineation needed to be made, lines cut and crossed so that we'd stop hurting one another. Of course, it was another problem I had no hope of solving today in my current predicament with Rachel and Mason.

Taking a deep breath, I firmed my own resolve. "You're right. Thanks for the advice."

"Of course," she said, and I could hear her nails clacking on the keys through the receiver. "Sorry the baseball thing didn't work out. That had to be a long month."

I grinned, thinking back to Alec. "Technically, I met up with an old friend when we were in Seattle."

"Oh, sounds like you had a good time with that old friend."

"True." Wanting to change the subject because I didn't know what the rule was about meeting back up with your clients as it pertained to the business side of things, because what Alec and I had, and last month what Wes and I had, was personal, private, and had nothing to do with me being an escort. "You gonna keep me in suspense about where I'm going next?"

"Oh my dear child, this is going to be fun. Ever been to Hawaii?"

Surf, sand, and suntan lotion. "Seriously? I'm going to Hawaii?"

"Yes, dollface, and get this... You're going to be a model!"

I groaned. "Like I was for Alec?" It was fun being a muse, but that experience tore into my subconscious and the issues of my past. The last thing I needed was another round like that on the job.

More clacking could be heard, and then she tsked. "No, honey. You're going to be modeling swimsuits for this top fashion designer in swimwear. His name is Angel D'Amico. He wanted you because he's followed you in the smut mags. Seen that you're getting attention and making the rounds with some pretty big names. This does well for someone who's bringing something new to the table in his profession. Not to mention he's making suits for real women."

"How so?"

"His line doesn't start out at a size zero. It starts at a six and goes up from there. He wants more curvy woman in his ads. Women with some meat on their bones. You know, a woman with a pair of breasts that couldn't fit into a two-inch speck of triangle-shaped fabric. He loved that you were a thirty-six D cup in the bust and were a classic hourglass shape. He has some motto about proving beauty comes in all sizes, or something to that effect."

Huh. That actually sounded really cool. A fashion

designer who was actually focused on more realistic sizes. "Sounds like fun. Plus...Hawaii! Awesome." I started dancing around my room, not believing I was headed to an island.

"It's going to be a long flight, sweetheart. Six hours from Boston, and then another five from California. Want a layover in California for a couple days, hit your home?"

I thought about Wes and how I could see him if he wasn't on location. Then instantly tossed that idea out the window. It would just make more drama, more emotional crap to think about. No, I wanted to have fun, enjoy Hawaii. Hook up with some random island dude for the sole purpose of fucking his brains out. Yep, that was going to be my new plan.

"No, make the layover for two nights in Vegas so I can see Maddy, Ginelle, and check in on Dad." Gin had told me that Maddy was close to taking the plunge with her new beau, and I thought she might need her big sis around for some face-to-face time. "I'll make sure Gin sets up the appointments again for the required beauty stuff."

Aunt Millie sucked in a breath that seemed to skate through her teeth with a hissing sound. "About that. You're going to have get waxed."

"I always do," I reminded her.

"No, honey, I mean *everywhere*. Full Brazilian. You're going to be doing bathing suits. There can be no tuffs of hair peeking out or against the fabric showing when you're shooting in the ocean."

I groaned. "That sucks. And it's going to hurt." It was as if I could already feel the strips of sticky goo being slathered onto my sensitive parts and then being ripped away. Ouch!

"Yes, dollface, it does. But the good news... The designer is a fifty-year-old Italian. Married to an ex-model named Rosa who works with the girls. And you're not going to be on point every second. You'll work a standard day or two modeling and then have most of the week off. I know they have around one to two shoots per week planned. The rest of the time will be yours. Even confirmed that you'll be staying in a rented two-bedroom bungalow right on the beach."

"My own place? I don't have to stay with them?"

"Nope, and they won't be providing you with clothing. That's the tradeoff. Since you will only be shooting ads and maybe attending a couple of parties with the couple, you'll have most of the time to yourself, so you'll wear what you want. You get to keep the bathing suits though."

Sweet! A month in Hawaii. My life just got a hundred times better. "Think I could bring Gin and Maddy?" From the extra twenty from Wes and Alec, I had enough saved to be able to pay their way. They could stay with me, so really we just needed plane tickets and food.

"As long as you make your shoot days, you can do whatever you want. Should I book them some tickets?"

"Yeah, but I'll get back to you on when. I need to see when Maddy's break from school is for the spring and find out if Gin can take some time off. Oh my God! I'm going to Hawaii, and my sister and my best friend are going to get to come. This is the best day ever!" I squealed into the line, and my aunt laughed.

"I'm glad you're pleased, dollface. Just remember that when you're getting every speck of hair ripped off your neither regions."

I snorted in reply.

"I'll send over an e-mail with your flight plans and information. You want the first flight of the day out again, right?"

"Yep. I like to leave early." Really, I just liked to sneak out before my client knew I was leaving. It's worked the last three times, and I saw no reason to change it now. "Love you, Aunt Millie."

"You, too, dollface," she said and then hung up without saying good-bye.

Now that that was settled, I just needed to find a way to get Rachel and Mason back together.

Just as I was putting my cell in my back pocket, it rang again.

"Hello?"

"Is this Mia Saunders?" a serious yet quiet voice asked.

"Yes. May I ask who's calling?"

"I'm calling from Mass General Hospital on Cambridge. We've got your boyfriend, Mason Murphy, in our ER."

"Oh my God." I glanced around, already a panic setting in. I spied my purse on the dresser, grabbed it, and started down the stairs and out the building. "Is he okay? What happened?"

"He's got some bumps and bruises and is being treated for a concussion. Was in a small car accident with a couple of other players who are also being treated. Can you come down? He also asked for someone named Rachel Denton, but she's not picking up."

"I'll find her. Is he really okay though?"

"Yes, ma'am. He'll be out of here tonight. Getting patched up now. Doctor will probably release him in a few hours. Would be good to have someone here to pick him up."

"Of course, of course. I'll call his family, too, just in case."

"Sure thing, ma'am. See you soon."

I clicked off and then stood outside on the Boston street in front of Mason's brownstone and had no idea where the fuck to start. I didn't know his dad's information, and Rachel wasn't answering my calls. Then I remembered his brother worked at Black Rose. At the very least, someone there would be able to get me info on his brother.

I called information, and they connected me to the bar.

"Black Rose Pub. Brayden here," his brother answered the line, and I felt my knees go weak.

Sitting on the stoop, I pulled myself together. "Brayden, it's Mia. Your brother's been in a fender bender and is at Mass General on Cambridge."

"What? Is Mason okay?"

"He's fine. A concussion and some bumps and bruises. I'm heading there now, but I need to find Rachel, his girlfriend," I said, instantly forgetting my role.

"I thought you were his girlfriend?" he asked with a timber to his voice that I hadn't heard before.

Sighing, I stood up and put my arm out to hail a cab. "No, it's all been for show. Rachel, the blonde from the other night, that's his real girlfriend, only she's pissed at both of us, thinks Mason cheated on her with me, and now she's not answering our calls. He's hurt and wants the woman he loves by his side. I need to find her."

Then Brayden did something I wouldn't have expected, based on the circumstances. He laughed. Hard.

"Did you not hear me?"

"Mia, Mia, that pretty blonde who's always hanging around him? Big blue eyes, thin, rocks a suit?"

Finally, a cab caught sight of me and drew up to the curb. I got in and prepared to tell him to go to the hospital, when Brayden chuckled and responded with, "She's here, in the bar. Drinking like a fish. You want me to cut her off?"

Looked like the universe was shining down on me tonight. Must be a full moon or something. This shit never happened for me. "Yeah, water down her drinks. I'll be there in fifteen.

"Black Rose Pub, and there's an extra twenty in it if you hurry!" I told the cabbie.

"You got it, lady. My wife was bitchin' about not having any extra. A cool twenty will be nice!"

"Get me there in ten, and I'll give you forty."

The cab screeched out into traffic, flipped a U-turn, and sped off toward the bar. He must have really needed the cash, because he got me there in eleven minutes. I didn't mince words about the minute. I paid the tab and threw the extra forty over the seat.

"Thanks, dude!" I hollered, jumped out of the car, opened the door to the bar, and started scanning patrons.

Sitting hunched over, her hair a wild mess falling out of its complicated twist, pieces flowing all over the place, was Rachel. Drinking away her sorrows.

"Thank God!" I yelled and made my way over to her.

She scowled. Even with her face pinched into a scowl, she was still unbelievably beautiful. One of those women you'd see while getting groceries or standing in line at the post office and think, *Man, I wish I could be as classy and elegant as she was.*

"Rach, thank God I found you!" I plopped into the stool next to her.

"Whoop-dee-doo." Her finger went into the air and made a motion like a tornado. "Can't say I'm happy you're here, boyfriend stealer!" Those blue orbs narrowed like slits at me, shooting daggers with extremely sharp blades. I hated that she looked at me like that.

"Rach..." I tried again.

She cut me off. "Don't you get enough men with your job? I mean, look at you." Her eyes seemed to scan me from head to toe. "You're perfect. The kind of woman who deserves to score a man like Mason Murphy. He's perfect, too, you know. Like and like go together. Birds of a feather and all that." Rachel sucked back a glug of whatever fruity martini thing she had in front of her and licked her lips. "You know..." She pointed a finger at me. "I'm glad this happened. At least now I know for sure I could never be with a man like him. Gossamer male specimens like him could never be happy with me. Not when they can have someone exotic like you!"

I groaned and held her shoulders.

She bit into her lip and finally stopped talking.

"Listen to me." I shook her. "Mason loves you. You!"

Her eyes widened, and she started to crumble before me. Her lips pursed, and those pretty eyes filled with tears that didn't fall. She shook her head, unwilling to believe.

"Yes! He does, and if you'd just listen to him for five flippin' seconds, you'd know it, too! Have you even taken the time to listen to any of the voice mails we've left?"

That's when she started to tremble and shook her head, tears slipping down her cheeks.

"Jesus, for a smart woman, you can be pretty fucking dense!" I accused.

Her shoulders slumped, and she crossed her arms over her chest and cowed into herself. "Just leave."

"I can't!" I roared and lost my temper. I could feel heat blasting out of every pore as I yelled in her face. "Mason's in the hospital, and he's asking for his girlfriend. His *real* girlfriend."

CHAPTER TEN

"I'm going to be sick." Rachel's entire face paled, and she put a hand over her mouth. Out of nowhere, a bucket appeared in front of her, and she lost it. Heave after heave she hacked into the bucket, releasing all the liquor she'd imbibed that evening. I rubbed her back and looked at Brayden. His face said it all. Sadness and concern.

Once Rachel was done, Brayden took the bucket and left the main bar, headed to the back room. I led a shaky Rachel into the ladies' restroom. She washed out her mouth, and then I shoved a stick of gum in to mask the tastes and smell. Then I pulled out the pins in her hair and let her curls fall. I dug into her purse. She hadn't even removed it from around her while she was drinking the night away. I found a brush and slowly worked out each tangle until it glistened like the spun gold I knew it to be. I handed her a wet paper towel, and she removed the streaks her mascara had left around her eyes and cheeks. Then I passed her some tissue to blow her nose. After that, I rummaged through her purse again and located lip gloss. It wasn't much. The woman obviously didn't carry makeup around with her, though she did have a small powder compact. I handed her both of those, and she fixed up her face as best she could.

"What happened to Mason?" Her words were shaky as she started to come back to the Rachel I had considered my friend.

"He was in a car accident with some of the other players. He has a concussion, but they're letting him out in a few hours. I haven't seen him. He wanted you, so my goal was to find you."

She choked back a sob. "He wanted me?"

I nodded and put my hand at her shoulder. "Rachel, I swear to you, nothing happened. We were drunk. Really drunk. So far over the limit we were breathing fire. Honest to God, I had no idea I wasn't getting into my own bed. We just fell into his and slept. That's it. Nothing else."

Her eyes closed, and her chin tipped down. "I believe you."

I took a huge, refreshing breath, letting out days of heartache and guilt. "Thank God. Mason has been so lost without you, thinking he'd never get you back."

"It doesn't mean we're meant to be together, Mia. Like I said, seeing him with you opened my eyes. He's not meant to be with some professional career woman. He's meant to be with someone who's fun-loving, can go to his baseball games, fly around the country with him, and be there by his side. I won't be able to do that much."

"You can't be serious. What about all those jobs? You're with his PR firm. You're his go-to for all the sponsors and stuff. He needs you close more often than not."

Her head tilted to the side. "There is that..."

The hairs on the back of my neck tingled. I was getting to her. "And who's going to prevent him from making an ass of himself at those meetings? You saw him in there. He's so green it's ridiculous. They'd take advantage of him in seconds if you weren't there. The only reason he's dialed in is because of you. Now that the deals are coming left and right, and they're going to keep coming, he's going to need a publicist who can work for only him. I'm certain of it. That person is you. He'd only trust you."

She pushed her hair out of her eyes, and her shoulders straightened. "You're right. He would have been taken. He's too giving and carefree. Even if he's not in it for the money, completely—I know he loves the sport—they were trying to lowball him."

"Exactly. And you knew that. You, Rachel." I pointed at her chest. "You're the one for him."

Her eyes glowed with what could only be described as a renewed sense of self-worth. "We have to get to him!" she said.

The two of us hustled outside the bar.

"Brayden, I'll call you when I find out what's going on."

He did a cool chin-lift move that silently said *sure thing* or something equally macho.

"Charge Mason for the drinks."

"Got it on his tab already." He grinned. "Plus this one." He lifted up a beer and put it to his lips and took a long pull.

I shook my head and headed out the door.

★ ★ ★ ★

The hospital was a madhouse when we arrived. Apparently a big rig had jack-knifed on the freeway and ended up causing a fourteen-car pileup. There were people everywhere, holding bandages to their heads, arms, and legs. I cringed and hit the info desk.

"I'm Mia Saunders. We're here to see Mason Murphy."

The woman looked up his name in the computer. "He's been moved to a temporary room. Level two, room 130."

"Thank you."

Rachel and I hit the elevator and waited and waited.

"Fuck this," I said, and instead we took the stairs. Two flights up, and we were on level two and searching for his room.

When we found it, we both slowed down. I held Rachel's hands, and for a moment, we were connected. Connected in the way that sisters do or best friends, sharing comfort and sending healing energy to one another. After a couple of slow breaths, we turned and opened the door. I entered first, Rachel trailing quietly behind.

Mason was in the bed, his eyes closed. The lights were low, and his dad sat in a chair in the corner.

"Mia, sweet girl, they finally got in touch with you," Mick said and hugged me. I kept my arm around his shoulders as Rachel stood near Mason's bed.

His eyes opened, and he licked his split lip. There was a row of stitches, no more than five or six, which stretched across his forehead. He had a series of cuts and scrapes along his arms, but it didn't seem like anything else was broken or damaged.

"Rachel..." His hand reached out, and she clasped it with both of hers. Those tears she had in check on the car ride over were renewed and sliding down her cheeks, dripping onto Mace's hand as she held it near her face. "Baby, I'm okay. You. I'm worried about you..."

"Uh, I think I'm missing something." Mick cleared his throat and held me tighter, as if he was protecting me. Such a good man. Concerned for his son and his son's pretend girlfriend.

I held Mick in return and shook my head. "It's okay," I whispered.

Rachel looked at Mick. A frightened, scared little mouse-type expression scrolled over her features.

Mason wouldn't have it. "Hey, pretty girl. Look at me. I'm sorry. Nothing happened. I swear," he said, close to the same words that I said to her earlier. "It never could. I only want you. You're it for me."

"Don't speak. You need to rest." Her voice was raspy, as if she'd chain-smoked a pack of Camel non-filters.

He shook his head and winced. Her hand came up and caressed the side without damage. From what I could see, his head must have hit the window, which split it open. The glass was probably the reason he was littered with tiny cuts and scrapes.

"I don't need to rest. I need the woman I love to listen to me!" he growled, and both his dad and I stayed very still and very quiet watching the entire thing unfold. For me, it was beautiful. For his dad, confusing.

"Mason..." She lost her ability to speak.

He pulled her hand to him, which brought her body closer. "That's right. I love you. I have since that first night. I'd never, never fuck that up. Not in the way you think. What happened with Mia and me was innocent!" His voice rose, and she placed two fingers over his lips.

"Mia already told me. And I believe you. I'm sorry I ever doubted you."

"You had your reasons. But, baby, after that wreck today, it could have been so much worse, and not having you by my side right now... I can't even think it..." His voice turned thick with emotion. "I need you. Always. By my side."

Rachel's big blue eyes were glassy and soft, focused only on the man in front of her. "Then I'll be there. Whatever you need. Because I love you, too."

I wanted to shout from the rooftops and jump for joy but

instead had to settle for a giant grin.

"Son..." Mick said, coming up to the other side of the bed. "You've got some explaining to do," he offered somewhat jovially.

"Dad, this is Rachel. She's gonna be my full-time publicist, if she'll take the job."

She nodded, grinning wide.

"And on top of that, she's my girlfriend. My real girlfriend."

She smiled so brightly, it lit the dark room up just like it had from the moment I met her. "Hi, Mr. Murphy. I'm Rachel Denton, and I'm in love with your son."

Mick looked from Rachel, to his son, and then to me. He hooked a thumb toward me standing behind them. "And what about her?"

"She's an escort," Mason responded simply.

I wanted to smash my head into the wall. His dad's eyes got so wide you could see straight through to his brain.

"Oh, no, no. Not like that!" Rachel tried.

"Dad, no, we hired her to help my image. I needed a girlfriend, and at the time, Rachel and I hadn't gotten together. It was Mia who encouraged us, actually."

Now that was true.

"Sorry for not telling the whole truth, Mick, but it was part of my role. Can you forgive me?" I batted my eyelashes in a way I thought looked pretty pitiful.

"Us?" Mason added with his own puppy-dog look.

Mick grumbled and slapped a hand at Mason's shoulder. Supporting his son. Always supportive. "Son, if this pretty lady is your girl and you love her like you say, I'm sure I'll love her, too. But you lie to me again, and I'll tan your hide even worse than that car accident did. You hear?"

At that, both Rachel and I laughed. Mason scowled. "Yeah, Dad. I heard ya."

★ ★ ★ ★

It was early. The sun hadn't yet broken on the horizon as I zipped up my suitcase and silently carried it down the stairs. Mason and Rachel were asleep in the master bedroom. After the doctors cleared Mason, we came back to the house, and his father puttered around making a late dinner. Claimed that you needed to feed a cold. Of course, Mason didn't have a cold. He was in a car accident, but none of us thought it prudent to make the distinction. I had a feeling his dad needed to do something to help, mostly just to spend some time making sure his son was okay.

Once dinner was done, each one of his brothers stopped by, Shaun with his newest girlfriend. Not the same one he'd showed me a picture of last time we were at dinner, but teens were fickle like that. Hell, I was like that. Hopping from man to man each month, not knowing where I'd be and when. His brothers stayed long enough to rib him about the accident, about having two girlfriends, which made Rachel extremely uncomfortable, not yet used to the attention from the Murphy clan, but I knew eventually she'd fit right in. Ellie had a lot to do with that. With the way Rachel looked, Ellie believe Rachel was a princess and not for pretend. Just like their mother Eleanor, Rachel was elegant, had a regal look about her, spoke softly, and was a classic beauty. I had a feeling these two would make it for the long haul and hoped even with everything that had happened toward the end of my stay, they'd be willing to keep the lines of communication open.

I walked through the dark house, made some coffee, and sipped at it while looking out the window. My time with Mason had been interesting to say the least. I'd had an amazing time watching his games front and center, meeting the players, getting to know the life of a WAG, but more than that, I saw the inner workings of a team. Men who supported one another through it all and played ball like a finely tuned instrument: each player no more important than the next and utterly beautiful as a whole. I was even more in love with the Red Sox team than I had been before I got to Boston, and I was a diehard fan then.

I'd miss the wives and girlfriends that I'd met as well. They had their own little clique, and I very much enjoyed being a part of their girl club for the month. Sarah, Morgan, and of course little Kris would not easily be forgotten. They were fine women who supported their guys one hundred percent. Silently, I sent good will and love out to them.

More than anything, though, I'd watched a couple fall in love. Two people who didn't believe they were right for one another found that the only thing that didn't work for them was being apart. In the end, Rachel and Mason complemented one another. They were their own yin and yang.

I couldn't be happier that Mason had lost his piggish ways. Overall, I think maybe they were his way of putting up a wall. One that would deflect good women, perhaps because he didn't feel worthy or good enough for a high-caliber lady. Once he made those life changes, started living for himself, finding who he was in the grand scheme of things, it was easier for him to see that he didn't have to put up a front. He could take a chance on being himself, and when he did, it opened up an entire world of happiness, namely in the sweet little woman lying by his side, prepared to take care of him in every way that matters: businesswise, physically, mentally, and emotionally.

For Rachel, I think it took almost losing Mason to realize that who she was and what she had was enough for him. More than enough. The woman she showed to the world is the exact woman that Mason fell in love with, the one that I was certain he'd take down the aisle one day.

Finishing my coffee, I got out my stationery.

Mason,

Something you don't know about me is that I don't like good-byes. They're messy and uncomfortable, which is why I'm leaving you while you are sound asleep in the arms of the woman you love. The woman you were meant to love.

I'm honored that you chose me to be your pretend girlfriend. I had more fun this month than I've had in years. And I learned a few things. I'm going to take with me the knowledge that you should always put your best self forward and be open to the opportunities right in front of you. Taking chances toward finding your special happiness is important, and far too often people get stuck in the daily grind or think that the life they are living just can't get any better, even when they know they aren't happy. You chose happiness, and that came in the form of a sweet, beautiful blonde. Do right by her. She's taking risks of her own by giving herself to you completely.

Rachel,

Take care of him. He needs a strong woman who won't put up with his crap. I know you're that woman.

I'll miss you both and think of you often. Thank you for showing me how life could be if I'd only choose happiness. One day, I'm sure I will find what I'm meant to, and when I do, and

the time is right, I'll never let it go.
   Don't ever let one another go. All my love,
   ~Mia

I left the note on the kitchen counter and rolled my suitcase out the door and down the stairs, where I met the taxi.

"Logan International Airport, please."

The city flew by as the sun started to slide up over the horizon, lighting the sky in soft hues of blue and gold. It had been a good month. Between baseball games and hanging out with Mason, Rachel, and the rest of the crew, I'd had a blast. I also had the opportunity to get my feet wet in planning a charity event, one that was beyond successful and would help a lot of women get the help they needed to fight breast cancer. Overall, I'd rate this month as one of many that I'd never forget.

The cabbie dropped me off at the airport. I checked into arrivals, went through security, and then found a Starbucks to sit at and have more coffee and a slice of lemon bread. Something kept nagging at me, and the more I tried to push it away, the more the annoying thoughts crept up and prodded me.

I pulled out my phone, and my heart stuttered to a halt. A text from Wes. We hadn't spoken since I'd hung up on him over two weeks ago.

To: Mia Saunders
From: Wes Channing
Still friends?

For a long time, I thought about those words. Still friends. Were Wes and I friends? Lovers, yes. Friends... Before finding out that he was sleeping with Gina, I would have said yes. Definitely. Friends with benefits, absolutely. I thought about Gin and what made us friends. Trust. History. Commonalities. But ultimately, it came down to what would my life be like if she wasn't in it. And that answer was horrible. I'd feel lost without the anchor of her friendship. Did I have that with Wes?

The answer unequivocally was yes. Yes, I did. I knew for a fact that if I called Wes right now and told him I needed him, he'd drop everything, get on a plane, and be there for me. Same as Hector or Tony, or even Alec would. Definitely Mason. Because they were my friends. People I shared a portion of my life with that made an impression on my soul. They were now a footprint on the path in my life.

With quick fingers, I typed back.

To: Wes Channing
From: Mia Saunders
Yes. We will always be friends. I can't imagine my life without you in it.

I walked through the airport, picked out a magazine and then waited at the gate before my phone dinged with an incoming message.

To: Mia Saunders
From: Wes Channing
I feel the same. Is there still room for more or have I lost you?

To: Wes Channing
From: Mia Saunders

You could never lose me. For now we go our own way.

To: Mia Saunders
From: Wes Channing
Stick with the plan?

To: Wes Channing
From: Mia Saunders
Yes.

To: Mia Saunders
From: Wes Channing
When I can see you again?

To: Wes Channing
From: Mia Saunders
The next time you're meant to see me.

With that last text, I turned off my phone and boarded the plane to Vegas. A quick couple of days with my sister and best friend would be exactly what I needed to get me ready for a month in Hawaii. I could hardly wait. Sun, surf, and suntan lotion. Bring on the heat.

May

CALENDAR GIRL

CHAPTER ONE

Layover hell! I'd flown from Boston, stopped in Chicago, and then into Denver, where I thanked the Almighty I'd donned my well-worn biker boots as I ran as fast as my feet would take me through the Denver airport, barely making my flight. As in, I was the straggler everyone knew was in the airport somewhere and were waiting rather impatiently for me to board.

Over a hundred and fifty pairs of eyes threw daggers my way as I maneuvered my carry-on through the horde of disgruntled passengers to get to my seat. Things were not looking up from there. I was placed in between a very rotund man and a nosey eight-year-old girl who was flying alone. Her parents were divorced, and she now had two families. She hated the woman she referred to as "stepmonster" and the woman's older daughter who, according to her, was a meanie.

Her destination was her mother's, where Mom was a showgirl on the Strip. No surprise there. When you lived in Vegas, meaning in the heart of Vegas, you either worked the casinos, served food, or performed some type of act or service to the tourists. If you lived outside the city, there were other employment opportunities available. I knew all this about little Chasity because she made a point to tell me everything there was to know about her. And I mean everything. Her favorite color was purple, but not the dark kind, only the light kind, which I deduced was lavender. Animals were her *thing*, especially horses. Best part of being at her dad's in Denver, apparently, was that he had land that included animals. Big draw for an eight-year-old. But there was Stepmonster to deal with, and that knocked the pegs of visiting her dad down several notches. And then there was the guilt. Chasity's mom had very few friends and no family. The small child felt it was her role to keep her mother company. Because, "no one wants to be alone. People need people." At least according to in-your-face, well-meaning Chasity.

When the pilot announced that we were twenty minutes from landing, I actually sent a little prayer up to the Big Guy that Chasity and her mother would find their way to a happy medium. I also thanked the medical professionals for the awesomeness that was birth control. Being with an eight-year-old for a determined length of time solidified the notion that I was nowhere near ready to procreate, and I might not ever take that plunge. It took a special kind of person to mother a child, and I felt I'd already done that with my baby sister, Maddy. The next kid I raised would likely be a hellion or a demon spawn. Best not to leave that kind of thing up to Lady Luck. As I'd already determined...a cold- hearted bitch, that lady. No need to ruffle any feathers unnecessarily.

At baggage claim, I hauled my extra suitcase of amazing Boston Red Sox gear, jeans, and the rest of my loot from Chicago, figuring I could leave it at Dad and Maddy's. That way Mads could have the pick of the litter and feel like a princess in all the clothes Hector picked out for me, along with the hip, casual duds from Rachel.

A litany of pings trilled from my cell phone the second I hit the power button.

To: Mia Saunders

From: Mason Murphy

Your letter was cool, sweetness, but your saying good-bye in person would have been better. Rach and I wanted to take you to the airport. She's hurt. I'm pissed. Find a way to make it up to us.;-)

Not the first time a client, or I should say "friend," was upset with my style of good-bye. Wes seemed to anticipate my ninja-like departure. Alec went with the flow, and Hector cried. That gay Latino sent me a sobbing message about how I ruined the perfect good-bye. Something about seeing it on a movie once, and he'd had it all planned out, with flying doves and shit. I don't know. Tony must have grabbed the phone at that time and interrupted the message. He had added his own brand of irritation that I'd left him with a sniveling fiancé to deal with and that I owed him one.

The next message was my ride.

To: Mia Saunders
From: Skank-a-lot-a-Puss

Yo. Your ride is outside. Circling. Don't make me stop and a get a ticket for your ugly mug.

Laughing, I hefted my bag and caught sight of Ginelle's Honda. I waved, and she came to a screeching halt at the loading zone, parking cock-eyed.

"Word up, Biz-natch!" she said as I shoved my giant suitcase and smaller carry-on into her back seat. When I jumped in the passenger side, her blonde locks bounced against her neck, and a shock of bright-green chewing gum was pressed against her white teeth.

I lifted my chin. "Hi, honey. Thanks for picking me up," I cooed smugly.

With a flick of her wrist and a turn of the wheel, she squealed out of her spot and into the moving airport traffic. One could never mistake Ginelle for a good driver. Could she drive for NASCAR? Probably. Her maneuvers were second to none, alongside her ability to make millisecond decisions when behind the wheel. However, she took a lot of chances. So far, they had been okay. I held on to that little nugget as I clung to the oh-shit bar until we got onto the freeway.

Slowly sucking in a breath, I leaned my head back and just enjoyed the silence of being with my best friend. We didn't need to talk, and that's what made the two of us perfect BFFs. Being comfortable in shared silence. The sounds of the freeway and her gum smacking, and the scent of her lemon shampoo, almost had me tearing up. Home. This was familiar. This was good. This was what I'd known my whole life. It didn't mean it would always be my final destination, just that when I was here, I loved it with my whole heart.

Ginelle drove me to Maddy and Pop's. She could tell I was contemplative and didn't fill the car with idle chitchat, but she did glance over at me, grab my hand, and hold it against the console between us. Sister solidarity. She might not be my blood, but she was by far the next best thing in the entire universe.

"I love you," I whispered, not realizing I was busting out with the emotional shit.

Her eyes caught mine, her face so lovely and sweet. Her pink lips puckered in a way I thought she was going to say those three words right back. Instead, she used two. "I know."

And then I laughed. Hard. Leave it to my Gin to know

exactly what I needed after a long fucking day of travel, a hard escape from my last client—who I now thought of as my *brother from another mother*—and the knowledge that I only had three short days here before I had to get on a plane to my next client. I'd pushed the limit of my time in Boston by two days. Usually I was required to stay approximately twenty-four days so that I had around six or so to take care of personal business and the two travel days needed to get to and fro. I hadn't even been back to California since January, and here I was, three days before the start of May. Another month, another hundred thousand dollars off to Blaine.

I handed Ginelle the envelope with a check in it. "Drop this off with the admin at the hotel? Save me a stamp?"

"Sure thing, babe." She grabbed the envelope that had Blaine's latest payment and tucked it into her purse as she pulled up to the curb of my childhood home. "You must be hungry. Mads is making a homecoming dinner. Meatloaf, mashed potatoes, corn, and Pops's famous chocolate cherry pie for dessert." Then she opened her door and went around to her trunk and pulled out a case of beer.

"I really do love you." I looked at the case of beer and then at my shack of a home that had a tiny porch with a bare bulb for a light. Behind the lace curtains, I could see my sweet baby sis plating the table. For me. Because I was coming home. Nothing beats that.

Gin put her arm around my shoulders and tugged me toward the house. "I seriously know this shit already. Didn't you hear me the first time?" She rolled her eyes and huffed for emphasis.

I shook my head and hugged her tight.

I opened the door, and the mouthwatering scent of cooked

meat, veggies, and garlic instantly hit my nose. "Mads, I'm home!" I called out, dropping my purse on the scratched-up side table, and waited for the squeal. Maddy was always good for a little-girl squeal when she was excited. This time was no different.

The squeal was followed by my tall-assed sister plowing into me. I held strong, barely keeping myself up. "Baby girl, I missed you." I hugged her lithe body so tight. It had been close to two months since I'd seen her, and already she seemed like she was filling out, losing those teenaged ridges and coming into our mom's side of the womanly curves. Her boobs definitely had grown, and her hips seemed a bit fleshier. When I pulled out of her arms and away from her cherry-almond scent, I looked deep into her eyes. That huge smile I adored spread out across her lips.

"Prettiest girl in all the world. But only when she smiles," I said, mimicking the phrase I'd said to her for close to a decade. That lovely blush rose across her cheeks, and she pulled me into another hug. This one was much tighter and held the sense that she didn't want to let go. "What's the matter?" I held her cheeks and looked into her eyes.

Maddy shook her head, letting the too-long bangs across her forehead fall into her eyes. "Nothing. I'm just really glad you're here. I made your favorite."

"I can smell it." Right then, my belly decided to make my lack of eating a well-known fact, grumbling extraordinarily loud.

"Soup's on," Maddy said, pulling my hand toward the kitchen.

Ginelle followed behind us. Yep, this was good. Being home was exactly what I needed.

★ ★ ★ ★

"We're going to Hawaii!" echoed through the room at a decibel level that could shatter glass.

"Jesus Christ! Cool it, will ya?" I held my hands over my ears.

"Are you fucking kidding me? I'm going to Hawaii? I haven't even left Nevada except to visit you in California, and now I'm crossing a motherfucking ocean with whales and fishes and all kinds of shit! Fuck me!" Ginelle screamed, popping in a new piece of gum and following it with a huge glug of beer. Gross. I chose not to say anything about the questionable pairing, because she wasn't smoking, and that, above all else, was serious progress.

After sipping my own beer, I set it down on the Formica tabletop. "Calm down. Yes. I'm paying for both of you to come to Hawaii this month. You have to find out between the two of you when it works best. Come for a week or so, stay in the bungalow they are providing me." I held up my hands to stop both of them from interrupting. "Now, I don't know what the accommodations are going to be like, so it may be three of us in one bed, but I figure hey... free trip, right?"

"Fuck yes! I'll sleep on the motherfuckin' floor!"

I groaned. "Gin, cool the f-bombs around Mads. Jeez."

"Oh please, I'm not a little girl. As a matter of fact... I'm officially a woman as of last weekend." Maddy's tone was haughty and informative and not at all what I wanted to hear come out of my baby sister's mouth.

I closed my eyes, my hand knocking my beer across the tabletop. Gin caught it before it spilled everywhere. "Mads..." I whispered.

She pursed her lips together and smiled shyly while tracing a finger along the tabletop. "Can we talk about this later?" Her eyes flicked to Ginelle. As much as Ginelle was my sister from another mister, she and Maddy weren't as close. They loved each other, but not in the "confide completely in one another"-type friendship, or I should say sisterhood, that Maddy and I shared.

Ginelle overtly looked down at her watch. "Well, look at that. Time to go!" she said loudly. "Looks like I've got some bathing-suit shopping to do. Oh, and tomorrow at one o'clock, we have the spa day to get all your shabby bits back into prize-fighting order. Three of us again. Cool?"

"Gin... Thank you. For everything. You know that..." I started, but Ginelle, as usual, didn't take offense at Maddy wanting to talk to me alone. She wrapped an arm around me, giving me a hug, and kissed the top of Maddy's head and ruffled her hair. "See you bitches tomorrow!"

"Bye!" Maddy and I said in unison. The tension in the room thickened, but not in an ominous way. More like the "you've got shit to say, say it" way.

"I didn't mean for it to happen..." Maddy started, and tears filled her eyes. "I wanted to talk to you first, but we've been having such a good time, and he really loves me, and I love him, and..."

Covering her hand with mine, I looked into her pretty eyes. "And...what was it like?"

She licked her lips and tipped her head. "It hurt. I bled a little, but he went so slowly. So much that he shook with the effort. He was afraid to hurt me, and really, it only hurt for a little bit."

I smiled, tears filling my own eyes and falling down my

cheek. My baby girl had grown up. "Did you enjoy it?"

Instantly, she nodded. "We've done it two more times since then." She giggled. "And those times were like, a million times better!"

I laughed and nodded, knowing what that's like.

"So what about your relationship. How's he acting now? Still cool?"

Her eyes lit up like a birthday cake filled to the brim with candles. "Oh, he's so cool! Tells me every day how I'm the most beautiful girl, and how much he loves me, and how one day we'll get married." She clasped her hands in front of her chest and wistfully looked off to a bare spot on the kitchen wall. "He's everything, Mia. Everything I ever wanted. Everything you told me to find before I took that step. I couldn't be happier."

I scooted over my chair and pulled her into my arms, needing her close. "I'm so glad you had a good experience and that the man you're with loves you for you. He does, right? Love you for all the true beauty within you, not just the beauty on the outside?"

Maddy's head nodded frantically against mine as I petted her hair. "I think so. He tells me all the time. He actually wants to talk to you. I told him he couldn't tonight, but maybe tomorrow you would be willing to go to his parents for dinner. They want to meet my family, and well...you're all I have."

That sent a fresh wave of remorse through my veins— anger at our mother for abandoning us and sorrow that our father couldn't get his shit together long enough to be there during the important times in our lives. At least for Maddy. She's the deserving one.

I held my baby sister's cheeks and kissed her softly on the lips. "I would love to meet your boyfriend's parents and have a sit down with your guy."

Once more, that face that could light a hundred cities shone with excitement and joy. She hopped up and went over to the coffee pot. I could see her dumping in a few scoops of Folgers decaf while she wiggled from side to side to a song only she could hear. "This is cause for a celebration... A chocolate celebration."

"Sounds good, baby girl. I have been dreaming about the chocolate cherry pie since you made it for my last birthday."

That night, we talked sister to sister, catching up on everything. I told her about each client and how much I'd come to care for all of them. Being a Red Sox fan, she was most impressed with Mason. That was going to make the signed shirt, hat, and headshot all the more fantastic when I finally gave them to her. Of course, I promised her that one day, I'd introduce her to Mason and all the other guys, if the opportunity arose.

When the topic of conversation got to Wes, I laid it all out. It was almost as if I needed to.

"That bastard!" she swore when I told her that the star of his movie answered his phone and he admitted to banging her.

I shook my head. "It's nice that you think so, and believe me, I did too when it first went down. But really, think about it. Should Wes wait for me to get my shit together, have fun with whatever guys I want, while he sits back in California carrying a torch?"

Her face turned contemplative. "That's not really fair," she admitted.

"No, it's not. I won't say that it didn't sting, and for a full week or so I stewed hard over it, but in the end, I get it. And to top it off, later that month, I met back up with Alec, and you know, one thing led to another."

Maddy's eyebrows narrowed. "What do you mean, you met up and one thing led to another? How did he even know you'd be in town?"

I looked off into the distance and sipped my coffee. "Um... the details are hazy." I tried, but she wasn't buying it.

"Bull honkey! You straight up called Alec to hook up, didn't you?" Her accusation held laughter within it.

"Hook up? What does that even mean? I believe the official term is booty call, and I will tell you, dear sister, that man has one of the finest booties known to mankind!" I sat back, feeling smug and owning every second of it, and shoveled a bite of my second piece of cherry chocolate pie into my gullet.

Maddy's cute little snicker had me giggling. She was so young and naïve to the ways of the world. I just hoped this boyfriend of hers was a stand-up guy and he wouldn't take advantage of her. I guess I'd find out tomorrow night when I met the parents. A tremor of unease swept across my chest.

Is this what fathers and mothers think when they meet the parents for the first time? I mean, it's not like the guy is proposing. It's just dinner. Normal families do that, right?

I had no flippin' clue.

Later that night, when we were finally in bed, I pulled out my phone to contact Angie, Tony's sister. We got close back in Chicago, and if anyone would know about dating and meeting the parents, she would.

To: Angelina Fasano
From: Mia Saunders
Hey Angie, it's Mia. Sorry so late. Question for ya. When a boy's parents invite the girlfriend's parents over for dinner, is it

a big deal?

Surprisingly the phone dinged right away. I chanced a glance at the clock. It was three in the morning here. Five her time.

To: Mia Saunders
From: Angelina Fasano
Hi girl. Weird question, but yeah it's usually some type of formality. They want to make sure that the girl is good enough for their son by checking out the family. Why?

Fuck. I'd call Hector tomorrow and find out what to wear. He'd know. First defense, look like a normal, responsible older sister. Do not mention the job. Do not bring up the fact that dear, old, drunkard Pops is in a convalescent hospital paid for by the state because the ex-boyfriend, the loan shark, beat him within an inch of his life. Christ, it sounded super fucked-up, even in my own head.

I groaned into the too-quiet room and typed out my response to Angie.

To: Angelina Fasano
From: Mia Saunders
My sister's first real boyfriend. Uggh.

To: Mia Saunders
From: Angelina Fasano
Sucks to be you! Lol

CHAPTER TWO

After a day of being pampered like the true Hollywood socialites Gin and I pretended to be, the last thing I wanted to do was spend an evening with strangers. More than that, I didn't want those strangers to find me or my familial genes lacking. I'm pretty sure I groaned repeatedly while getting ready for the big dinner with Maddy's boyfriend's family. Maddy, though, was fluttering around the house, stopping to check herself in the mirror, smoothing down her flowing sundress, and putting nonexistent pieces of hair back against her slick ponytail without a care in the world.

She looked young, carefree, and beautiful. Vegas at the tail end of April was warm enough to rock the summer wear, which, on her, seemed effortless. I looked her over. She was the epitome of the girl next door. Golden-blonde hair and pretty green eyes, the one and only feature we had in common. One day, she'd make a good man the perfect suburban wife. As far back as I could remember, she'd always wanted to get married and have the white picket fence and a gaggle of kids. Exact opposite of my dreams.

"So what's Matt's major?" I asked, curling the last strands of my long black hair.

"Plant sciences, remember?" She sighed and sat on the bed, clasping her hands in front of her.

I nodded and caught her gaze through the reflection in the mirror. "Did you decide on your major? I know you were waffling in the sciences a couple months ago?" Internally I chanted, *Please no forensic science, please no forensic science.* I could just hear the question now. *What does your sister do for a living?* "Oh yeah, she cuts up dead people." A grimace stole across my face, but I hid it quickly, not wanting to sway her one way or the other. As much as I wanted to make all her major decisions for her, rationally, I knew I had to let her go to some extent. My sweet baby sis was an adult, and it was time I started treating her as such.

She sucked in a breath and pulled up her leg and sat on her foot. "I have, actually. Biochemistry."

Turning around, I let the word roll over my brain. Biochemistry has to have something to do with biology, but that doesn't mean forensics. "Okay, so what exactly is that, and what would you be doing with that type of degree?"

Maddy licked her lips and settled in. As she spoke, she became more animated, smiling wide, her cheeks pinking and her eyes sparkling. I tuned out most of what she said because honestly, she started speaking geek and my filter was on. "So basically, biochemists study aspects of the immune system, the expressions of genes, isolating, analyzing, and synthesizing different products. I could work with cancer mutations, mange a lab, or lead a research team. The options are endless."

Hearing the wide variety of options that were on the horizon for her made my cheeks burn I smiled so large. "I'm so proud of you, Mads. Biochemistry sounds difficult but right up your alley. How much schooling? You're still going for master's level, right?"

She bit down on her pink lip and looked away.

"Maddy, now I know you're worried about tuition, but you don't have to. I've already paid your tuition this year and the remainder of last year's."

Her eyes widened, and her jaw dropped open.

I grinned, loving that little surprise. "By year's end, I'll have saved Dad's ass, and I'll have enough money to put you through another several years of school. I do not want you settling. At all!" Not like me, I wanted to add but didn't. My lot in life was uncertain. For now, I was going with the flow and making the money I needed to in order to help my family survive.

Maddy jumped up, ran over to me, and wrapped her arms around me, tears filling those gem-like eyes. "I love you. When I'm a rich scientist, I'm going to buy you a house right next to me so that no matter where you are, you will always know where your home is. Close to me."

I petted the side of her head as she kissed my temple.

"Now, don't worry. I'm also going to be submitting for some scholarships, because to go where I want to go in this field, I'm going to need a PhD."

PhD. That one acronym sent a rush of adrenaline through my chest and out each limb. The hair on my arms stood at attention as I let myself freak out. "A doctor!" I said with pure awe and motherly pride in my tone.

Maddy rolled her eyes and nodded, pulling that pouty lip of hers into a smirk. "Yeah, sis, a doctor...of philosophy," she said with a snicker.

"Fuck, I don't care what type of doctor. My baby sis is going to be a doctor and a scientist. You've made my year, sweet baby girl." I shook my head and thought about the future. Maddy walking the stage getting her degrees, settling into some company wearing a white lab coat that screamed authority. Yeah, my girl was going places, and I'd do anything in my power to make sure she got every last one of her dreams met. Wistfully, I stared off into space and then jolted when Maddy tickled my bicep.

"Figured you'd like that plan. Now, can we go? I'm dying to see Matt."

Matt. The boyfriend. The one she just gave up her v-card to. He better be worth his weight in gold, or I'd steamroll his ass so fast he wouldn't even see it coming. Nothing was going to prevent Maddy from succeeding. Nothing.

★ ★ ★ ★

Matt's parents were right up there with those old-school TV parents everybody wanted but nobody had. Matt Rains, on the other hand, did have the perfect parental units. His mother, Tiffany, was tall, with dark hair and dark eyes. His father was a good foot taller, also with brown hair and a set of stunning, clear-blue eyes. Matt, the young man my sister was looking at with googly eyes, was smokin' hot in that nerdy-chic way. He wore a button-up shirt that fit tight against what looked to be nicely defined muscular shoulders. Definitely took good care of himself and worked out. His dark hair was wavy, yet styled away from his face in a sleek manner. Perched on his straight nose was a pair of thick, black-rimmed glasses. Nerdy-chic. Like his dad, he had those crystal-blue eyes. Ones that hadn't focused on anyone but my sister all through dinner.

"Mia, I understand your father is in the hospital?" Trent Rains asked when dessert was being served.

I nodded. "Yeah, he had an unfortunate accident. He's been in a coma for a few months now, but we pray every day that he'll wake up."

Tiffany's features turned soft, and she laid a hand on my shoulder. "I'm sorry to hear that. It must be tough on two young women to be managing alone." She shook her head, not really in pity but almost sadness.

A retort that wasn't altogether kind was on the tip of my tongue. With effort, I choked it back down. They were being nice. What I wanted to say in response and sat like acid, burning a hole through the tip of my tongue, was I'd been managing on my own since I was ten years old and I was doing just fine, thank you very much. Unfortunately, I had enough sense not to be a bitch. Instead, I smiled and sipped my decaf. Damn, even the coffee here tasted better than what we had at home. Probably some fancy-brand stuff they had to grind daily.

"Okay, everyone." Matt stood up and held my sister's hand. She looked up at him with diamonds in her eyes. "I have an announcement to make."

Anytime a person claims they have an "announcement" to make, it usually means some shit is about to hit the fan and hard. I watched in horror as Matt tugged on my sister's hand and pulled her to his side, holding her close—too close, in my opinion.

Matt's head tipped down toward Maddy's. Complete and utter devotion filled the air. "I've asked Madison to marry me, and she's accepted!" he said with bravado and a huge smile.

Squeals of excitement came from his mother, and a loud clap and a response that sound like Santa Claus saying his "ho, ho, ho," echoed around the room from his father. Me? I about pissed myself.

What. The. Fuck.

Maddy, smiling like I'd never seen before, looking the most beautiful I'd ever seen her, flashed her gaze toward me.

Then her smile dropped, her chin shook, and that lip I knew all too well started to quiver. Tears pooled in her eyes but hung just at the lash line.

"Please, Mia..." I heard her whisper, and I shook my head.

I stood up, walked right out of the room, straight out the main door of the house, and into the cooler desert vista seen clearly from the Rain's family porch. Had I stayed at that table, I would have lost it. Ripped my baby girl away from the clutches of suburbia and not stopped until I got her clear of this ridiculous notion that she was going to get married...at nineteen. Fuck.

I paced back and forth, my entire body aflame, sweat prickling against my hairline and upper lip. While stewing and trying to come up with a reasonable way to not look like the evil sister in this scenario as I hauled my sister out of here, I heard the screen door catch and slam behind me. Twirling around, I came eye to eye with Matt. His face showed remorse but not enough for me to believe he'd take it all back.

"I'm sorry I didn't ask you first, but after last weekend..."

"You mean when you stole my baby sister's virginity!" I roared, not recognizing my own voice. It sounded like a banshee's wail.

His head shot back as If he'd been struck. "Not that it's any of your business. Madison is a grown woman, one whom I love very much. What she gave me was a gift, one I'll treasure always. One I never want another man to have in this lifetime." His statement was said with conviction, and I could almost see him standing a little taller when he released the words meant to bring me to his side of thinking. Not happening.

Tugging at my hair, I leaned against the railing. "What makes you think you need to marry her? Right now?"

He walked over and stood in front of me. "Not right now. We're going to get our bachelor's degrees first. That's two full years away."

That declaration instantly made the fear start to slowly ebb away, the anger shrinking back down to a manageable size.

"I just wanted the commitment. For her to know that I'm hers and she's mine. And I want her to have something concrete, because we're planning to move in together... Soon."

And then the frustration rolled over me again like a pin smoothing out dough. "Seriously?" I growled.

He nodded. "I don't like where she lives, especially there all alone. When she didn't have a car, I about lost my mind knowing she was walking through that neighborhood at night. Then you got her the car, and that was great, but your father isn't there, Mia. And *you're* not there."

That last sentence hit me like a frying pan to the face.

Matt's face turned hard, almost cold, his tone gravelly. "She's alone, unprotected." He shook his head. "Unacceptable." Matt finished with a huff, as if he was a grown-ass man and not a twenty-year-old wannabe man.

My shoulders drooped, defeat filling the edges of reality. He had a point. A very good point. I didn't like Maddy being alone any more than he did. I loathed it. It had been a constant source of stress these past few months. It was the same reason I had Ginelle drive by the house on her way home from work every night to make sure everything looked okay.

Breathing in slowly through my nose, I let it out even slower. "You're right. It is unsafe."

Matt nodded but kept silent. I respected him for letting me have my say, giving me the time to express my concerns. This was Vegas. They could have just run off and hit one of the million chapels on the Strip if they were determined. Gripping the railing, I dug my nails into the white wood and looked out over the desert. "I just don't want her to make a mistake. You guys are so young."

"And we're going to take it slow. Live together first, see how that goes. Support one another through school and get our bachelor's together. We both have two more years after this one."

I jumped on that because it wasn't exactly true anymore. Maddy was going to be a doctor. The first in our family. "And Maddy wants to go for her Master's and PhD. What then? You gonna support her through that as her husband?'"

Matt nodded frantically. "Absolutely. It was my idea! She's top of her class, much higher than even me, and I work my ass off. Her natural talent and brains are unparalleled in the program. She's going to be an amazing scientist, and I get to be the guy who rests his hand on her back when she accepts those awards and makes those speeches she will undoubtedly be asked to do in the future. I get to stand by her side and cheer her on, as she will for me." Matt placed his hand on my arm and forced me to look him in the eyes. "We're not taking this lightly, and we're not stupid. But we are in love, and I don't want to risk losing her for anything."

Matt's blue eyes held such a strong conviction, I couldn't be angry any longer. It all seeped out like water swirling and flowing down the drain during a shower. It left me feeling wrung out and defeated.

"Is it okay to come out now?" Maddy's voice sounded small through the screen door.

"Yeah, baby girl, come on out. Let's see the ring." I shot playful daggers at Matt, trying to make a little bit light of the situation. "There better be a ring!" A scowl slipped across my face, but I couldn't hold it when Maddy came hopping out of the house with her left hand out.

The ring wasn't huge, but it wasn't small either. It looked antique.

"It was my grandmother's. Mom gave it to me the first day I brought Madison over for dinner." He laughed.

"It's lovely." I looked up at my baby sister, who seemed incredibly nervous and unsure of herself. Man, I hoped Matt taught my girl some confidence. If he could go up against a bat-shit crazy sister who had the helicopter-mom syndrome on lockdown, he could teach my sis how to be more certain of herself.

Tears dropped down Maddy's cheek. "I'm so happy, Mia. Please be happy for me. I can't handle you being disappointed."

Ever since she was little, and especially after our mom left, I was her only female influence. Over the years, she couldn't handle thinking she'd let me down or hurt me in anyway. That girl would rather walk across a stretch of hot coals than hear I was disappointed in her decisions.

"Oh you sweet, silly girl. Come here."

I pulled her into my arms. She cried softly into my neck, letting her nerves and fear go while I petted her hair and hummed her song. "Three Little Birds" by Bob Marley was the song I'd learned off a CD Dad listened to after Mom left. Mostly he listened to "No Woman No Cry" over and over again in a drunken haze while I took care of Maddy and me. But that one song made me believe that things would be all right... eventually.

Maddy pulled her face up, and I wiped away her tears with my thumbs. "I'm sorry I reacted the way I did." I hedged a glance at Matt. "Your parents probably think I'm a fruitcake."

He chuckled. "No, I think they probably can relate to impulsivity and the response from the family. They met and got married within three months of knowing one another. To them, I'm just following in their spontaneous footsteps. I promise you though, Mia, this is not spontaneous. We're going to finish school first. I just want my ring on her finger and her safe in my apartment directly across the street from the school."

"You live across the street from the school?" That motherly side of me that only came out when it came to my baby sis started flashing brightly like a lighthouse beam to a boat lost in a dark ocean.

He smiled wide and nodded, pulling Maddy into his arms. "You okay, sunshine?" he whispered in her ear but loud enough for me to hear.

I focused on the care and concern with which he touched my girl. He was a good guy. Probably a true angel in a sea of sinners here in Vegas.

"As long as Mia's okay with all this I am." Her eyes flashed to mine.

I groaned. "Fine, I give my blessing."

That got a reaction.

A jumping, squealing, teenaged reaction to be exact.

After a few more lectures from me, we went back into the house. Tiffany and Trent Rains were waiting patiently in the living room.

"My boy will take excellent care of your sister, I can promise you that." Mr. Rains beamed with pride. "He's got his head on straight, but you can't deny a man in love. When the Rains men fall, they fall hard and fast and for life." He looped an arm over his wife's shoulder. "And that's a fact," he said with gusto.

I sat down and looked at the happy couple. "Maddy and I didn't have it easy growing up. We've only ever been able to count on one another. So hearing that my baby sister was going to marry your son, at the young age of nineteen, something inside me just snapped. I didn't handle that well, and I apologize."

Tiffany stood up and sat next to me in the love seat. "No worries. It was a bit of a shock when Matt mentioned his intention to us earlier this week. I mean, I knew he loved her. They haven't been away from one another for the better part of two months."

Two months. They've been together two months and are engaged. I couldn't wrap my head around it.

"It seems awfully fast..."

"Things like that happen in the Rains family." Tiffany grinned while looking at her husband. Love, adoration, and loyalty filled her brown eyes. I wanted my sister to have that, and maybe by marrying into this family, it would be hers one day. Please God, just let it truly be after she gets her degree.

Tiffany ran her hand up and down my back in a soothing, motherly gesture I hadn't received in more years than I could remember. "It will be okay. They'll finish their bachelor's, and then we'll plan a wedding! We've got time."

Time.

Seemed these days that was the last thing I had a lot of.

★ ★ ★ ★

The rest of my stay in Vegas was a complete whirlwind. Gin,

of course, thought that Maddy getting engaged was absolutely hilarious. That skanky ho knew exactly how to push my buttons and kept at it the rest of my visit. Making comments about how Matt and Maddy would run off and get married on the Strip, or end up pregnant in a few months. That little joke had me giving Maddy a sit down and chat about the importance of never missing a birth-control pill. She swore she'd never miss a day and took it right before bed each night. After that embarrassing conversation—for her, not me—I made her pinky promise that she would not get married without me. That was the only recourse I had to ensure things would stay as planned. In her nineteen years of life, we had never, not once, broken a pinky promise to one another. It was sacred, and I believed her when she kissed my pinky, and I kissed hers, that she wouldn't let me down.

As I sat on the plane, I thought about how defensive and upset I'd gotten when I heard the announcement that the teens were engaged. Was it that my sis was getting her happily ever after before I did that was the problem? That's what Gin joked. But no, that wasn't it. I never wanted the things she did. If I really dug deep, the answer was simple.

I couldn't lose her.

I'd been responsible for Maddy for as long as I could remember. Her living with a man, leaning on him for support, would be only the first loss. His family had informed me that they paid for their son's apartment and that the only thing Maddy would need was spending money. They were happy to contribute extra to their son's food bill for his fiancée because they already thought of her as family. Simple as that. They now had my sister as *their* family and were supporting her.

Putting a roof over her head, feeding her, those things were *my* job and had been for almost fifteen years. I didn't know how to handle that. For one, I knew that I'd keep up the rent at my dad's place, and I'd send her several hundred bucks a month for incidentals and supplies for her coursework as well as for her to play with. She deserved that. My sister worked her bum off, and I didn't want that to change by her attempting to get a job. I wanted her to stay on that fast track to future success. Now, I just had to accept that Matt Rains was going to be holding her opposite hand through this journey.

Well, at least nothing had changed about the Hawaii trip. Matt seemed crushed when she told him, which made me secretly thrilled. Yep, bona fide bitch here, and I was not sorry about it. According to Maddy, he understood the need for "girl time" and that the news they'd shared was a bit shocking. At the end of the discussion, the sweet bastard was congratulating me on the idea and giving *his* blessings. Like I needed it. Funny boy, he would learn real quick who was boss. I just hoped in the end, it would still be me.

CHAPTER THREE

Black tribal tattoos. Drool-worthy, thick, corded muscles wrapped in intricately weaving designs cascaded all over tanned, toned, male skin. From the top of his left shoulder, down his bulging bicep, over his ribcage, waist, dipping into the sarong that covered his male essence and beyond. The black ropes of ink and then scaled down from his tree-trunk-sized thigh, along a tight, carved-out calf, to stop bluntly at the ankle. I could barely feel the sand burning the soles of my feet as I stood there in awe of the magnificent creature before me. He turned sideways, giving me a lickable view of a strong, well-formed back, one that could easily lift me and two friends and toss us into the ocean just beyond where he stood. A camera clicked repeatedly, and then he looked at me. No, he didn't look at me. His eyes sought mine across the thirty-foot expanse between us. Brown eyes—the color of the deepest, darkest cocoa bean—sizzled as they took in every ounce of my form.

The stranger's gaze slid over me like a burning caress, so heated I fanned my face trying to remove the searing feeling that encapsulated my skin. An Italian-accented voice called out some commands, and finally, Mr. Tattoo looked away, releasing the hold he had over me. I was freed but felt an odd, niggling sense of loss instead. The way this man looked at me was a calling, a beacon of desire needling at my psyche. One I was all too familiar with, as the space between my thighs swelled and softened. I stood and watched as the man behind the camera took a dozen more photos and then abruptly made a slashing gesture with his hand.

"*Finito!*" he said, followed by: "*Perfetto.*"

Ripping my gaze away from the overly delicious male, I watched as the photographer twisted around, his face turned toward me. He had on a woven, brown fedora-style sun hat, cargo shorts, and a white linen shirt that was held together by a single button that did nothing to hide the svelte body underneath it. He smiled wide and trudged over to me, sand kicking up with each step. I stood stock-still where the limo driver had suggested when he parked and pointed at the tent on the beach. He said my boss was behind the camera. I hadn't anticipated my client would also be the man taking the pictures for the campaign. Either way, it didn't matter much to me. Work was work, and as long as it came with a hundred-thousand-dollar check, I was all in.

As he came closer up the beach, I could see a soft smile, white teeth, and small wrinkles at the edges of his kind blue eyes, with more around his mouth. His handsome face showed he'd aged well, and his salt-and-pepper hair spiked out from under the fedora.

"*Bella donna,*" he said, grasping my shoulders in a warm embrace and leaning forward and air kissing both cheeks. "I am Angel D'Amico, and you are more beautiful than I anticipated when my wife said we must have you for our campaign."

At the mention of his wife, a statuesque Latina exited a white tent, her brown skin glimmering in the sunlight. A fiery red sarong-style halter dress wrapped around her curvaceous form and flapped in the breeze. Her dark hair was long and whisked out as if she had a personal fan blowing directly on her to accentuate her features. Talk about beauty. This woman had loads of it.

Angel clapped his hands as the woman headed our way. "Ah, my wife. Takes away breath, yes?" His Italian accent was more prevalent.

I nodded because she had stolen my breath. She was that stunning.

A huge smile graced her lips. "Mia, it is so lovely to have you as part of our project." She also leaned forward and air kissed both of my cheeks.

Now that she was close, I could see she had also been kissed by age, but it did not take away from her beauty. Aunt Millie had told me that the designer and his wife were around fifty. These two could easily pass for early forties.

"I am Rosa, Angel's wife. We are excited to have you here."

I tugged my bag up my shoulder and pushed my hair off my forehead. "I'm happy to be here. The island—well, what I've seen of it coming from the airport—is beautiful."

"It is. You can take the next couple of days getting acquainted with it. We just shot Tai and will plan to do singles of you." Angel looked over his shoulder as Mr. Tattoo pounded back a bottle of water and grabbed a shirt from someone who looked like an assistant. "Tai, come. Meet your partner for the month."

Partner? Millie hadn't said anything about having a partner. Just as I was about to question his comment, the man they called Tai moved to meet us. When I say moved, really the entire Earth might as well have split open and separated, carving out a path for him. All sound seemed to disappear, and the entire environment zeroed in on nothing but this man's progression across the sand. He was breathtaking. The muscles in his giant thighs pulsed and tensed with each step.

A fine layer of abdominal squares rippled, the skin indenting around each shape with his movements. His chest shone like an opal, smooth, swirling with colors. Then again, that could be the heat and my vision ebbing around his shape.

When he reached the small huddle we'd created with our three bodies, the addition of his giant frame had me almost stepping back, the space now seeming far too small. Hell, the beach was far too small when you had such animal magnetism and male perfection standing on it. The ocean probably cried its own salty tears, wishing he'd grace its silky depths with his presence.

Angel stretched out a hand in front of me. "Tai Niko, meet Mia Saunders. She's going to be staying in the bungalow next to yours and doing all the couple shoots with you this month. We're presenting you as the tropics couple for the 'Beauty Comes in All Sizes' campaign."

Tai's brown eyes locked on to mine. He licked his plump bottom lip seductively and made a sound as though he was kissing his teeth before those lush pieces of pink flesh pursed. I did my best not to swoon, but the heat generated by this man felt like a wall of fire. He sucked in a slow breath, his nostrils flaring as his gaze swept all over my body. I didn't say anything. Couldn't even move or breathe under his scrutiny. "You're radiant. I will enjoy working you," he said, but his eyes said far more than "working" with me. Wait... What?

"You mean working *with* me?" I clarified, shaking my head.

Once more, his head tilted down, and his gaze stared at my feet. In that moment, I realized he was lacking hair, as in almost all of his hair. He had a scruff on his dome, much like the way the Rock kept his lack of locks. Looking him over, he very much resembled the actor, Dwayne Johnson. Huge, latte-colored skin, darkened even more by the sun's tropical rays, tattooed, only Tai seemed far more traditional in his Samoan features and heritage than the actor.

Tai puckered his sexy lips together and smirked. "No, that's not at all what I meant."

Damn. This month was going to be one helluva ride. Hopefully that ride included being on top of or under a six foot godlike Samoan man named Tai.

★ ★ ★ ★

A ray of light split through the room and landed on my face, waking me up from the most glorious dream of naked Twister with a sexy Samoan. I got up and padded through my morning routine, making coffee, and snacking on some fresh pineapple and other various island fruits from the fully stocked fridge. The bungalow the D'Amicos had me in was the type of place people dreamed of staying in on vacation. South of Honolulu, we were right on Diamond Head Beach. As in, I could open the sliding door and touch the sand with my toes within ten feet. An unobstructed view of the ocean was my backdrop. I opened the doors, letting in the morning ocean breeze and the sound of the surf.

Not able to wait any longer, I pulled on a white bikini, grabbed a towel, and made for the ocean. It had been far too long since I'd been on a beach. The last time was when I was with Wes.

Wes. I wasn't going to go there. When I'd gotten to the airport in Vegas, there had been a picture of Gina DeLuca on the cover of a tabloid with the heading "New Love Interest for

Gina," and the image below it showed a picture of the beautiful actress having lunch with none other than my Wes. Well, not my Wes, but I'd had him first, so by ownership rights, that would make him mine, right? Then again, she had him now, and possession was nine-tenths of the law. What the hell was I thinking? I didn't own Wes any more than he owned me. He might have a piece of my heart maybe, but not the whole enchilada. We'd made that very clear, even though there were still some feelings brewing. We both agreed to leave that in the background while we lived our lives. And that was what I intended to do.

Live my life.

Dropping my towel on the sand about thirty feet from the ocean's edges, I looked out over the aquamarine water. It was so clear you could see straight through to the stand at the bottom for at least a hundred or so feet before the water got deeper. There was one lone surfer wearing a pair of black board shorts catching some serious waves out in the distance. He definitely had mad skills I watched for a while, mesmerized by the movements. The man caught a few ankle busters and then made a 360, slamming his large body back onto the board and paddling back out. Within moments, he was up on his board and hitting a magical A-frame wave, rushing through it like a pro.

Before long, the surfer headed my way on a snapper wave. It seemed like it happened in slow motion. The black swirls from shoulder to ankle caught my eye first. Then my gaze roamed up the wet, slick surface of the widest chest I'd ever had the pleasure of seeing. Tony, back in Chicago, was the largest by far and definitely no slouch. Still, even he had nothing on this giant. A man like Tai Niko made a woman like me, five foot eight and a curvy size-eight body—bordering on a ten when you factor in the giant tits and junk in the trunk—feel miniscule in comparison. I loved feeling small.

His board hit the beach, and he popped off perfectly, hitting the sand as if he did it every day, before leaning over and yanking up his board. He carried it under one bulging bicep like it weighed nothing.

"Hey, *haole,*" he said, and I narrowed my eyes.

Mental note... Look up the word haole *on Wikipedia.*

"Didn't realize that was you out there. You're good." I nodded my chin at the ocean, trying to find any reason not to stare and drool over his magnificent frame.

His sculpted jaw ticked as he smirked. "I should be. I teach surfing on the days I'm not modeling or working the shows with my family."

"You teach?"

"Why? You want a lesson?" His tone was alluring and seductive.

That was most definitely my cue to flirt back. "You gonna teach me how to ride?" I arched a brow into a fine point.

His mouth pushed into that delectable purse as his eyes seemed to walk all over my bikini-clad curves. "I'll teach you how to *ride* all day and all night, girlie." When he said the word girlie, it didn't sound the way a woman said it to her best friend. No, from him it sounded more like a growl, where he enunciated the "grrr" sound, giving it a "grrrlllleee" vibe. One that pinpointed lusty spikes straight through me to the point that my toes curled instinctively and my hoo-hah clenched delightfully.

"Is that right? We still talking about surfing?" I called his bluff.

I meant it to sound playful. Though I imagined playing with him in other ways would be a lot more fun. My vagina and I were definitely on board for that ride.

"What do you think?" His dark eyes turned pitch black. Lust swirled in those inky depths, and my feminine side jumped for joy and did the chicken dance.

"Go big or go home" is the catch phrase people used in moments like this. Well, I intended to make that fucker my theme song, because I was definitely going "big" before I went home. "Baby, I'll take whatever ride you're offering," I responded boldly, knowing I was poking the beast. This time, I wanted whatever came from it. Wanted it so badly, my knees were weakening.

Tai's nostrils flared as he sucked in a noisy breath. With a loud thud, his board hit the sand, a large paw looped around my waist, and I was slammed against his chest, his lips crushing mine. The kiss was savage, brutal, filled with nothing but an insatiable hunger.

We ate from one another's mouths. Stinging bites of lips, and nips of tongues. Fluttering licks meant to consume, taste, and plunder as we took from one another. Without question, comment, or discussion, Tai lifted me, slid his hands over the ass he'd been squeezing, and yanked me up his body. I wrapped my legs around his waist and held on, unable to let go of his addictive taste for even a moment to see where we were going. It wasn't until my bikini top was off, my back hit a cloud like surface, and Tai's lips clamped on to my nipple that I realized we were no longer on the beach. At that moment, I didn't care. I wanted him more than my next breath.

Holding his nearly bald head to my breast was extremely satisfying. Not as much as digging my nails into his dome and leaving crescent-shaped indentations on the prickly sphere. He was not bothered by my aggressiveness. He was far more aggressive in his own movements. His teeth sank into the tightened bud, and I cried out. Tai released my swollen breast, grinned maniacally, and clamped on to its twin, giving it the same delightful torture from his hot mouth. His hands were all over me. Plumping my other breast, clenching the rounded skin of my bum, and finally locking behind my head when he took my mouth again. With Tai, it was all about the taking.

"Gonna take you hard, and then soft, and finish with something in between. Then I'm gonna do it all over again," he growled, pulling off my body. He reached a long, muscled arm to his nightstand for a foil packet. Thank God someone was thinking clearly. My mind was a haze of lust so intense, I just wanted him to stick his sizable erection so far into me I'd forget my own name.

Tai's board shorts dropped to the tile floor, and I leaned up on my forearms. That sight would fill future fantasies for decades. His tattoo did not stop at his midsection. No, that beauty covered the entire left side of his body. Black patterns formed so many symbols and images I couldn't grasp them all. Tai grinned wickedly, wrapped a hand around his flesh, and lazily stroked his massive cock. When I say massive, I mean, it's one of those that you know for a fact will hurt the first time going in, but you will accept that pain like a badge of honor and not complain. And you will take it again and again because nothing will ever come close to the fullness. "Jesus, you're a big boy...everywhere." I gawked at his sculpted perfection.

He continued to watch me squirm, hips rotating uselessly, my body getting hotter and pussy getting wetter with every stroke of his delicious flesh. I could no more stop my mouth from watering or my response to his naked form, nor did I want to.

Wanton. Achy. Swollen.

Those were the predominant feelings rushing through my overheated skin as I looked at him.

"Remove your suit." He practically growled his request. No, not request... *Demand.*

I should have balked at his dominance, but I was so worked up I simply acted by pulling the two strings and letting it fall open, along with my spread thighs.

"Wider. I want to see your flower open and wet." Tai sucked in a harsh breath when I acquiesced.

I bit down on my lip to hold back a moan as I revealed myself to him in a way that could be considered demeaning, but with him, it somehow felt forbidden, hot, and ramped up my desire for him to a scalding burn.

Tai continued to look his fill while stroking his dick. A pearl of liquid coated the top, and I licked my lips.

"You want a taste, girlie," he offered in that gravely tone that sent shivers racing down my spine and my oversensitive skin.

I couldn't respond. The room had faded into only him and my need to press every single inch of my body to his. I nodded, and he stopped his strokes.

"Lick me. Taste what you do to me."

Scrambling forward and getting on my hands and knees, I leaned forward, and just when my lips were close enough that he could feel my breath on him, I looked up. His eyes were dark as night, his bottom lip pinned between even, white teeth. Keeping my eyes on him, I flicked out my tongue and lapped up his essence. The tangy, salty sensation sent a wave of fresh liquid to pool between my own legs.

He inhaled loudly. "I can smell your flower, girlie. Smells like liquid sunshine." He let out a long breath. "I'm gonna feast on your body until you pass out. You want that?"

Instead of responding, I engulfed his member and guided it down my throat. His hand threaded through my hair, not quite tugging, more like his fingers flexed against my scalp as I pleasured him. The fingers gripping my scalp without pressing was an entirely new, pleasant sensation. Balancing on my knees and one hand, I lifted my free hand to wrap about the base of his manhood. He was far too large for me to take him any deeper than halfway, and I prided myself on my ability to take a man down my throat. It was a skill I had, one I'd been told many women didn't. With his size, half was all I could swallow. The thought that this cock was going to be splitting me open soon had me doubling my efforts.

"Slow down, girlie." He pulled me off his cock with a wet plop. Then he maneuvered himself onto the bed, his long body stretched out like a buffet. I didn't know what I wanted to taste next: more of his succulent cock or the dip between each square pec. "Straddle me. I want to eat you while you suck me off. And you *will* take every drop."

His tone was forceful, but more in the I-am-the-boss-in-the-bedroom way. And with him, I gotta admit, it worked. I straddled his wide shoulders, and he gripped my hips. Before I could even move my hips down toward his mouth, he'd already tipped his head and sank his tongue deep between my folds.

"Oh fuck, Tai," I yelled out wildly, bucking on his face as he pressed on the back of my thighs, widening me farther, spreading me so wide that I must have looked like a frog about to jump off a lily pad. I was definitely about to jump...into a mind-numbing orgasm. He had me riding his face, pleasing him completely forgotten as I ground my sex onto his face. Tai was a world-class pussy eater. *World-class.* Hands down, one of the three best I'd ever had, right in line with Alec and Wes. Only with Tai, he gorged like a man who'd been locked up for a decade and the only thought for those ten years was the taste of my pussy.

Within minutes, I was coming all over his tongue. That seemed to egg him on. Through the noisy way he ate me, I could hear small grunts, or words.

"Sugar."

"Soaked."

"Mmm."

"All day."

"Eat you all day."

That was the last thing I heard before I came down from the first high, falling against Tai's body to land near a rock-hard cock that almost poked my eye out. Lifting up weakly, I wrapped my lips around his massive dick and went to town the second I got that burst of his flavor. I licked, sucked, nibbled, and stroked, giving it my all until he was lifting up his toned hips to meet my downward movements.

His dick turned dark, angry, hinting that he was about to go off. I gloried in my ability to give this giant pleasure, take him there the way he was taking me. When he pressed two thick fingers into my sopping center, my body strung up tight as a drum. One more pluck, and I was going to lose it. *It* being a hurricane-sized orgasm the likes of which I'd not experienced since my time with Frenchie. Those fat fingers of Tai's knew exactly what to do and zeroed in on that hidden nerve inside and put the tickle pin on it. Titillating it with the pads of his fingers over and over, until I had no choice but to lock my lips around the head of his cock and suck like my life depended on it. At that moment, I gave Hoover vacuums a run for their money.

Tai's hand pressed deep, and his lower half lifted off the mattress to go farther into my mouth. It felt like I was riding a wave. Rolling warm waves rushed over me as I came against Tai's fingers and mouth just as his essence shot down my throat in long, ropey bursts. When I sucked him dry and he finally removed his hand from between my thighs and laid his head flat against the mattress, we both sighed. A bone-weary release of pent-up sexual tension. As if I weighed nothing, he spun my body around, maneuvered me against his non-tattooed side, and held me close.

"Next time we use this." His tone held mirth as he held up the unused condom between two fingers.

"Deal," I laughed, cuddling into his side. He smelled of the ocean, sex, and me. A delectable combination.

There was another man who always smelled of the ocean, and I closed my eyes, trying not to bring him into this moment. I'd just had incredible sex and was planning on having a lot more of it and soon.

Not now, I reminded myself. *Enjoy the sexy Samoan while you can.*

Tai slid his hands up and down my back and then up and into my hair, where he rubbed my scalp. I was pretty sure I purred like a kitten under his talented hands.

"You like that, *haole*?"

I anchored my chin on his chest and traced some of the ink over his heart. "What does *haole* mean?"

He smiled, leaned forward, and pressed his lips to my

forehead. It was an incredibly sweet gesture for someone who'd just manhandled me like a Dominant in a BDSM club. Well, probably not. I didn't know jack about that lifestyle, but he definitely had the dominant nature down.

"*Haole* means foreigner."

"I much prefer girlie," I grumbled and licked his nipple.

His resounding laugh at my sarcastic comment rumbled against my ear and shook me to the core. I could already feel the stirring of desire once more. Just from his laugh. Boy, was I in trouble.

"Noted, girlie," he said in that timber I was beginning to love.

He lifted me up and took my lips. And I mean took. Tai Niko did nothing half-assed in the bedroom. It had become abundantly clear in the time we'd already spent together that he put his all into giving pleasure. He owned that kiss as if he was competing for an award, which he would have won.

CHAPTER FOUR

Oddly enough, we didn't end up using that condom as planned, because just when our last kiss started heating up, Tai got a call. And then another, and another, and another. Apparently Sunday night dinner was a big deal in the Niko family. So now, after only one day of knowing Tai, which consisted primarily of the two of us going down on one another, I was about to meet his family. His *entire* family.

"Now, Mia, my family is cool. The coolest. However, you are white, a mainlander. So if they make a comment on your being *haole*, just go with it. Our people are very proud of our culture, our heritage, and our family lines. They will treat you well and welcome you with open arms...as long as they don't think we're in a serious relationship."

"That should be easy. We're not. I'm here on a job for just under a month. End of. I'm happy to reconfirm that. If we play a little on the side"—I knocked his giant bicep playfully with my own—"then that's a bonus. Right?"

His lips twisted into a grin so sexy I wanted to smother it with my mouth and gobble it up. "You got that right, girlie. Now come on. In my home, you meet my father before anyone else. Then you'll meet my brothers, and then my mother."

My eyebrows narrowed of their own accord. "Why is your mom last?"

He shook his head. "We save the best for last," he responded, but I thought that just might be a line to prevent me from kicking him in the nuts.

When we arrived at our destination, to say I was surprised would be an understatement. For some reason, I'd expected something far more tribal and island-looking. This home was painted as blue as the sky above and had white trim and a wraparound porch. Sprawling green lawns with palm trees everywhere dotted the property line. There was a long, wraparound driveway with no less than twenty cars. *Twenty.* For a family dinner. If you invited my entire family to dinner, we could all arrive in the same car.

The moment we walked up, I could hear a dull roar. Voices all around. Inside and farther away, as if they were somewhere out behind the house. Overall, I was floored by the best sound of all—the rounds of laughter coming from all directions. Joy. I felt it the moment we walked through the very modern plantation-style home located deep in the heart of Oahu.

Tai wordlessly held my hand and led me from room to room. There were people in every corner. All of them looked up, watching our progression through the house with smiles across their brown-sugar-colored faces. There was no judgment. There was nothing but a sense of curiosity that tinged the humid air as we passed.

Eventually, we made it out back, which was where the party was really being held.

"Is this a family dinner or reunion?"

Tai kicked his head back and laughed out loud. Several heads turned our way at the sound of Tai's rumbling baritone. "Mia, this is the same every Sunday night. My family is very close. Everyone participates, brings a dish big enough to feed around forty to fifty people. They take home whatever they can in the same dish they brought their own offering in. No mess."

I clinched his hand. "But we didn't bring anything." I worried my lip with my teeth, suddenly concerned that we weren't following Samoan protocol for a good party.

"Of course we did. What do you think you are?"

"Me?" My eyebrows pinched together so tightly that a tiny spike of pain shot through my nasal cavity.

He pulled me into his warm body. I loosely wrapped my arms around his form, clasping my hands over his rock-hard ass. Jesus, I wanted to take a bite out of that ass. Once again, I bemoaned the fact that we had been interrupted and we didn't get to finish our romp the way I would have liked. Meaning me having trouble walking tomorrow.

Tai licked his sinful lips, pressed his forehead against mine, and his voice got low, so low I felt it in my hoo-hah. "Don't look at me like you want to fuck me, girlie, or I'll be nailing you to the closest wall, and fuck all who hear us. And they would hear you. Nothin' beats making a woman scream out in pleasure when you're buried balls-deep in her flower."

Yep. That pretty much stunned me silent, until Tai stood in front of another mammoth of a man. This one had his shirt off, wearing nothing but a pair of board shorts. I glanced around and noticed that everyone was wearing similar beachwear. Tai, however, was in a pair of cargo shorts and a polo. It's a look Hector, my Gay BFF back in Chicago, coined as "golf chic." Tai could wear anything, or better yet nothing at all, and look good enough to eat.

"*Tama.*" Tai announced our presence using a Samoan word that had to mean dad or father to the man who stood near the barbeque. He lowered his gaze, and I followed suit, not knowing what was appropriate.

"Son, who is this you have brought to our home?" His

tone was welcoming and friendly.

Tai looked up and smiled. "*Tama*, this is Mia Saunders. Mia, this is my father,

Afano Niko."

I held out my hand, and he shook it.

"She is working with me on a modeling campaign."

His father's eyebrows rose up into his hairline. "Another model? I thought you'd learned from your last mistake," he grumbled, his voice now concerned, holding judgment. Obviously something had happened in the past that his father did not want Tai to repeat.

"Mia is not my girlfriend, *Tama*. Just a close friend. She's only on the island for the month. Then she will take her leave."

That seemed to perk the grump right up. He slapped a hand onto Tai's shoulder and squeezed. "Well good, good. Then she should eat and talk with the family. Learn of the Samoan culture while she can."

Tai smiled wide and proud. "My thoughts exactly."

I met Tai's brothers, all massive, all good-looking, and with different variations of parts of the tattoo that I'd seen on Tai. The sunburst on the ball of Tai's shoulder was the same as his father's, with the rays of light reaching down his arm and out onto his chest. On Tao, Tai's older brother, I saw the same turtle tattoo. Another couple of his brothers shared similar black bands of ink around the forearm and leg. There were a variety of patterns I hadn't had a chance to evaluate in our rush to get dressed and out of the house. Once I'd been razzed and hit on by each of Tai's three brothers, he led me through the house back toward the kitchen. I was on number two of the Niko family's special beverage they called Lilikoi's Passion, which Tai told me roughly meant "passionate for passion fruit" or something equally silly. All I knew was that it was yummy and made my belly feel warm and my mind feel free. The last time I drank, I ended up in bed with my client, Mason Murphy, in my skivvies. Which didn't end well for his girlfriend, though nothing happened. Mace was like a brother to me. And like all good alcoholic beverages, random thoughts of all the people I needed to reconnect with popped into my head, friends like Hector and Tony, Mace and Rachel, and Jennifer, the director's wife back in Malibu. She should be a few months pregnant by now. And of course...Wes. We texted and for now, that was enough. Seeing the picture of him and Gina supposedly dating front and center on the cover of my favorite smut mag didn't help my thoughts on reaching out. Nope. I was in Hawaii to work and have a good time. Work started in a couple of days, and the fun part was already happening. In the warm, sculpted arms of my own personal version of the Rock.

Tai stopped in front of a tiny speck of a woman. Her black hair was long and braided intricately. Her forearms appeared strong as she stirred something in a pot.

"*Tina,*" Tai said loud enough for her to hear. Again, he lowered his eyes, which I'd learned was out of respect. I noticed while talking with the brothers that every elder was treated with the same respect. I didn't know if that was a Samoan thing or just a Niko family gesture, but either way, it bespoke an extreme veneration of their elders, which likely meant they had earned such a gift.

The small woman spun around on bare feet. She wore a bursting bright-orange island wrap skirt that hit her ankles, a matching tank, and a sheer white overlay, which I suspected was to give a level of modesty. The young women in the family had no such problem showing skin and a lot of it. All of them were built well and wore bikinis while standing around chatting up their relatives. Of everyone, I probably seemed overdressed in a pair of white shorts and a green tank top. At least my hair had a natural wave due to the humidity, adding body and shine. I was definitely made for the tropical climates. My hair rocked, and I didn't have to do anything to make it so.

"My boy. My sweet, pure heart." She petted him over the heart, pulled his neck so he'd bend his large frame down to meet hers, and kissed each of his cheeks and then his forehead.

Her brown eyes were identical to Tai's and filled with a mother's love. I couldn't remember the last time I saw that look from my own mother...if ever.

"*Tina*, this is Mia Saunders, my friend from work. I'm showing her around the island and sharing our culture while she's here. Mia, this is my mother, Masina."

"Um, I thought her name was Tina?"

They both laughed, Tai's a throaty one I felt coil through my body, making even my toes curl in delight, but his mother chuckled sweetly.

"*Tina* is mother in Samoan. My children use our language when addressing someone of our culture."

I waved a hand, and I could feel the skin of my cheeks flame as I responded. "Oh, sorry. I haven't been around anyone who spoke Samoan before Tai. It's nice to meet you Mrs. Niko."

I put my hand out, and she grabbed it lightly and tugged me into her arms. Then she softly kissed each of my cheeks and then my forehead. Her hands cupped my cheeks, her thumbs pressed against my temples. "You are very lost and on a great journey. Never fear. You will find great joy in the experience before committing to your forever."

At this point, a small breeze could have knocked me

over. I stood there stock-still, incapable of moving or really responding. The best I could come up with was an: "Uh."

"*Tina...*" He chastised his mother and then pulled me into his side. "Mother has a bit of a spiritual way about her. She's been blessed with sight."

"Sight?" I clenched tighter onto the side of his body and glanced at the lovely woman.

He nodded begrudgingly, and she patted my shoulder. "Everything will be as it should, Mia. Do not let my boy mix up your forever with his. Sadly, they are not linked." At that time, she frowned, puffing out her thin lips. "You have but a short time. Make it last." And then she smiled brightly. Her wide nose and high rounded cheekbones made her seem ethereal.

Tai sighed. "Mia is not my girlfriend. We are friends spending time together for a month and working together."

Masina nodded. "I know, pure heart. Do not expect more, for it is not to be yours." Her tone was dead serious. A mother's warning, definitely one we should heed. "Now go." She flicked her fingers out, effectively excusing us. "I have much to do for dessert."

Tai looped an arm over my shoulder and led me out back again. By this time, I'd sucked up the remains of drink number two and was passionately needing a third. I shook my glass, and we hit the open bar, where tall see-through jugs sat filled with the strawberry-colored liquid.

★ ★ ★ ★

Back at the bungalow after way too many Lilikoi's Passions, we sat out on the beach, toes and bums in the sand, dark ocean the only sound around. The waves crashed hard against the shore, the white foam and silky ocean reflecting a perfectly bright moon. The ocean seemed endless from where we sat, the murky depths ready to swallow us whole at any time. I loved and feared the ocean in equal parts. It was something I had a great deal of respect for. It was also something I never underestimated.

I leaned back on my forearms and crossed my ankles, looking at the shirtless man next to me. "What do all the tattoos mean?" I asked.

"All of them mean something, girlie. Which spot in particular has your attention?" His eyes were as dark as the ocean behind him but not as scary. I could willingly be taken prisoner into those beautiful black pits.

Sitting up, I traced the sunburst on his shoulder, allowing the point of my finger to caress each ray of light. Goosebumps rose on the surface of skin I touched.

"That was my first. It was an incredible honor. In my culture, the sun typically stands for riches, brightness, grandeur, and leadership. For me, the way the rays reach out across my heart show my desire to lead with my heart. To be rich in the ways of love like my *tama*. And one day, I hope to serve as a great man at the head of my business and my family. Again, like my *tama*. That is why I asked my father to share it."

"That's really special."

Tai's chest shifted and puffed out more as he inhaled. "In the way of Samoans, if you want to get *tatau*—or the ink—you must earn it. And you must have a willing member of your family who will share it with you so that your lives will forever be linked. He stood up and dropped his shorts, leaving him completely naked. He turned to the side, his cock semi-erect and nothing close to the levels it reached when he was really turned on. With a sweep of his hand, he traced down his ribs to a crescent shape with a circular pinwheel design in the center.

"These markings I received for my brother, Tao. It was his wish to find harmony in his life. He fought a lot. With our parents, me, our sisters, brothers, kids at school. When he found his way, he wanted to share that journey in his life with me."

I pulled my knees up to my chest and hugged them. "And the turtle?"

He grinned and ran his hand down to his abs. Not abs. Lust squares. Each square ab on his body made me lust after it. I wanted to lick and bite my way through every inch of that torso and midsection, tattoos and all... Hell, especially because of the tattoos.

"Another request of mine that I share with my youngest brother. The turtle symbolizes longevity, wellness, and peace. It's something I desire for my family and myself."

"What about the waves and swirls? Do they mean something, or are they just filler?" I asked honestly, and he laughed.

Shaking his head, he used a finger to trace the swirls all over his body. By this point, his shaft had hardened, and I was ready to get story time over, but I was interested in why he would tattoo an entire half of his body and leave the rest pristine...devoid of ink.

"The ocean in our culture is very prominent, not only because we are surrounded by it, literally at its mercy, but because historically, Samoan's believed that the ocean is where you went when you died. Since I surf, and my culture is to always be near it, I give it a place in the story of my life and my family's lives." He continued and showed me bits here and there that were for a couple of cousins, his other brother, and so on. He even broke the rule and got the same flower every woman in his family had on her foot.

I'd noticed it at the party but hadn't mentioned it. At the time, I did find it odd that every woman in that house had the exact same tattoo on her foot. Turned out it was their lineage. It was the female version of paying the same respect to the family by permanently marking your body.

"My last question, I promise!"

He rolled his eyes and sat his bare bottom on the towel we'd brought with us. I bit down hard on my lip while feasting my eyes on his erect cock. I wanted that massive appendage in me like I wanted that million dollars to pay off Pops's debt.

"Go head, girlie. Ask it. But while you do, remove your clothes. Slowly."

I looked around, as if someone was magically going to appear on a private beach. Hey, I was a Vegas girl. You never knew when a creeper was hiding behind the bushes. Of course, here there weren't any bushes. Just miles of palm trees and sand. Standing up, I tugged off my tank, unbuttoned my shorts, and let them both fall to the sand.

"Continue."

"What, the question or the removal of my clothes?" I added seductively.

His eyebrow quirked up. "Both."

I unclasped the hooks at the back of my body, my bra loosening so that I was holding it in front of me. "Why is the entire right side of your body free of *tatau*?" I tried the Samoan word for tattoo on for size. He grinned at the use, so I must have said it correctly. Go me!

"Melons."

"Huh?"

"I want to see your melons. Drop your arms."

I let go of my bra and let the girls bounce free. Nice size Ds that were pretty damn perky in my opinion. My hands instantly fondled each large globe brazenly.

Tai groaned and leaned back, widening his legs. "You seeing this, girlie?" He shook his head in mock indignation.

"I sure do. Now tell me so we can get to the happy ending of the evening."

He wiggled a finger, and I shook my head. He used that come-hither finger again, and not being able to deny the wet coating my thighs nor the desire racing through my body, I walked over. He slammed me down onto his lap. Without a word, two of his fingers slipped between my folds and sank deep, his thumb pressing hard into the knot of nerves aching for attention. My head flew back, and I arched on his lap, giving him perfect access to my breasts, which he took greedily.

Tai had me bouncing on his lap, forcibly digging his fingers deep and fucking me beautifully with those fat digits. When he bit down on my tender nipple while simultaneously twirling his thumb around my O-trigger, I lost it. *It* being my hold on one helluva orgasm.

Once I came down, he took my mouth, kissing me hard, long... Mesmerizingly. When he pulled back, I felt drunk all over again, only this time I was drunk on him. Ready to be his willing slave if he'd just give me another sip of his sweet pleasure.

"I left the side of my body pure for me. That half of my life is mine alone and will only be shared with my future wife and children. When the time is right, I will share the markings of my sons' lives and hopefully their sons."

My hair fell against his face when I pressed our foreheads together, lips barely touching. Just enough so you could feel the slight humidity when sharing one another's air. "You can't even be real," I whispered against the moisture on his lips. "Men aren't ever that selfless."

"Oh, honey, I'm far from selfless and plan on showing you when I take what I want from your wicked body."

"Yes, please."

With that, he gripped my ass and walked me to my bungalow.

CHAPTER FIVE

Cock. Specifically, Tai's cock, left an impression. A big one. The space between my thighs was swollen and well-used after last night's sexcapades. His hunger for me was insatiable. He took me so many times that my pussy felt empty, devoid of the fullness he gave. Last night was one for the books. A night of pure, unadulterated, dirty, filthy sex. The kind every woman wants but rarely gets.

A grin slipped across my face, so wide it was impossible to hold back as I made my way up the stairs to the beautiful beach house, which was the location of my first photo shoot for D'Amico Designs and the "Beauty Comes in All Sizes" Campaign. When I held my hand up to knock on the door, it opened and a scrawny, overly thin hipster-type guy greeted me.

"Thank God you're here. Mia, right?" he said and gestured with a wave to follow him in.

I took in his appearance. He wore all black, and his skinny jeans looked glued to stick-like legs. A black T-shirt that was tucked haphazardly into his pants revealed that his waist was the size of my thigh. I followed him at a fast clip, my flip-flops flapping loudly along the tile floors.

"She's here," he said to the room as we entered the living area.

A few looked up and nodded, but that was it. The living room didn't look like your normal comfy living space with couches and TV. It had been transformed into a workspace for makeup, hair, and wardrobe. Racks of swimsuits and cover-ups lined one wall. Another had a wall of mirrors with seats that mimicked stations at a salon. Several heads were being worked on while upbeat music played in the background.

The man who had yet to introduce himself slapped his hands over the back of a leather chair. "Sit."

I did as instructed, mostly because I didn't know what else to do. I could see through the open French doors and windows that led out to a massive pool and garden where Angel, the designer and photographer, was setting up equipment and ordering attendants around. When I modeled for Alec, it was mostly just me and there wasn't much in the way of hair and makeup. That wasn't what his art was about. This reminded me of an upper-scale shoot like I'd done for a few ads and commercials during my brief sojourn into acting prior to becoming an escort.

"I am Raul, your stylist, makeup artist, and hairdresser all in one. I am everything and a bag of Cheetos." He winked.

I scaled his thin gothic look and thought he could use a bag or *twenty* of Cheetos right about now. The only color on his body was his light-brown skin and purple hair. It was shaved on the sides and smoothed into a pompadour style. With the length of the hair that fell over the back, it made me wonder if he spiked it up into a Mohawk. He pulled my hair off my neck and into a ponytail, making quick work of my makeup. We chatted idly while he did my hair, weaving beautifully bouncy curls into the long tresses.

Raul called a few orders out to other people standing around until one googly-eyed, super tall, incredibly skinny woman brought over a bathing suit, handing it to Raul. He looked her up and down slowly, licked his lips, and thanked the girl. She preened for him and turned to help another stylist.

"Your girlfriend?" I asked as he made finishing touches to my hair.

"Not yet," he said confidentially. "Working on that. She's shy. Don't want to scare her off, but we're going out this weekend."

"Good for you!"

I smiled, and he grinned, fluffing and spraying his masterpiece, making sure nary a hair was out of place.

With one last poof of the hair and burst of spray, he announced I was done. I looked in the mirror and barely recognized myself. I looked frickin' awesome! My hair was shiny, filled with body and loose curls that swayed elegantly as I moved my head from side to side. The makeup was nothing short of a masterpiece, Michelangelo quality. My green eyes were popping and so bright, I gasped at how beautiful they were. The rest of the look was very sun kissed and bronzed, seemingly natural only with an entire face full of makeup to achieve said "natural beauty."

"You're a genius."

"I know," he said and handed me a shimmery black bathing suit. The top was a tankini-halter paired with bottoms that had two white strings at each hip. More coverage than my normal bathing suits, which was nice for my first run. "Go change over there where the other girls are going."

I entered the room to see a variety of women of many shapes and sizes in various stages of undress. Assistants were mingling from woman to woman, spraying things on their skin and sealing bathing suits to specific areas.

A curvaceous black woman approached me. She had on a complex white suit that crisscrossed at the breasts into larger swaths of fabric that covered her stomach and then nipped at the hip where the design went into a boy short. On her shape, and with her espresso-colored skin against the white, it worked, and she was definitely comfortable with her curves. "Hey, girl. I'm MiChelle," she said, pronouncing it as "Me-Shell" and holding out her hand.

I shook it with a smile. "Mia." I looked around the room, and the other girls waved.

MiChelle locked an arm around my shoulder. "Okay, that hot blonde beeotch is Taylor." She pointed to a woman who was having her very large breasts taped into a bathing suit. Her blonde hair was gorgeous, falling down to her ample booty. My guess, girl was a solid size sixteen, possibly even an eighteen, and looked smokin' hot in the black suit. She waved. "That right there"—she pointed to a brunette with cropped hair that was slicked back into a Robert Palmer girl, complete with the bright-red lips—"is my girl Lindsay." She was probably a tad smaller at a fourteen or sixteen.

She took me farther into the room, where a set of identical twins were sitting, their hair being pinned in complicated designs, both wearing the same bathing suit in a different color. Their red hair was a deep mahogany, with striking swoops of caramel blonde running through it. Each had one blonde swoop of hair left down to curl around their face. "Hi," they both said at the same time and then giggled like teenagers. Actually, the more I looked, the more I realized they were teenagers, just with a lot of makeup on.

"Misty and Marcia, our twin babies. We all watch out for them. Keep them out of trouble... Don't need them turning into some island hoochies. Right, girls?"

They giggled once more, and it reminded me of Maddy.

I couldn't wait for my sister and Ginelle to come at the end of the month. The twins were also considered plus-sized, along with everyone else, but they couldn't be more than a size ten. I was barely smaller, and not by much.

MiChelle led me over to a spot and held my suit while I dropped my clothes. She continued updating me about the models. "The twins are only sixteen. Here without family, even though they have a chaperone designated to them from their modeling agency. That glow-in-the-dark motherfucker is never around. Their dad back home is single and works to provide for his girls, but as you can see, they're gorgeous and got picked up without trying. This is a huge gig for them and will set them up for college. Only reason their dad allowed 'em to come."

Once I was suited up, a female attendant sprayed something on my bum to make sure the suit didn't ride up in the pictures and taped the suit to my chest, keeping the look exactly where they wanted it for the shoot. Then she poured some oil onto her hands and proceeded to rub me down to a nice shine. MiChelle stood with her ebony arms out in a T, her legs in a wide-legged stance as the same thing was done to her.

A brisk knock on the door had all of us quieting down. "Mia and MiChelle, you're up!" a booming voice hollered through the door.

"Showtime," MiChelle said.

Angel was an amazing photographer and human being. Working with him and MiChelle on the first shoot was the highlight of my day. This ad was going to be labeled "Yin and Yang," based on the opposite colors of our skin tone, and he positioned us into lying head to toe, curving our bodies into a crescent shape. He took the photos from up above. At one point, he had us holding one another's hand and ankle, stretched out into a complicated design, but the end result was philosophical and thought provoking.

Once finished, MiChelle and I hung out with the other girls, pigging out on pizza. Probably not what models should be doing, but MiChelle made a point to note that the pizza did have spinach, artichoke, tomatoes, green peppers, olives, and chicken. All healthy things. That explanation was good enough for me and every other girl. Besides, we lamented that we were plus-sized models and got the gig based on the figure we had, not the size society wanted us to be.

★ ★ ★ ★

Over the next couple of days, I did single shots and group shots with the girls. Tai had been off duty. Unfortunately, I worked from dawn until I couldn't stay awake any longer. Modeling was no joke. These women worked their asses off. I mean, there were parts that were really fun, and each shoot started out that way, until you've had to keep your toe pointed for over an hour, your chest arched up, your booty tucked in so you weren't looking like a girl at the club, and repeated slight adjustments to your form, as well as your hair, makeup, and environment. I'm pretty sure I had a permanent cramp in my right foot from attempting to make the shape of a Barbie foot all day with my very real flesh-and-bone, non-plastic limb.

Today, I was meeting up again with Tai. I smiled, thinking about all that male, warm, yummy skin and how he'd wrap it all over me. Hopefully we'd have another night full of meeting one another's carnal desires. However, he was dead set on showing me the island. As much as I wanted to lie in bed with him all day, I did want to explore my surroundings and get the full island experience.

The first spot we hit was a place not far from Honolulu, located in the center of the lower half of the island, called Pali Lookout. At the top of the mountain, there was a panoramic view of the windward coast of Oahu. The trade winds were so fierce there, my hair was lashing against my face until Tai handed me his baseball cap.

"Amazing, isn't it?" he said as we took in the magical view.

"It's something I'll never forget."

While at the lookout, I found out that it was the location of one of the bloodiest battles in Hawaiian history. During the battle of Nu'uanu, almost four hundred soldiers defending Oahu from being overtaken by Kamehameha the First were trapped in the valley and later pushed over the cliff to their deaths.

"So sad," I said, thinking about all those people who had died in the battle, while we walked back to our car.

Tai stole his cap back, allowing my hair to fall in tumbles down around my shoulders and back. "Better." He grinned and then plopped it back on his own head. "If that made you sad, we'll be skipping Pearl Harbor."

"Good idea."

"You hungry?"

"Absolutely."

"You like Hawaiian beer?"

"Doesn't everybody?" I retorted, narrowing my brows for emphasis.

He took me to a place on the far south side of the island called the Kona Brewing Company. It sat located in what seemed to be a shopping complex, so I didn't have high hopes that it would be as fantabulous as he hinted. I was never happier to be dead wrong.

The waitress led us through the normal restaurant to a back area that felt as if it hovered over the bay. Boats were docked down below. Patrons could park their boat, walk up, and have a meal. The view was just as amazing as Pali Lookout, only different. Each side of the restaurant was wedged between a mountain range on either side of the water. Bright bursts of green, yellow, brown, purple, blue, and every other color in the rainbow filled the landscape, as if an artist had rendered it. Now I knew why so many people painted these mountain ranges. They were incredibly beautiful and inspired peace in those who were lucky enough to gaze upon them.

We ordered plenty of beers as we sat talking about everything from island life, to the Samoan culture, to my life back home, surfing, and the future. Tai drank a beer labeled the *Big Wave,* a golden ale, and I stuck with the fruiter option of the *Castaway.* Somehow, the names of both beers seemed to fit our lives. I felt like a castaway, just floating through this year of my life, bopping from place to place, while Tai was always in search of the "big wave." The part of his life that would make him feel complete. Secretly, I figured that would happen when he chose a mate and settled down, but I was rather content to enjoy being his number one for the month.

"All right. We've seen the lookout, you've partaken of the local food and drink... How about something to feast your soul on?"

"My soul? You think you can provide something that will serve my soul?"

He grinned and took to the road. We drove for a little over a half hour, but it felt like mere minutes, my eyes were so focused on the breathtaking views. With every mile, the view seemed to ebb and flow and adjust to the lush landscapes, each beach we passed different than the last.

Eventually, we turned into a place called Valley of the Temples Memorial Park. Tai drove us through what seemed to be a cemetery, only it wasn't like something you see back home, with concrete or bronze plates in the ground. No, this was unlike any memorial park I'd ever seen. In many of the areas, large black marble squares with etched gold writing stood up like sentinels guarding the resting place of the human below. It was evident in the views and markers how Hawaiians revered their dead. For a place that should feel filled with death and sadness, I was consumed with compassion and love for the people allowing me to share their final resting spot.

Tai stopped in a parking area, and we got out. He led me by the hand through a long path until we came to an outcropping cut into a mountain. There stood a red Japanese-style temple.

"The Byodo-In Temple," Tai said, his voice low, almost a whisper. "It's a non-practicing Buddhist temple. All faiths are welcome to mediate, worship, or just enjoy the grounds. Come on. Let's get a closer look."

He had to drag me. I was so in awe of the building in front of me. It sat perfectly in front of a giant mountain range behind it. A bamboo forest flanked one side, and another, the cemetery. Saying it was one of the most beautiful places I'd ever seen would be downplaying the rapture it brought to your body, mind, and soul. The sense of peace and humanity here filled my pores, moistened my eyes, and hugged my heart.

"Never seen anything like it." I turned to Tai, and he leaned down and gave me a soft kiss.

"I'm glad. You have yet to see the best part."

We walked through the gravel paths, stopping to check out the koi ponds all over the grounds. Little pathways were covered with drooping trees, adding to the secret-garden feel. At the mouth of the temple stood a giant bell. Next to it was a log. When I say a log, I'm actually referring to a tree trunk having been cut and turned onto its side, where it was tied up level with the bell. Visitors to the temple could pull back on the heavy rope attached and hit the enormous bell with the tree. Of course I had to do it.

On my first try, I pulled back and the wood barely moved, only slightly dinging the bell. Extremely unsatisfying!

"Hold up, girlie," Tai said, handing his phone to a Japanese couple waiting their turn to access the bell.

The man lifted up Tai's phone, getting ready. Tai looped an arm around my gut, the other around the rope, and pulled along with me, using his superhuman strength. That log swung back and crashed into the bell, making a resounding *gong,* and then it swung back and hit it again. *Gong.* A little softer and one more time. *Gong.*

I jumped up and down, clapped, and wrapped my arms around his neck, giving him a grateful, sloppy kiss. Tai hooked me closer and took my kiss to a whole other level. He was sucking and biting my mouth as if he were trying to eat my excitement directly from my lips. Someone cleared their throat, and once again, I'd forgotten where we were. The small Japanese woman standing next to her husband smiled and gave me the thumbs-up symbol behind her husband's back. I covered my mouth and tried to prevent the piggy snort from making an appearance.

Tai thanked the man and pocketed his phone. Then he held my hand, and we walked up the wooden steps and platform to the entrance to the temple. Tai instantly removed his shoes, and I did as well, kicking off my flip-flops and holding on to the back of his T-shirt in the darkened space. There wasn't anyone else in here that I could hear as we walked through to stand in front of the most breathtaking Buddha statues. It was huge, standing nine feet in height on a raised platform. In the center was a young, contemplative Buddha, resting in a meditative pose.

"It is a depiction of Buddha himself and known as the largest statue of its kind outside of Japan. Famous sculptor Masuzo Inui designed it. I love how he is sitting within a lotus flower." Tai's voice held veneration and awe.

"Why is it gold?" I asked Tai, my eyes flicking from spot to spot, attempting to brand this beautiful sculpture into my mind for a lifetime.

"To highlight its beauty. It was painted with three coats of gold lacquer and then gold leaf. See all the figures surrounding him?" He pointed to a couple.

I nodded, squinting, trying to get as close as possible without going past the rope.

"There are fifty-two bodhisattvas, or 'enlightened beings' surrounding him, floating on clouds, playing music, dancing. They represent the culture of Fujiwara's aristocracy."

After the history lesson, we both lit a small sprig of incense and set it in front of the statue.

"Now say a prayer, or a wish, or send out love and light to whomever you think needs it."

Tai sat down in front of the raised platform and crossed his legs in front of him. I followed suit. He pressed the palms of his hands together and held them close to his chest, as if in prayer. Then he closed his eyes and bowed his head.

I too closed my eyes and bowed my head, but instead of picking one prayer, wish, or sending out love, I did all three.

Please, God, don't let my father die.

I wish for Maddy to get everything she wants in life.

Buddha, I would like to send light and love to Wes so that he never feels alone, even when in a crowded room.

CHAPTER SIX

Tai drove around the island for the rest of the evening. We stopped on North Shore and had Mexican food of all things. It wasn't anything like the Mexican food I got in California, but it was spicy and hot, and it made me feel comforted and full, just what I needed after an evening of watching the beaches pass us by. I put my arm out the window and played with the wind for a long time. Tai was content to drive and hold my other hand. The radio was playing some soft Hawaiian music. I couldn't hear the words but enjoyed the background noise anyway.

"When do you think you'll settle down?" I asked him out of the blue.

He tilted his head and pursed his full lips. "I dream of it nightly, but I have no answer." The frown that followed his response seemed to go bone deep. Honestly, this seemed to plague the sexy Samoan.

Tai was one of those men a woman would meet and marry. Sure, we were having fun, but it was about sex and friendship, not love and commitment. The latter was something I knew he wanted in a big way.

I squeezed his hand, sending my support. "What did your mom say? You said she could see things, future things. And what she said about me, well, I can only hope it's fact."

He sighed. "*Tina* says I will meet my mate unexpectedly." He dipped his head shyly and looked at me adoringly with those coal-like eyes. "I thought maybe you were her."

I shook my head instantly.

"I know, I know. We're destined to be friends. Besides, *tina* would have been all over you if you were the one. It's frustrating to wait. I feel as though I am living half a life, my other half living somewhere without me."

God, this man was a saint. I was convinced he'd get everything he wanted. People who are that kind, that good, and came from solid families usually came out on top. Tai deserved that. "You'll find her."

"Well...*Tina* did share a couple of hints."

My eyes widened, and I turned in my seat, pulling a knee up so I could view his profile fully. "I'm waiting..." I punched his arm and shook my stinging hand. "Damn. Lay off the weights."

He snorted. Yes, Tai piggy snorted. "You're the first woman ever who has told me that."

"Stalling. What did Masina say about your true love?"

He ran a hand over his prickly dome. I could almost hear the pointy hair growing back scrape along his calloused hand. "She said her eyes would be the color of fresh-cut grass and her hair will be a golden yellow like the sun."

I opened my mouth and laughed. "We're looking for a blonde with green eyes!" That was awesome.

Tai shrugged. "Means she will not be Samoan." He frowned. "That will be difficult for the family." His tone seemed tired and uncertain.

Rubbing his shoulder, I moved close and leaned against it. He wrapped an arm around me. "True love always is. I think you have to go through some trials and tribulations to get to the happy ending, to find that happily ever after."

"Think so?"

"Know so." I smiled, turned my head, and kissed the ball

of his shoulder.

He groaned. "In the meantime, I will enjoy a sultry brunette from the mainland." Tai shifted so that his hand moved from my knee up my inner thigh, where he cupped my sex aggressively.

My voice was husky and filled with desire when I replied. "Now *that* sounds like an excellent idea."

★ ★ ★ ★

Instead of turning off toward Honolulu and Diamond Head Beach where we were staying, he turned left and took the Jeep up a long hilly road until nothing but dense trees were the only view out the window.

"Where are we going?'"

Tai squeezed my shoulder. "You'll see. Trust me."

I pouted, scowled, and groaned obstinately.

"Hey, hey, turn that frown upside down, girlie."

"I would if we were home and you were fucking me right now," I retorted.

His eyes blazed with heat in response to my graphic reply. "Trust me. It will be worth it."

"Worth missing out on a Tai Niko orgasm? Doubtful," I grumbled playfully but not really. I wanted to get laid. It had been days, and I was ready for a dose or two or three of Tai lovin'. The song "All Night Long" by Lionel Richie ran through my mind.

Finally, the car stopped at the top of a clearing. It was pitch black around us. Only the light of the moon and the entire city of Honolulu below made it possible to see. The view, as I was coming to expect from any location in Oahu, was incredible and worth the side trip. Tai led me to the front of the Jeep, laid out a beach towel, and sat me on top of it. Then he went back to the car, rolled down the windows, and turned up the music. Hawaiian music oozed from the car as if on tropical winds. The night was warm and slightly humid. My skin felt a tad moist to the touch but not uncomfortable. Tai turned off the car and came back with a bottle of champagne. Where he had been hiding that, I had no clue.

"Where did you get that?" I asked.

"Real men have secrets their women don't get to know about."

I laughed and accepted the tiny Dixie cup filled with sweet, bubbling champagne. "Am I your woman?" I asked the loaded question. Like his mother said, Tai could not fall for me, nor I him. We had to be clear about the parameters of this thing we had. Fun and friendship.

"For the next seventeen days you are. Then you're some other schlub's problem," he joked, and I opened my mouth and laughed out loud.

"Wicked burn!"

"Thank you very much. I learned from the best," he said and winked.

We sat for a long time and drank champagne until I got tipsy. Champagne was always good for loosening my inhibitions. I watched Tai out of the corner of my eye. He was sitting on the towel, leaning back on his forearms, enjoying the view. I knew he hadn't drunk as much as I had because he had to drive. I turned on my side and traced his jawline with one finger until he turned his head. The man could make grown women weep at his perfection. He was just that good-looking.

I licked my lips while tracing his. The tip of his tongue

came out and flicked my finger. I inhaled noisily and gasped when he bit down on the digit. You wouldn't think a finger would be sensitive. Right then, it felt as though it had a direct connection to my clit. As Tai swirled the finger with his tongue, sucking it into the heat of his mouth, I could feel my panties getting wetter by the second. I pressed my legs together and squeezed, moaning with the pleasure of putting pressure on the achy space between my thighs.

"Your flower is ripe," Tai said, trailing a hand down between my breasts. He lifted up my skirt and zeroed in instantly on my clit, swirling his finger around it before plunging fully into my cleft. I laid on my back, Tai's hand moving smoothly in and out. He added another finger. "I can smell that nectar, girlie. Can I taste it? Right here, out in the open?"

I nodded frantically and clasped his strong shoulders. "Please," I whimpered when a third finger slid in to meet the first two.

"How about I strip you of all your clothes and take your body hard right now. Ever been taken on the hood of a car, Mia?"

I shook my head. "Only a motorcycle," I admitted shakily, and tipped my head back when he moved his hand faster, finger fucking me like it was his job.

"Really?" His surprised tone had me groaning. "You'll have to share that story later." He removed his fingers and pulled me to my feet in front of the car. He pulled off my panties and stuck them in his pocket. Then he lifted my tank over my head. I yanked at his shirt, needing to feel that brown-sugar skin against my erect nipples. Once removed, I clutched at him, slamming my mouth to his in a brutal kiss. He returned it with fervor. As with our previous sexual encounters, it became heated and dirty real quick.

Tai pulled away from my mouth, lifted me back up, and set me on the warm hood. Enough time had gone by so it wasn't nearly as hot as it had been when we first parked. "Lie back. I want to see you spread out naked on the hood of my Jeep."

I did what he said, arching my breasts up, needing to do something. The desire firing through my body, the need for him to touch me...anywhere, was hitting epic proportions.

"Give your tits some attention. I'm going to be busy tending to the flower between these creamy thighs and the sweet nectar sliding down the crack of your ass."

Jesus. The things he said, I felt straight through my body to my clit, where they crash-landed, throbbing in reply to every filthy word. My Tai was graphic yet beautiful and raunchy at the same time.

Placing my hands over my breasts, I squeezed the heavy globes. The moment I pinched each nipple between thumb and forefinger, Tai plunged his tongue deep. He growled, and I moaned. Between the two of us, we sounded like a pack of wild animals fighting in the woods. When Tai goes down on me, it's as if he's tasting the most decadent dessert for the first time. He licks, sucks, nips, bites, and presses in all the right spots. When he set those plump lips around my clit, twirling around the nub with his tongue, pushed open my inner thighs wide enough to feel a twinge of pain, his black eyes lifted and our gazes met. He gripped my thighs hard, opened his mouth, laid the flat edge of his tongue against my O-trigger, and rubbed. I whimpered, begging him with my eyes. With the force of my legs, I tried to lift up but was completely at his mercy. He lifted his mouth for just a moment, and I wanted to cry. Tears actually formed in my eyes, and my body shook with the need to come.

"Don't close your eyes. Watch me take you to bliss," he growled before licking me from slit to clit, setting his lips over my tender bundle of nerves once more, lifting his gaze and sucking hard. My entire body clenched with the powerful orgasm that ripped through the very fiber of my being. I couldn't move. He had me restrained by the legs with his righteous man hands. When I couldn't come anymore, I gripped his head with both hands and pulled. My tiny red clit slipped from between his lips, looking like a small little cherry. I couldn't move him any farther, but he left the bundle alone and pressed his tongue deep into my cleft, tasting my true essence.

He was feral in his desire to lick up every drop, and he did, taking me to the point where I was almost over the edge again before he pulled away. His eyes were white hot, and his cock was practically punching out his shorts. He removed his shorts, and his heavy cock looked painfully erect. I started to move off the car to wrap my lips around it and return the favor, but he shook his head. He handed me a foil packet. I ripped it with my teeth, removed the condom, and ran it down the length of his massive cock.

Tai yanked my knees high up on his ribs so quickly that I had to slam my hands down behind me to hold my body up. He centered his cock and rammed home. I screamed out at the sheer size and girth. The man was huge everywhere, and his manhood matched the enormity that is Tai. Within seconds, he was gripping behind my knees and pressing higher, going impossibly deep. I clung to his shoulders and neck the best I could. My nails must have left claw marks in his back, neck, and head, but he didn't stop fucking me. Then he pulled out and flipped me over so my knees were on the hood. I braced myself by leaning forward and holding on to the cooled metal of the hood near the windshield wipers. He tugged my ass back and lined himself up, pressed my lips wide, and slammed home once more. He was so deep, it was as if he was fucking unchartered territory.

"Gonna fuck you wide open, girlie. Make my mark so you miss this cock when you leave. You hear me?"

"Yeah," I moaned as he slid his cock all over every internal nerve I had. Shivers of pleasure rippled along my veins. The walls of my sex clutched and pulsated around his stiff length.

"You gonna miss my cock one day?" he practically snarled, wanting to imprint me somehow.

"Fuck yeah, Tai. Just fuck me," I screamed as he pulled my hips back and I held on with all my strength.

Tai kept a furious pace. Then he propped a leg up on the bumper for more leverage, pushed my lower back down with one hand, and then brought the other to my tender clit, where he gave it a little massage. It didn't take much until I was barreling into my second orgasm.

Soaring. Flying. Weightless. That's what I felt, though somewhere I could vaguely feel Tai fucking me like a rock star, his hips pistoning, sweat dripping down on his chest until he climaxed on a mighty roar.

★ ★ ★ ★

I didn't remember the ride back or how I made it into my bed when I woke for work the next day. As Tai expected, my hoo-hah was sore and sensitive to the touch. Even my undies grated against what Tai would call my "tender petals." Snickering, I took a shower, letting the hot water soothe and relax the tissue. When I looked down, I swore out loud. On the front of each thigh were four quarter-sized bruises and then another around the back.

"Fuckin' great. How the hell do you explain this shit to a bathing-suit designer? *Um yeah, I had crazy sex out in the open on a mountain on the hood of a car. And you know that giant Samoan you hired, yeah, it was totally his fault for getting wild and bruising my thighs while he went down on me.* I groaned and grumbled while I got ready for work.

When I showed up at the set—on the beach down from our bungalows, thank God—my attitude hadn't abated at all. Tai looked up and smiled when he saw me enter.

"Hey, girlie. You look..." His words died on his tongue as I shot daggers at him from a good ten feet away.

I set down my bag and proceeded to ignore him stupidly. It was adolescent and silly, I knew, but still, my soon to be very embarrassing story as to why Angel D'Amico fashion designer extraordinaire has to airbrush bruises out of his photos was not going to go over well. Tai set a large paw on my shoulder, and I flinched it off and glared at him.

"What happened between last night when I put you in bed and you showing up here?" he asked, full concern in his tone.

"You happened with your big man hands!" I grouched, lifting up my dress and showing him the ten finger-shaped bruises on my thighs.

When I looked up, expecting him to be truly apologetic and sympathetic, he absolutely was not. In fact, he was chuckling, holding a hand over his mouth and everything. My entire body turned hot, and I placed a hand on each hip.

"Are you freakin' kidding me?" I whisper-yelled. I was mad, but I was still a professional and didn't want to be the model chick who caused issues at the shoots.

At that moment, Raul walked up to me. This time, he wore white from head to toe. Turned out he wasn't actually gothic. As he'd explained it, when he chose a color for the day, he committed wholly to it. So from the tip of his toes to his neck he'd wear entirely the same color. Today was white. Even his shoes were white Converse. The purple hair remained. He said that was him being whimsical.

"What's the problem here?"

I narrowed my eyes at Tai. "Nothing," I said through clenched teeth.

"She has bruises on her thighs," Tai admitted immediately, and had there been a knife close, I would have stabbed him in the eye. As it was, the makeup brushes were looking like a good possibility as a weapon of convenience. "We got a little crazy last night. You know how it is," he said, clasping Raul on the shoulder. "Think you can fix it?"

Raul's lips barely twitched. "Let's see them."

I rolled my eyes and lifted up my dress. Raul came down to his knees, held my legs, and looked closely. "I'll need ten spoons put into the freezer now!" he said behind him.

The girl he'd been dating the last week and a half jumped to it with a "Got it!" over her shoulder.

"No problem, honey. I'll lighten the bruise with the cold spoons and then cover them up."

"Oh, thank God. I'd hate to have Angel have to airbrush the images."

Raul's eyes turned hard. "Honey, Angel D'Amico will no sooner airbrush a picture he's taken of a woman wearing his designs than he would cheat on his hot wife, Rosa. He's an artist first. He would never edit his photos. It's important to him that every image is raw."

"Oh. Okay, but you can help, right?" I looked at him with my best puppy-dog eyes.

He led me into the chair for hair and makeup. "For you, anything."

"Thanks, Raul." I leaned up and kissed him on the cheek.

"What about me? I'm the one who asked him," Tai added from behind me.

I cringed and flipped my hair off my shoulder. "You're the one who went all man-hand crazy on my thighs!" I challenged.

Finally, he looked appropriately apologetic, but as soon as the look came over his features, it left. "You know, I don't regret it. Would do it again in a heartbeat. You saying you regret last night, your thighs wide open, you naked on the hood of my car, the air kissing your sweet, wet..."

"Fuck..." Raul stopped, his hand holding a comb directly above my head, his eyes glazed, and a rosy hue lighting his cheeks.

"Shoot. Forgot where I was. Sorry, man." This time, Tai actually seemed sorry.

Raul shook his head. "Nah, it's okay. Hey, how about you tell me where you parked. Yeah?"

Again, Tai clapped Raul's back. "Sure, bro. We'll talk later. See you in the water. We're doing the 'sexy swimwear couples fondling one another on the beach' shoot today." He waggled his eyebrows at me.

"Seriously?" I asked, not believing him. It had to be a coincidence.

"Yep. I'm going to be all over you."

"Wouldn't be the first time," I huffed.

"Won't be the last, girlie."

CHAPTER SEVEN

Angel D'Amico was a genius. Not only did he have Tai and me working the camera as if we were a couple that had been together for years, but the lighting, the background, the swimsuits—all of it gave the shoots a new, fresh feel. He had a unique perspective on how to take a huge issue like women and their body image to a new plane of existence. This campaign was cutting edge. There was no other way to describe it. I served as the smallest model, somewhere between a size eight and a ten. The rest were anywhere from ten to eighteen, maybe even a size twenty. All beautiful women with buxom shapes they were proud of and should be. They were *real* women with real bodies.

"Come, girls. Gather 'round the hunk, eh?" Angel said, his Italian accent still thick and cultured. "Now, Tai, you will place a hand on Taylor's bum and the other on MiChelle's hip. Mia, you will stand off to the side here looking very...um...how you say this... Pissed?"

Rosa, his wife, positioned Taylor and MiChelle exactly the way Angel wanted. "Mia, love, you will stand over here with your hands on your hips looking poised, beautiful, but also very mad. Or as my husband so eloquently said...*pissed.*"

I chuckled and got into position.

"Marcia and Misty, come over here, my darlings." Rosa waved the twins over.

Their red hair flowed out behind them as they ran with

sixteen-year-old exuberance.

"Oh, *si, si*. I see, my love. I see you beautiful, intelligent woman. I shall worship you," Angel said to his wife, getting behind his camera.

"When don't you worship me, my love?" She smirked and winked. He held a hand over his heart and looked at her adoringly for long minutes. "Get to work," she said over her head while fluffing the twins' hair, making it just so.

"*Si, si*. Now, Tai, you have got your hand caught in the cookie jar." He laughed. "But you are looking at the young girls, too, and your true love, Ms. Mia, catches you. Okay?"

Tai nodded and gripped the women's flesh. A jab of jealousy sprang through me as I saw his fingers dig pleasurably into their flesh. Each of the women got into position, posed accordingly, and I followed suit. It wasn't hard to look angry. I pulled from my frustration over Tai giving me ten lovely bruises to contend with, the feeling of hopelessness about not knowing if my dad was going to pull out of his coma, and my irritation at seeing yet another magazine with a kissy-face picture of Wes and Gina. Casual relationship, my ass. I'd taken a picture of the magazine and kept it so that every time I felt even a smidge of guilt, I'd look down at that image.

"Good, Mia. You are projecting much anger and frustration." The camera clicked crazily.

Then Tai went off the plan and pushed away from the women. They looked taken aback, but then Tai fell to his knees before me. The camera continued to click like mad.

"*Si*. Tai. *Perfetto!*" Angel called out.

Tai leaned forward and kissed my thigh, gripped my hips, and looked up at me like he was genuinely sorry. I smoothed my fingers over his head while he smirked, seeming very confident that he'd pulled one over on my character. Just as he thought I'd forgiven him, I pushed off his shoulders, and he fell back on his ass. Then I turned, facing the camera, cocked a hip, laid my hand over said hip, and winked at the camera.

Angel fell back with glee, kicking wildly in the air. "This too much! This will be one for the blooper reel!"

The group laughed, and once the chuckling abated, we got back to doing the shoot. Overall, we had a great day. Tai and I, of course, made up through the humor and teamwork on the job. We left holding hands, walking down the beach toward a night at the bungalows. Tomorrow, my sister Maddy and my best friend Ginelle would arrive. I could hardly wait.

★ ★ ★ ★

The taxi cab pulled up to the bungalow as Tai and I waited out front. I had been sitting on the stoop and jumped to my feet when they arrived. Ginelle flung open the door, her petite form barreling at a dead run toward mine. Then she jumped midair and slammed into me, both of us falling to the grass. "You stupid cunt! I can't believe you have been living in paradise without me! I'm here now, biznatch." She kissed all over my face. I could hear Mads chuckling behind our yard acrobatics. Then two very tanned feet and one tribal-filled leg came into both our views.

Ginelle looked from me to the feet and up, and up, and up. "Holy mother of all things fuckable. Where on God's green earth did you come from, you sexy beast. Jesus." Gin looked down at me. "Is this your client?" Her eyes turned hard, and I shook my head. She looked up again. "You better be fucking this hotness." She glanced down at me, where I was still pinned to the ground. I nodded happily. "No chance I can take a ride on the Samoan side?"

At that, Tai tipped his head back and laughed loud enough to almost echo off the palm trees. I shook my head and frowned.

"Biznatch, you get all the guys. Not fair," she said on a pout, and stood up.

Tai held out his hand. "*Aloha.* You must be Ginelle."

Her blonde hair flew behind her head. "You've been talking about me." She puffed her chest out. "All good, I hope."

"All warnings," I added and took Tai's hand as he helped me up. Then I pushed Gin out of the way with my hip to get to my sweet sister. "This is Madison. Our Maddy. My baby sis and the pride of my life. This is Tai."

She smiled so wide at the compliment.

"See?" I pointed at her face. "What did I say, Tai?"

"Prettiest girl in the world," he offered. "*Aloha*, Madison."

"Damn straight!" I hugged Maddy to me. "How are you, sis?" I pulled back and set my gaze on hers, taking in the pale-green eyes that matched my own. They looked happy.

"I'm good, really good. Worried about Pops. He doesn't have anyone while we're here. Matt and his family, though, are going to check on him."

Of course they were, because they were like the best family in the universe. I wanted to hate them for their perfection, but since my girl was going to join the Rains clan in a couple years, I needed to cut them some slack. They meant well. Hell, they meant very well because they were really good people.

I clucked my tongue and looped an arm around her waist. "Well, that's very nice of them. Have the doctors said anything recently?"

Maddy shook her head as Tai grabbed their bags. *All*

of them. In one trip. Shivers of lust slithered through me at his male virility and prowess. I licked my lips, staring at his beautiful back while he led the way to my bungalow.

"I wish Pops would wake up," Maddy admitted, taking a seat on a barstool.

I trotted around the kitchen area, getting out the alcoholic beverages and mixers. Vacation mode meant cocktails.

"Do they know why he hasn't? His body has healed," I said.

Gin's eyes widened at all the variety of liquor and mixers I set out while Maddy responded. "The docs told us that he'll wake when his body wants to wake. With the level of head trauma he received, they keep telling us not to be too hopeful."

Ginelle's lips pursed together. "Sucks. I know you guys are freaked."

Maddy stood abruptly and walked over to the French doors, opening them wide. The tropical breeze from the ocean blew into the room, filling it with the scent of the ocean. I would miss that breeze and smell when I left here next week.

I scanned the drink options and then pulled out the ones I wanted. My days as a waitress and backup at the bar made me somewhat of a cocktail connoisseur, with an emphasis on the *cock* part. Snickering to myself, I grabbed the citrus vodka, peach schnapps, triple sec, some OJ, pineapple juice, and the sweet and sour mix. Quickly, I dropped ice into four glasses. Tai watched me, his large body leaning up against the counter, giant arms crossed over one another, a speculative gaze on his beautiful face. Gin openly ran her eyes all over him. He didn't seem to mind. With a body like that and the employment positions he'd chosen, I imagined eyes all over him was commonplace.

"Gin, really, don't do the skeevy eye fuck all over Tai."

She pouted, looked away, and then as if drawn by magnets, those eyes were back on him. Her tongue came out to lick her bottom lip.

"Gin!" I shook my head, and she crunched her eyes closed and pressed her palms into the sockets.

"Sorry, sorry. It's just he's the epitome of eye candy. Tai, really, you are crazy good-looking."

He tipped his chin in that cool way men do. "You ain't so bad yourself, tiny," he said in that low grumble that made my panties wet. Gin, however, practically melted—she put a hand over her chest and slid down her barstool dramatically.

I elbowed Tai in the ribs.

"Ouch! Wha'd I do?" He rubbed at the spot I'd tagged.

"You're encouraging her." I glared, and he laughed.

Finally, I added all the ingredients into each glass and handed them out. Maddy, Gin, Tai, and I held the glasses up. "To fun in the sun...Hawaiian style!" I said, and we clinked glasses. The drink, called "A Fuzzy Thing," slid down my throat, and the three different types of alcohol instantly commingled, warming my belly.

"Ready to hit the beach?" Tai asked.

"Bathing suits for everyone in the room. You girls are going to die when you see all the options I've collected from the shoot!"

Both Maddy and Gin squealed and ran off down the hall to the master bedroom.

"You really going to give them any suit they want? Those are designer. Probably a few hundred a pop."

I shrugged my shoulders. "So. I love those two women more than I love anything, including money or free designer

AUDREY CARLAN

clothing. Gotta share the wealth, right?" Which, I knew for a
fact, he did with his family.

In the background, we could hear the whoops and hollers
as the fights began like true sisters.

"You're too tall for that stretch!"

And Maddy's reply, "Shut up. You're just pissed because
you're height challenged."

Then another screech. "You shut up. You're jealous
because I'm fun-sized! Everyone loves a little something to
nibble on!"

Tai pulled me into his arms and rested his head against
my forehead. "Girlie, your family is loco."

"Not something you need to tell me."

I laughed and kissed him soundly. It went on for a while,
our tongues dancing, his hands creeping down to fondle and
squeeze my ass. He pressed his thick erection into my pelvis,
and I groaned.

"Continue this later tonight, when the girls are crashed
from jet lag. At your bungalow?"

"Hell yes."

★ ★ ★ ★

The next day, Tai and I did another shoot, but we were off by
mid-afternoon. Gin and Maddy spent the early part of the day
sunbathing. Tonight, though, Tai was taking us all to a luau,
where he and his family performed. I'd been here almost three
weeks and hadn't seen him perform. Surf and model, yes, but
not his fire-knife routine. I could not wait. I didn't have a clue
what fire-knife dancing was, but it sounded exotic and exciting.
Two of my very favorite things.

The three of us girls got ready, wearing maxi dresses in varying lengths and colors. Each of us left our hair down and pinned the flowers Tai had left for each of us on the kitchen counter. I thought that was really sweet and gentlemanly. A direct opposite of how ungentlemanly he was last night when he fucked me hard against his wall and then bent over his kitchen table. Apparently he'd missed me and showed it.

We arrived at the five-star resort where they were performing. Tai had left us tickets to the show. We handed our tickets to the man at the entrance and were surprised to find our seats located directly up front, right next to the stage.

We were served incredible selections of traditional Polynesian food, including teriyaki chicken and beef, lau lau—which was a boneless wrapped pork dish—Hawaiian poi, tossed greens, some taro rolls, and every fruit you could imagine. Seriously, the fruit in Hawaii was the best, and I lived in California, where the produce was as fresh as you could get. I'd basically give my left tit to have mangos fresh from Hawaii every day.

"This is amazing," Maddy said, shoveling in a huge bite of pineapple. "I can't get enough of it."

"I know, right?"

Gin, Maddy, and I ate, chatted up the folks we were seated next to, and watched the sun go down. The stage was set with a perfect view of the open beach behind so the diners could appreciate the view until it was dark enough for the show to start. Once the sun set, the heavy drums started building a beat that I could feel in my chest.

Tai's father, Afano, came out. He was dressed in a sarong that barely covered his man bits. His tattoos were clearly on display and magnificent. Pieces of grass leg adornments were wrapped around his calves, hanging over his feet. We were so close that I could hear the whisk noise of each long blade as it dragged along the stage floor.

Afano introduced the drummers, located off to the side, who did a quick drum ditty that had the crowd clapping and smiling. He welcomed the crowd to share in the Samoan culture. Then he introduced the first act. I was shocked to see all of the female relatives, including Tai's mother, Masina, enter the stage. The older woman wore a complicated sarong dress, and the young ones wore coconuts over their breasts and short sarongs that showed off their young, toned legs and bodies.

The music started, and the women had the entire crowd enchanted with their routine. It was beautiful and something that I had only ever seen in the movies. It included the hula and other Hawaiian-style dances where the women delicately brought their hands above their heads, turned from side to side, swayed their hips, and moved their feet. It was lovely, and every eye in the crowd was glued to the ladies as they danced.

After they completed two different dances, they asked for volunteers. Gin and I held up Maddy's thin arm, much to her disagreement, and they picked her and a handful of other women. Masina stood next to my girl and winked at me. I held my hands in a prayer position and tipped my head, saying thank you. Having my girl with Tai's mother was exactly as I would have hoped. Each professional on the stage taught the audience member a small routine. Maddy seemed to pick it up right away, as I knew she would. The girl was gifted in everything, including dance. Masina cued the music, and the audience members followed along with their instructor. Before long, Maddy was smiling and waving her arms in the air like she'd been there all her life. I loved seeing her up there having fun, knowing I was giving her this memory. The first time she left the state of Nevada, and it was with me, to Hawaii. She'd remember this forever, as would I. it was something that she'd be able to tell her kids about. *Please, God, let that be years down the road, after she becomes a doctor.*

The music stopped, and the audience members received a loud applause. The show continued, and the longer it went without Tai, the more nervous I became. Usually the last ones in a performance like this meant it was the most dangerous.

Finally, Afano came out wearing different garb but still showing just as much skin. His tattoos looked sharply black and oiled, reflecting the fierceness.

"And now I give you our most desired performance. It takes a warrior's heart to handle the fire knives, and my sons..."—when he pounded his fist against his chest, it was so loud you could hear the smack against his flesh—"...my sons are pure of heart and have cleared their minds to bring you this piece of our culture. Men!" He roared, and that's when Tai and his three brothers came onto the stage. Afano and Tai stood at the front, the three brothers in the back. Each held a long stick. Masina came out in a beautiful white dress that flowed in the breeze. She held a torch and lit each end of the stick, patted her guys one by one on the cheek, and returned to the side of the stage. The men stood, legs wide apart, grassy bands around their calves and elbows. Each wore a small blood-red sarong.

"Oh sweet Lord, how am I to control myself when all that is standing right in front of me," Gin whispered, and I shoved her shoulder.

"Behave."

"No promises."

We both laughed, but my eyes were on Tai. I felt as though my heart was in my throat as Afano called out commands and then the men made a huge *hut* sound and stomped their feet. The two lit ends blazed on in front of their faces, and then they began to spin the stick. The fire stick. In my head, I had to repeat it because I couldn't believe it.

Spin. The. Fire. Stick.

Just as I thought I would die with worry, clearly believing they were going to get burned, they all threw the sticks up in the air, caught them, and then flipped around and wove through one another, spinning the fire sticks the entire time. I had my hand over my mouth and my other fisted in my lap.

The guys did several moves that defied gravity, all things holy, and set a fear so deep within my soul I could hardly breathe.

Then it got scarier.

The four other men backed up and stood in the very back, their legs out wide, their hands holding the sticks above their heads as if they were lighting the stage. The drums pounded loudly, shaking my chest with every *boom*! And then Tai was alone in the middle of the stage. That's when shit got real.

My Tai flung that stick high in the air, did a couple of flips, caught it, and spun it around his body, weaving it through his legs and behind his back. The grass blades of his costume could catch on fire at any moment. He flung that thing around the back of his neck, twirled it like a baton with two fingers, and then held up a hand. Afano, from behind, threw his fire stick in the air. Tai went down on a knee, lifted his arm, and caught the second one midair. I gasped and closed my eyes. Once I opened them, he was spinning both fire sticks. The audience was clapping wildly as I just sat there in shock. Frightened out of my mind.

After what seemed like an eternity of Tai doing complicated twists, throws, and flips, the noise of the drums hit a booming roar that I felt deep in my chest, making my toes curl into my wedged sandals. The brothers made a *hut* sound over and over, while stomping toward Tai, and then threw all of their sticks into the air at different intervals. Tail flipped, landed on his back, and then bounced each one of them from his feet as they fell from the sky to his hands, where he caught them one after another. Then he stood up holding all five fire sticks and made a perfect H symbol. Two sticks in each hand and the last one flat held between his thumbs. Each brother hugged Tai, wet the flames, and then bowed.

The entire dinner party of several hundred people stood up and screamed their excitement, joy, and adoration of the performance. Afano had his family all came up onto the stage, where everyone bowed. Tai's eyes were glued to mine. Tears filled my eyes and spilled down my cheeks as I clapped so hard my hands were burning. He grinned that sexy Tai grin that melted the hearts and panties of every woman within a mile radius before they left the stage and the emcee announced that the luau was over.

"Your May boyfriend is crazy talented," Ginelle offered while hugging me against her side.

My *May boyfriend*.

I guess if I thought about it, that's what he was. And Alec had been my February boyfriend and Wes my January. I didn't want to think about what that meant. Most women didn't have multiple boyfriends in a year like that, but what else would you call a monogamous relationship you have for an entire month, where you're committed to the same man, you go out on dates, meet their family, have fun together, tell each other your hopes and dreams, fall asleep together each night, and so forth. If that wasn't the definition of a boyfriend, I didn't know what was.

"Yes, he is. Let's go thank him for the tickets."

When we made our way to the back, the family had already picked up what they needed and Tai was in a pair of board shorts and nothing else. His chest was still slicked with oil, showing off every delectable inch of his muscular body.

"Can I have one of his brothers?" Gin asked, taking in the three guys whose eyes were all over her.

Tao, his eldest brother, looked at Gin as if she was a nice hearty steak and he was starved. Watching her eyes, the feeling was absolutely mutual.

"Go for it, hobag. Rock his fucking world. Why not?"

"Man, you guys are making me miss Matthew." Maddy pouted prettily.

"Oh, so you now know the joys of sex."

She grinned and nodded her head a bunch of times.

"Great. That blows. And not in the good way," I chastised her before she could comment. I didn't need to know if my little sis was blowing her man. God help me, please don't let her ask for pointers.

Tai walked up when he noticed us in the distance. His form was so manly. Cut muscles everywhere that felt as good as they looked and bulged with each prowling step forward.

"Enjoy the show?" he asked.

I nodded numbly but couldn't hold back anymore. I wanted to take a bite out of him so badly. Lust swirled in my veins, moistened my sex, and made me wanton in a way that was indecent. I flung myself at him. He caught me in the air just as my lips crashed over his. He growled his appreciation and took my mouth hard, his tongue swooping in to taste. I sucked on every millimeter of those lips, rubbing my core against his now-hard length through his shorts.

"Girlie..." His voice was a rumble against my lips. "Not the place. But don't you worry. We're going to continue this back at the house when the girls are asleep." His lips moved to my ear. "You will suffer so much pleasure for making me get this hard and having to wait to take you. Be prepared. Be prepared to burn up the sheets with the fire you've set." The way he said it was more than a promise. It was a fact.

CHAPTER EIGHT

"Oh God, no!" I screamed. "No more. I can't any... Oh sweet... Fuck me!" I howled, pressing my hips up into Tai's mouth and my hands down on his head. He held the globes of my ass and sucked another orgasm from me. I didn't think it was possible. He'd eaten me raw. I'd lost count of how many orgasms I'd had against his tongue. All I knew was that if he didn't put that huge cock inside me quick, I was going to pass out from sheer exhaustion alone.

Tai growled low in his throat, sounding like a wild animal. I now knew it as his I'm-about-to-lose-my-mind precursor to pounding me into oblivion. He flipped me over on my stomach and pulled my hips up and back so I was on my hands and knees. "Grab the headboard. I'm too far gone. Need to take this tasty pussy hard."

He gripped my waist, leveled his hips, pressed the tip of his cock to my soaking entrance, and slowly eased in. One steely hard inch at a time. I held my breath, expecting a wild thrust, but he surprised me by going in soft. It wasn't for long. "Yeah, nice and easy. Get my dick fucking wet with that juicy pussy."

He eased in and out slowly, and I took long breaths, relaxing my neck down to watch him enter and exit. The condom was coated with my essence. I moved one hand and reached down to feel where he entered me over and over.

"Aw yeah, girlie. You like to feel me splitting your flower

open. Nothin' better."

One of his hands came up to my breast and tweaked, pulled, and elongated my nipple. With that, I started pressing back into him with enough force to knock his hips back.

"What? What do you want? You have to ask for it, *haole*."

I hated when he called me *foreigner*. He knew it pissed me off, which was why he used it during the height of our lovemaking. Though, you really couldn't call it making love with Tai and me. There wasn't even one time where we'd had a slow, drawn-out session with candles and chocolate or anything remotely related to romance. The closest thing to that was when we sipped on champagne before he took me hard on the hood of his car last week. Nope, Tai and I fucked, and we fucked each other with abandon. I loved *that* about Tai. We were friends, and I would be friends with him after I went on to my next adventure, but for now, I was going to enjoy getting pummeled good and hard with Tai's fat dick.

"Fuck me with your Big. Samoan. Fat. Cock!" I roared and shoved my hips back, piercing myself onto his member.

"You ready to walk funny tomorrow, huh, girlie?" he goaded.

"Is my ass white?" I asked flippantly, looking at him over my shoulder, wiggling said ass.

His eyes were focused on my cheeks. His fingers were clenched around my hips. "Oh yeah," he said, grinding into my cleft, reaching that high spot I dedicated personally to his dick.

"Then don't ask me stupid questions." Criminy, these men I bed are always asking me dumb... "Fuck!" My pussy clenched down like a vise as Tai's cock rammed home.

I screamed soundlessly, no air coming out of my mouth as he pounded mercilessly into me. His balls smacked up against swollen flesh, adding an element of pain that felt so good I arched up, holding my body aloft and bent back. Tai roughly ran a hand down my chest while he pinched my clit between two fingers. Not pressed and rubbed. No, he pinched, adding more pressure with each mighty thrust. The pleasure rose so high, I cracked, broke, and shattered while he held me together long enough to find his own release. This time he hollered his release in a lion-sized roar. So loud I was certain Gin and Maddy had to have been awakened, because the walls seemed to shake with the sound.

That was the last thing I recalled before I blacked out. When I woke, he was wiping the space between my thighs with a warm cloth, cleaning me.

"Did I hurt you?" His eyes were flat, cold, and black.

I shook my head.

"Do you want to go back to your bed?"

Again, I shook my head, still having a little trouble speaking through the sated buzz zipping along every nerve ending.

"Are you sure?" His voice cracked a bit, sending warning flares to my mind.

He sat down next to me, and I got up and crawled into his lap, his arms coming around me tight. "You didn't hurt me."

"You passed out," he said in a tone so emotional I left the comfort of his warm neck, where I'd snuggled, to look deep into his eyes.

I cupped both cheeks, forcing him to look at me and really see the truth in my words. "Tai, that was some of the best sex of my life. I'll remember that until I die. You didn't hurt me. Last count, I had six orgasms. *Six.* That's unheard of." I didn't tell him that I had a couple other guys who could go rounds like that, but with Tai, it was unique. Different intensity, different body parts, words, thoughts. All of it good but special to him, to what we had in this bed.

Tai tunneled his fingers at the nape of my neck and up into my hairline. "Mia, I lost control."

I shook my head. "We got heated. Hey, you're the one who said we were going to burn up the sheets. I'd classify that round...or rounds"—I grinned, and he smiled on a huff—"as burning up the sheets. Wouldn't you?"

He tilted his head and inhaled. "As long as you're truly okay."

"Oh, honey, I'm more than okay. Give me a good night's sleep, and I'll be ready to take you on again. Only this time...I get to be on top!"

Tai laughed, laid me back under the cool sheets, and wrapped me in his warmth. Exhausted, we both crashed.

I woke up the next day with the sun shining in my eyes, the sounds of the beach, a cool ocean breeze kissing my skin, and a sinfully sexy Samoan's face between my thighs.

Hawaii.

Best. Month. Ever.

★ ★ ★ ★

The walk of shame wasn't too far since Tai and I had connecting bungalows. I snuck in on bare feet, holding my wedge sandals in one hand and tiptoeing through to find Maddy pouring a cup of coffee and smirking at me. Damn. "Good night?" she asked, and I grinned, my face flaming. "My Mia blushing? Could it have been the, 'Oh God, fuck me with that big fat Samoan cock' that put that smile on your face this morning?"

My mouth dropped open. I could have caught a hundred flies with the amount of shock that slammed into me.

"Oh yes, big sis, I heard it all. Did you not know that the guest room shares a wall...with Tai's bed!" She laughed so hard, her entire face turned beet red with the effort.

I shook my head. "Um... I... Hmm, not really sure what to say here."

"I had to go sleep in your bed. Jesus, I can't wait to have crazy sex like that all night. Seriously, does your hoo-hah hurt?"

I sat down on a barstool, set the wedges on the counter, and poured myself a cup of coffee. "Are we really having this conversation?" I cringed, and she nodded. "Yeah, my lady bits hurt, but only in a good way." I pressed a hand to my forehead and massaged my temples.

Maddy twirled a finger around the rim of the cup. "Matt and I have had, you know, sex, like ten times, and it's never been like that." Her face held that rosy hue as she focused on her cup. "I mean, don't get me wrong, it always feels really, really good, but I'm never screaming out. Maybe I'm doing something wrong?"

I laid my hand over hers. "Oh honey, no."

"I mean, I've never heard Matt scream out in pleasure. He usually just tells me he loves me and grunts a little."

Leaning over, I banged my head onto the counter a few times. Last thing I ever wanted to do in life was talk about good or bad sex with my baby sis. Times like these made me hate our mother even more. She should be the one having these conversations with her daughter, not me.

Pulling up my metaphorical boot straps, I stood up straight, puffed out my chest, and flung my hair back behind me, readying for a conversation that was uncomfortable but necessary. Mads wanted to know how to please a man. I'm her sole female influence. I'm going to lead her in the right direction. Lord, help me through this.

"Let's go sit outside on the lanai."

She jumped up, grabbed the plate of fruit she'd cut yesterday, and took it to the table outside. Thankfully, my sunglasses were lying there, so I plopped them on and stretched out my legs onto the opposite chair. Maddy sat across from me, waiting patiently as I thought about what I wanted to tell her.

I sucked in a breath and let it out. "Okay. With men, I've found that they like an active partner. So don't just lie there. Touch, kiss, do what feels natural."

She nodded and stayed silent.

"Have you experienced anything other than missionary position?" I groaned and looked up at the sky, letting the sun's rays warm my face.

"No." She frowned. "But I want to. How do you tell them that you want to try something else?"

Oh, thank God. An easy question. "Talk about it when you're alone but not having sex. Like maybe after dinner, sit on the couch and tell him your desires."

"I don't know what those are."

Sucking my bottom lip into my mouth, I bit down on the flesh. I could do this. "Tell him, or better yet, when you're on the couch, just hop up in his lap and straddle him. Then, you know...ride him that way." I gagged in the back of my throat and swallowed. Fuck, this was hard. Sweat broke out at my hairline, and I wanted nothing more than to go throw myself into the cool, calming ocean in front of us.

"Men like that? A woman on top in their lap?"

I nodded. "Yeah, sitting or while he's lying down. It will be good for you, too. Just take it slow because it's deeper that way."

"Deeper!" Her eyes got wide. "I already feel like Matt is splitting me in half!" she said and twisted her fingers together. At least her soon-to-be hubby wasn't lacking in the genitalia department. Once she got used to having sex, that would be in the plus category for good ol' Matt. "What else?"

"Don't you watch porn?" I groaned, not wanting to hear that answer.

She shook her head.

"All right. How about doggie style? You on your hands and knees, him taking you from behind. Try that."

I swear if she had a notepad, she would have been writing this down. My sis, the analyzer. Always taking notes, approaching situations analytically as well as scientifically.

"And how does that feel?" she asked.

My shoulders dropped, and I sighed. "Good, really good. That's how Tai was taking me last night when things got loud," I admitted.

She smiled shyly, and once more her face reddened.

"You know, you guys need to just explore one another. Do what feels right, and who cares what others do or how they do it, or whether or not they are louder than you in the bedroom. What you have with Matt is between the two of you, and obviously he likes it, because he put a ring on it!" I laughed.

Her smile in return was so bright I needed another pair of sunglasses. "That is true," she said.

"So don't worry about it. You and Matt will find your way together. You don't need me telling you how to please a man. Only you are going to know what Matt likes and doesn't, and you are the one who will ultimately be giving it to him. Just be honest with him. Talk to him about the things you think about or fantasize about. And for God's sake, read some sexy books or something. I'm dying here!" I admitted. My skin felt like it could break out in hives at any moment.

That had Maddy giggling like the nineteen-year-old she was. Though not for long. Shit. What day was it? Hawaiians move at their own pace, and the days feel like they slip by in a tropical haze. "What day is it?"

Maddy tipped her head and smirked. "May nineteenth." She turned her head and looked out over the ocean.

Fuck me. Her twentieth birthday was tomorrow. "Someone is leaving her teens tomorrow." I grinned. "Going to have to blow the roof off this mother for that!"

She squirmed in her chair, doing a little happy dance. "I'm pretty excited to be in my twenties. Though Matt's really bummed that he can't be here to enjoy it with me."

"Oh pish-posh. He'll get all the rest of your birthdays. Twenty is mine, just like all the ones before it." One thing I'd made sure of, as Maddy grew up, was that I made a huge deal about her birthday. Our mother left when she was five. Even at eleven years old, I did what I could to make sure she had an awesome sixth birthday, and every single one after that was as amazing as I could make it. We didn't have much in the way of money, but we made do. Well, I did.

I'd have to talk to Tai about some options. I wanted this first birthday in her twenties to be something she'd never forget.

I heard the door open behind me. Thinking it was Tai, I turned around and waved. Nope. It was Gin, wearing the same dress she'd worn to the luau. That bitch was doing the walk of shame! Oh, hell yes. This was too good.

"Hey, Gin. I thought you were still sleeping." I played along as she plopped down into the chair next to me, her blonde hair shining in the sunlight. She stole my cup of coffee and slugged it back.

I scanned her face and down her body. There were red rash-like marks dipping deep into her cleavage, her neck had a full-on hickey just under her ear, her hair was a tornado, and her lips looked twice their normal size.

"Good night?" Maddy asked her the same question she'd asked me, and I busted out laughing.

"What?" Gin groaned, covering her ears. "Must you say things so loud?"

Oh, this was awesome. Hung over, too? Love it!

I sat up and pulled a knee to my chest. "I'm guessing you look like you were rode hard and put away wet for a reason?"

Gin waggled her eyebrows, reached her hands above her head, and pointed her toes, stretching out even while sitting at the table. "Oh yeah." Her eyes were gleaming with sexual bliss. "If your Tai is anything like his brother Tao, whew." She pressed a hand against her chest and fanned her face with the other. "He fucked me six ways from Sunday and then started all over again. Never in my life..." She lost her words and slumped back. "I never want to leave. I'm just going to stay in Hawaii and be Tao's sex slave. I'll clean his house, make his meals, and he can pay me in dick," she said crudely.

I stole back my coffee, and she pouted. "Gin, Jesus. You whore. Watch what you say." I tipped my chin at Maddy.

"Really, Mia? After the conversation we just had?"

"What conversation?" Gin asked, and I groaned.

"Well, Mia had a night much like your own. Only I could

hear every last word and scream of her night in the sack with Tai."

Gin's gaze flashed to mine, daggers in place. "Hypocrite!"

"Shut the fuck up! I didn't know!" I crossed my arms over my ample chest. My sore nipples screamed out their discomfort. Tai had been a sucking machine last night.

Maddy continued, undaunted by Ginelle and me bickering. We did it so much, it didn't even phase her. "So I asked Mia for pointers on how to please a man. You know Matt and I have only had, well, missionary, so she was giving me tips."

Ginelle thought that was absolutely hysterical, if the way she howled with laughter, kicked her feet, and flailed her arms in the air like someone stuck out in the middle of an ocean who couldn't swim was any indication. "And how did you handle it?" Her gaze sought mine. "I bet you would have rather had white-hot pokers seared through your eyes rather than have that discussion." Gin smoothed my bicep, still laughing.

I shrugged her off. "I hate you."

"You fucking love me!" She pulled my hand up and bit along my arm, making *nom nom* noises like Pac Man, until I laughed hard and playfully pushed her away. Gin just had a way about her. There was no way in the universe I could ever stay mad at her and no one I'd rather have in my corner fighting off the battles that came upon my world.

"You can just ask me, Mads. I'm happy to share all the wonders of sex and everything in between. I could tell you a trick on how to suck a man off that will have him begging for mercy..."

Maddy's eyes went round and large while she nodded and moved her chair closer to Ginelle, as if she was about to hear a secret.

"The fuck you will!" I roared.

"Oh come on. Don't be a spoilsport. Maddy has to learn how to suck dick or she'll never keep a man." Ginelle turned to Maddy and clasped her hands. "Let me tell you right off, baby girl, a man loves it when you swallow. They don't mind if you spit, but something about them marking you and you taking that nasty slime down your throat gets them way the fuck off."

I stood up and put my hand over Ginelle's mouth. "Ginelle's done speaking out of her ass right now. Time for a shower." I pulled her out of her chair and lifted her tiny body into a princess hold.

"No really. Get on your knees and take Matt's cock as far down your throat as possible," Gin continued talking as I hefted her over the sand and toward the ocean. Maddy must have been following from behind, because Gin kept running her mouth.

"What else?" Maddy giggled.

"Hold on to his hips and let him tug on your hair and fuck your face, and for God's sake, keep those teeth wrapped—" was the last thing we heard before I tossed her into the ocean.

Ginelle sputtered and laughed, spitting water out, and then floated on the top, letting a wave push her close to the sand.

I looped my elbow with Maddy's. "Come on. Let's get some breakfast."

Maddy looked over her shoulder. "Think she's okay?"

"Let the bitch in heat cool off. She'll be fine."

We could hear Ginelle laughing in the background, splashing in the water, as we trudged through the sand back to the house.

CHAPTER NINE

Nothing but green, as far as the eye could see, enclosed the small valley we rode our ATVs through. Mountains on both sides so high you had to crane your neck to see where the mountain met the misty sky. Fog and clouds swirled around the wetter portions of the mountain like cotton sticking to Velcro. Tai and Tao led us through the Valley until we were directly in the middle, and they stopped. Each of us turned off our personal ATV and hopped off to look around. Everything in Hawaii was beautiful, but this, this felt like a hidden gem that we'd just uncovered. Seeing God's Earth undeveloped from mankind stole a piece of your soul, making an imprint that would only ever be filled by this experience.

Tao sat on his ATV, pulled out a small ukulele from his backpack, and started to strum a tune. He hummed along for a while until his rich, baritone voice smoothed over my senses like a cool breeze fluttering through the valley. He sang a song I recognized Tai playing in his room called "Drop, Baby, Drop" by Manao Company.

Maddy sat on her ATV and swayed from side to side, entranced by his song. Then she giggled when he said the best line. "I love you like a mango." It was also my favorite line.

Tai pulled my hand and brought me close to his body. "You're leaving in two days," he whispered, holding me close, moving his hips in a smooth shimmy as we danced to Tao's music.

"I am." I held his hand close to my face and pressed my lips to his fingertips.

"What if I didn't want you to go?" He said this with a twinge of emotion I knew, after having spent the better part of a month with this man, was held tightly in check.

"But you know I can't stay." I rubbed my nose into his neck, inhaling his ocean and fiery, woodsy scent. He must have practiced his fire-knife routine this morning, the scent of the fire and wood sticking to his skin, melting into his pores.

Tai pressed his forehead to mine. "But it's nice to be told, yes?"

"It is." I bit my lips and let the truth out. "I don't want to leave you either, but you know...you know, Tai, that we're not each other's forever."

He sighed and kissed me sweetly, his lips dragging softly across mine. It was a kiss of longing, one of a future we both knew was not meant to be. He deepened the kiss, holding me tight. I clung to him, doing my best to imprint him into my soul the same way this secret valley had. It wasn't love that kept us clinging to one another. It was friendship, lust, and ease. Being with Tai, the two of us together just worked. It was easy. I'd not had a month with a man yet that was as smooth as it had been with Tai.

"You're going to make a man fall to his knees and thank the Heavens above when he secures you forever."

I laughed. "One can only hope. Don't you think your forever is right around the corner?"

Tai hugged me to him again and continued to dance with me. It was as if there was no one else around—only us, the tinkling sound of the ukulele, and a song about dropping all your love and loving your one like mangos. "Sometimes, I wonder if it is this lifetime that I will find her."

I pulled back, cupped both his cheeks, and stared deep into his dark eyes. "I promise, you will."

★ ★ ★ ★

After ATV trail riding, Tai took us to some friends of his, who owned the Kualoa Ranch. The five of us were loaded up onto horses, and his buddy Akela led us through a tour of the four thousand square foot ranch.

Maddy was having a little trouble leading her horse but soon got the hang of it. I treated my horse, aptly named "Buttercup" for his caramel color and black hair, reminding me of a Reese's Peanut Butter Cup, just like I treated my motorcycle Suzi back home. I petted him, spoke softly in his ear, and braided his awesome hair and my own so we were twinsies. Every time I looked at Tai and he caught me lovin' on the horse, he'd close his eyes and shake his head. Whatever. I hadn't had any pets growing up. This was an awesome treat to be riding something so majestic and real.

"Can it," I growled and then petted Buttercup and told her how annoying and devastatingly handsome Tai was but how that didn't make up for his bratty ways. Then I warned her about the hot inked ones and to be careful because I could see the black stallion with his amber eyes had the hots for her.

Ginelle trotted up on her horse as if she'd been riding all her life. "What? Mine's a dude horse. It's no different than riding a man. It's all about the control in your thighs. Isn't that right, baby." She petted her horse, and Tao pulled up to the side of her and responded.

"I can attest to that. You could crack coconuts with those

thighs, blondie."

She grinned and waggled her eyes.

I rolled mine. "Gross."

"It's true. I probably could crack some nuts with these thighs. Maybe we should give it a go tonight, big boy," she said to Tao, and I noisily made gagging sounds. "What? You think it's fair you're the only one getting hot Samoan meat between your legs. Hell no. I'm going to ride this guy like a prized bull rider to-night!" She emphasized the last word, making it two.

"Keep it to yourself, Slutty McSlutty."

"Says the woman who was on her back within what, a day of meeting Tai?" she shot back, her arrow hitting the bull's eye.

I flung my braid over my shoulder and shot daggers at her. "How the hell did you know that?" I put a hand to my hip yet kept the other firmly on the saddle.

Gin guffawed and cackled. "It's true!" Her eyes widened with utter glee. "You're just as bad as me! I have no problem admitting I jumped on that"—she hooked a thumb toward Tao—"the very first night I could get my greedy hands on him. Fuck me, look at him. No..." She looked at Tao. "Fuck me. For real, I want you to fuck me." She giggled and grabbed her breasts and gave them a squeeze and a jiggle for his pleasure.

I smacked her arm, almost pushing her off her horse. "Bitch, keep that shit behind closed doors. I swear you're like a cat in heat."

She opened her mouth, and I knew, I just *knew* she was going to say something about pussy.

In a wild rush of words, I said, "Don't you dare talk about your hoo-hah," and let out the rest of my breath.

Gin closed her mouth and pursed her lips. "Party pooper."

I shook my head and maneuvered my horse off to Maddy,

who was listening intently to Akela and the information he shared about the ranch, the land, the trees, and the movies that were filmed on the island and on this ranch specifically. Turned out the big blockbuster hit *Jurassic Park* was one of them. She was completely enthralled, asking questions and commenting on pieces of information she learned in her plant courses. When my sister spoke about school or the things she'd learned in school, that sense of extreme pride coated my aura. I loved hearing her spew off facts and details about something we'd probably never discuss or see again. But the fact that she knew exactly what these things were, what they did, where they were indigenous, if the plant could be used in medicines and for holistic ailments, was mind boggling.

"Your sister is very knowledgeable for someone so young," Tai complimented.

"Yep, she is. I've made sure she's been a professional student since graduating high school as valedictorian. Me, I barely graduated, working two jobs while going to school."

Tai nodded. "I know what you mean. My family has been performing since I was very little, but *Tina* made sure that it never conflicted with our schooling. She wanted her children to have choices, even though none of us have ever left the island for work or to find something different. It just doesn't seem like any of us want to make that leap. We live to be with one another."

I totally got that. I lifted my chin to Maddy. "I live and work for her, but I'm trying to find what is mine and mine alone. I'll let you know when I find it."

He chuckled.

"Do you worry that you won't find your mate because she may not live on the island?"

His shoulder slumped a bit. "All the time. Especially now that *Tina* says my future mate is blonde and green-eyed. That is not a common combination of islanders."

I thought about that. He was right. Hawaiians, Samoans, and most of the Polynesians who are born and raised within the islands are dark. Skin, eyes, and hair. Exactly opposite of what Masina described. Tai continued explaining his fears.

"She might very well be a tourist. What happens if I miss meeting her?"

"You won't. What's meant to be will be, Tai. Just go with it."

"Just go with it," he repeated.

★ ★ ★ ★

Later in the day, Akela led us to a private beach. He pulled out his backpack and handed each of us a turkey and cheese sandwich and a bottle of water. Individually, we found a nice shady spot to sit and snack on our lunch.

Maddy stood looking out at the ocean. I walked over to her, put my arm around her shoulder, and knocked our heads together. "You having a good birthday, pretty girl?"

"The best." She smiled, and we munched, looking out over the cerulean waters. Fish flicked around, going in and out of shells and coral that had washed up closer to the shore. The beach around us was deserted for as far as I could see. "I think maybe Matt and I will come here for our honeymoon. I'd like to show him these places."

"Yeah?" I tried to sound positive, but the thought of my twenty-year-old baby sister being tied down made me incredibly nervous. She hadn't lived enough yet to be that committed.

"Oh." Her eyes lit up and became a brighter green. "Maybe we'll have a destination wedding! I don't have much family and only a few friends. That might be cool. What do you think?"

I had always pictured her in the big white dress, walking down a long aisle to marry her prince. Maddy was my princess. "You don't want the big white dress and wedding?"

She shrugged. "Honestly, I've always wanted the white coat more than the white dress." She raised her eyebrows, and I laughed.

Her eye was on two prizes now. She still wanted that lab coat, and having Matt didn't change that. Getting married was just a bonus to her. Sharing her life with someone was great, but she'd do it and still make sure she kept her dream, the one thing she'd worked her ass off for.

"Mads, honestly, honey, I'm so glad to hear that. I think my biggest fear with you accepting Matt's proposal had nothing to do with the guy or your age. He's wonderful and seems to adore you."

"He does."

"I know that. I just freaked thinking that you might consider throwing away everything you'd worked for and choose to be a wife and mother and not a doctor. The time to be a wife and mom will come, but the doctor thing... You gotta go for that when you're young."

Maddy held me close. Her eyes were serious as she focused on me. "I'm not going to let anything take me away from my career goals. Matt is encouraging everything I already want. It's just now, I have someone besides you to share it with."

Someone besides you.

That struck deep, cutting right through bone and tissue to

pierce and rip open my heart. I knew she didn't mean it that way, and it's part of letting someone you raised go, but did it hurt? Hell yes.

"It has only ever been us." I choked back my tears and pushed a golden lock of hair over her shoulder.

Maddy sighed like the entire weight of my love was pressing into her, holding her down, not lifting her up. "I love him. I want to be with him, but I don't want to lose what we have either. You're always going to be my sister. Heck, you've been more my mother than a sister for as long as I can remember. It's time to let me make some decisions for myself. Make mistakes. Take chances that don't affect you."

"Everything you do affects me," I responded automatically.

"That's not how it should be, Mia. You need to live for you now. I'm fine. Yes, I still need help with the schooling tuition, and one day I'm going to be able to pay all that back..."

"The hell you will," I shot off, instantly angry. "Being able to provide for you, for your future, has been the highlight of my life. Knowing that you are going to succeed where I didn't, it's the only thing I've ever done right. That's my one claim to fame."

"That makes me sad. I want more for you."

I inhaled hard, not able to catch my breath, tears threatening to consume me. I yanked her over to my chest and hugged her. "You've always been my everything."

"I know. But now I'm going to be Matt's everything, and he will be mine. You need to find that too."

My little sister's words hit home. She wanted me to find a new everything. How did one change the core of their being so easily? I didn't know if I could. Regardless of where I was, what I did, I was always going to be worried about her, thinking of her, missing her. I couldn't begin to even comprehend what my life would be like if I didn't always base my decisions on how they would affect her life and future.

In the end, I knew she needed something. She was worried about *me*. "I'll try, baby girl. I'll try."

"That's all I ask."

"Come on, we've got more partying to do!" I tugged her hair and held her hand, walking up the beach swinging our arms like we used to as kids when I would walk her home from school. Every day, I'd get out an hour earlier than she did and wait at the door to her classroom to walk her home.

My baby sis was all grown up. She was in college, twenty years old, and had a fiancé. She didn't need, or want, her big sis hovering over her all the time.

What the hell do I do now?

★ ★ ★ ★

The rest of our tour was incredible. We were taken to a place that gave us a cool view of Mokoli'i Island, otherwise known as Chinaman's Hat. We learned that Mokoli`i translates from Hawaiian as "little lizard." According to mythology, the island was the remains of a giant lizard's or dragon's tail that was chopped off and tossed into the ocean by the goddess Hi`iaka. I found that incredibly funny since there are no lizards native to Hawaii. That I learned from my smart-as-hell sister. The nickname, Chinaman's Hat, is obvious to anyone who looks at the tiny island, which seems as though it's floating on the water. It looks exactly like an Asian conical hat.

After the tours, Tai and Tao took us to Duke's Waikiki Beach. We ate outside and had the best burgers ever. Tiki torches lit the outside area, making the space glow, and each of our happy faces shone with soft light. We ate and watched the sun set over the horizon at the tableside ocean view. Once it got dark and we'd finished our meal, we went upstairs, where Duke's had live music.

The three of us girls danced the night away. The two men watched, fascinated, as our bodies swayed provocatively on the floor. It had been a long time since the three of us girls had gone out and let our hair down.

At that moment, I let it all go. My sadness over leaving this island and missing out on having Tai in my life on a regular basis. The anxiety I'd been harboring over Wes moving on with Gina—whether they really were in a causal relationship or not, I hadn't a clue anymore. My nerves over my sister getting married and finishing college. I realized that all of these things were outside my control. There wasn't much I could do but take my own advice. The same words that I gave Tai earlier that day rang through my mind.

Just go with it.

That's what I decided I'd do for the rest of my time here and into the rest of my year. I was determined to save my father. Determined to make sure Maddy got through school, and determined to find what was out there that was meant for me. I had spent so little time focusing on my own wants, dreams, and desires that I didn't even know what they were anymore. For a half a year, I thought it might be acting, and I did okay at it. I think mostly I was just trying to escape Nevada. Get the hell away from all the men who had hurt me over the years. Escape the father who'd tried his best but really wasn't ever enough to truly take care of us, leaving me to pick up the brunt of the workload at a very young age.

Maddy was right. I needed to find what my everything really was. What did that look like? What did I want to do with myself after this year was up? It was as if I was asking myself the same question that adults ask you when you're little. What do you want to be when you grow up?

I'd turn twenty-five this year, and I had no flipping clue what I wanted out of the rest of my life.

Time for some serious soul searching.

CHAPTER TEN

Before the taxi picked Maddy up, I sat on her bed and helped her get her stuff together. "Here." I handed her a tiny wooden Hawaiian box. It had a beautiful bird of paradise flower on it painted by a local artisan.

"What is this? Another present?"

"Well, technically I didn't give you a gift you could hold in your hand for your birthday yesterday. This is that and to commemorate our time here."

She opened the box, and inside were a sea shell and a piece of pink coral I'd found while walking along the beach yesterday. Also inside wrapped in tissue was a white-gold charm bracelet. One charm sat dangling at the end. It was a heart that said one word.

"Sister?" She smiled and held it up. The light bounced off its shiny surface. I held up my own wrist, where the identical bracelet sat.

"Now anytime you miss me or want to think about your big sis, you can wear your bracelet and know I'm always thinking about you. And we can add to the bracelet, filling it up with pieces of our future. Individually, and when we're together."

She tugged me into her arms, tears running down her cheeks. "I'll wear it every day because I miss you every day. I love you, Mia. You're the only one I can't live without."

"Me either. Wouldn't ever want to."

We pulled apart when we heard the car honking. Together

we grabbed her things and headed to the front. I hugged Gin and Maddy once more and watched as they got into the cab and it drove away.

One more day on the island with Tai. I needed to make it a good one.

★ ★ ★ ★

As I was getting ready for my last night out, my cell phone rang.

"Hello?"

"Hi, dollface!" Aunt Millie's smooth, sultry voice came through the line.

I breathed heavily into the phone, wanting her to hear my frustration. "Took you long enough. I was worried I'd be headed back to Vegas or California."

"Sorry I didn't call you sooner. I actually hadn't had you booked for June until today."

That admission sent a ribbon of fear rushing through me. I could not have a month off. I had to pay Blaine, or he'd kill my father and go after Maddy. "That scares the shit out of me, Millie. What do you mean? The last e-mail I got from you said I was booked up for the year."

"Yes, all but June at that point. I had no worries, honey. I could have easily called a couple of your last clients, and they would have booked you right away. That Frenchman, Alec, told me he'd take any month where you had a cancellation."

"Really?" I needed to talk to Alec about that.

"You're surprised? He wasn't the only one. The first one you fell all over yourself for, Weston. He said to call him if any monetary problems arose or you needed assistance in any way. Interesting how your first two clients made a point to ensure your well-being."

Interesting was right but not something I was prepared to get into right now. I sighed deeply and finished putting on my mascara. "So where to this time?"

Millie was silent for a bit. "Well, that's the downside. It's nothing like Hawaii, and unfortunately, I can't promise you a stud. This situation might feel a bit icky, but I promise you, you don't have to sleep with him, and he's a really nice guy."

"Ugh. Is he a dog face?" Images of a giant man with a beer belly and sour breath filled my mind.

"No, not at all. I think he's incredibly handsome. I'd hit that so fast your head would spin."

"Wait a minute. You would hit that? You have never said that about any of my clients. Always hinted that I should hit it and quit it, especially to make the extra cash, but never have you eluded to the fact that you'd go there. What's going on?" My nerves hit epic proportions. Liquid courage was definitely necessary. I made it over to the kitchen and pulled out the Malibu Rum, poured a shot, and sucked it back, chasing it with a huge bite of fresh pineapple. Rather unsurprisingly, it tasted damn good. I licked my lips and poured another. "You gonna talk or what?"

"Well, he's not as spry as your usual clients."

Oh no. I groaned loudly, tossed back another shot, and finished off the hunk of pineapple. The rum did its job, soothing the frayed edges of my nerves. "Lay it on me, Aunt Mil."

"How many times do I have to tell you to call me Ms. Milan?"

"You're avoiding..."

"How about I just e-mail you?" she offered in that sweet tone that did absolutely nothing for me.

"How about you just tell me what I need to know right now before I get on a plane and take my happy ass right to LA and your doorstep?"

She tsked. "Fine, he's older."

"I need a number, Millie. Forty? Fifty?"

A noise came through the receiver, sounding as though she was sucking on the inside of her teeth. "Maybe late fifties, possibly sixty."

"*Gross!* Seriously? He's going to be a creeper, isn't he?" Man. Just when I was starting to love this job, I get a pervy old guy. "He probably has a daddy complex in reverse. This sucks."

"I know, I know. But he was very pleasant on the phone. Mostly he wanted a woman of your caliber to attend functions with him. Apparently, if you're old DC money, you have to have a hot trophy girlfriend. He has several senators and investors to schmooze, and he needs pretty arm candy. By the sound of it, he's working on something that has him lobbying for a type of governmental historical building he needs to amass support for. Blah blah. Does it really matter?"

"Not really. I need the money regardless. As long as he doesn't think he's going to be getting into my pants, I'll be fine. You made that clear, right?" A sour taste filled my mouth, making me want to spit. "He's older than Pops!" I shivered, trying to wipe the ick factor off my skin.

"Actually, he made that clear to me. Said that he didn't know what type of escort services you offered as a whole but that he would not be partaking of any sexual offerings."

"Well, that's a relief," I deadpanned, but in truth, it was a huge relief. Knowing that I was going to have a sex-free month kind of sucked, but I'd survive. Probably. Maybe. Hell, I better make sure my B.O.B. had new batteries.

"Okay, I'll send the details. Name is Warren Shipley."

"That name is familiar."

"It should be. His son is the senator from California."

"No shit. Now that guy is hot. Youngest senator in history at thirty-five, right?"

"You got it, dollface. And last I checked...he was unattached."

Now the son had possibilities. I recalled making that check mark next to the name Aaron Shipley, voting for him in the last election, and not just because he was hot. Though he was that. Tall, dirty-blond hair, and kind brown eyes. And the way that man wore a suit made a woman like me think of all the ways I could get said suit off his body in two point five seconds flat.

"Send the details via e-mail. I've got dinner with Tai."

"Tai? Who's that?" Her tone was clearly confused.

"One sinfully sexy Samoan. Ta ta, Auntie!"

★ ★ ★ ★

Tai held my hand from the moment he arrived to pick me up, to the car, from the car, into the restaurant, and all the way until we sat down for dinner. He was having a hard time letting me go.

"Hey, big guy. Can I have my hand back?" He let it go as if burned. I leaned over and rubbed my hand over his large, muscular thigh. "It's okay. Everything is going to be fine."

He shook his head. "How can you say that? You're leaving tomorrow."

"Yes, I am. So let's make tonight count, okay?"

He closed his eyes, took a soft breath, and then opened

them, focusing all his attention on me. "Mia, it's just... I've never met a woman like you. Not ever. You're funny. Smart. Beautiful." He leaned closer and whispered, "A mountain lion in the sack..." He shook his head and stopped. His beautiful dark eyes held such beauty and longing. "I don't know how to say what I feel."

I held his hand on top of the table. "I'm going to miss you, too. More than I want to admit."

"Yes, exactly," he admitted.

"And we're going to keep in touch by phone, text, and e-mail. You're going to tell me everything that's going on with your crazy family and with work and the shows. Send me videos of any cool new tricks you've learned with your fire-knife dancing, and me, well... I don't know what I'll send you. Probably selfies of me doing stupid shit in random places."

Tai tipped his head back and laughed, heartily, deeply. So much so that it filled my heart with such joy to hear it. I leaned forward and place a kiss on his cheek.

"We'll stay friends?" he asked tentatively.

"The best of friends," I agreed.

With that, the happy-go-lucky giant clapped his hands and pushed his chair out. "I'll get some champagne! We need to celebrate your last night!" Just as he stood, the chair tipped on its legs under the pressure of his big body pushing it back, and it flipped over and fell to the ground. Unfortunately, a waitress was passing by at the same time with a tray of wineglasses filled from the nearby bar. Her foot hit the chair, and her tray went flying forward along with her. Tai reached for her, and they both tumbled. She fell directly on top of him, straddling his body.

All I could see was a broken chair, a lengthy blonde, and

Tai's brown hands surrounding her small waist. She lifted up on her knees, her skirt rising up. His hands went to her thighs to steady her. I was going to help out until I saw her face. She was facing me, and Tai was on the ground looking up toward her, lying at my feet. Her entire face turned rosy in color. The waitress pushed a hand through her hair, and that's when I noticed a pair of startling green eyes. Her lips were wet where she'd bit into them. A touch of blood pooled there. Tai sat up and pressed a finger to her plump bottom lip to staunch the blood flow.

For long moments, he just stared at her face. The girl didn't move a muscle, focused solely on him. The entire room could have imploded, and neither one would have noticed. It's like they were in a trance. And it hit me the moment Tai pressed one of his big hands to her face and she automatically leaned into his palm.

"Are you okay, sunshine?"

Sunshine.

Holy hell. This was his girl. Blonde hair, kissed by the sun. Green eyes the exact color of brand new cut grass. And he'd called her sunshine.

I held my hands to my chest and didn't make a sound, wanting to watch this play out before me like my own personal love story.

"Um, sorry?" she offered in a small embarrassed voice.

Tai petted her bottom lip with his thumb. "You're bleeding."

She flicked her tongue out to lick her lip and ended up licking Tai's thumb. They both gasped in unison, only Tai's sounded far more feral and growly alpha male that I loved. I watched as his eyes heated. Her own gaze didn't leave his. I could see her fingers press into his shoulders reflexively. This was almost better than watching a movie because it was live. Damn, I wished I had popcorn.

Finally, the woman shook her head and tried to stand. Tai lifted up, holding her close to his giant body. So close that when he stood up to his full height, she ended up sliding down his body until her feet met the floor once more. He groaned, and I knew that sound. He was turned on. I wanted to kick my feet and squeal with excitement. There was no denying the attraction.

After a couple more moments of holding one another, she pushed off and put her head down. "Shit." She looked around at the huge mess. "I should have watched where I was going. I'm going to get fired." Her lip trembled, and the tears started up.

I stood up and moved into motion. "Oh, thank you so much, miss. We didn't mean to knock your tray over. We'll pay for any drinks we spilled."

At that point, the manager came over, his face a look of barely contained aggravation.

"Sir, thank God you're here. This woman saved my friend here from getting an entire tray full of drinks splashed on him. The big guy is sometimes so clumsy. Right, Tai? The way you jumped up and knocked your chair over at the same time that..." I snapped my fingers at the waitress for her name.

"Amy," she said meekly.

"...that Amy here was coming by. She could have really hurt someone if she wasn't so light on her feet, trying to avoid slamming into my friend, making sure all the patrons around her didn't get tagged with the drinks. We'll be recommending your establishment to all our friends."

"Ah, well yes. Thank you. We only hire the best. Amy, good work. I'll have a busboy come clean this up while you get to your tables."

Amy held out her hand to me. "Thank you." Her eyes were apologetic, but really, it was Tai's fault.

"Nothing to be sorry for. I'm Mia, and this very available hunk of a man is Tai Niko."

"You mean, you're not a couple?" She covered her mouth, as if she hadn't meant to ask that.

I smiled and looked at Tai, but his eyes were stuck on Ms. Amy. "Nope. But we are really good friends, and I'm moving back to the mainland. I'm sure he could really use a new friend. Have you lived here long?"

She shook her head. "Moved here this week with my dad. Didn't want him coming alone, and it's just the two of us, so here I am. I don't know anyone yet." She picked up her tray and several pieces of broken glass until the busboy took over.

"Well, now you know one another. Do you have your phone on you?"

Her eyes narrowed as she reached into her back pocket and pulled out an iPhone. I snatched it quick, added Tai as a new contact, and then texted him. His phone buzzed, and he pulled it out.

"Now Tai has your number. He'll call you tomorrow."

Tai opened his mouth, but I gave him The Look, the one that puts the fear into any man that is on the receiving end of it, and he wisely chose to keep quiet. Amy looked from me to Tai and back again.

"Do you like surfing?" I asked, knowing that our time to chat with Ms. Amy was limited.

She shrugged. "Never been."

I beamed and hugged her into my side. "Tai. Isn't that horrible? Amy's never surfed, and what do you know? Tai teaches surfing."

"Really? Sounds fun." She brushed off her skirt and straightened her apron. Tai's eyes never left her movements. "I gotta go. It would be really great to make a new friend. And I'm really sorry about running into you."

He put his hands in his pockets and rocked from his heels to his toes, playing it cool. "You can make it up to me by going out with me tomorrow night after I drop Mia off at the airport."

Of course, Tai didn't know that my escape plan didn't include face-to-face good-byes.

Her eyes sparkled a crazy bright green. "I look forward to your call, Tai." She blushed and turned to walk away.

"Oh, hey, Amy?" I called. She turned around. "One last thing. How do you feel about tattoos?"

She walked close to me, whispered in my ear, thanked me, and strutted off to the bar to get new drinks for her tables. Thank God we were in Hawaii and not some hoity-toity place in New York. We'd all have been kicked out for dragging our feet and having a conversation over spilled wine and crushed glass. Here in Hawaii, people just minded their own business and walked around the mess.

Tai and I sat back down.

"So champagne, then?" I reminded him.

His eyes turned black, and he practically growled. "What the fuck did she say to you?"

"About the tattoos?"

"No, about the pope. Yes, about the tattoos." He looked incredibly nervous, which was awesome since Tai hadn't really looked anything but perfectly comfortable in his own skin for most of the time I'd known him—aside from that one crazy night where he fucked me until I blacked out.

I leaned forward conspiratorially and looked around to make sure that no one could hear. "She loves them. Says they make her so hot. And get this..."

He moved closer so that my lips were touching his ear.

"The entire left side of her back, dipping down to her ass, is covered in a tattoo. Though, it's not tribal." I sat back and enjoyed the look of pure hunger in his eyes. "Cherry blossom branches with the blooms and sprigs all running sexily up her back and down to her ass. Hot, right?"

His nostrils flared, and he breathed long and slow for a couple of breaths. "Yes. Absolutely hot as hell."

I waggled my eyebrows. "I figured you'd like that."

"And you setting me up. Isn't that kind of weird?"

"Why?"

"Because we've been fucking for a month."

His reasoning was sound, but I didn't care if he thought I was crazy. He needed someone and pronto. Besides, I was convinced she was the woman Masina spoke of.

"Yeah, and it stops after tonight. You're going to send me off with a night I'll never forget and vice versa, and then tomorrow, you'll start your new life. Did you not see her hair, eyes, and body? She is your forever!"

"You don't know that."

"You tell me you didn't feel something when she ran into you and you had your hands on her thighs, her waist, her cheek and lips?"

"No, I can't say that I didn't feel something." He narrowed his eyes and then laughed as I gloated.

"I'm so happy for you!" I shimmy danced in my chair.

"Let's say fuck dinner and order dessert and the bottle of champagne you promised!"

"It's your night, girlie. And tomorrow is your forever."

★ ★ ★ ★

Good thing I'd had enough foresight to pack my bags before dinner last night. Tai thought my plane left in the evening. I'd told him it left at eight. What he didn't know was that it left at eight in the morning. Good-byes and I just didn't go well together.

I pulled out the package I had made near the shop that designed Maddy's and my sister bracelets. I set the framed image of the Samoan symbol for friendship on the counter. A local artist had been painting images when I left the jewelry store. I'd asked her about the symbol. She'd known exactly what I wanted. She'd painted the symbol, which, to my untrained eye, was very similar to a wide cursive L with bigger swirls at each end. The symbol was about four inches in size. Under the symbol, I'd used a black pen and drew a heart and wrote my name next to it. Then I framed the entire thing in a small five-by-five-inch shadow-box frame.

My stationery was the last thing to come out of my handbag. I sat at the barstool and wrote to my Tai:

Tai, my sinfully sexy Samoan,
Thank you for giving me one of the best months of my life.
You filled my world with such joy, laughter, and pleasure.
I'll never be able to forget you. Not that I'd ever want to. When
I came here, I was down about a lot of things. My family, my
relationships, and my work. You changed that for me. With a

wink and a smile, you took away all the dark and brought me light. Sunlight.

Through my time here, I learned to enjoy what life brings as it comes. To just "go with it." Let life happen and appreciate the moment. I can honestly say I had the most fun with you than I have had in a very long time. You reminded me that I'm young and still have plenty of time to figure out what my forever looks like. I know you are aching to find your forever, and in my heart of hearts, I believe you may have. Call it women's intuition. Things happen for a reason. We just might not know what the reason is.

I'm glad I met you that very first day. Every moment with you was a new experience, an adventure. Thank you for giving me that. I'm sad to go and will miss you terribly. Please keep in touch.

Your girlie,
~Mia

As usual, I'd slipped out of Tai's bed, written my letter, left his gift, and walked out to the cab waiting at the curb without waking the hunk of a man. I wondered what awaited me in Washington, DC, with Mr. Warren Shipley, old money and politics, with an emphasis on the old part. Who knows? Maybe I'd get to meet his too-hot-to-trot son, Senator Aaron Shipley. If not, oh well. I was getting a hundred thousand smackaroos to play trophy chick on the arm of an old guy who didn't want sex. Ohhh, maybe it was like Tony and Hector and he was secretly gay? That would be too coincidental. No, there was definitely something fishy about why he'd hire an escort when he was a rich, good-looking old guy. There were tons of vipers ready for a go at an old geezer. He didn't need to pay a hundred large for an escort when he could get arm candy for free.

Taking my advice and just "going with it," I lay back in my seat on the airplane and instantly dreamed of white stone steps, phallic symbols in the sky, and a dead marble president who sat in his chair silently watching over a concrete city.

June

CALENDAR GIRL

CHAPTER ONE

June in Washington, DC, felt oppressive. The air made your clothes stick like a second layer of skin. Muggy and miserable. I worried that if I pulled my tank away from my chest, it might pull off an additional layer of flesh with it.

The first step out of the airport delivered me into an overcast, sunless sky. This was not at all what I was used to, having spent the last month in Hawaii.

I scanned the rows and rows of cars waiting. One tall fella stood in front of a shiny black town car holding a sign that said "Saunders." I figured that was my ride.

"I'm Mia Saunders." I held out a hand, and the driver shook it.

"I'm James, your driver. I'll be taking you where you need to go throughout your stay with the Shipleys." He took my suitcase and tossed it the trunk before opening my door.

I climbed into the vehicle, trying not to allow my sweaty thighs to imprint the smooth leather. The flowy skirt I'd worn on the plane seemed like a great choice at the time. I should've gone for the standard yoga garb. I slicked the palms of my hands down the backs of my legs, wishing I had a dish towel.

"Is it always so humid?" I asked while pulling my phone out of my purse and hitting the power button.

"In June? Eh, it can be hot has the dickens, raining, or really quite lovely. You'll probably experience it all this month. I will concede it's been unusually warm this year."

My phone blared. Rapid dinging signified the messages that had arrived while I was in flight.

To: Mia Saunders
From: Sexy Samoan
Girlie, you've got some explaining to do. You bailed. Not cool.

I scrolled down to read the other messages. Apparently Tai hadn't cooled down after his first message.

To: Mia Saunders
From: Sexy Samoan
The gift... No words.

To: Mia Saunders
From: Sexy Samoan
I'm so mad you stole my kiss good-bye.

That's when my fingers raced over the keyboard.

To: Sexy Samoan
From: Mia Saunders
Kiss your forever. That will heal all that ails you.

An unladylike snort left my mouth, and the driver's eyes popped up to mine in the rearview mirror. His eyebrows rose, but I just shook my head and looked back down at the other messages.

To: Mia Saunders

From: Wes Channing
*Are you ever going to talk to me? It's been a month. Don't
make me come after you.*

Flying phalanges once again. There was no other way to
express how quickly I typed back the most flippant message
possible.

To: Wes Channing
From: Mia Saunders
*I'm sure Gina kept you busy. I saw you happily sucking face
on the cover of HotDirt smut mag.*

After twenty minutes of stewing in my own irritation
and glancing down every two seconds at my phone, he finally
responded. He being Wes, not Tai, but I ignored it, trying to
force myself to be cool. Instead, I thought back to my sexy
Samoan.

Hopefully Tai was getting ready for his first date with
Amy right now. My heart fluttered, thinking about how the
universe dropped her into his lap. Literally. She landed in
his lap at dinner that night. I sure hoped she was the one.
Mentally, I made a note to touch base with Tai in a week to
double check their progress. Something told me that she was
it. His forever. As for me, I didn't know when that was going to
happen. Definitely not before this year was up. Thinking about
Tai or the future did not help me forget the burning desire to
read Wes's message.

To: Mia Saunders
From: Wes Channing

Jealous?

Was it possible for a woman to cut a man's dick off from three thousand miles away? Maybe, if I hired out a hit man.

I had some extra money in the bank for emergencies. That made me snicker. Have his dick lopped off with the extra money I got from *fucking* him. I shook my head.

What game was he playing? Should I respond or just let him stew in it? Obviously he didn't like the month-long forced break. Served him right. He was hitting the sheets with model-perfect Gina DeLuca, while I was banging my own sexy Samoan.

It. Doesn't. Matter.

I could tell myself that over and over and over again, but the end result still slapped me upside the head. It was impossible for me to stop caring. Wes would *always* matter to me. Not knowing what he was doing and who he was doing it with ate at me like a piranha nipping at raw meat. With Tai, I had an awesome diversion. Fun. He made every day more exciting than the last and every night more scorching hot than I dreamed possible. It was easy to put my issues with Wes on the back burner because I was filling my mind with everything that a young, almost-twenty-five-year-old woman should be enjoying. Now, though, it wasn't working.

"Is it going to be much longer?" I asked James.

He tipped his hat. "Sorry, miss. Traffic is atrocious at this time."

Forty-five minutes. Plenty of time. If Wes wanted to chat, I'd give him his time. Technically, we were friends after all.

I pulled out my phone and hit his number, forcing a level of calm into my mind that I didn't feel.

"She lives!" Wes's California-soaked breathy timber came through the line, instantly stirring up some serious vibes.

"Hardy har har. What's this shit about me being jealous? You know I'm not." *Lie.*

Wes sucked in a slow breath, possibly even a sigh. I could hear the sounds of the ocean in the background. He might even be on the beach having just finished surfing. Hearing those comforting sounds, even filtered through the phone, made my heart ache to be home. "I figured if I provoked you, you'd call."

"Wes, what's the deal?" Even through my own ears it sounded catty and a bit bitchy, which wasn't at all what I intended.

"You tell me. Did you have fun in Hawaii?" His tone seemed to feed off mine.

I thought of Tai and licking those tribal lines from the tip of his shoulder all the way down his chest, ribs, hip, and thigh. All month, it had been my favorite pastime. Yum. A sultry, "Yes," left my mouth before I could filter the inflection.

He chuckled. "That good, huh? Client or local?"

The tension between us broke briefly.

I closed my eyes. "Does it matter?"

"Everything about you matters to me. Haven't you gathered that yet?" His tone was sincere but dipped in regret. He was failing miserably at playing it cool, and we both knew it.

"Wes..."

He sucked in a breath through his teeth. "No, I'm not going to pretend I'm not upset you were off in Hawaii fucking whoever you wanted, yet you're pissed at me for doing the same with Gina."

He had a point. An excellent one. But that's the thing

about the heart and the mind. They are rarely balanced or realistic. He could make more sense than Deepak Chopra's teachings, but it didn't change the facts. Him being with Gina hurt. Badly. We were both hurting one another, and neither of us could find a good way around it.

My throat felt strained, tight, when I responded. "Look, Wes. I'm sorry. I get what you're saying. I do. And you're right."

"Does that mean you're going to come home?" Two heaping spoonfuls of hope laced his question.

Home. Where was home? In California, the tiny apartment I hadn't stepped foot in within the last five months, or Vegas, in my childhood shack of a house, or was it on the coast of Malibu in the arms of a very dreamy man who likely owned more of my heart than I'd care to admit?

I licked my lips and huffed loudly. "Wes, you know I can't do that."

He groaned softly, each rumble sticking a knife in my gut. "Not true. You can. You won't." He emphasized each phrase.

I shook my head trying to clear the cobweb of emotions running a marathon through my mind. "I can't let you pay my father's debt."

"Again," he sighed, "you can. You won't."

He sounded tired, weighed down by each word. And it was all my fault. I was doing this to him, to us. These chats were getting harder every time, and I still had half a year to go. It was anyone's guess where we'd be at the end of this year. So far, we weren't fairing too well as friends. We were constantly hurting one another without even trying.

An enormous pause lingered between us as I tried to think of what to say next, yet I was coming up with nothing.

"When can I see you again?" he broke the silence to ask.

He still wanted to see me? I didn't understand this man. Hell, I didn't understand most men, especially not this one. "Um, I don't know. I've just landed in Washington, DC. Arm candy for an older gentleman."

Wes's laughter rang through the line. "A geezer? At least I know you won't be giving it up to an old guy with a prescription for Viagra."

"That's not nice!" I playfully scolded. "Besides, he has a hot son who's a senator. You know me and powerful men..."

Wes's laughter died instantly, that brief moment of peace shattered. The tension rose between us again. "You're joking?" he asked.

Hook. Line. Sinker.

"Nope."

"Fuck me," he groaned.

"Gladly," I shot back without thinking.

"When?" He didn't miss a beat.

"When I see you next, silly."

"Which will be?" He kept it going, but I was no longer sure he was playing around anymore. This thing between us zigzagged, twisted and turned. It was never an easy road to maneuver.

"Don't know. I guess I'll see you when I see you," I offered.

"Why me?" His voice was loud and frustrated, sounding like a man who'd looked up at the sky, held his arms wide, and yelled at his maker. "Why the hell did I have to go balls-to-the-wall crazy for a nut job like you?" Then he laughed that throaty, beautiful chuckle that belonged only to him and him alone. The one that made my heart pound so hard it felt like it might burst out of my chest if I didn't press my hand to it.

I shrugged, but he couldn't see it. "If the universe deals

you a shit hand, bet against the dealer. Bye, Wes."

Instead of waiting for him to say good-bye, I ended the call and took several calming breaths. *It is time to get your eyes back on the prize, Mia. Warren Shipley. Your next client.*

★ ★ ★ ★

Warren Shipley did not greet me at the entrance to his mansion. No. The man who stood at the top of the stone steps when I exited the town car looked like he'd walked out of *GQ* magazine. Aaron Shipley, the Democratic senator for California, leaned against the white column. I'd been around beautiful men. I'd been around giant alphas who could chop wood with their bare hands, but I'd not yet seen a man who wore a suit the way this one did. Pure perfection.

The dark-charcoal fabric clung precisely to his broad shoulders, trim waist, and long legs, as if it had been tailored to fit his exact measurements. Probably was. His eyes were shaded behind a pair of black Ray-Bans. Thick-looking, dirty-blond hair was coiffed into that messy bedhead yet styled look that was so popular right now. On him it worked, and it worked hard. It gave him that put-together appeal with a hint of whimsy. It was a lethal combination for a girl like me. Hell, for any girl.

As sleek as a steel-gray jaguar, he took one step at a time from the top of the stone stairway down to the gravel drive below. Most people would make the attempt to meet him halfway up the dozen or so steps. I'm not most women, and he was definitely not most men. I enjoyed watching him move. He had an air of authority that clung to him like a fine, crisp cologne. I watched him take each step with grace and agility, exuding so much power I almost melted on the spot. The earlier complaint of humidity paled in comparison to the sweat I could feel beading at my nape, a single drop running down the length of my spine, shooting sparks of desire out each nerve ending.

"You must be Ms. Saunders." His tone was straightforward yet welcoming as he held out his hand. The moment our hands touched, an electric charge zapped my palm. I tried to pull away. He clung tighter. "Curious. I rarely feel someone's essence just from a single touch."

"My essence?"

A secretive smile stole across his kissable lips. They weren't too thin or too plump. Like Goldilocks and her three bears, those lips would fit mine just right. He still hadn't let my hand go. Instead, he turned it over, keeping our palms touching. Just that simple skin-on-skin contact was enough to have me salivating for more. He pushed up his glasses into his hair, a move that was far too cool for someone of his political stature. Men like him were supposed to be dull, boring, and all about government blah blah blah... My thoughts were interrupted by the depth of his brown eyes positively searing into mine. They were like identical Hershey's Kisses, melting *me* instead. I sighed as his thumb brushed along the top of my hand.

"Your essence is your life force, your magnetism. When we touched, I felt the charge. Did you feel it?"

I nodded numbly, staring into those chocolaty orbs, focusing on the straight nose, the high cheekbones and chiseled jawline.

"When I press our palms together harder"—he placed his other hand over the top of the one he was holding, forcing them closer together—"it's much stronger now." His eyebrow quirked at the same time I licked my lips. Those eyes went straight to my mouth, and my knees weakened.

It took every ounce of strength I possessed not to lick my lips again.

"Come," he said, and I swear that one word alone sent a bolt of electricity directly to my pleasure center, where it throbbed and pulsated, ticking to its own clock. He said something else, but I lost track after the word *come.* He let go of my hand and reached up to cup my cheek. Oh, man, I liked that a million times better, but it also forced me to focus on my surroundings. "Mia, are you okay?" His gaze roamed all over my face. Worry and concern were prevalent in the line that appeared between his brows. "I said come on. Father is waiting."

I blinked a few times and then focused. "Oh, yeah. Sorry." I shook my head attempting to clear the remaining lust fog. "It was a really long travel day. I was in Hawaii and came straight from there to here, with a couple layovers in between. I've been up all night." Layovers meant mad dashes to the gate so I didn't miss my flights. I could have killed Aunt Millie for booking flights with fifty-minute layovers in between. It left absolutely no time to get to your next plane. Potty breaks were completely out, and the captain didn't let you go before takeoff—and definitely not until you reached a certain flying altitude. Then there was the one several-hour stint where I didn't land until morning the next day. Not my best travel experience.

Aaron tsked and shook his head. "That sounds dreadful. Let's introduce you to Father, and then I'll have James show you to your room so we can have a quickie."

"What!" I stopped at the top of the stairs and pressed my hand into my temple. *A quickie?*

"I said I'll introduce you to Father, have you settled into

your room, and then let you rest. The time-zone change can be quite tricky."

"Oh, tricky." I closed my eyes and laughed internally.

"What did you think I said?" He smiled showing a row of the most beautiful teeth known to man. He could easily grace the cover of magazines. Oh wait, he already had. Never mind.

"I thought you said we could have a quickie." I laughed, and he stopped in his tracks, this time at the top of the steps next to the front door.

A sly smirk slipped across his lips. "Well, that could be arranged as well, though I don't know that Father would appreciate me dipping my hand into the cookie jar before offering you a proper meal and a date." He winked and then grabbed my hand. That same sizzle of excitement zipped through our touching palms, stirring the magnetic energy again.

Aaron shifted, glancing at me sideways while leading me through the entryway. "You feel it, too?"

Lord, I wish I didn't. Instead of lying, I closed my eyes, held my breath, and nodded.

★ ★ ★ ★

I'd thought the sprawling mansion from the driveway up was amazing. It had nothing on the inside. In the foyer was a double staircase lined with yellow carpet. It reminded me of the yellow brick road and how Dorothy would skip along to her destination. If I wasn't dead tired, I'd be skipping, too. This place was beyond lush. Wes's Malibu home was beautiful, lived in, and probably cost a mint. Alec's warehouse was incredible and kitted out. Tony and Hector's penthouse apartment was swank, but this was a whole other type of rich. When Aunt Millie had said old money, I honestly didn't know what I was heading into. I thought politician, government? It would probably be a nice place. But this felt like something Britain's Queen Mother could be comfortable living in. The walls curved, had crown molding, and there were giant windows with thick, wine-colored drapes. My feet sank into the carpet, making me want to remove my sandals and go barefoot just so I could dig my toes into the plush pile.

"This is amazing."

Aaron smiled and looked around. seeming unimpressed. "My mother was good with décor."

"Oh yeah? She must really be proud of this. It's beautiful."

"She passed long ago, but she definitely appreciated the many admirers and home journals that shot different rooms here. She made the cover a few times. This home was her pride and joy—once I left for university that is." He grinned and winked.

It looked like Aaron Shipley's ego was perfectly intact. I followed him quietly, taking in my surroundings until we were in front of a set of double doors. Laughter rang behind the door, as if someone was having a jolly time. Aaron knocked sharply but didn't wait for the greeting, opening the door as if he had a right to.

"Ah, Aaron, my boy! Come, come. Kathleen and I were just discussing last week's debacle with the kitchen." He pointed to a woman in a navy pencil skirt with a white frilly apron tied around her middle and a cream silk blouse tucked precisely and buttoned up to the neck. She had to be staff. "You see, the caterer for last week's event thought I wanted—"

"Father..." Aaron cut him off abruptly, which I found

rather rude and unappealing. His hotness just got kicked down a notch. "Ms. Saunders is here." He tugged my arm forward, and I came face-to-face with an older carbon copy of young Shipley.

"Well, aren't you even more beautiful in person than I saw in your profile. That Ms. Milan knows exactly how to impress. She is going to do perfectly, don't you think, Aaron?"

Aaron's gaze roamed my body from head to toe. "Yes, she's definitely the ideal candidate to gain the attention of your consorts."

"Come here, my dear. I am Warren Shipley," he said jovially. Instead of a handshake, he pulled me right into a fatherly hug. "You are not at all what I was expecting." He moved away and smiled while looking directly into my eyes. Dirty old perverts would be looking down at my breasts in this position. Seemed as though what my aunt said was true. He wasn't interested in me in *that* way. "Thank you for coming. The situation is unique, but Ms. Milan assured me that you would be a great candidate. Just by your look alone...I can already tell I'm going to have them eating out of the palm of my hand."

CHAPTER TWO

"What do you mean, just by my look?" My eyebrows narrowed of their own accord.

Aaron huffed behind me and placed a hand on my lower back...very low. It was low enough to feel the curve of my bum through my skirt. Then he patted my behind and came around to the front of me, arms crossed over one another, to sit on the edge of his father's desk.

I was about to filet him for patting my ass like the little wifey, but he took that moment to explain. "Father has hired you because you're beautiful, young, and will look drop-dead sexy in a cocktail dress. You've heard the term 'arm candy,' right?" His lips pursed as his eyes trailed over my body. I wanted to hate the way it made me feel, but I couldn't. Something about the open admiration was forbidden coming from someone of his caliber and status. A rich politician sizing up an escort was fucking hot.

"So I'm going to pretend to be your what, Mr. Shipley?" My gaze went to Shipley Senior for clarification.

Warren Shipley glanced at Kathleen, who lowered her gaze and looked away, a pained expression crossing her delicate features. "I think I'd better take my leave and let you discuss business." Her voice shook as she made a hasty retreat. The woman strode out of the room, so light on her feet I didn't even hear her footsteps. I guess if you were a house attendant, you learned how to be quiet and not disturb.

Aaron's father held up a hand to say something to the woman, but Aaron grabbed his hand and pressed it back down to the desk where they leaned. Warren pushed his shoulders back and tipped his head. "My dear, the type of men I consort with are all members of the One Percent, like myself. They have more money than a thousand people would ever need in their lifetimes and use it to control big business. I am merely playing along with their game."

That confused me, because the only one percent I knew about was an outlaw biker gang outside of Vegas.

I set my hands on my hips and cocked one out to the side. "That explained nothing about why I am here."

Warren cleared his throat and rubbed his hand over his chin stubble. He seemed incredibly uncomfortable with continuing this conversation.

"You're to be Father's whore," the senator confirmed blatantly, not even a hint of tact in his tone.

My head slammed back, and I instantly crossed my arms over my chest. "Excuse me? I do not copulate with clients unless I *want* to. Emphasis on the want."

"No, no, no, my dear. I don't want that..." Warren sounded as uncomfortable as I felt and looked to Aaron for what I could only assume was assistance in explaining.

Aaron rolled his eyes and stood. "Mia, these men have a woman on their arm. Usually they are gold-digging whores. Meant only to look pretty, take as much money as they can, and fuck the men whenever and wherever."

"Jesus, son. Must you be so crude?" Warren stood and came over to me. His eyes were filled with something akin to shame. "Mia, I will not treat you badly, but I do need to stay on the good side of these men in order to move forward on my building plans and mission for the new program. All of them have very young, beautiful women on their arms. It's a disgusting status type of thing, if you will. I don't care for it, but I will play whatever game is necessary to advance my agenda. In order to do that, I need the backing of several very prominent men in business and government. Without it, they could crush the program, and all plans are shot."

"Sounds like you've put a lot of thought into this."

"That, money, and time. More than I'd care to admit," he confirmed.

Again, Aaron shook his head. "Father is a modern-day vigilante. He's building the headquarters to offer medical services to third-world countries. In order to do that, he needs to have trade opened up to countries that offer specific vaccinations for a fraction of the cost. In others, he needs access to government as well as immunity to have his people travel to these locales. It will take legislative acts of governments to approve the organization coming in and out of the US, sending doctors, medical professionals, etcetera, much like a Red Cross, Lions International, and Doctors Without Borders."

"You want to help save people in third-world countries? I don't see how this is a problem. Shouldn't government officials be jumping at the chance to help, especially if it's not at the taxpayer's expense?"

Warren cupped my cheeks, looking deeply into my eyes. His brown orbs were warm and kind. "Some are, my sweet. Some are. But there is a lot of red tape. More than you can possibly imagine." He dropped his hands and stepped back to lean against his desk. "In order to have that tape cut, I need to get a few powerful fellas on board. There are also others who want special favors from my family that we cannot accommodate." He turned his gaze to Aaron.

Aaron inhaled and tipped his head down. Warren wouldn't dare put his son's political stance in jeopardy with his plan. Right then, I knew Warren Shipley was a good guy. The jury was still out on his son.

I shrugged. "So where do I come in?"

That's when Aaron came over to me and cupped the back of my neck. His hand was warm and held just the right amount of pressure when he squeezed. "At the events and gatherings. Look incredibly gorgeous, smile, hug on Father as if you're his young plaything, and your job is done."

I wished I had one of those big red buttons that said "That was easy" for him to press.

"And what about you?" I licked my lips. Again, he watched with an intensity I rather liked. If his father hadn't been there, I was certain I'd be pressed up against the nearest wall with his lips all over mine.

He made a humming noise deep in his throat. One I could feel all the way down to my toes. He leaned close to my face, so close I could feel his breath on my cheek as he whispered into my ear. "Me. Well, I get to chase my father's hot young plaything in private." His eyebrows quirked before he stepped back and winked.

I held out my hands and slapped them against my thighs. "When do we start?"

★ ★ ★ ★

A few days later had me at one of Mr. Shipley's fundraisers, looking around like the wild gazelle caught in the crosshairs of a hunter. With Wes, I had him to anchor me to the environment, make me feel as though I fit in. Not this time. Mentally, I gave myself a hefty dose of self-confidence, setting my goals straight and readying for battle. Scanning the room reminded me of being back in Malibu with Wes at one of his stuffy events, except a far higher level of class. I wasn't wearing sparkly sequins. No, I wore a dress designed by Dolce & Gabanna as a personal favor to Mr. Shipley. One that was entirely cut out from nape to ass but covered everything in front. Warren blushed and said nothing about the closet full of designer threads. I had taken pictures of the dresses and gowns and sent them to Hector, my gay BFF back in Chicago. His text message went something like: *Chica, you own the universe. How do I get a ticket to Heaven?*

I looked around the room, and honestly, I was shocked by the number of men over fifty dressed in fancy suits with women young enough to be their daughters—possibly even their granddaughters—on their arm. Stealthily, I pulled out my phone and took a snapshot of the giant room, patrons included. We were at a local fundraiser for one of Warren's "friends." I use the term lightly because as Warren admitted, very few folks in the One Percent were actually friends with one another. That friendship only extended as far as the next business deal. If the deal didn't bring them closer to a goal or make them a bucketload of cash, that relationship no longer had any value. No longer good pals. Honestly, it sickened me, but I was being paid to be here. Hypocrisy was something I was working on.

To: Skank-a-lot-a-puss
From: Mia Saunders
Caption this?

From: Skank-a-lot-a-puss
To: Mia Saunders
Easy! It's bring your daughter to work day on Capitol Hill!

I almost lost it. The laugher bubbled up so fast, I ended up choking on the champagne I was sipping, forcing me to wobble on my stilettos. God, I loved that woman.

"Careful there." An older gentleman clasped me around the bicep and held me up. "That's the good stuff you're choking on. I guess there are worse ways to go than to choke to death on five-hundred-dollar champagne." He chuckled as my eyes watered.

I ended up spraying the liquid still in my mouth across the plant in front of me. I hacked and coughed, trying to get my bearings. A waiter walked by at that moment with glasses of water. The gray-haired old man stole one and handed it to me. I slugged it back gratefully, clearing out the champagne that had gone down the wrong pipe.

"I'm so sorry." I cleared my throat and put my lip out, giving my best pout.

The man, who must have been at least sixty-five or seventy, shook his head and petted my cheek like I was a favored pet. "No worries, little girl. Who's your daddy?" One minute he was grandfatherly old guy and the next, a true predator.

Without realizing it, my eyebrows narrowed. "I'm not sure what you mean?"

"Don't be dense. Who takes care of you?" He licked his dry, cracked lips. The old man breathed with his mouth open, and the stench of cigars and liquor wafted over me. I cringed, gulping back the need to vomit.

Someone cleared their throat behind him. "I believe you have found something that belongs to me." Warren Shipley's face twisted into a scowl. His eyes were hard as stones as he took in the man's hand holding on to my arm.

"Warren, I didn't know you'd finally taken a lamb." The man grinned, and his eyes traced wantonly over my curves. "And what a perfect little pet. Do you share her?" His tone was smarmy. Holding down that vomit was getting harder by the second.

Warren laughed out loud. A full-bellied laugh that could be heard far and wide. "'Fraid not, old friend. Bit selfish in my old age, Arthur."

Arthur let go of my bicep. Instinctively, I rubbed at the spot.

Warren clocked the move, and his jaw tightened. He came over and put his hand lightly around my waist. "This is Mia, under my care. Mia, Arthur Broughton." Warren squeezed my waist, and I held out my hand.

"Pleasure to meet you, Mr. Broughton." I cuddled up to Warren for good measure. He held me closer, his body a pillar of strength, firm and standing tall. A strength that belied his years.

Warren leaned down and kissed my temple. "Mia, you look parched. Go on ahead and get a drink. I'll be there in a moment."

I nodded, and he tapped my ass lightly. You couldn't really say it was in a good-game-type way like the way Mason, my old client and friend, did with his Major League Baseball buddies, or me, for that matter. It was more coddling. At least he didn't grope like some of these men did.

I made my way through the veritable buffet of old dudes

with tight, pretty, young female bodies clinging to their arms. I could almost imagine the tiny manacles holding the women close, making sure they were never far from the men's wallets. Gross.

The bartender offered me a new glass of champagne. I pounded it, set the glass down, and asked for another.

"Easy, tiger. You don't want to be falling down drunk and ruin Father's image," Aaron said as he settled onto the stool next to mine.

I shook my head and pursed my lips. "I don't get what I'm here for."

"You're already doing it. Looking good, showing these old-timers that Father is one of them. See how he's talking animatedly with Arthur Broughton?"

I cringed at the name of the guy who had gripped my arm. "Yeah."

Aaron nodded toward the duo. "He owns the ports Father wants to take the meds through. He has the port authority in each country he serves in his back pocket. Father needs that guy in order to park his ships."

Exhaling, I pushed out my chest and adjusted my shoulders. "But why? What he's doing is good, kind, and humanitarian."

Aaron chuckled. "It is, but it doesn't make any money, and it's dangerous to take Americans into these countries and set up medical facilities. And I use the term 'facility' lightly. They're more of a bunker-tent-type situation. It's only one step. That's *if* he gets Arthur to agree to allow the ships to come in and out and lose that revenue in trade plus manpower for the cause. Not an easy feat. He also has to get the freighter company, the doctors, missionaries, armed forces for protection, etcetera.

There's a lot more at stake than you think."

Wow. Warren really was a modern-day superhero. Taking medicine to third-world countries, taking dangerous risks for the good of mankind. It's extremely powerful, and for once, I felt really good about being with this client.

"So, how can I help?"

Aaron lifted a hand and petted my cheek with his thumb. "You can relax. Being here, you're making him one of the big boys with his pretty toy."

I was certain my eyes blazed white-hot fire when he said that, because Aaron laughed and quickly responded.

"Not that we think you're a toy. Jeez. Touchy one."

I rolled my eyes and huffed. "Sorry. Maybe I am a little off my game. This is different than what I'm used to."

He leaned a bit closer, enough that I could smell the sweet notes of apples and expensive leather from his cologne. "And what are you used to?" His tone was alluring and spoke directly to the woman in me.

Tipping a bare shoulder and looking over it, I batted my eyelashes. "It's different for everyone."

"Is that right? And if I wanted to test the waters of *different* while you're here... Would that be something you are interested in? With me, not my father."

I pinched my lips and inhaled audibly. Tipping my head, I looked directly into his chocolate eyes. This man was not shy. Desire, lust, want, and greed softly traced every inch of my skin at the way he looked at me. Shivers of excitement rippled from my chest to rest heavily between my legs. He moved his hand to my knee, making slow circles over the bare skin. That excitement I'd felt mere seconds ago was turning into a swirling pot of nervous energy. Anticipation was a fun game the debonair Aaron Shipley seemed to enjoy playing. He was definitely stellar at the art of seduction. I was seduced...big-time.

Before I got completely lost and leaned forward and took a bite out of what I now had a burning need to sink my teeth into, Warren came back. A huge smile lit his slightly wrinkled face.

He clapped his hands. "Champagne, good man. We have reason to celebrate!" he announced.

The bartender handed him a glass of the bubbly.

"Is that so, Father? Do tell. The anticipation"—his eyes flicked to mine, a heated look still burning bright—"is positively stifling."

Warren spent the next half hour breaking down the agreement he'd come to with Arthur Broughton about the ports. Turned out that Arthur needed a solid charitable write-off and the positive press for his company. He'd been dealing with some bad media about his trades with Asia. News that he would be offering his ports to import medical necessities, supplies, and professionals to countries in dire need of Western medicine was a good business decision and one he couldn't afford to pass up.

"Thank you, Mia. You're already helping me get where I need to be with the program."

I turned my head and frowned. "How do you figure? I didn't do anything."

"On the contrary. Arthur had been avoiding me because he thought I had an issue with another business deal he was making with a competitor of Shipley, Inc., which is completely apocryphal."

Aaron nodded. I pretended I knew what apocryphal

meant but gathered it likely had to do with something being false or untrue.

"You gave me a perfect road to open conversation with him. We spoke of you momentarily and then moved right into business matters. Worked like a charm." He smiled wide and drank the rest of his champagne.

There was really nothing more I could say. This entire scenario was outside my comfort zone. Rolling with the punches would be my only option. I held up my glass in a mock cheers. "Glad I could help then." I laughed and finished off my drink before we took our leave.

The night had been long and the conversations boring. A few weeks of this was going to be as dull as the historical section of a local library. It was going to be full of nothing but old men, business deals, and gold-digging skanks. I needed to figure out a way to be more helpful.

I pondered that very question while I walked through the vast, dark halls of the mansion later that night in search of the kitchen. A soft light shined at the end of one stretch of hallway. Art and sculptures from different centuries were displayed every ten feet. The house felt more like a museum of art than a home. There were no snapshots or photographs of the family donning the walls. No memorabilia that I could attribute to Aaron's youth. There were just stodgy antiques and pricey artifacts that didn't seem to have any personal value. They were clearly relics of times forgotten by the house's inhabitants or just used for opulent decoration. It made me sad because some of these pieces were true gems. They should be elevated and highlighted, not placed to fill space in a vast and mostly empty mansion.

The hall ended up leading to a lavish, grand kitchen.

Stainless-steel appliances, with four glass doors you could see through. One set of doors had milk, cheese, fruit, and veggies. The normal suspects you'd see in a fridge. The other set had fresh flowers of all varieties.

"Oh, I didn't see you there," came a lilting voice from my side. I turned and found the house manager, Kathleen.

I smiled and waved. "Couldn't sleep. I haven't really adjusted to the time change yet."

She entered the room, went over to the cabinets, and pulled down a couple of plates. "Would you like a sandwich?"

My mouth watered. "Boy, would I ever. I've only eaten gourmet foods the last two days. A plain old turkey and cheese would be heavenly."

Kathleen smiled softly, but it didn't reach her eyes. Every couple of moments, her blue eyes would glance my way. With practiced ease, she made us both a sandwich. Still, she didn't say a word, but I could tell something was on her mind.

"You know, you can ask me anything. I'll answer honestly. I'm getting the feeling you don't know why I'm here."

She shook her head, crossed her hands over her robe-clad chest, and dropped her gaze.

"I'm an escort. Warren hired me," I answered honestly.

Kathleen's eyes went as wide as an endless blue sky. Her hand went to her heart, and she braced herself on the butcher-block counter. "I see."

I couldn't help myself. She obviously had something going with the Senior Shipley. "It's not what you think..." I started, but she backed up until her bum hit the fridge.

"Doesn't matter what I think. I'm uh... I'm just the help." Her eyebrows narrowed, and she whispered again, "I'm just the help."

Leaning a hip against the counter, I waited until she looked at me. Tears pooled in her eyes, and it broke my heart. "I'm not sleeping with him. It isn't like that."

Her head snapped back. "But you're an escort. You just said—"

I cut her off. "I said I was an escort. Hired to attend functions with him, as his personal arm candy, not his bedmate. It seems he already has that part covered." I smiled, and she blushed.

"I don't know what you mean." Kathleen grabbed the lapels of her robe and covered more of her chest, even though not even a speck of skin was visible.

"Sure you do." It was becoming very clear to me. On top of the table sat the two sandwiches she'd made. One was twice the size of the other. Uh-huh. "Who's the sandwich for?"

Again, those sweet cheeks of hers turned a nice shade of rose. "I'm quite hungry."

"Yeah, I'm hungry after a round of great sex, too. Go take your man his sandwich. Your secret is safe with me." I grabbed the plate with the smaller sandwich and turned to go back to my room. Late-night TV was calling my name.

"Mia, he doesn't want anyone to know. It would hurt him."

That got my attention, and I spun around on a toe. "Hurt him? How?"

Her shoulders sagged. "I raised Aaron after his mother died. He wouldn't understand. His father and I agreed not to tell him. Besides, I'm not a woman of wealth. All the men in business have wives who are in the life. I'm a nobody."

I reached out a hand to her, but she backed away.

"It's fine. I chose this. If I wasn't madly in love with him, I'd have left already. It's better that I have him under the cover of night than not at all."

Of course I disagreed wholeheartedly, but when I started to reply, she clasped my arm and got close.

"Thank you for your concern, but you don't know either of us. We'd appreciate your discretion in this matter." She waited while I stood there, not certain what to say.

"If that's what you want," I finally said.

"It is. Thank you. We'll visit in the morning. Mr. Shipley notified me he has a list of events that he plans to take you to. I'm glad I know why you're here. Thank you for your honesty, Mia. It is a refreshing trait around these parts." Her lips formed that small smile I'd seen in the office when I met her yesterday and now twice this evening. I had to admit, it worked at keeping me calm. She left me standing there with my sandwich and a potential side project. Of course, I needed to find out if Warren felt the same about the lovely housekeeper as she did about him. I'd also have to feel Aaron out as to his thoughts about Kathleen and their history.

I had a strong suspicion that feeling out young Shipley was going to be a tough job, but someone had to do it. I snickered at my own lame joke and headed for the maze of hallways leading back to my room. Tomorrow was a new day.

CHAPTER THREE

Half asleep, I walked through the doors of what I assumed was the dining room. Eureka! I'd found it. As soon as I entered and took in the space, a groan spilled from my lips. Kathleen approached, fully dressed in her pencil skirt, silk blouse, and heels, looking freshly pressed and pristine. Her graying blonde hair was pulled into a tight twist, not a strand out of place. It was seven in the morning, and her face revealed a light dusting of makeup. Tasteful and suited her age and grace just right, but it was seven in the morning. Who looked that put together so early?

Kathleen showed me to a place setting at Warren's left. I sat like an elephant and blew the layers of loose hair off my forehead. Warren tipped the corner of the newspaper down and smiled.

"Morning, Mia. I trust you slept well?" His eyes took in my camisole and cotton pajama pants. Of course I'd brought the bubble-gum-pink tank and multicolored striped pants, looking every day of my twenty-four years. I could be this man's grandchild, and here I was, serving as his date.

I huffed. "I know *you* did," I said knowingly. He set his paper down into his lap and rested his elbows on the solid oak surface.

"It seems you have become aware of some very private information. Would you care to discuss it?" His tone was straightforward with absolutely no hint of concern.

Kathleen looked away as she poured me a cup of coffee and refilled Warren's.

"Not especially. Would you like to discuss why you hired an escort while your girlfriend serves your breakfast?" I answered boldly, knowing I was stepping way over what would be considered appropriate for a woman in my position. The last thing I needed was to lose my bundle of cash before I could ship it off to Blaine, the dirty rat bastard ex of mine.

Warren grimaced, and his mouth tightened, so much so that his lips turned white. "You'd do well to remember your place. Personal matters are none of your business."

He had a serious point. "I apologize. You're right." I wanted to ask Kathleen for a slice of humble pie for breakfast instead of the eggs and bacon she set in front of me. Instead, I cast my head down and picked up the fork. It was heavy and solid. Probably cost more than a month's rent.

Shoveling in the food, I sat and tried to mind my manners. The second Kathleen left the room, I set down my fork and turned to Warren.

"Look, I'm sorry."

Warren folded up the *Washington Post* and set it on the table.

"I guess it's hard for me to understand why I'm here when you have a perfectly beautiful woman ready to do as you bid."

His gaze held mine as he seemed to think about my statement. "Kathleen has been with this family since Aaron was a young boy. She helped raise him when we lost his mother. Only recently have we begun something more." Warren inhaled and then sighed. "Honestly, I'm not even sure how to broach this. Having an affair with the help wouldn't look good for me—or the business. I'm uncertain whether Aaron would accept it or not. He loved his mother deeply. Her passing hit this family hard."

"But it was Kathleen who helped hold it together right?"

"Yes, absolutely. Things would have been much worse without her here to pick up the pieces."

"So then you owe her in a way." His eyes burned at that comment, but I continued. "When I chatted with her last night, I figured it out. She didn't tell me, by the way."

"I've been with Kathleen for over a year, and she's not mentioned anything to a single soul. I know she's trustworthy."

"Then why don't you trust her with your heart? Bring her out into the light. Has she not earned that?"

He ran a hand over his chin as his jaw tightened.

"Maybe you don't love her like she does you? Is she just someone you use to get your dick wet?"

Warren stood up abruptly and tossed his napkin on the table. "I will *not* have you address me with such crude language or accuse me of something so heinous. My time with Kathy is special and...and wait... Did you just say she loved me?" I nodded, and he put his hands in his pockets and rocked back and forth on his heels. "Really? Did she actually say the words?" From angry to pensive in twenty seconds flat. That may be a record for my matchmaking skills.

"Yeah, last night. Said she wouldn't stay with you in a hidden arrangement if she wasn't madly in love with you."

This time Warren sat down in a heavy heap. "I'll be damned."

"You mean you didn't know?" I'm certain my tone was quite shocked, because I was. I'd been there two days, and I'd figured out the woman was head over heels. How could he have been bedding her for the last year and not know? Maybe it was that politician side to him. Always thinking someone had an agenda of their own. The world would be a lot better off if everyone said what they thought and believed in living the Golden Rule.

Warren shook his head and placed a hand over his mouth. "This whole time..."

"Yep. You could have been hitting that for a lot longer." With that, he let out a huge chuckle. "Mia sweetheart, you are definitely a handful all wrapped up in a pretty package, aren't you?"

"A handful?" I shrugged. "I've been called a lot worse." I grinned, and he placed his hand over mine.

"Thank you. I'm not yet sure what to do with this information, but I do know that I need to proceed with my plan. The project will suffer, and after last night's win, we need to strike while the iron is hot. You understand? I need you to do what I've hired you to do."

"You got it. Whatever you need."

"Good. Review this list and plan for the next few week's events. The rest of the time will be your own. I believe Aaron has offered to show you around DC proper if you're interested."

I nodded vigorously. There was no telling when I'd be in our nation's capital again. I wanted to soak up all the sites I could.

Again, he patted my hand. "I'll be busy until Friday. We have a dinner to attend, hosted by local United Nations ambassadors for different nonprofit organizations. Saturday, you're attending a tea held by Arthur's current lady friend. There will be at least ten other women I need you to make friends with. If you're in with them, I'll be invited to events that their men are hosting. Access to these men within their inner circle is crucial to the next phase. Are you up for the challenge?"

I placed my hand at my forehead and saluted him. "Aye aye, sir!"

"Definitely a handful. In the meantime, enjoy spending time with my son. Seems he's rarely around anymore, but with you here, I've already seen him twice in two days. Interesting to say the least."

"Mmm, interesting," I concluded and finished up my coffee. "See you Friday, Warren."

"Until then, Mia."

★ ★ ★ ★

To: Mia Saunders
From: Sexy Samoan
To remember you always.

The text message from Tai was cryptic until another text came through with an image. It was his right shoulder. A shiny brand new black tattoo shone through the image. It was placed on what used to be his bare right shoulder. The Samoan symbol for friendship. The same symbol I'd left for him in the picture I'd had done by a local artist. Tai had tattooed it on his body. For me. On the side that he'd said was just for him. It was large, tribal, and one of the most beautiful things I'd ever seen.

I pressed my contacts and clicked the send button. It rang a few times before a female answered. "Hello, Tai's phone," the female giggled sweetly.

"Um, hi. This is Mia. Tai available?"

"Mia!" the woman responded with a heaping dose of

enthusiasm. "Babe, it's Mia!"

Babe. This woman called him Babe in a way that could only be interpreted as proprietary. I crossed my fingers and waited.

"Who's this?" I asked, hoping I was guessing correctly.

"It's Amy. Remember, you set Tai and me up at the restaurant last week?"

The desire to fist pump couldn't be stopped. Silently, I jumped in the air and did a solid touchdown dance, air fist pump included. Once I'd shimmied enough, I focused on the phone. "Yes, of course. How are things going?" I asked conspiratorially. Never once did I claim I wasn't a typical girl. At least in some aspects, like when we wanted to get the goods.

"Oh Mia, just amazing." Her voice got very low. "I'm totally..." She inhaled. "Just...you know...he is so..." She hesitated again.

"Perfect?" I offered the word-challenged, lovesick girl.

"Yeah. Mia...this last week... It's been unreal. Thank you." Her voice turned breathy, as if she was choked up.

I smiled and swung my arm out and looked out the window onto the rolling landscapes of the mansion. "Don't thank me. It was fate. I'm glad you're hitting it off."

"Tai wants to talk. Bye," she said, but it sounded as if it was yelled down a tunnel, the voice fading out until I heard the most welcome growl.

"Girlie, I see you got my message."

"The tattoo... Tai, that is beautiful."

"As are you and what we had."

That hit me hard, right in the chest where I could practically feel his arms holding me close, bringing me comfort.

"Just because what we shared has changed, it doesn't

mean I want to ever forget it or you. You'll always be welcome here in Oahu as part of my family. Mia, we are friends. Friends to the end. It is the Samoan way. It is my way. Understand?"

I shook my head, smiling wide even though he couldn't see it. "Yeah, Tai. I understand, and I love that about you, your Samoan culture, and your traditional values. So now tell me... How is it with Amy?"

"Been gone less than a week and already diggin' for dirt, eh girlie?"

I loved how, when he used my nickname, it was always a growled "girl" followed by a long "eeee."

"Some things never change." I laughed, and he chuckled.

"So far so good. I think you were right. I may have found it."

Prickles of excitement and that psychic chill one gets when they know something intense is about to be said shuddered through every pore.

"Yeah?"

"Yeah. I found my forever. And Mia, it's so much more than I could have ever dreamed."

My chest tightened, and my heart pounded. "Oh, Tai, I'm so, so happy for you. You deserve it."

"So do you, girlie. When are you going to try and find it?"

"I don't know, Tai. I don't have a psychic mother telling me my future, now do I?"

We both laughed. "Tai, does Amy know?" I pulled at a strand of my hair, tugged it across my face, and bit down on the thick chunk. Disgusting nervous habit and one I usually controlled. Not now though. Both of us knew that the only way we could ever stay friends was if Amy knew about our relationship the month I was there and she was okay with it.

"Relax, girlie, she knows. After the third date, before things got you know...uh...heated."

I giggled but held my breath, wanting to hear it all.

"Before we went there, I told her. Everything."

"Everything? The Jeep, the ocean, the wall?" Mortification swam along my vision, and I could feel the prickles of embarrassment chase their way up my neck and flush my skin.

"No. Christ. I'm not stupid. I was honest. Told her we'd had something very intense—life-changing, even—but it was done, and in its place was a friend for life. Amy gets it. She's not jealous. What she and I have already experienced in a week of being together is so right. Mia...I'm going to marry this girl. Soon. Probably next year you'll be coming back out to the islands."

"I'll be there. Tai, I couldn't be happier. This is well-deserved."

"Thanks, girlie. Do you like the tat?" His voice was a sultry grumble, fishing for compliments. It reminded me of when he'd fished for something else only a week ago, but that had to do with getting into my panties and often.

"Very much." So much so it gave me an idea, a crazy amazing one. Something I'd never done before that would stay with me the rest of my life.

"Thank you, Tai. Tell Amy I said congrats, and let me know when you pop the question. But give it at least a month, okay, lady-killer?"

He laughed that big Samoan timbre, the one I missed terribly after not hearing it for a week.

"Will do. Take care of yourself, and I want regular updates. Every week or two. Promise me."

"Okay, okay. I promise."

"Anything happens to you, Mia, I'm on the first plane out to kick serious ass. I'll protect you, girlie. You need me, I'm there. Amy knows and agrees. What you're doing, your job, it can be dangerous, but I get it. Family's first."

"Yes, Tai. I don't think anyone else gets it the way you do. Family's first."

"Take care of your *tama*, girlie." He used the Samoan word for father. "But until you get a man to be your forever, I'm there. The big Samoan brother you never had."

"From lover to brother?"

He chuckled. "You get the drift. Promise me you'll be safe."

"I'll be safe. Love you, Tai."

"I love you, girlie. Friends for life."

"Friends for life."

I hung up and blew out a long breath. Everyone around me was moving forward, everyone but me. I had another six months to go to finish this with Blaine so Pops could be free. Even though it wasn't what I would have picked for my life, serving as an escort to rich men wasn't really so bad. Thinking back to the very beginning, I'd actually been pretty lucky.

Weston Charles Channing the Third. I snickered recalling how much crap I gave Wes about the numbers at the end of his name. Wes played the dutiful son card well. He was devastatingly attractive, laid-back, hard-working, and took the time to enjoy the simple things in life. My time with him was so much more than I'd ever have believed it could be. He'd made a very scary situation a cake walk. I'd learned to surf and had been shown that not all men are cut from the same cloth.

The men I'd been with before him, the ones I'd devoted

myself to, had completely hurt me, broken me, and made me cynical about love. Wes had restored my faith in men, in the belief that I, too, could have something that every woman in the known universe dreamed of having. True love. Only I couldn't have it now. But with Wes, I'd experienced being made love to for the very first time, and it was something I'd never forget or forsake. That night was the most beautiful moment of my life. I finally felt whole...loved. No matter what the future brought, I would always have that.

Alec Dubois, my filthy-talking Frenchman, was the second. God, he was lovely. From his long hair to his unique man-bun, coupled with the beard and mustache combo, he was nothing but yummy. The reminder of all that thick, rich hair sent bubbles of desire tickling along my spine. Thinking back, I'd spent most of an entire month attached to his hip, and I didn't mind. The work he'd done, the art he'd created, would show the world a piece of me that I'd never been able to demonstrate. The vulnerable, the imperfect, the lonely, the wanton, and the lost woman I'd become over the last twenty-four years was so clearly visible in his work. The entire Love on Canvas campaign was me, and for the first time, I'd felt beautiful. He'd made me see myself in a new light, and I'd liked it. Too much. Better yet, I was okay with the world seeing it, and I strived every day now to live up to it.

Tony Fasano and Hector Chavez, my Chicago guys. Odd, but just thinking their names made me feel lonely. With them I knew companionship. I learned that no matter what love looked like or how hard I had to put myself out there and take risks, it had to be done. If what I wanted in life and love was meant to be, it would be worth it in the end. That's something I was holding on to so tightly. I could only dream that one day it would ring true for me.

Mason Murphy, the arrogant, hot-shot baseball player who had a heart of gold if you dug deep enough, ended up being the brother I never had. He liked to pretend that he was someone else, the same way I did, but really, when you got down to the heart of him, he wanted the same things we all did. Friendship, companionship, and a place and a person to call his own. And now he had it...with Rachel. She'd be that and more for him. My time with Mace helped me to realize that trying to be something I wasn't only hurt me and the others around me.

And then there was my sweet, loving, sexy Samoan. God, the space between my thighs ached, remembering how long, thick, and hard he was. He was the biggest I'd had by far, and Wes and Alec were no slouches in the sack. With Tai, it was all about the fun, friendship, and fucking. I'd had more sex with him in one month than most single women—or couples for that matter—probably had in a year. We couldn't get enough of each other. It was as if we'd both had something to prove. After all was said and done, that time together cemented our friendship in a way that we never could have without that physical connection. I knew for the rest of my life, he'd be there. His culture and the type of love he gave his friends was all-encompassing and didn't have time limits.

Remembering each month of this past year and the experiences I'd had solidified my idea. If I didn't do it now, I'd never do it.

Leaving my room, I fled down the staircase and skidded to a halt.

James looked up from his desk in the sitting room. "Ms. Saunders, do you need a lift?"

"I do! Do you have time now?"

He tipped his chin. "Of course." He held out a hand, gesturing that I walk ahead.

Once we were in the Town Car, I pulled out my phone, did a Google search, and found exactly what I was looking for.

"Where to?" he asked as we drove down the long, winding estate road.

"Place called Pins N Needles."

"The tattoo shop?" he said with surprise.

"Yep. Hurry, too, before I change my mind."

CHAPTER FOUR

The buzz of the tattoo needle filtered through the low hum of the shop. A few stations had patrons sitting in black leather seats similar to mine. One guy was getting lightning bolts tattooed along the side of his head where he'd shaved off all his hair. Only a thin patch of fuzz ran straight down the middle of his dome. There were nickel-sized gauges in his ears and more metal on his face than the crotch rocket he'd ridden in on. The bike was sweet. Made me miss Suzi back home. Again, I looked at the fella who thought it a good idea to tat his head.

While the needle bit into my flesh, I wondered what the guy planned to do about those earlobes when he was seventy. They would certainly be hanging flesh by then, especially if he stretched them any farther. I guess that wasn't something a twenty-year-old skinhead type cared about. Probably didn't even think he'd live to see seventy, and by the looks of him, twitching like he had somewhere to be right this very second, he was on the fast track to an early grave.

Down the aisle, there was a Barbie-doll-looking chick getting what was probably her man's name inked into a decent tramp stamp. I snickered under my breath, knowing that the moment a person got a tat with their man's—or woman's—name, it was the kiss of death. The person getting the tat didn't think it applied to them, and they could test fate with it. Not wise. The laughter caused my foot to jiggle, and I winced as the artist held on tighter to my left ankle. The black swirling text was almost finished, and then she'd start the dandelion.

The skin of my foot was already numb. The pain for the first twenty minutes had been a piercing, gnawing sensation that irked as much as it pleasured. That saying about pain and pleasure being flipsides of the same coin was very true. At this point, I was used to both. Every time the artist picked up the gun for more ink and pressed that fiery tip into my skin once more, a little jolt of excitement lit up my nerve endings like sparklers on the Fourth of July.

"So Mask is an unusual name, especially for a chick," I said simply, attempting to strike up a conversation with the small Asian woman working on my tat.

Her smile reached her eyes. It was like looking into a pitch-dark galaxy with nothing but tiny specks of white lights where the starry gases burst into flames. She had bright-red lipstick and a tiny silver hoop through the side of her bottom lip. Her Asian heritage was strong in the pretty shade of her smooth skin against the stark ebony of her hair that she had pulled back into a sleek bun at the nape of her neck. If she didn't have the lip piercing and two tatted forearms, she'd fit perfectly in any of these downtown Washington, DC offices.

Mask tilted her head and focused on the letters of ink she pressed into my skin. "It's short for Maskatun. Mask is easier for Americans." Her voice didn't have even a hint of an Asian dialect.

"You're not American?"

"No, I am. My family and friends can say my full name easier than the tourists and locals who come in to get some ink." She smiled softly.

"Well, I think your full name is beautiful, but Mask is badass, so I'm going with that."

"My family comes from Brunei, in the middle of Southeast Asia, but I'm American."

"I think it's cool."

"Thank you," she said and then sat up and inspected her work, turning my foot this way and that under the bright light. Along the entire side of my foot, from about an inch above the heel to the toe, was the text I'd settled on. It's just above an inch from the sole where I walk. When Mask asked me what I wanted, I knew instantly. We chose a font that suited my tastes, and now that part was done. "Check it out before I start on the dandelion."

I flexed my foot this way and that, grimacing when the skin pulled at the marred flesh. It was beautiful, exactly as I'd pictured it. "I love it."

"Okay, so the dandelion goes here." She ran a finger up the bare spot just above the heel and up the side of my inner ankle about four inches.

I nodded.

"Then the petals blowing in the wind will have each letter you chose as part of the stem. Incognito, right?" Her gaze met mine, and she grinned.

"That's right."

This time I laid back and let Mask do her thing. The prickling sensation started anew the second that gun touched my ankle. It stung, sending a sharp bite of pain through my leg. I gritted my teeth and waited for that pain to turn to pleasure once more. After about ten minutes, I was flying on pure endorphins.

"I've got the W and the A done."

Mask pointed at my foot, where two little wish petals were blowing across the text alongside several others. Only, these two were unique. One had the letter "W" to represent my time with Wes and the other an "A" for Alec.

"How did you want to do the T and the H again?"

"If possible, I'd like both of them somehow intertwined on the same petal wish-type thingy."

Mask looked at my foot, again rotated it back and forth in the light, and nodded succinctly and went back to work. "Finished with the M and the single T, too. I put a couple more plain ones here and here." She pointed to the simple ones interspersed between the special ones. "But you mentioned that you might want to add to this later in the year, so I left some space down the foot."

I nodded. "Yeah, if the year goes as planned, I could have several more petals with new letters to add."

"I think this looks good and doesn't look incomplete, but you can easily have an artist add to it, though I'd prefer it was me. Kind of like having my tats be mine, you dig?"

I held up my hands in peace. "Absolutely. I'll be back toward the end of the year if I need to add to it. I promise." I held out my hand, and she shook it.

"Well, all right. Check it out?"

The dandelion was incredible and realistic. It framed the text so beautifully, showing exactly how much I wanted the saying to pop yet flow with the meaning behind making wishes. Along a gust of wind, you can see each dandelion petal. Five of the fifteen interspersed had a letter intertwined in the stem of the blown petal. Wes, Alec, Mason, and Tai each had a single letter etched into the movement of the stem. Tony and Hector were a TH combo on the same tiny petal.

The importance of having a piece of each man with me, treading that path each day, was not lost on me. It's something

I knew in my heart I needed to get me through the remainder of the year. Having those men, the first letter of their name, hovering around the text that had become my own personal theme was utterly perfect. I looked down at the text, admiring the statement as it became a part of my life and truth, forever printed on my body.

Trust the journey...

★ ★ ★ ★

My foot ached as I made my way back into the house and limped up the stairs toward my room.

"Sweet heavens, what happened? Did you hurt yourself?" Kathleen rushed up the steps and took hold of my shoulder, cradling me into her chest as I limped up the remaining steps. She helped me get to my room, which took an inordinate amount of time. Every step hurt more than the last and more than the entire process of getting the tattoo altogether.

I hopped on one foot once we made it to my room and landed in a heap on the bed.

"What's wrong?" she said, inspecting every inch of my body until finally settling her gaze on the shiny area of my foot where Mask had slathered petroleum jelly. "Oh, my. It seems you've done this to yourself, then." She leaned down close and inspected the area. "It's very beautiful, and it looks like the meaning behind the text is very important to you."

I smiled around a grimace. "It is. Thank you. I don't know. I woke up today and just knew what I had to do. Since I don't have to be at an event for another few days, now was the best time," I told her.

Kathleen nodded prettily. "I'll get you some tea and

cookies. Here, let's get you set up." She lifted a pillow and placed it under my foot delicately, being extra careful of the raw ink. Then she patted a pillow and, with two fingers, had me leaning forward to place one behind my back. "That better?"

Laughing, I tilted my head and took in the lovely woman. Any man worth his salt would scoop her up and keep her for his very own, not hire an escort so he could save face with the big wigs. Momentarily, my opinion of Warren plummeted, but really, it wasn't my place to judge.

"You know, I'm not sick. I just got a tattoo." We both chuckled as she smoothed the blanket around my legs.

"True, but you're in pain. Let me care for you. It will be a nice change of pace for me to spend time taking care of a woman rather than two prickly men who think they can take care of themselves." She winked and treated me to that soft small smile I'd begun to recognize as her own way of communication. Kathleen was a kind woman with a strong will and a gentle manner. I found I liked the quiet way she handled things. For me, she was the epitome of grace. Maybe I could borrow a page or two from her book.

When Kathleen returned, she was not empty-handed. Her arms were filled with items, including wine, not tea, snacks, magazines, and chocolates.

"What's all this?" I asked as she set the tray down.

"I rarely get a girls' night, and if you don't mind, I'd like to get to know you better."

I smiled and shimmied in place. "Heck yeah. Hand me a glass of the good stuff."

Her eyes lit up and sparkled like a ten-carat diamond. "And it is the good stuff. Taken directly from Mr. Shipley's private stash."

My eyes widened. "Are you sure we should be drinking it? He won't get mad when he sees a couple of bottles missing?"

She shook her head emphatically. "I'm sleeping with the boss. I have my ways of buttering him up. 'Sides, he said I could have whatever I wanted, and I happen to know these have been sitting awhile. He doesn't like Zinfandel as much as I do."

"Aww, I see. How does that work anyway?"

Her eyebrows rose in question.

"The part about banging your boss?"

I chuckled, and she followed suit. Though I knew damn well how it went to hit the sheets with the man paying your salary. Then again, I hadn't stayed with any of them longer than a month, whereas she's been around for decades.

Slowly, she inhaled and sat down on the bed next to me, propping herself up with the plush pillows. She sipped a bit of wine and seemed to mull the question over. "It's not as bad as it sounds. Warren and I have been friends for thirty years. I was enamored with him when he was still with his wife. And then when she died, well, he needed me. It wasn't until years later that we started a covert relationship. Now, I share his bed most nights." Even though what she said sounded like they were in a full-blown relationship, there was something she was hiding.

"Then why do I get the feeling that things aren't what they're cracked up to be?"

She shrugged and sighed. "I guess I just figured by now, we'd be out in the open. That he wouldn't be embarrassed to be with me." Her eyes got glassy, and she sniffed softly.

I shook my head. "I do not get the impression that he is embarrassed to be with you. But I will say, I've been to these events, and you'd be the odd duck out for sure." I looked over her beautifully pressed blouse, her frilly apron, and her figure-flattering pencil skirt. Definitely. She was leagues above the young tarts the men in Warren's group paraded around. Women just like me. With effort, I choked back a gag.

"I see," were the words she said, but they could have just as easily been a cursed challenge, except that she was far too classy.

Placing my hand on her forearm, I held her tight until her gaze reached mine. "You don't see, but I'll show you." Looking like a woman with ants in her pants, I reached back under me and yanked my phone out of my back pocket. Then I pulled up the image I'd sent Ginelle last week. "This is what you're up against." I handed her the phone.

For long moments, she inspected the image. "These women are young enough to be their daughters." A slightly shaky hand lifted in front of her mouth. "Some possibly even their granddaughters."

I nodded. "Yep. That's why I'm here."

A horrified look crossed her face.

"No, nuh-uh, not because of what you think. His reasons are actually really altruistic."

That's when her do-I-look-stupid face graced her features, along with an eye roll.

"Okay, it's weird, but I get it. He needs his own bimbo"—I ran my hands in the air closely over my form—"to make him look like he's one of them. It's all for a good reason, though. He has this project that he needs these rich guys and a bunch of stodgy politicians to support so he can get medicine and vaccines to third-world countries."

Recognition must have dawned on her because she started to nod and lean closer. "You know, he mentioned this project. It's been in the making for years. I honestly thought he'd given up on it." Then she huffed. "Yet another thing he's doing in *her* memory." The tone when she said "her memory" seemed put-out and on the ugly edge of scathing.

My eyes narrowed. "What do you mean, 'in her memory'?"

Right then, Kathleen responded in a way I would have never pictured. She tipped her wine glass up to her lips and glugged back the crimson liquid until it was gone. "Ketty Shipley."

"Who's Ketty Shipley?" I asked, completely lost.

"Warren's dead wife."

"Oh, *that* Ketty Shipley." With that, I sucked back the last of my wine and waited a moment. "So why the nastiness?"

Kathleen rubbed her forehead and pulled out the hidden clip. To my extreme surprise, a wild mane of long hair fell well past her shoulders in beautiful, big, bouncy waves. With a shake of her head, she ran her hands through it a couple of times and groaned. "It's not that I didn't like her. For a while, she was my best friend. It's that I don't like that she's been dead for twenty-five years, and Warren is still in love with her. You can't win the man's heart when it still belongs to his dead wife."

Her shoulders slumped, and I looped an arm over hers and locked her to my side. "Honestly, it can't really be that bad."

"Oh no," she said mockingly. "You think I'm full of piss and vinegar, then?" With a burst of energy, she was up and out the door. I sat there completely dumbfounded. What the hell did piss and vinegar have anything to do with it anyway? I swear, older folks said the weirdest shit.

A few minutes went by, and I worried that I'd offended her. I played out the conversation, and although it was uncomfortable at best, I hadn't said anything inappropriate that would cause her to rush out of the room. Before I could go over it again, the door was flung open and she pushed in a food cart. The same kind that you get when you are staying in a really fancy hotel and the bellman brings your dinner.

"What's this?" I asked, even more confused.

In a second, she was at the side of the bed. "Come now. Let's hop along." She patted the top of the cart. "I have to show you something that will prove my point."

"What point?" I hopped up, and then she helped me sit down on the cart. Then she pushed me out of the room and down the hall.

"The point that he's not over Ketty!"

Gripping the cart, I cringed. "If I say I believe you, will you not scare the hell out of me by dragging my gimpy ass around this McMansion on a deathtrap? If you accidentally push too hard, I could end up flying down the stairs."

She stopped and then patted me on the back. "I used to run Aaron around the house in this all the time. He loved it. It's perfectly safe. No worries. Besides, we're heavily insured. You'd end up set for life if you were truly injured while in the Shipleys' employ."

That did not make me feel any better. "Not if I'm dead!" I countered.

"Relax, we're here." She stopped at a set of double doors at the end of a very long hallway and pulled out a set of keys from her apron. When I say a set of keys, I mean a ring filled with so many keys it could keep a locksmith with fattened pockets for another couple of decades.

With a quick flick of her wrist, she unlocked and opened both the doors. I slid off the cart onto my good foot and then tiptoed into the space. The taut skin still smarted, but the wine had helped.

Once I got into the center of the room, I stopped and looked around. The room was gargantuan. It seemed to take up the entire end of this side of the mansion. It had to be two thousand square feet alone. Along two full walls was picture after picture of a dark-haired, blue-eyed young woman, spanning what looked like her teenaged years all the way to approximately her thirties. I slowly made my way to one of the walls and fingered a couple of the framed images. The woman shared an amazing resemblance with Aaron. In some of the photos, the young lady was holding Aaron, who looked no more than three or four.

As I scanned the rest of the space, I saw there was a vanity set up. A brush, comb, makeup, and other lotions and perfumes sat, as if waiting for the woman who owned them to sit and prepare herself for a night out. Moving along the side, I saw that another area hosted a wide glass case. The case was at least six feet in length by two feet wide. Within were incredible sets of earrings, necklaces, bracelets, rings, the likes of which would be found in a high-end jewelry store. They were all top-notch, obviously very expensive pieces that would sell for tens of thousands of dollars and possibly more.

Farther down the room was rack after rack of women's clothing. None of them had even a speck of dust on them, even though they had to be decades old, yet they were hung as if ready to be worn by their owner.

More things hugged the walls, books, knick-knacks, picture after picture of Aaron as a small boy, all the things that would have made a home were in this one room.

"What is this place?" I asked Kathleen, practically losing my ability to speak as shock closed my throat, the words coming out whispered and breathy.

Kathleen leaned against the vanity and traced the golden-handled brush. "Exactly what it looks like."

With a sarcasm-laced tone, I responded. "Jesus Christ! It looks like a shrine to a dead woman."

"Ketty Shipley lives on, even though she's been dead for twenty-five years."

CHAPTER FIVE

"What the hell are you two doing in here?" the irate voice of none other than Warren Shipley growled behind me, and I spun around.

"Um, I'm sorry, Mr. Shipley," Kathleen started to explain, but I cut in.

I shrugged and hopped over to him. "Sorry, Warren. I got curious. It was the only door in the whole house that was locked. Now I know why. Kathleen was just telling me how inappropriate it was for me to enter your private space." Plastering on an apologetic smile, I glanced at Kathleen and patted Warren's chest as if what I saw was no big deal. It was. Huge, in fact. "Your secret is safe with me," I added and moved to the hallway. "Uh, my foot hurts, so I'm going to turn in."

Warren must have gotten over his shock at being caught with a shrine to his dead wife and stopped me with a hand to my arm. "What happened to you?"

"Nothing." I lifted up my foot. The hall light shined on the black ink. "Got a tattoo today."

Apparently shock was an easy thing with this guy, for he gasped and held my foot aloft, taking a gander at the ink. I was getting tired of holding it up, when he lifted me up in a princess hold and set me back on my cart. "Convenient this food cart with wheels is sitting right here, isn't it?" His bushy eyebrows lowered in a frown.

"Um, yeah. I was going to find the kitchen and make

myself a meal, but trying to hop on one foot and carry a plate would have been a disaster." I smacked the metal cart and was satisfied when it made a gong noise. "Found this baby, and voila! Figured it would work like a charm. Plus, I can lean against it and push off with my good foot." I gave my best grin-pout combo.

"Uh-huh," he mumbled, unconvinced. Based on his tone, I didn't think he bought my layer of lies, but so far, he hadn't stopped me.

Kathleen, however, wasn't about to play games. "Sorry, Mr. Shipley. I'll take Mia back to her room to rest."

"I expect to see you back at my room so we can discuss this, Kitten."

Once we were out of earshot, I tipped my head back and looked at her upside-down as she pushed me along the hallways. "Kitten?"

Her lips moved into that sweet, small smile. "Nothing out of you. You're getting me in all kinds of trouble."

That got my attention. "Me!" I scoffed. "You're the one who just had to show me how he wasn't over the dead wife. That we got caught was all on you! I tried to save your ass."

Kathleen chuckled softly, and it sounded like tinkling little bells. "Oh sweetie, if I wanted my ass saved, I wouldn't still be here after thirty years, now would I? I'm perfectly happy with the location of my ass as it is."

There was an undertone of discontent. That shrine proved he was, in fact, not over Aaron's mother. Maybe some people just never got over their first love. Shit, I hoped that wasn't the case. I'd had a pretty shitty first love. I'd had a lot of pretty stellar dives in the crap pool that was my love life. Hopefully, God would take pity on me and send me the right man. The man who would take it all away and everything with him would just be...effortless.

My phone buzzed in my back pocket, startlingly loud against the metal of the cart. Both Kathleen and I jumped out of our skin and then laughed about the silliness of the situation. We'd been caught trespassing into a very whacked-out, secret space. She was pushing me around the McMansion on a food cart after I'd permanently marked my own body, and now we were scared of things that buzzed in the night. The scene was comical. No doubt we could make some money on Broadway with this shtick.

When we reached my door, I thanked Kathleen for the lift, hopped into my room, and fell to the bed, phone in hand.

To: Mia Saunders
From: Wes Channing
I dreamed about you last night. We were in my pool again. Sky was nothing but midnight and bright stars. You were laid out, legs spread wide, and my mouth was doing that thing you loved. Remember that? Remember how easily I could make you melt? Make you come with just my mouth? God I miss that. Your taste on my tongue. Like pure honey. Tell me, are you thinking of me right now?

To: Wes Channing
From: Mia Saunders
Yes.

To: Mia Saunders
From: Wes Channing
Prove it. Show me.

Holy mother of hot men. I read Wes's words at least five times. Enough that I felt twitchy, like my body was roasting from the inside out. He wanted me to show him. I'd never sexted before. The idea had some serious merit. I was horny, and he obviously was. What would it hurt? That little voice inside my head that said this would only complicate things prodded at my subconscious like a woodpecker against the trunk of a tree.

Tap, tap...tap, tap...tap, tap.

Like the idiot I was, I pulled out a mental BB gun and shot that woodpecker off its perch and shimmied out of my clothes, leaving nothing on but my bra and panties. A hot-pink set that had scalloped lace edges. He was going to lose his mind at this getup. Holding the phone at my chin, I crossed my legs, making sure they looked casual yet sexy in the soft light, and took a picture.

To: Wes Channing
From: Mia Saunders
How's this?

I sent the picture and started caressing my thighs with just the tips of my fingers, running them up and down my legs and higher. Once I reached my breasts, I cupped them and squeezed more roughly than I would normally, but I was imagining the way Wes would touch them. He couldn't get enough of my body, and often, when he was insane with lust, he'd hold on to me like I was the last woman on Earth. Roughly and with manly intent. I loved those times. They made me feel desired, wanted, like nothing in the world would come

AUDREY CARLAN

between us.

The phone pinged, and I scrambled to lift it up. Oh sweet baby Jesus and all things good, kind, and delicious.

To: Mia Saunders
From: Wes Channing
Now you've made me hard.

The picture he attached mimicked mine, only he was in a pair of swim trunks that were delightfully tented. His abs were on full display, and at that moment, I would have given anything to run my tongue along each ridge of muscle, especially the very large appendage raising his shorts.

Wetness pooled between my thighs. Ribbons of heat and desire roared through my limbs. I rubbed my thighs against one another, attempting to relieve some of the tension, but the friction just added to the need.

To: Wes Channing
From: Mia Saunders
I wish you were here. I'd take care of that big problem you've got.

To: Mia Saunders
From: Wes Channing
Would you now? Looks like we're going to have to use our imaginations. Starting with your hands. Pull down the cups of your bra and touch your breasts. Christ, they're sexy and soft. Remember how it felt when I'd push the fabric down and lift each one to my mouth? How I'd bite just enough to get you squirming? Pinch those sweet pink tips for me. Wet your fingertips and start

soft, and then hard, just like I would.

Jeez Louise. The man was three thousand miles away and had the power to make me come with just a simple text. Lost in the haze of lust that only Wes could pull off from this distance, I pressed down the fabric of my bra. My breasts were full, heavy, and ready to be worshipped. Licking my fingertips, I closed my eyes and swirled them around the erect peaks. Then, like he'd said, I wrapped thumb and forefinger around the tips and tugged, elongating them before pinching the tissue. I cried out at the intense sensation that rippled through my chest to settle heavily between my thighs. The material of my panties was soaked, my pussy clenching around nothing but air, feeling empty, needing to be filled.

Another text came through.

To: Mia Saunders
From: Wes Channing
Are you wet, sweetheart? Achy, ready to be fucked hard?

My fingers fumbled, and my breath came in heavy pants as I typed back.

To: Wes Channing
From: Mia Saunders
This is torture.

To: Mia Saunders
From: Wes Channing
I know, baby, but just stay with me. Slide your hands down your tiny waist. Swirl a finger around your belly button and

tickle the skin the way I did. You remember? Of course you do. Slide that hand down to where you miss me most, but don't enter that bit of heaven just yet. Play with your hot little clit. I'll bet it's hard as a rock for me. Small, tight, rounded flesh. If I was there, I'd lick it until you came. I'd swirl my tongue around that hot button of nerves and suck so hard your legs would clamp around my head, caging me in, keeping me there. Play with yourself now.

Gone. Completely lost in the fantasy, I did exactly what he said. Tickled my stomach, sliding a wet fingertip around my naval the way he'd lick me on his path to what he called Heaven. My breath was labored, coming in soft pants. I could feel the wisps of hair against the tingling tips of my breasts, jutting out, the nipples zipping with the need to be touched, sucked, and bitten. Slowly, I allowed my hand to trail beneath the lace covering my sex. Wet. Practically dripping. Only Wes was capable of doing that to me. Just words in a text turned me into a melting pot of pure need. The need for him to touch me. Taste me. Make love to me. Doing as he said, I played with my clit. Flicking the little button teasingly the way Wes always did before he went to town.

Another text came in.

To: Mia Saunders
From: Wes Channing

I'm imagining your taste and stroking my cock thinking of you, of your pussy. Your cunt would be warm, sweet, and juicy, like a peach off the tree. Remember how I'd cover as much of that tasty pussy as I could with my mouth and suck on you...

Oh fuck. His words lit a fire so hot it was burning through

three thousand miles of space. I continued reading while pinching my clit, tugging on it, rocking my hips back and forth.

To: Mia Saunders
From: Wes Channing

Suck so hard you'd scream. And when you came, I'd start all over again. By the time I was done with you, your cunt would be crying to be filled. Is it that way now? Ready for my dick? I'll bet it is. I know that greedy pussy. It wants to be jammed full of hard cock. Don't be shy. Push two fingers in hard, sweetheart. Pretend it's me thrusting into you that first time.

I couldn't stop. It was as if I was a marionette and he the puppet master. I shoved two fingers in hard, just like he'd instructed, and cried out at the small sting of the fast intrusion. The pain only lasted a second. It was just enough to trick my mind into thinking he'd entered me, except that two fingers were a very small comparison to Wes's package. Right now, it would have to do.

To: Mia Saunders
From: Wes Channing

Do your fingers feel good, sweetheart? Not as good as it would feel to have me there. Now thrust those fingers in and out. Take your other hand and pluck that little clit I love to nibble on. Fuck yourself until you come. Come for me, sweetheart.

I was helpless to resist. My fingers moved on autopilot, my mind using the images he'd conjured. Tingles broke out over my skin as a fine mist of sweat tickled the surface. Every pore gasped with the intensity of pleasure ripping through my

AUDREY CARLAN

system. Heat built until pleasure coiled low, spiraling from the center and out until nothing but sparks of multicolored lights blasted across my closed eyelids. As the orgasm took hold, its claws scratched and shredded along my nerves until the euphoric edge hit home and the release splintered through me.

A few more jerks, my hips arched off the bed, and the newly inked skin screamed in agony as the last dredges of bliss spiraled along each limb. I finally came down into a lifeless heap.

To: Mia Saunders
From: Wes Channing
You asleep?

I laughed at Wes's last text.

To: Wes Channing
From: Mia Saunders
Sorry. You took me for quite the solo ride.

To: Mia Saunders
From: Wes Channing
I was right there with you, sweetheart. You weren't alone. Came harder, imagining you touching yourself thinking of me, than I have since Chicago.

And that was all it took to pop the pristine little bubble of happiness he'd created for me.

Chicago.

That was the last time we'd been together physically. Three long months ago. Since then, I'd had a booty call with

Alec and a month with Tai. All the while, he'd been with the sultry actress, the same one who all the celebrity mags were calling this year's most beautiful woman alive. And my Wes was fucking her. Regularly. It was only a matter of time before he cut me loose. Maybe I should make it easier for him. Cut him loose first.

If I was being honest with myself, I didn't know if I could cut off Wes forever. There was too much there. Things left unsaid and undone, all while attached with the weight of a promise for more. A promise I'm not sure either of us could keep for another six months. For such a short time with him, it felt like years of history sat between us.

I couldn't do this over text. With a deep breath and a sigh, I hit the "Call" button on my phone.

Wes answered, a sleepy timber to his voice. "Hey, beautiful. I figured you'd be avoiding what happened between us for at least a week or two?" He chuckled, and the sexy sound went straight to my overtaxed libido. Criminy, all the man had to do was breathe, and I wanted him with a fierceness that was unmatched by any other.

"Wes, we should talk about this. What we're doing to one another..." I let the statement hang heavily between us.

He sighed aloud, a deep rumbling noise. It reminded me of when I would lie on his bare chest and listen to the beat of his heart and the sound of his breath moving in and out of his lungs. One of the most soothing places in the entire world was being lost in his arms. If only the rest of life could be that comforting.

"Let's not make this more than it is. Two people who have a mutual affection for one another, taking the edge off."

I huffed. "So that's how you want to play this?"

"I'm not playing anything. Nothing has changed. You know where I stand. I know where you stand. That doesn't mean we can't meet in the middle now and again to remember how good it can be."

The man had a point. "I'm so tired."

"What's the matter, sweetheart?"

Wes had a way of lulling me into complacency. Making me believe that this thing between us could just be. For now, I had to trust in him and in that. "Washington, DC is filled with nothing but gold-digging whores and stuffy old dudes with too much money and far too much power."

He laughed out loud. "You speak the truth. So what's the problem? The guy you're with want you to be something more than an escort?"

I shook my head and made a gagging sound, which was reciprocated by his rich laughter. I loved every bit of it. Without even trying, he made the air seem lighter. "Warren is a good guy. Not at all interested in me in that way."

Wes scoffed. "I find that very hard to believe."

"I'm not his type."

"Mia, sweetheart, you're *every* man's type."

I rolled my eyes and twirled my hair, inspecting my tattoo while I thought about what he said. "Whatever. It's just being here is weird. I'm not exactly sure of my place."

"How so?"

"Well, he's hired me to be the pretty piece on his arm so that he fits in with the other rich old dudes. They all have a young woman clinging to them. But he has this woman at home who he's been with for years, and yet he hides her away."

"Huh. That is odd. Why do you think that is?"

I shrugged. "I don't know." The image of the shrine came

flashing across my mind. "Not sure he's over his dead wife. But she died twenty-five years ago. It's weird. And he has this house attendant he's been having a hidden relationship with for years, but he keeps it under wraps. I don't know, I guess the fact that he keeps a woman as his dirty little secret doesn't sit right with me."

"Me either. Think you could maybe make him see the error in his ways? You're pretty good at that."

"Probably be more fun than sitting around his McMansion with nothing better to do than go out and spontaneously get a tattoo." Wes was quiet for so long I had to check the display to make sure the call didn't drop or the phone battery hadn't died. "Wes?"

"Sorry, sweetheart. I was just imagining you with a tat. Shit, you got me hard again."

I grinned. "Maybe we can do something about that."

"Oh yeah?"

"Yeah. Close your eyes and imagine me kissing my way down your chest..."

CHAPTER SIX

"Honey, you spend a spell with the other ladies here while the men and I talk business," Warren said while dropping me off at a table with seven other women.

All of them were dressed similarly. Tight little dresses, hair long and luxurious, and some serious sparkles all over their ears, necks, wrists, and fingers. These women were kept and didn't have any bones about flaunting that fact.

I waved awkwardly. "Hi, I'm Mia."

All but one looked at me with daggers in her eyes. "Hi, I'm Christine Benoit, the only one here married to my guy. The rest of the girls are a little bitchy. They don't like sharing the limelight, do you, ladies?" She puckered her lips, sneered, and lifted her hand to shake mine and nearly blinded me with the size of her diamond wedding ring.

"That's a serious rock!" I exclaimed, grabbing at her hand, lacking total grace or tact. I really had never seen a diamond quite so large.

Her entire face lit up as she held her hand aloft. "I know, right? My *daddy* takes good care of me. Five karats on top another five surrounding my princess there." She pointed to the square-cut diamond blinding me. I needed a pair of sunglasses to view the thing. The rays of light bouncing off seemed to have their own zip code.

"Shut it, Christine. Just because old man Benoit finally put a ring on it doesn't mean you need to rub it in our faces."

I looked over at a scowling brunette. Her ring finger was, not surprisingly, bare of giant jewels. I'm guessing her attitude had absolutely nothing to do with it. I rolled my eyes covertly, pretending to fawn over the ring some more. "It's beautiful, Christine. You said you're married to Mr. Benoit? You're visiting from Canada, right?" A huge buzzer went off in my head.

Ding. Ding. Ding.

Benoit was one of the names that Warren wanted to talk up. Apparently the man had ships set all along the Eastern side of Canada. A port in Yarmouth he said was located on the Gulf of Maine in Southwestern Nova Scotia. It was the perfect location to transport supplies from Canada to the United Kingdom, where they'd be loaded into freight vehicles that could run all the way down to Mali, one of the poorest countries in Africa. I knew this moment was not fate. My opportunity to help had just hit me upside the head in the form of a ten-karat diamond ring on a tiny little blonde.

Christine's surgically enhanced lips widened. "Yes! We're from Canada. My Frances is here on business. I saw you were with Mr. Shipley." She nudged my shoulder. "He's probably the most handsome of all the men here...aside from my husband."

Her head tipped up, gesturing to a man who couldn't be more than five foot eight on a good day. Thank God she was petite. In my heels, I'd dwarf the guy. He had a gray mustache and thick gray hair. At least he had hair. The ratio of hair to men was about fifty-fifty in this crowd. I tipped my head to the side and looked at Mr. Benoit and back at the woman who had to be at least thirty-five years his junior.

"If you don't mind me asking, how old is your husband?"

Her eyes glittered as much as her diamond. No concern

with my question showing on her pretty face. "He'll be sixty-six this year."

"And you are?"

"Twenty-five."

I chewed on that information and sipped at the full glass of champagne I'd tagged before Warren handed me off to the wolves. "And forty-one years' difference in age doesn't bother you?"

She shook her hand. "Gosh, no. He's so good to me. Pulled me right off the streets, set me up with a place to live, helped me get my GED, and then put me in college. Now I have a bachelor's degree and work at Benoit Shipping Inc., our headquarters."

I nodded, once again unsurprised by her story.

"I run all the new marketing campaigns. We share an office, play a little hide the pickle when we're stressed, and then get back to it."

Hide the pickle.

"Did you just say hide the pickle?"

She nodded without any concern for who heard our conversation. The phrase "an open book" rang true with this one. "Yeah, when we get tired, bored, or you know, just want to fuck, he bends me over my desk or his, and then fucks me stupid. He's crazy good and makes me come harder than any partner I've had before. I think it's because he, like, takes those little blue pills. Makes him rock hard all the time. I'm happy to oblige. And you want to know a secret?" The lovely thing was alight with energy and excitement.

A secret. From the woman who fucks a man almost old enough to be her grandfather, who uses the phrase hide the pickle, and has a ridiculously active sex life with an old guy...

Yes, yes, I do believe I wanted to know her secrets. I was certain they were going to blow me into next week.

Christine leaned close to my ear. "We're expecting our first baby."

You know that moment in the cartoon where Yosemite Sam blows his top and smoke comes out of his ears? I felt like that happened to me on hearing she was pregnant by a guy three times her age. It started with a buzzing sensation and the need to sit down. Once settled, she felt my head.

"You're a little warm, Mia," she offered, looking absolutely concerned for my welfare.

"Maybe you can lead me to the rest room and we can chat there." I needed to get this hot tamale alone. Her husband owned the shipping company Warren needed to transport goods to the UK. I took it upon myself to help make that happen. If befriending the pregnant wife was going to help, I'd take one for the team. Besides, she was really nice—if a little misguided.

★ ★ ★ ★

"So you see, these vaccines and medicines are going to save countless lives."

Christine gasped, her hand going over her still-flat stomach. "My goodness. We have to help!" she said with conviction.

I nodded. "Well, maybe you could put in a good word for Warren with Frances?" I suggested, thinking that was the best way.

She shook her head. "Oh no, I'm going to do better than that. She pulled out a cell phone from her purse, clicked a few buttons, and held it up to her ear. "Franny, snookums..." She giggled. "Sure, I'm always ready for your big cock, baby. You know that."

The thought of her getting plowed by the old guy made my mouth sour, the same way it does right before you vomit.

"Oh, I know, snookums. I want it hard too. Real hard. So hard my teeth rattle, but I need to talk to you about something."

I waited while she shared pretty much everything that I'd shared about Warren's project and how they could help. "Yeah, snookums. We'll make it this year's charitable contribution, and I can even run up a campaign about the good work we're going to do with Shipley, Inc." She said another few "uh-huhs" and "mm-hmms," and then turned to the side. Her hand slid from her neck down to her breast, where she cupped it boldly. "Yeah, they need to be squeezed. Thinking about you fucking me here, right now, is making me super needy. Can you come down and lick me? The baby is making me so horny. I know you already fucked me twice today"—she sighed and then whined—"but I need your mouth this time..." She practically jumped up and down and clapped. "Okay, Franny. I'll be in the ladies', wet and ready. Don't keep me waiting, or I'll start playing without you."

Then she snapped off the phone. Her chest was heaving. "We're totally going to do the shipments for the Shipleys."

I wanted to jump up and down and celebrate, but she started grabbing at her boobs in a brazenly wanton way.

"You into threesomes?" she asked distractedly. "Franny loves when we add another one of my friends. Fucks us both really good, and I'm okay with sharing as long as it's not in my marital bed. That's just for us."

I opened and closed my mouth almost as if I couldn't

catch my breath. I really couldn't breathe. The images that were jumping all over each other as I tried to process what she'd said. Christine had just propositioned me for a threesome with her husband—her old, granddaddy-like husband—in a ladies' bathroom. I shook my head. "Um, nope, but I'm really excited about telling my own, uh, daddy, about the Benoits' involvement."

"Cool." And that's when she put a finger to each strap of her already miniscule dress and let it drop to the floor, leaving her standing in nothing but a tiny red thong. Absolutely *nothing* but a thong. What the fuck? I turned around to give her some privacy at the exact moment that old man Francis Benoit entered.

"You starting without me, pumpkin?" he said, sizing his almost naked wife and me up.

"Can't wait. Give me your cock, Daddy. I want to suck on it while you suck on me."

"Girl, what have I told you about getting naked in public places," he scolded, though he didn't sound that upset. "I'm going to dock your allowance for this transgression."

She groaned. "But I can't help it. I need you."

That was most definitely my cue. "Uh, I'm going to go and see my uh...Warren," I said, not able to call him "Daddy" again. It just grossed me out.

When I was just at the threshold of the ladies' room door, I heard Christine sigh and moan. "Gonna ride you so hard. I love you, Franny. I love you. Love fucking you."

"Get on it, pumpkin. That's right. Fuck me until you come hard enough to last until tonight. Jesus this pregnancy is going to kill me," I heard her husband say, his Canadian accent thick and strong. If it was me, I'd definitely be worried about his health. The heart-attack years were definitely upon him, and if he was downing those blue pills with alcohol and tons of rough sex with a twenty-five-year-old, he definitely had something to worry about.

When I exited the bathroom, Warren was waiting for me. His eyes seemed troubled as I grabbed on to his wrist. "Let's get far away from here."

"Why? Francis said he wanted to talk to me about using his ships for the supplies I need to go to Mali."

"I know. I set it all up with his wife. But they're indisposed, and if you go in there, they are going to invite you to join their little public sexy time," I warned.

He cringed. "I see. We should wait for them at the bar, then. You can tell me all about what was said. Shall we?" He held out his arm like the perfect gentleman. Definitely the way a grandfather would to his granddaughter and not his hot piece of ass. Classy guy. At least I'd gotten the good one. Though Francis didn't seem half bad once I got past the fact that he'd married and impregnated a woman three times younger than he was.

I shivered, and Warren stopped, took off his suit jacket, and draped it over my shoulders.

"Thank you."

"Anytime. Now tell me what happened."

★ ★ ★ ★

Apparently scoring the Canadian ships was a huge part of the go-live plan for Warren's project. Together, we sat at the bar at the stuffy event and had drink after drink of incredibly expensive top-shelf whiskey. Even Christine sat with us and sucked on her nonalcoholic drinks, happily enjoying herself. I guess once the edge of her horniness was dulled, she really was a lot of fun.

At nearly two in the morning, James the driver had to hold both Warren and me up as we walked up the stone steps singing a ridiculous rendition of "I'm Henry the Eighth I Am" so loud that, when the foyer lights went on, we were both shocked. Kathleen leaned against a bannister, arms crossed over her chest, lips pinched tight.

"Good night?" she asked, her tone indecipherable.

Warren moved over to her with the quickness of a man half his age. He pulled her into his arms, pulled each hand out, and started dancing with her. Swinging her from one side to the next, dipping her low. I clapped and swayed and then grabbed hold of James, who took pity on me and twirled me around the foyer alongside Warren and Kathleen. The four of us danced for a bit until both of our dance partners led us up the stairs.

"Oh man, wait. Warren, buddy...don't forget to tell Kathleen about that score!"

He laughed as I slumped into James. Without further comment, James lifted me into a fireman's carry, my body a dead weight. I smacked his surprisingly firm ass. "Nice!" I said, and then remembered I still wanted to say something. "Wait..." I smacked his ass again, and he stopped laughing and tried to grab my hands. "And tell her about the gross bathroom sex they had!"

Warren started laughing so hard he sat down in the middle of the floor. I wanted to go help him up, but I was already upside down in my own predicament.

"Kathy, honey, you'll never guess what old man Benoit and his saucy little wife did!" he said.

She petted him on the shoulder. "I'm sure you'll tell me all about it, but first we need to get you to bed."

"You know I'd never share you, right?" he said seriously to her, and James started walking again.

I smacked him hard on the ass again, and this time, he retaliated by doing the same to me.

"Will you stay still? You're heavy enough as it is."

I leaned up, trying to get a glimpse of his face. "Are you calling me fat?"

"Hardly. But drunk off your ass, you're not light as a feather!" he quipped.

Like a child, a cross between a groan and a whine left my lips. "But they were getting to the best part. He was telling her he loves her."

James shook his head and held me tight. Time seemed to fly as he took me to my room more quickly than I would have thought possible. Evaluating the passage of time wasn't my strong suit in my inebriated state. "Everyone knows he loves Ms. Kathleen. He's loved her for ages."

"But the shrine," I countered, my liquor-loosened lips flapping in the wind.

"He didn't know what to do with Ketty's things. He thought maybe Aaron might take on a wife, kids, and want some of that stuff. Besides, he didn't want to hurt his son. He's more sentimental than he lets on." James huffed, seeming almost put out. Regardless, the information definitely changed things. James flopped me onto the bed. He walked over to the dresser and pulled out a tank and pajama pants and tossed them on the bed. "There's your nightclothes. Please tell me you don't need help."

I gave a sexy smile. "You're not offering?" I quirked my

lips again, the whiskey making me stupid.

"Hell no. My wife would take strips off my ass and feed them to our dogs. After her brothers broke every bone in my body," he laughed.

"Aww, you have a wife?" I asked and snuggled into my pillow.

"Yes, I have a wife, a very mean one who rocks my world. I'd never be unfaithful." James unbuckled and pulled off my heels. "Cool tattoo, by the way. Good thing the shoes didn't rub it. Looks almost healed."

"That's good," I said about his wife, not the tattoo. Then, just like any drunk chick who's lost her mind, I shared personal information that I wouldn't normally share in different circumstances. "You know, I have a Wes." I thought back to our sexting earlier in the week, and my body got hot once more.

"You have a Wes," he reiterated, his tone rife with amusement. "I'm guessing that's a man." He said it with a laugh, handing me the bed clothes he'd laid out. More like smacked me in the face with them.

"He's not really mine, but he's more mine than anyone else's."

"I see. Sounds complicated." Boy, he didn't even know the half of it.

Finally, he helped me lean up.

"I think I'm gonna be sick."

He grumbled and helped me to the toilet, where I spent the rest of the night vomiting violently. At some point, James left and Kathleen was there. Like aloe to a burn, she laid a cool washcloth over the back of my neck and soothed me with calm words and light caresses against my hair and spine. My knees ached from pressing into the tile for what felt like hours. I had no sense of time or space. All I knew was that I felt like death.

When the morning rolled around, I had a hangover the size of Texas. My robe hung off my shoulder precariously, and I couldn't be bothered to care. There seemed to be a construction worker jackhammering into my skull with every step I took. I reached the dining table and found that Warren didn't look much better. For the first time, he wore a pair of men's satin pajamas and not a suit. If I had been of sound mind, I would have cracked a joke, but all humor and wit had left me with the last bout of dry heaves.

"You look like shit," I said while assessing him through one eye. The other eye had a piercing nail ripping through my cornea every time the light touched it. Keeping it closed worked best.

Warren's bloodshot eyes looked me over from the rumpled pjs to the top of the rat's nest that I once considered a great head of hair. Not now. Now I couldn't even run a comb through it. When I tried, the strands felt as though tiny little hair gnomes were tugging on each strand individually, trying to separate them from the root. It was a no-go zone until after I dumped a healthy dose of conditioner on it.

"Takes one to know one," Warren grated through his teeth while placing a hand to his temples. "Christ, how much did we drink?"

"Um, I'm going to go with more than our fair share."

Kathleen entered with plates loaded with bacon, sausage, and biscuits and gravy. This was the hangover food for any true drinking champion. I wanted to bow down and kiss her heel-clad feet.

"I so love you." I looked at her like she was the second coming.

She petted my head like I was a faithful pet. "I know, dear. You told me several times last night while you promised you didn't have a threesome with Warren, the Canadian, and... what was the last one...oh yes, the prego."

Warren choked on his coffee, and I groaned. "Sorry about that. I was way over my limit. As in, at least five shots over the threshold."

"You also kept talking about James."

"Our driver?" Warren asked.

"Yes, dear. You said he was hot, nice, and had a mean wife who rocked his world." Her lips turned up into that small smile I'd grown to love.

I shoveled in a huge bite of biscuits lathered in gravy and pointed my fork at her. "That part is true. He admitted that!"

They both laughed, and we settled in to eat. Warren and I both groveled like the useless drunkards we were last night. It was by far one of the strangest breakfasts I'd had in a long time. After that, I hit the shower and went back to bed to sleep off the whiskey.

CHAPTER SEVEN

A tickling sensation sprinkled along my ankle and then up my calf, as though someone was running just their fingertips along the bare skin. I rolled over, and there he was in all his sun-kissed glory. The light hit his shaggy blond hair. And his eyes... Oh good Lord, his eyes shone like perfect pools of cerulean blue. Everything he didn't say aloud could be seen so clearly in the bottomless depths. I wanted to look into those eyes for eternity.

"You're here," I whispered.

"I'm always here." He trailed a calloused finger over my chest where my heart lay beating from within. His touch was like a match, igniting and setting off an explosion within that burned far too bright to contain.

In a blur of limbs, he had me straddling his trim waist and his mouth was on mine. He tasted of the earth, the ocean, and all things beautiful. I nipped, sucked, and licked at his skin as though I'd never get another taste.

"Wes," I said against his lips, my mouth hovering.

"Mia." His lips moved lightly against mine as he spoke.

That was all that needed to be said. Our bodies moved over one another instinctively. Hands trailed over heated flesh. In a whoosh of fabric, my nightgown was up and over my head, leaving me in nothing but a pair of sodden panties. Muscled arms lifted me up until I was hovering over him on my knees, his head so close to the space I wanted him more than anything.

I didn't wait long. Wes lifted up his head and covered my sex, panties and all, putting that talented mouth to work. It seemed as if he had radar on my clit, because his eyes were closed, and when he pushed the bit of fabric to the side, his tongue was all over my O-trigger, flicking the swollen, aching knot of need until I was fucking the air. I grappled for the headboard, my fingers digging into the fine wood as I arched into his mouth, grinding wet flesh all over his face. It only made him hungrier. Wes liked it went I lost control.

"More," I cried out.

"You'll get what I give you...and it's going to be plenty. Widen those legs, sweetheart. I want to taste you deep."

Wes growled and sank his teeth into the fleshy patch at the top of my thigh as he tugged on the thin strings of my panties until the fabric seemed to disintegrate. I howled, my hips jutting forward as I followed his command. Within moments, his mouth was all over me.

Ravaging. Devouring. Claiming.

Each and every time with Wes was unlike the last. Between the two of us, we lost ourselves in one another so much so that there was only one body consisting of two souls.

The ticking sensation tingled against my hip in a swirling, circular pattern.

I twitched and inhaled, my mind trying to bring something to the surface.

A strong hand slid along my ribs, over my breast, taking hold of the back of my neck. "Come back to me, baby. I'm right here." Wes pulled me down while he pressed up, dragging his muscular chest along mine until the tips of my nipples ached and throbbed. His mouth covered one rosy cap. Bursts of pleasure spiraled out and along every nerve. A fresh wave of arousal coated the heart of my sex, readying for the ride of a lifetime. I wanted him. I needed him to fill my body and my soul with his essence.

Wes leaned me back, licking his way from one breast to give attention to the other. He flicked just the tip of his tongue against the tight bud. It tightened and darkened, from a pale dusky pink to a deeper hue. He encased as much of my breast as he could, kneading the heavy tissue surrounding it for good measure. Definitely a breast man, he worshipped the twins like two goddesses to bow down to, and he did, often.

Time seemed to pass, and I looked around, the room no longer familiar. The edges were blurred and hazy.

"Hey...I'm right here. Stay with me. Let me love you."

I shook my head. The tickling sensation crawled up my spine and niggled at the edges of consciousness.

"I don't know how," I whispered, admitting my biggest fear, tears pooling in my eyes.

"I'll show you." He lined up his cock with my center and entered me, inch by glorious inch, until I arched back, laid my hands on his chest, and let the connection bind us. "That's it. Just go with it."

Rocking my hips, I slid up on my knees and then took him back into my body. Again and again. I watched as he closed his eyes, though I wished he hadn't. Those eyes tethered me to him, had a hold on me, but when they weren't there, things changed.

I picked up the pace, roughly jolting up and slamming back down. He groaned and moaned. The room spun as pleasure peaked, and I lost my breath, panting hard, riding him savagely. I cried out and opened my eyes. Everything was a blur as the ecstasy ebbed and flowed, searing through my body on a wave so big I knew it would end me. End the passion, the pleasure, the...the dream.

The tingling sensation warped into a warm hand sliding up and down my back, but it wasn't Wes's. Pleasure spiked hard between my legs, and Wes's body bowed, his hands holding my hips in place as he ground into me. I came, hard, bouncing on his cock as he bathed my womb with his seed. "I miss you." I whispered against his lips, sucking each one separately.

His eyes flew open. "Don't go. I need you," he said at the same time I heard another's voice.

"Wake up, Mia." Then I felt a hand curve around my bare breast. Again, it wasn't Wes's.

Wes shook his head. "Remember me."

Then I opened my eyes, and no longer was I naked and on top of Wes. No, I was still very naked, but this time a cold hand covered my breast, rhythmically squeezing as the other hand slid down my torso and to the thin thatch of hair between my legs.

"Mmm, I like this. Very sexy." The low tone hit my ears. A heavy body weighed me down. The smell of apples and leather permeated the air. I pressed hard into a wall of the finest fabric.

Aaron lifted up, his eyes nothing but dark ponds of lust. "You're awake." He grinned wide and stood.

I gripped the sheet and tugged it over my chest. "What are you doing here, and why the fuck were you touching me?"

Aaron rotated his shoulders, letting his suit jacket slip off his shoulders. Then he folded it and set it neatly on the bench at the foot of the bed. The rational side of my mind wasn't working properly after a night of drinking and a dream involving making love to Wes.

"Don't act like you weren't enjoying it." His tone was

a sneer. "I heard you moaning, sighing, licking those sweet lips"—he tugged the knot of his tie and loosened it—"rubbing your legs together wantonly, as if you were ready to be taken. I have to admit it was enticing as hell." Tie removed, he set it on his jacket and then proceeded to open the buttons of his shirt.

I blinked a few times, trying to clear the cobwebs. "What are you doing?"

His shirt lay open, exposing a broad chest, chiseled abs, and a smattering of hair. If I wasn't so confused about what was going on and half asleep—not to mention the double dose of hangover I had going—I'd have reacted much more quickly.

With his shirt open wide, he placed a knee on the bed, and my eyes widened. "I had a meeting to attend to with Father, but he was busy. Needed a few minutes." He continued to crawl along the bed. "Thought I'd be a good son and check in on our guest." Aaron caged me in, arms on each side of my hips. "To my delight, you were thrashing around in bed, naked, clearly needing something to assuage the tension I could plainly see in your body." He ran a finger along my arm, from my shoulder to my wrist, where I still held the sheet, and I shivered, but not in excitement.

"Aaron"—my voice shook, and his eyes narrowed—"I'm not feeling well. Your father and I drank too much last night. I need to sleep it off. You shouldn't have come in my room without knocking."

He leaned close and ran his nose along my hairline, inhaling my scent. Goosebumps rose along each pore, and the warning bells blared loudly. "I knocked. You didn't answer."

"Because I was asleep."

"I know, but now you're not. Now you're very much awake and very naked. I think we should do something about that."

His lips came down and pressed into the skin of my neck. "Mmm, you taste sweet. Like pure honey."

Pure honey.

I swallowed hard as the vomit rose from my gut and up my esophagus. If he didn't move, I'd throw up on him, which would serve him right for the stunt he'd pulled. I pushed hard against his chest, falling out of the bed, where I barely reached the trash can next to the desk and threw up my breakfast.

"Jesus, you really are sick." Disgust was thick in his tone. He didn't even try to assist me as I heaved into the can, gagging and coughing. I heard the sound of clothes rustling, and I could only hope he was putting his back on. "Kathleen!" Aaron bellowed. "Kathleen, come here. Mia's sick." He continued to holler, the noise piercing my already tender brain.

A clacking noise started out far away and then got closer as Kathleen, in her prim heels, rushed into the room. "Oh goodness gracious. Mia, you poor dear."

Her cool hands on my back were comforting and welcome. Quite the opposite of the way Aaron had touched me, uninvited.

"Handle her. I'll be with Father. Until next time, Mia," he said coolly, leaving the room.

I gagged again. After several minutes of dry heaves, Kathleen helped me up and into the shower.

"Sweet girl. I'm worried you've got alcohol poisoning. Perhaps I should take you to acute care."

I shook my head. "I don't have medical coverage." Actually, I might have coverage now that I worked for my Aunt Millie. I'd have to check. Either way, I was not going to the hospital from drinking too much. "It's okay. Sleep, water, and food are what's going to fix this problem. That and not drinking again for another decade."

She smiled shyly. "Okay dear. Let's get you settled."

Kathleen helped me put on a pair of yoga pants. I insisted on a sports bra this time and a T-shirt. That was the last time I'd sleep naked in this house.

"What was Aaron doing in your room while you were naked and throwing up in the wastebasket?" Kathleen asked softly. Not even a hint of judgment appeared in her tone.

I swallowed and sighed. "I don't know. I think he likes me or whatever. But honestly, he was inappropriate. Touching me while I was asleep. It was creepy." A shiver accompanied the memory.

Her eyes widened, and I knew instantly that I should have kept my mouth shut. A blush rose up from her chest, carrying on to her neck and over her face. Her brow furrowed, and her eyes squinted into little slits. The skin around her lips turned white as she snarled, "He touched you while you were sleeping?"

"Um, not the way you're thinking." Well, technically yes, the way she was thinking was accurate, but it wasn't enough of a something for me to do anything about it.

"That's sexual assault. His father is going to go berserk!" Her tone was so sharp I swear it could cut glass.

I shook my head and placed my hands on her shoulders. "It's okay. I'm fine. He was a little inappropriate, yes, but we'd been flirty the last couple of times we'd seen each other. I handled it. Everything is fine. There is no need to make a big deal out of this. It won't happen again."

Her eyes were glacial, hard. "Mia—" she started, but I stopped her.

"No, Kathleen. I've got this. I shouldn't have said anything.

I took care of it, nothing to worry about." Only that was a lie as well but something I'd rectify as soon as I was feeling better and had a moment with the younger Shipley.

She took a deep breath, and her shoulders fell. "Are you sure? Warren would never stand for a man touching a woman without an expressed invitation."

I nodded quickly. "I know, and I get it. I think it was implied before, and he may have reacted on it at the wrong time. That's all. No harm done. I'm okay, and I'll talk to him." I got close to her face, making sure she saw the sincerity in my eyes. "I'll handle this, okay?"

With a tip to her head and a slow breath, she pulled me into a hug. "Okay. Just let me know if you need anything. Anything at all." She patted my back as though I was one of her children. I wondered if she had children of her own but figured I'd ask her later, when things weren't so heavy.

"I will." I squeezed her thin frame tightly, enjoying the motherly feel of her.

When she left me to my own devices, and after cleaning up the mess I'd made, I sat on the bed and put my head in my hands. How far would that have gone? Would he have really taken advantage of me? The entire scenario played out in my mind as if I had a rewind and fast forward button. If I hadn't been sick, would he have stopped? I abolished the thoughts. Going there was going to bring nothing but heartache and self-doubt. When I had a chance, I'd talk to Aaron. Tell him how inappropriate he was and make it clear that whatever there may have been between us, the attraction or whatever, it was completely gone now, with no hope of ever coming back.

Now what the hell did I make of the dream about Wes? It had to be because of the sexting we'd done last week and the booze doing strange things to my subconscious. Right? The dream was so real. I could still feel the flutters of excitement when thinking back to the things we did.

Groaning, I pulled out my phone and dialed my girl.

"Ugh, do you have telepathy or something?" she groaned into the phone.

"What's the matter?" I asked, becoming more alert now than I'd been all day. Gin didn't do the whole woe-is-me thing like other people. If she was unhappy, she told it like it was, and she definitely didn't stew in it for any given length of time.

Ginelle paused and then clucked her tongue. "I was just sitting here flicking an unlit cigarette, telling myself not to light it."

I knew that tone. Regret.

I closed my eyes. "Gin, babe, it's been how long now?"

"Three months, two weeks, and two days." She rattled off the numbers as if she'd really been focused on every single day of being smoke free, the same way an alcoholic does of their sobriety.

"And you're doing so well. Don't do it. You've been so happy not smoking, and remember that peanut butter cup you texted me about? The one that you ate and felt like you tasted for the very first time now that your taste buds weren't destroyed from the cancer stick?"

A heavy sigh filled the receiver. "Yeah, that was really tasty. I still can't believe how good it was. I mean, who isn't a fan of Reese's Peanut Butter Cups? They're like the most perfect food in the entire world..."

"True."

"...and it was as if I'd never tasted anything so good. Smoking kills your taste buds," she said, matter of fact.

"And remember, hot guys do not want to fuck chicks who smoke." That was my ace in the hole. Gin had hot-guy-itis and wouldn't dare risk messing up her chance with sexy men.

A long, drawn-out groan hit my eardrums. Then I heard the sound of gravel crunching off in the distance.

"What was that?" I asked.

"That was me destroying that ciggy. I can't believe I almost fucked up hot-guy kisses. You really are my best friend."

I tipped my head to the side and smiled. "Hey, someone has to protect you and ensure you're still gettin' it from the sexier sex."

"I guess I'm just missing you, missing Maddy."

Concern slipped through my tone. "What's going on?"

"Now that Maddy's got Matt, she doesn't want to hang out. You're gone, and the girls in the show are just catty bitches. I don't know..." Her voice sounded really sad and downtrodden. "It was like I had the best time in Hawaii with the two of you. Then you went off to DC to hang out with an old dude, Maddy went back to her guy, and I'm stuck with the dicks who drool over the show."

"You're lonely?"

After a long pause, she relented. "Yeah, I guess so. It's been a long year. When you left to go to Cali, I thought I could handle it because I planned on coming out eventually, but I don't know... Sometimes I wonder if I'll ever leave Vegas."

"You will, babe, if you want to. How about this? When I finish this year, no matter where I go, I'll scoop you up and take you with me."

"Even if you choose to be with a guy?"

I laughed out loud. "Yes, even then. We don't have to live in the same house, do we?"

"I don't want to share a bathroom with your filthy ass. You're a goddamned slob. I can't imagine anyone wanting to live with you."

That's why the man I'm with will need a housekeeper. Judi will handle that problem.

"Fuck..." I swore, realizing where my thoughts had gone.

"What?" This time, her tone was concerned.

I closed my eyes, deciding if I wanted to admit what had been running through my mind. Shit. Ginelle was my best friend. She was the only one I could tell and would set me straight. "When you said that about the bathroom thing..."

"Not sorry. That shit is totally true."

"I know it is. When you said that, I thought about how Wes has Judi and she cleans the house, so I wouldn't have to worry about a clean bathroom."

Her gasp was loud. "No, you didn't just go there. How the fuck are you going to get through the rest of the year if you're thinking like that?"

I groaned and ran my hand through my hair. "I know, and it's worse."

"Whaaaaat?" she said, long and drawn out. "Lay it out there. Come on."

"We sexted last week, and then I had a crazy sex dream about him." I said this really fast, as though if I said it fast it couldn't burn me.

"Really? Sexting? Huh. Can you send me the thread?"

Seriously? I'm bearing my soul here, and she wants to see the texts? "Are you fucking kidding me? Hello...BFF, be one!"

"Oh yeah, okay, okay. Sorry, I got sidetracked. That's hot shit. Anyway, for realz this time. Did you like doing it?"

"Yeah, but that's not the point."

"No, but was it fun?" she continued.

"Yeah, I think we both had a good time."

"And was the dream fun?"

I laughed and answered honestly. "Yeah." Of course it was, until I woke up. I wasn't about to tell Gin that part though. She'd lose her mind and overcharge her credit card to come here and kick some politician ass.

"Do you feel like you owe him something? Like your loyalty?" I thought about that until she added, "Is he going to stop seeing the actress?"

"No, he's not. Not that I know of anyway." Just hearing Gin mention her felt like a stake in my heart. A bout of anger prickled along my hairline, forcing my blood to heat.

"But end of story is, you had a good time with him?"

"Yeah," I admitted, not sure where she was going with this.

"Then why does it have to be anything other than that? Just a bit of fun. Didn't you tell me you learned that in Hawaii with Tai?"

My bestie had a point. A really excellent one. Even Wes said to let it be what it was. Enjoy what we had. Remember how good it was. And boy, had it been good.

"No, you're onto something. I'm just having trouble keeping it all separate. It's like when I'm with a guy, I'm one hundred percent with him, and when I'm not, I'm not. But with Wes, it's just...there's always something there, haunting me."

"You love him," Ginelle said, simply stating what she saw as fact.

Instantly, panic sheared through my body and my subconscious. Even the air around me felt charged with a nervous fear. Not being able to respond, I took the coward's way out. "Gin, babe, I gotta go. The boss is calling for me. I love you, skank. I'll call soon. Bye!"

My fingers shook as I pressed the "End" button.

CHAPTER EIGHT

I thought long and hard about what Ginelle had said on the phone today. Did I love Wes? Of course I had very strong feelings for him. More so than I'd ever admit to him, but I was leery to call it love. With Alec, Mason, Tony, Hector, and even Tai, those three words—I love you—slipped so easily out of my mouth, but not with Wes. Why? What was holding me back? I think somewhere deep down, I knew that if I said the words, the feelings of hope and loyalty would build. I wouldn't be able to move on to new experiences, finish off the year with a new guy every month, and pay off Pops's debt.

Even though there was something there between Wes and me, there was no way in hell I'd confirm it. Putting words to what we had would destroy us, or at the other end of the spectrum, it could very well bring us closer. Either way, my fate would be sealed, and with six more months of earning the money to pay the debt, I didn't have the liberty of making that type of decision unless I wanted Wes to bail me out.

No matter how much Wes wanted to pay off my father's debt, I knew I'd regret it for the rest of my life. I'd be beholden to him. And what if we didn't work out? Then he'd have paid a million dollars—well, five hundred thousand now—for my family and me to be free, and I just walked? I'd owe him with no way possible to pay that kind of money back. Aunt Millie gave me this opportunity to fix the wrongs that my father made and the guilt I had over ever introducing Pops to Blaine. I had to take this opportunity for what it was and recommit to my decision.

Mia Saunders was an escort. I'd be an escort for another six months, I'd pay off my father's debt to the prick of an ex, make sure my baby sister was still happy with Matthew, and then I'd decide what there was left for me.

Resolve firmly in place, I went over to my closet and scanned the contents. A slinky gold number caught my eye. It would be perfect for the huge charity event tonight. Warren had us flying into New York and staying over for a few days so he could meet with some big wigs and talk shop about his project. Shipley, Inc. also had a base in NYC, making the trip even easier. I'd been to New York with Mason on business, but still, I was pretty stoked. I only had a little over a week left with the Shipleys, and then I was off to my next location. Which reminded me that I hadn't heard from Aunt Millie.

Instead of waiting for her call, I decided I'd give her a ring this time. I punched in her number while pulling clothes from the closet and setting them on the bed. Kathleen told me to lay out the items I'd planned to take and she'd make sure everything was handled. The way she spoke, it sounded as though she wouldn't be taking the trip with us. Not sure why that was. I'd have to ask Warren about it. He'd been opening up to me a bit more since we'd had our drunken celebratory evening when we landed the Benoit assistance in Canada.

"Exquisite Escorts, Ms. Milan's office, Stephanie speaking. How may I help you?" a perky voice answered.

I rolled my eyes. Every time I heard my aunt's fake name, it gave credence to how very fake the entire business was. Don't get me wrong. I was very thankful for the opportunity to make the cash I'd made and pay off Pops's debt, but it's not something I would have chosen if we weren't in dire need of making a lot of money in a small amount of time.

"Hello, Stephanie. It's Mia, Millie's niece. Is she there?"

"Millie? Who's that?"

I sighed and smacked my head up against the palm of my hand. "I apologize. Millie is a nickname I use for my auntie, Ms. Milan," I lied.

"Oh! Okay, how fun. Let me ring her."

Her chirpy voice grated on my overtired nerves. If I could, I'd rip that singsong birdie from her throat and set that sucker free.

"Ms. Milan will speak to you," she said when she came back on the line.

I wanted to say, "Duh, I'm her family," but instead held back my snark, ending with, "Thank you, Stephanie."

"No problem at all!" She giggled, and the line buzzed before the sultry voice of my auntie came online.

"Mia, dollface, how's my favorite niece and escort?"

My eyebrows rose of their own accord. "Now I'm your favorite employee?"

"Yes, darling. Of course you are. We are making a mint off your little month-long jaunts. Makes me wish we'd planned them for two-week intervals and charged seventy- five a pop."

I'm going to bet that my eyes popped out of my head the way those wacky stress balls do. You squeeze the body, and the eyes darted out garishly. "Really?"

"Yep. Not only are you booked for the rest of the year, I now have a waiting list with a backlog of six gentlemen who would like to take any of your months if we receive a cancellation."

It took a few slow blinks and a moment for my brain to catch up with what she'd shared. "That's crazy. I can't imagine one wanting my company for a hundred K, let alone six on a waiting list. Wild."

"Hmm. Just proves that good company is hard to find. Especially with the special ability to not only help business but know their place and look exceptional doing it. How is our nation's capital treating you?"

I sat down next to the clothes I'd gathered and fingered a few of the threads. They really were quite extraordinary, made with the finest-quality fabrics and tailored to fit me perfectly. Each piece looked incredible and gave me a feeling of confidence that I didn't feel while duded up in sweats and a T-shirt. There was something to be said about dressing for the job you wanted, not the job you had.

"Fine. Warren is happy, I think."

"Oh, he is. Very much so. Received your fee a week in advance with an extra twenty-five thousand. Is there something I should know about?"

"What the fuck?" That baffled me. There was no reason he should have sent an extra twenty-five thousand. "We didn't sleep together. I have no idea why he sent it. Maybe it was a mistake?"

A bunch of clacking noises could be heard in the background as I gripped the cell phone so hard in my hand, it ached where the side dug into my palm.

"Nope. Ah, here we go. It's a bonus."

"A bonus? I don't get it."

"The fine print does state that if the client is exceptionally happy and wants to send additional monies by way of a bonus for services rendered, they may." She laughed. "Usually that's how we track the money you receive when you have relations with them, but he clearly states in his e-mail that the extra is to be given to you because of some account you single-handedly secured."

"The Benoits," I whispered.

"What's that, dear?"

"Oh, I...um...hit it off with one of the young wives. The woman got her husband to agree to the use of something that my client really needed in order for his project to be successful. I didn't know it was so important that he'd send me a twenty-five-thousand-dollar bonus."

Immediately, I knew exactly what a huge chunk of that money was going toward. My baby sister's wedding to her dream man. I'd save at least ten or fifteen of it and make sure she'd get the wedding of a lifetime, paid for by her own family, not his. The Rains were amazing people and obviously loved the idea of adding my sister to their growing family, but she was *my* sister. My responsibility until that ring was on her finger. I couldn't wait to tell her!

"Anyway, dollface, you're going to get a kick out of your next client."

I crossed my fingers. "Please tell me he's a hottie and somewhere warm?"

"Oh, honey, only a picture is going to do justice. E-mailing now." I heard the sound of her nails hitting the keys again. "His name is Anton Santiago, but get this... He goes by Latin Lov-ah." She snickered and must have tried to cover her mouth, because the noise turned muffled.

"Latin Lov-ah? Why the hell would he go by that name?"

"Did you pull up the image?"

Looking at the display, I hit speaker. "Okay, you're on speaker. Let me check my e-mail." I clicked a few buttons, brought up my Gmail account, and clicked on her message.

A picture filled the screen. You know how people say that a picture is worth a thousand words? Right then, no truer words had ever been spoken. "Oh my, lickable Latino. That's my client? Isn't he..."

"A famous hip-hop artist, yes," she said bluntly, but it really didn't resonate. I was too busy mentally licking my cell phone screen.

The image was a svelte man wearing sagging black jeans that showed a solid inch-wide bit of fabric that was obviously his underwear. The stark red band with black writing that said "M&S," which I now knew was Mark & Spencer Fashion out of the UK. Hector, my BFF—Boy Friend Forever, as he claimed it meant—taught me enough about the designers to get by. The lovely cotton hugged Anton's enticingly trim waistline. I traveled up the stairway of one helluva cut abdomen that was slick with sweat up to the pair of square outlines that boasted seriously tight pecs. His neck was corded as he leaned up against what seemed to be a push-up bar. His wrists were wrapped in that white tape that boxers used to protect their wrists as he gripped the bar.

All of this was absolutely delicious, but nothing prepared me for the face. Angels could have wept at a face like that. Mocha-colored skin with fierce black hair and pale hazel eyes stared back at me. The eye color was a cross between green and brown but light enough against that dark skin to stand out as uniquely as my own. And I wasn't being conceited. I'd heard my eyes were incredible since birth. If I'm out and about, I'm told every day by random strangers how amazing, or cool, or neat they thought the pale-green color was. This guy, my next client, Mr. Latin Lov-ah himself, had eyes that dazzled.

I took in the pic in its entirety. A gold bulky necklace hung around his neck with a chunky heart layered with diamonds covering its surface sat at his sternum. On anyone else, it would have been gaudy or tacky. On him, it added character and fit the persona of the heartthrob Latin lover he claimed to be. A pair of pouty, cherub-like lips formed a sexy smirk, and I knew just from this one picture that I intended to get me some of that.

"Day-um," I said in my best Latina accent.

Millie cackled. "Figured you'd like that. Am I forgiven for the oldie but goodie?" she asked, referring to Warren, my sixty-five-year-old client.

"Oh yeah, big time."

"Good. I'll send the details and make the arrangements. You'll be headed to Miami, Florida, for this gig."

Miami? I held back the woot woot.

"Was there anything else?" Millie asked.

"Oh yeah, one more thing. Why is he hiring me?"

The line went very quiet. I let myself fall back onto the bed. "Auntie..."

"He wants you to be the lead in his new video. Some single he's releasing later this year."

"A video? As in a music video? Like where I'll have to dance and act?" The acting part wasn't so bad. At least it was closer to what I had originally planned on doing with my life.

"Yes, darling. You'll do whatever they want. I don't know. Look hot, pretend to love Mr. Love-ah, dance, you know, whatever the youngsters like seeing nowadays."

A noise like a cat dying escaped my lungs. "Auntie, I don't dance."

She smacked her lips. "Well, I guess they'll teach you, won't they? He wants you. Saw your art from the Love on

Canvas campaign, apparently bought one of the pieces. When he saw the Hawaiian campaign come out and the pics of you with Weston Channing and Mason Murphy in the smut mags, he said you were his ideal flame for the shoot. Whatever that meant."

I shook my head and blew a loud breath, the force expanding my cheeks with the effort. "Okay. I guess I'll just see what happens. Miami sounds fun, though."

"Glad you think so, dollface. I need to go. I have a client waiting."

"Okay, but oh crap! One more thing: Maddy's engaged."

"Excuse me? I just sent the girl a present for her twentieth birthday. A gift card to Starbucks that should keep her in coffee for the year. What do you mean, she's engaged?" Her tone was a tad hostile, and I understood why. Aunt Millie did not believe in the sanctity of marriage. Hell, I wasn't sure I believed in it after what my parents and Aunt Millie had gone through.

"Says she's in love with the guy. Just moved in with him, too. I've met the guy and the family. They're really nice...uh, normal, even. Very much a perfect TV family."

"Those are the ones who are the most fucked up." She cursed, which she didn't often do.

"I know, but I've got a really good feeling. Besides, they are going to finish their bachelor's and then get married in a couple of years."

Millie huffed loudly, sounding very put out by the news. "Unless she gets pregnant first. Then her dream of being a scientist and all the work you've put into paying for her schooling is gone. Poof. Disappeared in the blink of an eye and replaced with a snotty, shitting, crying ball of flesh that ties you down for the rest of your life."

"Wow, tell me how you really feel," I threw back, trying to lighten the heaviness that had taken over the conversation.

"I feel she's too young to be committing to some college prick with a loaded dick."

I pursed my lips and thought about the best way to approach this. "I'll make sure she's taking care of the baby factor and that the doors are firmly locked down. But they really are waiting for a couple more years. The moving in together bit, I can't help but be relieved about."

"If it's about money, I'll send her whatever she needs to get through the year."

"It's not about money, Auntie. It's about her being in love and feeling safe. The neighborhood is not the best, and she's all alone in Pops's house. Ginelle drives by the house, but like you said, she's young and of course beautiful and naïve. I don't want her getting hurt. If playing house with her fiancé is going to keep her safe, I'm all for it."

Aunt Millie inhaled audibly, her breath sounding even more ragged than before. "Fine. I just worry about her."

"Me too, but it's all good. I'll keep you posted."

"Please do."

"Love you, Aunt Millie."

"I love you, too, my darling girl." And the line went dead.

Well, fuck me running. That was an incredibly uncomfortable call I hadn't anticipated. Of course, the highlight was the sexy Latin Lov-ah. I made a mental note to download some of his songs on my iPod so I could listen on the plane and get up to date with his tunes before I became the face of his next music-video love interest. The only problem is that this white girl cannot dance. I didn't even know what the hell people were talking about when they said "raise the roof," or "drop it like it's hot." One song I shimmied with said something about, "She hit the floor... Next thing you know... shorty got low, low, low, low, low." Why was it sexy to smack the floor and get low? Did the woman sit or kneel? I guess kneeling could be sexy if the girl was mimicking giving head, but I couldn't imagine that would be a popular dance move.

Oh well. Perhaps I'd look up some of his videos on YouTube so I could hit the floor and get low without embarrassing myself.

★ ★ ★ ★

Once my things were laid out on the bed, I took a trek through the enormous mansion in search of Kathleen or Warren. I found Warren first in his office. Lightly, I knocked on the door, not wanting to be too disruptive.

"Come in." His grumble came through the hardwood door.

I entered, and he looked up and stopped whatever he was writing. "Are you ready to fly out tonight?"

"Yep. Hey, I had a question, if you don't mind me asking."

His bushy brows rose. He gestured for me to sit in the chair opposite his desk.

"Is Kathleen coming along on the trip?"

He shook his head. "No. Why?"

This time my eyebrows rose. "I guess I just find it odd that you aren't taking your girlfriend with you."

He set down his pen and clasped his hands into a steeple, resting his chin on his fingertips. "Frankly, it never dawned on me that she would be interested in going."

"When was the last time she took a vacation?"

Warren's gaze drifted over to the window as he thought about it. "I can't say that I recall."

"And when was the last time you took her out to dinner."

His head jerked back. "Dinner? She makes dinner for me. It's part of her job. Why ever would I take her out to eat?"

I closed my eyes, exhaled slowly, and counted to ten. "Warren, this is going to sound harsh, but it's for your own good, and I think you can handle it."

As his eyes slanted, a line appeared at the top of his nose. Clearly, he was distressed.

"You are not treating her well."

His shocked expression surprised me. This couldn't be news to him. "I beg to differ. Kathleen has run of the house, sleeps by my side every night, buys the finest flowers, food..."

"That's all for you!" My tone came out biting, and he opened his mouth and then closed it again. "I'm sorry." I leaned forward and put my hand over his. "Warren, you're keeping her locked in this house as your staff, not your girlfriend. You don't take her on dates, buy her flowers." He opened his mouth to speak, but I cut him off. "You let her buy flowers for the house. That's not the same as a man who cares about you bringing you a bouquet he picked out or sending you some himself."

He leaned back in his chair. "Go on. You obviously have more to say. Say it."

I licked my lips. "The woman loves you, would do anything for you, yet you keep her here as if she's a secret you're embarrassed about."

His entire face got red. "Did she say that?"

I shook my head. "Not in so many words, but that's the gist I got. You come home to her every day. You let her serve your meals, don't eat with her, and expect her to lie down with you every night and just be okay with it?"

"I... I... Huh. I believe you have me at a disadvantage, dear one. I'm not even sure how to respond to that." He ran a hand through his salt-and-pepper locks.

"It's just, I see the way you look at her. You're in love with her, right?"

Without even hesitating, he responded, "Of course I love her. I have for years. I would never be unfaithful to her."

"Then why are you parading me around like your little tart, when you have a beautiful woman who would love to play dress-up and stand by your side if only to give you support? And furthermore, take her out on a date. Buy her a present. Get her some flowers, even if you pick them from the gardens." I pointed out the window to the green landscape beyond. "Tell your son about her. Stop hiding her in the dark. She wants nothing more than to be with you, *really* be with you in all the ways that matter most."

Warren nodded and glanced out the window, his mind obviously now on something else. I could only hope he'd consider what I'd said and make some moves. Faith was all it took, and I had faith that he'd make the right decision.

I stood up and moved to leave.

"Mia?" The hairs on my neck tingled, and I hoped he wasn't about to filet me for being incredibly intrusive about his love life.

Turning around, I faced him.

A soft smile slid across his handsome face. "Thank you for being bold enough to put an old man in his place."

That earned him a huge grin. "Of course."

"When you see Kathleen, ask her to come to me."

"I'm pretty sure she'd have no problem with that." I

winked and then skipped out of his office to find his girl. Things were about to change in the Shipley household, definitely for the better.

CHAPTER NINE

New York City was everything I'd ever dreamed of and more. The city was teeming with people, lights, towering buildings, and the best part...diversity. Every nationality, color, creed, ethnicity were all represented in one giant melting pot of mankind. I loved it. Every blessed second of the noise, the grit, the bodies pressing and pushing, weaving like mice in a maze trying to get to the other side of wherever they were going felt like an experience. A part of my life I'd not be able to forget if I tried. There was too much life to be had and seen in a place this vibrant.

"Mia, honey, are you coming?" Kathleen asked, holding open the door to one seriously fancy hotel.

The Four Seasons was known for its ostentatious price tag that only celebrities and one-percenters could afford. Looking out over this incredible city, seeing it through newborn eyes, I was in love. I didn't care that I was riding my client's coat tails, serving as an escort, looked at by this group as a gold-digging whore. Not a care in the world. In that moment, I felt nothing but blessed that I'd gotten the opportunity to experience something I might not ever have had otherwise.

"Yeah," I whispered, eyes still glued to the spectacle of square shapes piercing the sky with their flat and pointy tops. Unique, carved-out architecture gave every building an intricate feel, making them each one of a kind in a long line of smashed-together structures.

A hand closed around my bicep and tugged. "Come on, city girl. The view from our suite on the fiftieth floor will blow you away."

My eyes widened. "We're staying on the fiftieth floor?"

She chuckled. "Yep."

"How many floors are there?" I asked, craning my neck to view the top of the building. It wasn't the widest, only showing four windows across, but it had a charm to it. The architect definitely spent some time on the design, making it seem more special. Its lines weren't hard. They had a curved bull-nosed edge feel with a step-up approach from the bottom level to the top.

"Fifty-two. Warren wasn't happy that we didn't secure the penthouse, so don't mention it."

Like the thought would have popped into my head.

"A few of the other men going to the event secured the two top floors for their parties," she continued to explain while pulling me into the opulent lobby.

My heels clacked loudly against the marble floor. The dark marble was cut into a spider web-like design, with wide grout lines that were surprisingly white. You'd think something like that would get dirty, especially in a town where people were coming and going and the weather could be unpredictable. White stone columns dotted the space as a bellman led us through to the elevator. Warren had already taken care of check-in and was waiting for us at the luggage cart when Kathleen dragged me along.

Once inside the suite, I about swallowed my tongue. I'd never seen a room so beautiful.

"I take it the accommodations are to your liking, Ms. Saunders?" Warren asked, amusement evident in his tone.

There weren't words. Shock overtook my ability to speak. Instead of responding, I just nodded and took in our surroundings. White, cream, and gold were the prevailing colors, giving the space an ethereal yet comforting feel. As if a person could sit down and stay awhile...maybe forever. Windows surrounded most of the room, allowing an open view of the city in all its grandeur.

The room was nothing but utter brilliance. A shiny black piano sat in a corner as if waiting for a willing body to tickle its ivories. It made me wish I had a musical bone. I didn't. Technically, I could carry a tune. Most actors could, and I was no exception, but it wasn't as though I had a gift or anything. That pretty much summed me up in a nutshell. Jill of all trades, mediocre at best, gifted at nothing.

Kathleen flitted around the room, oohing and aahing adoringly, clinging to Warren's arm. Whatever relationship they'd had over the last several years was finally being brought out into the open. Kathleen literally beamed with joy. It seemed to burst out of every single pore.

Where that left me, I didn't know and really didn't care. As long as the two of them were happy and moving forward, and I still received my fee, things were golden as far as I was concerned. Though it definitely put a damper on what my position at tomorrow's charity event and what future dinners meant. Did I still pretend to be his arm candy, friend, and date? Would he take Kathleen along?

All these questions were instantly forgotten when I entered the bathroom. Talk about lush. Promptly, I walked into the room, traced a finger along the white marble vanity, and sat on the edge of the square tub. Yes, square tub, and it was as large as a full-sized bed. Two people could easily fit in there and get into some serious hanky-panky water action. In the mirror across from me, I noticed the frowning girl staring back. There would be no water sports for this gal in the magnificent, once-in-a-lifetime tub. Sighing, I stared out the floor-to-ceiling window...*in the bathroom*. I imagined the windows were glazed in a way one could only see out and not in. Someone with a telephoto lens would have a field day with naked celebrities otherwise.

Standing, I realized how tired I was. Not only bone weary from the travel, either. Tired of not knowing what I was doing. Tired of staying with strangers, even though they were kind and extremely generous and, for the most part, hot as fudge dripping along a cool scoop of vanilla ice cream.

Then, like concrete hardening into sidewalk, reality hit me hard. My life wasn't my own. My kid sister was off living with a man I'd only met once. Once! Even Pops wouldn't allow that. And Pops. I'd up and left my comatose father in a convalescent home. What the fuck was wrong with me? Granted, this entire year was his fault, and I should be pissed at him, I knew my father. He would never have wanted this for me. Uprooting my life, Maddy's, and for what? To pay off a goon I'd once fucked and thought I loved? No, he'd allow Blaine to kill him to protect me from living this life. The life of an escort.

I shook my head and trudged into the room that Warren had pointed out was mine. Face planting into the clouds of white reminded me of another time I'd done this very thing in a room three thousand miles away. That room was owned by a man I wasn't convinced could ever truly love me and would leave me. He would hurt me like the others, destroy the last speck of faith I had in the opposite sex for all of eternity. If I were honest, I think I was more afraid that he couldn't possibly ever compare to the man I'd made him in my deepest, darkest, fantasies, a man who could be everything in one. The devoted, worshipping, loving man I'd always dreamed of and spent my late teens and early twenties looking for, only to fail miserably. Now I didn't know what we were to each other outside of friends with benefits. I also knew I'd go to great lengths to avoid finding out. At least until I got past this year.

The goal was set and in sight. Blaine was being paid monthly, his blood money finding its way into his bank account, keeping my father, Maddy, and me safe. For now.

★ ★ ★ ★

If a terrorist group wanted to destroy the United States economy, all they had to do was take out Bryant Park that evening. Every major charity, not just one, was in attendance. They all had booths set up on the gravel perimeter surrounding the main grassy area in the middle. Rows and rows of lights had been extended and strung horizontally, high above the grass. Highboy tables with silver cloths and decorative lanterns sat every ten to fifteen feet, covering the massive ground. There were men from every major corporation you could think of. I was pretty sure I spotted Trump and Gates roaming around, along with celebrities and a horde of governmental officials. Famous movie stars glittered here and there, and I had to hold my tongue not to fan girl all over the place. It was a veritable feast of the richest of the rich.

As I took in the lights, people, and music wafting through hidden speakers, my body was jolted up into the air. I was spun around midair, slammed against a hard body, and squeezed in a vise-like grip. The scent of cologne mixed with a hint of familiar male sweat entered my senses, and I smiled.

"Let me go, you big lug!" I kicked and hollered as my body slid along a very firm, muscled chest I knew well but not intimately.

His hands cupped my cheeks, and the emerald-green eyes I adored sparkled. Coppery hair glinted off the overhead lights, and I ran my hands from his neck to his shoulder.

"Miss me, sweetness?" He kissed my forehead the way a brother does a sister he hadn't seen in a while.

"Mace..." I smiled and pulled him into my arms, holding on tight. He was something familiar in a sea of strangers. I held on to his lengthy, hard form like a leech, with no plan to ever let him go.

Mason firmly grabbed each hand and tugged me away. His eyes took in my face and then narrowed. "You look tired."

I huffed, blowing out a breath. Leave it to a man I'd spent a month with, one who became one of my best friends in the world, to notice when no one else had.

They don't know you, a little voice inside my head taunted.

"Is that another way of telling me I look like shit?" I pouted.

Mason's eyes did a scan of my body, taking in the tight little gold dress that hugged every curve, and I mean every curve. It hugged so much so that I couldn't wear anything underneath it. A very nonbrotherly look crossed his features.

"Wasn't referring to your dress, sweetness. The body is still a hundred percent bangable."

I shoved at his chest and made a gagging noise. "Where's Rachel?" I asked and then was greeted with her model-esque body as she walked up.

Mason watched her walk from the bar holding two glasses

of champagne. She was wearing a drop-dead gorgeous, white scrap of a dress. She looked downright chic.

"Never far from me, I'll tell you that right fuckin' now." His Boston accent took over as he licked his lips, that sexy smirk of his turning into a cat-like grin.

"You're a lucky man," I joked.

He winked and knocked my shoulder. "Don't I know it?"

When Rachel got a little closer, her entire face brightened. Her blonde hair positively glowed in the lights, and her cheeks pinked prettily. She handed Mace the glasses and pulled me into a hug. "Mia, my God. Whatever are you doing here?"

I leaned back and held her at arm's length. "Me? What are you two doing here?" I pointed to Rachel, and then Mason.

He shrugged. "All part of the image. Biggest charity event of the year." He looped an arm over Rachel's shoulder. "My publicist thinks attending these things will only solidify what I've been building on with my investors."

Rachel handed me one of the glasses she had probably gotten for Mason, but he didn't seem to mind. He was all smiles, looking from me to Rachel.

"She's right." I took the glass and sipped. "Thank you."

We caught up for a while. I had no clue where Warren and Kathleen were. He was probably introducing his *real* girlfriend to everyone. Me, I was just here mostly because we didn't want Warren to get any flack. If I was here, it wouldn't look as though I was mad or that he was carrying on with several women and piss off the Benoits. I guess it made me look expendable, but in reality, all the gold-diggers were, and that was not new to the men I'd previously met, with the exception of sixty-six-year-old Mr. Benoit and his twenty-five-year-old pregnant wife.

Thinking of her must have conjured her up. Christine

Benoit was waving at me from across the lawn.

"Guys, can we catch up in say...an hour? I need to network for my client."

Rachel hugged me again. "Mia, I didn't get a chance to thank you. To tell you how much what you did meant for me, for Mace. We...well, we just love you like family, okay?"

We love you like family.

Mason pulled me into his own hug as Rachel used her pinky fingers to dot at the corner of her eyes. "She's right you know," he whispered in my ear. "We do love you like family. Anytime you want to get away, come visit, there's always a ticket with your name on it. Okay?" He moved back and bent down low so that it was green eyes to green eyes.

I nodded, choked up.

"I mean it. You text saying you want to come to Boston, I'll ensure a ticket is waiting. Got it?"

I smiled wide and kissed his cheek. "Got it, brother." I winked and stepped back.

He put an arm around Rachel's waist, holding her close. That was a beautiful picture. So beautiful I pulled my phone out of my clutch and captured it for all time. One day, when I had a place of my own, I'd print that picture and put it on my own wall or mantle. An image to capture the moment that these people told me I was their family and that I was loved.

Turning around, I waved. "Catch up with you later on, okay?"

Both of them waved, and I turned, walking across the vast lawn to Christine.

As I sidestepped men in tuxes and women in the latest couture fashions, I thought about what they'd said. They loved me, and I was their family. Two people I'd only known for a month claimed me as theirs. As family. Clearly not the family I'd been born into—that would have been impossible—but by choice.

Friends are the family you choose.

Like Tai, Tony, and Hector had, they all in some way referred to me as their family. Wes and Alec were totally different when it came to their connection to me. With the other guys, *that* beyond anything solved the weariness and the concern I had over making this year-long journey. The part that was meant to be was the people I was taking into my heart, into my soul. The men and women who would stay with me...who would add to what was now *my family*. They were the reason for this journey as much, if not more, than the debt I needed to pay. Before, it had been me, Pops, Maddy, and Ginelle. Aunt Millie, of course, was there somewhat. But these people, they were the ones I now checked in with. Told funny stories to over the phone. E-mailed. Thought about when I was in a place or saw something that reminded me of them. The same way a person did with their own flesh and blood, only better because they had *chosen* me.

With a renewed sense of peace, I walked into Christine's arms. The tiny, pregnant, sex maniac was all smiles and billowy hair. The slip dress she wore accented the small baby bump her hand rested over. I yanked her hand away and turned her to the side.

"Holy smokes. I can see your bump!" I said, and she nodded vigorously.

Excitedly, her words came fast. "I know! Isn't it amazing! It just popped out a couple days ago, and all of a sudden you could see the proof of Franny's and my love. We find out what we're having in a week!"

Speaking of Francis Benoit, he came up behind his wife and placed his hand over her stomach. "How's my pumpkin and our little one?"

Christine's eyes lit up like a hundred candles on a birthday cake. It was clear in her body language how much she genuinely loved her husband, hugging him tighter to her, caressing his hand over her bump. It was odd, unconventional, and definitely weird to see someone over forty years older than she was gorging on her neck, but hey, who was I to judge? Okay, maybe I was judging a little bit. In my defense, anyone in their right mind would.

"I was just telling Mia about how we're going to find out about the baby."

He nodded and kissed her temple.

"Also, Mia, everything is in place for the project on our end."

My eyes went wide. "Already?"

"Yep. Franny and I know how important this cause is. We burned some midnight oil this past week and paid a few workers some overtime, but everything on our end is in place. When the product and people arrive, we'll plan for setting up the shipping schedule to the UK."

I ran my hand through my hair and held it back. "I can't believe you did that. Does Warren know?"

"Just finished telling him. He's looking for you, by the way. Everything okay between you?" Francis asked, uncharacteristically intrusive for a man like him.

"Perfectly okay. Thank you for asking."

I said a couple more congrats about the baby and the job and then scanned the area looking for Warren. My gaze landed on perfection in a tux instead. Senator Aaron Shipley's eyes were all over me. For a moment, I appreciated the obvious praise as he pushed evenly through other guests, steadily getting closer. A full tumbler of amber liquid accompanied him. About ten feet away, he lifted the glass to his lips and drained the entire lot. His eyes were glassy and hard, all traces of the sexy man I'd met earlier in the month gone. In his place was the predator that had touched me in my sleep.

Shit.

"Pretty, pretty, Mia. Looks as though your date has chosen another to fill his dance card."

His lips pursed as he came closer and put a hand on my hip, his fingers tightening. I tried to push back, but he locked an arm around my waist. Making a scene to pry his hands off me wasn't an option. He was the senator for California, and I was nobody.

I was a nameless face that had been attached to his father for the last few weeks.

"Can you let me go?" I pressed against his chest, trying to squeeze out of his grip. No dice. He held me tight.

"Come now, Mia. I just received the news that my father has been fucking my nanny for as long as my mother's been dead. Hell, possibly before. I'm in no mood for your antics."

I shook my head. "That's not true. That connection formed over decades. Talk to him, Aaron. Let him tell you how it came about."

His lips pinched together into white slits. He was walking us through the crowd, his grip bruising against the tender skin of my hip. I looked over my shoulder and caught Rachel's eye way in the distance. She looked concerned, and her hand went to Mason's shoulder as she stared my way. Unfortunately, he was busy talking to a group of men who might be fans. Talking to the star pitcher of the Boston Red Sox was a big deal, even if you were a ridiculously rich man and fan. Not to mention, it might open the doors to prospective new deals for advertising and sponsorship.

Before I knew it, I was steered past the green lawn, through the charity vendors camped around the lawns, and up the stone steps. Eventually, he ushered me up past the columns of the New York Library. The library was closed and dark. Several areas had blacked-out corners, which was where Aaron was leading me.

Finally, my champagne-filled brain realized that we weren't going for a little walk. He was taking me somewhere and was intent on whatever plan he had.

I turned my heel and yanked out of his reach. "What the hell, Aaron?" I spread my hands out and looked around. There was absolutely no one in sight. We were at least a good couple hundred feet or more away, and I cursed myself for allowing him to get me this far away from the party and witnesses.

"You think you're special, don't you?" The words were released with barely contained venom.

I shook my head and tried to sound calm. "Not at all, actually. The opposite is probably more true," I admitted.

He scowled and prowled forward until I was holding up my hands in front of me. He continued forward, and I found myself pressed up against the concrete wall of a darkened area. A few more steps, and his chest was against mine. I thought about the best way to handle this, but the champagne was fogging up my reflexes.

"Aaron, you don't want to do this."

His nose slid along my temple and sent shivers of dread down my spine, prickling the hairs at the back of my neck. "Of course I do."

I pushed against his chest to no avail. Aaron was not a small guy, and his bulk definitely prevented any slack.

He chuckled. "Trying to escape, little whore," he said with a drunken slur.

"I'm not a whore, Aaron. You know that."

He bit down on the space where my shoulder and neck met. "I know my father hired you to be his whore in front of his fucked-up rich friends. I know that you work for an escort service and get paid by the month. Time to get Daddy's money's worth," he said dementedly.

That's when I started to fight, but I didn't have much leverage. I got a nice fist to his mouth, cutting open his lip, before he restrained my hands with one hand and then groped my body with the other. He crushed my body against the concrete wall, so hard that I could feel the tender skin of my back being abraded and the skin being rubbed raw as he dry humped me.

I started to scream, but he put his mouth over mine. All you could hear was a person yelling as if they were under water. Then the sickening sound of his pants being unbuckled and the noise of the zipper going down was like my own personal death knell. I screamed louder, but he bit my lips and slammed my head into the concrete. Things got hazy, and I felt my dress being slid up to my waist. The cool air slithered across my bare flesh. Stars broke out across my vision from the staggering blow. Soft tissue slamming into a rock solid building did not equate to mental stability. I could feel fingers sliding down my stomach, and then he cupped my sex roughly. Bile rose up my throat, and I gagged.

"I'm going to fuck you so hard, take you like the whore you

are. Fucking white trash," he roared, spittle flinging against my face.

He was not the man I'd originally met when I arrived. He wasn't the same man with whom I'd enjoyed a few conversations, flirted with. No, this man was much like the one who touched me while I'd slept and had no remorse. That was my first clue that something was deeply wrong with the young senator.

I could feel the head of his cock resting against my legs as he ground it along my thigh. I whispered, "No," and shook my head, only to receive a gut-twisting grin in reply. He put a hand over my mouth as I screamed, muffling the sound. I bit down, and he cursed and smashed my head into the wall again. This time, I slumped against the surface, my body feeling almost weightless. I was going to lose consciousness, and then he'd take me. Maybe that was better. Not knowing what he was doing had to be better than being awake for every disgusting thing he would do to me. At that moment, I prayed for blackness.

CHAPTER TEN

"You ready to get pounded?" It was the last thing I heard and was said with absolute disdain. I wouldn't have thought it possible to come from the young senator who the world adored. A man who was on the fast track to becoming President of the United States one day.

I waited for him to strike. Instead, a burst of cool air covered my skin. My body was free from the weight that had pressed it into the wall. Scuffling, followed by grunting and feet scraping along concrete could be vaguely heard through the pounding of my head and heart. My knees bit into the concrete sidewalk when I slumped to the ground, unable to hold myself up.

"I'll show you what getting pounded looks like, you piece of shit!" Mason roared.

I looked up, confusion swarming like angry bees around my head as I saw Mason in a full-blown cage-style fight with Aaron. At some point, Aaron must have gotten his pants back up, because this fight lacked bare chests. The punches thrown were instead by two stunningly attractive men in tuxedos. I blinked as I saw Rachel running through the throngs of people in the distance, her heels crunching in the gravel and then clacking loudly up the stone stairs.

"Oh my God! Mason, where's Mia?" she screamed, and I tried to respond, but my voice wouldn't work. One too many blows to the head had temporarily robbed me of speech.

Mason threw a punch that landed solidly on Aaron's face. Blood sprayed out of his mouth and across the gray concrete, painting it red. My eyes rolled in my head, and I knew I was going to be sick. I gagged and heard Mason say something, but I couldn't distinguish it. I lay down on the damp, cool stone, pressing the side of my face and temple into it, needing relief from the pain taking over every speck of my form. Swirling volcanic acid in my gut squeezed my insides violently as vomit made its way up my throat. I wretched, barely able to move or lift my head.

"Mia, oh no. Jesus, honey." Rachel's voice penetrated the web of disorientation, and I felt her lifting my upper body onto her lap where she knelt. "Babe, she's naked from the waist down and hurt." She pushed my dress down, covering the bare lower half. Her fingers prodded lightly at the wounds on my back and the sticky substance on my head. Seemed the library wall took more than a chunk out of my back. "She needs a hospital," Rachel cried out, her voice shaking.

A mighty growl and fierce blows of flesh meeting bone could be heard in the distance. Fat wet drops of something hit my cheeks, one of them trailing down and touching my lip. I licked the salty flavor, realizing it was Rachel's tears.

Rachel leaned close and kissed my forehead. "It's going to be okay. We'll take care of you."

At some point, the blackness finally took me.

★ ★ ★ ★

The acrid smell of hospital anesthetic weaved its way into my senses. I licked dry lips and tasted nothing but a rough cotton sensation. Before my eyes even opened, a straw tapped against my lips, and I sucked the water greedily. The cut in my swollen lip—where Aaron had bit into the flesh—smarted. I opened my eyes to find Rachel tending to me. My hand felt warm, and a weight pressed into my side. I looked down at the blankets and found coppery hair and a large hand encasing mine. The knuckles were ripped with jagged edges and rimmed with blood. I moved my hand and dove my fingers into the silky goodness that was Mason's hair.

He lifted his head slowly, and his green eyes were dark and sad. I cracked as much of a smile as my swollen lip would allow. He held my hand and kissed my palm. "How you feeling, sweetness?"

I blinked a few times and took a mental assessment of my body. Knees felt bruised, back hurt like the fiery flaming pits of hell, but the bass drum in my head was the worst. "Did he...?" I stopped, unable to say the words.

Rachel petted the top of my hair, repeatedly whisking back the layer of swooping bangs, tears running down her face.

Mason clenched his jaw and shook his head. "No, he didn't. Thank God. Had he..." His face hardened into an evil look, one I'd not ever seen on Mason before. It was a cross between malice and pure hate. "I'd have killed him with my bare hands. As it is, he's in pretty bad shape. Cops arrested him for assault. He can kiss his fucking career bye-bye."

I closed my eyes and let the tears fall. "God, I wish I would have done something more when I woke up to him fondling me in my sleep..."

"*What!*" Mason's yell was so loud that the drummer in my head decided it was crescendo time and pounded so hard, I had to press my hands against my temples. Both palms felt sore and achy.

"Mace..." Rachel clasped Mason's arm and shushed him. "Her head, baby," she reminded him. "A concussion doesn't feel good, and she's in pain. I can see it on her face."

Mason leaned forward and kissed my entire forehead.

I had to admit, it felt really nice after the shitty evening I'd had. The tears, though, couldn't be stopped. They ran in rivulets down my cheeks. The skin of my face itched against the deluge of tears. He spoke words of comfort along my skin, whispering that he was going to take care of me. That family takes care of one another.

While Mason comforted me, I heard Rachel speaking. "Yes, she's okay. Had a rough night. Who is this? Oh yeah, she was with you in Hawaii. Yeah, some senator roughed her up, but she's okay now. Excuse me? You're going to what? Hello?"

"Oh no. Who was that on the phone?" I called out to Rachel.

She held the phone and looked at the screen. "It says Sexy Samoan."

I closed my eyes and groaned. "Did you just tell Tai that I was in the hospital because a senator hurt me?" I asked, my voice tight as a pair of size-six jeans on my more than size-eight booty.

"Was that a bad thing?" She smiled in that kind way that was purely Rachel. She had no idea the shit storm she'd just unleashed.

I held out my hand for the phone. Once she placed it into my palm, I was contemplating how to call off my big Samoan bad-ass when the buzzing increased, making me feel dizzy and on the edge of vomiting. Figuring I could call Tai later, I turned it off.

"No more answering my phone. No good will come of it."

Her eyebrows narrowed. "Why?"

"Doesn't matter. I'll take care of it." I closed my eyes, not able to keep them open any longer.

I was forced awake four more times through the night to keep watch on the concussion I'd suffered. I finally awoke on my own to a much larger hand holding mine. One was wrapped around my neck, the thumb firmly planted on my pulse point, and the other engulfed my smaller one. I smelled him before I saw him. The intermingling of fire, wood, and the ocean gave me an incredible sense of peace. I didn't even have to open my eyes, because I knew what I'd see.

"I can feel you, girlie." His thumb moved along the pulse point on my neck. "Open those pretty eyes for me." Tai's rumbling voice soothed every racked nerve I had. Tears accompanied my first look in three weeks at my sexy Samoan. His black eyes were fierce and blazing with barely controlled rage. "No one would tell me his name. Who put his hands on you uninvited?" He spoke in a sadistically quiet voice. It wasn't something I was used to with Tai Niko. When he spoke, everyone heard him. He was a big guy, and that timbre carried.

I inhaled slowly and winced as the pain rippled along my back and head. If possible, his gaze turned even blacker. Squeezing his hand, I tried to express what I couldn't through words.

He closed his eyes, leaned forward, and kissed me softly. "No one hurts my *'aiga*. My family." He hit his chest like a mighty ape. There was that word again. "Family."

"Tai, what time is it? Did you get on a plane right after our call?"

He nodded curtly, and I tilted my head down in shame. All these wonderful men, caring for me, taking care of me. It was a lot to take in, especially on top of the hell I'd experienced last night.

"I want you to come to Hawaii with me. Amy and I will take care of you. *Tina* will be thrilled to mother you." *Tina* was the Samoan word for mother.

"You know I can't do that, Tai. I have to work." I held my temples and squeezed. "This is going to be a shitstorm for the press. Fuck, what am I going to do? The Shipleys are huge, and Warren... Oh my God, his son." Tears poured down my face, and I covered my eyes.

"Warren is going to make sure his son is properly punished for his actions," came the booming voice of Warren Shipley himself. "Sweet girl..." he said, his voice filled with emotion as he walked to the side of my bed, Kathleen hot on his heels, though her hand covered her own mouth as she cried silently. "I'm sorry for what Aaron did. We'd have been here sooner but were detained by the police and the media frenzy. It's all my fault."

I attempted to clear my voice of the emotions clogging them, but it didn't work. "No, Warren, that was all him."

"I knew he was unstable when he drank. That's why he rarely did. In the past, he had a drinking problem and became violent when he was under the influence, but I thought that was behind him. Until, of course, the moment after I told him that Kathleen and I were an item. Then it was like something snapped in him."

"Something's definitely about to snap in him," Tai growled from his spot next to me.

Warren's eyes flicked to Tai and then roamed his form up and up as he stood. An astonished expression stole across Warren's face. That happened a lot around Tai. He was as unusually large and imposing as he was fine as fuck. "Friend of yours, I gather?"

Tai tapped his chest in a highly alpha move. "Family."

I smiled and patted Tai's hand, tugging his forearm, forcing him to sit once more. He sat quietly, focused solely on me, as if the other people in the room were insignificant gnats, annoying by their mere existence. God, I loved Tai.

"Well, as apologetic as I am, we're prepared to pay for all your medical bills, provide you with the best possible aftercare and any dollar amount you deem appropriate for your time and suffering. As much as I hate that this happened, and I do, Mia, more than you could ever know," he croaked, frowning deeply, the wrinkles in his face never having been more prevalent than they were now. "I have to think of the lives of all the people that I'm working to save. If this gets out about what happened, not only is it political suicide for my son, my project, but also the lives we planned to save..." He shook his head and lowered it in shame, unable to continue.

"Jesus Christ. They want you to sweep this under the rug. Because of a politician?" Tai's voice trembled as he spoke. "Girlie, that is *not* okay. Justice must be served—" he started, but I cut him off.

"Tai, there's more at stake than you know. And I'll explain it to you. Later. When we're alone, I promise." My gaze caught his, and I silently begged him to listen and cool his jets. His mouth tightened and an eyebrow rose, but he stayed silent and held my hand a little tighter. Then on a deep inhalation and a slow exhalation, I said the words I would never in a million years picture me saying.

I was giving a prospective rapist a get-out-of-jail-free card. It took everything I had in me to think of all the men, women, and children in countries all over the world who would never have the modern medicine that we had in the States. Without the help from Warren's project, they would never receive that help. He'd lose every single investor, especially Mr. Benoit, if the truth was made public. On the other end of the spectrum, the press wouldn't have to dig too deep to find out who hired me and why. It would negatively affect more lives than just the Shipleys or my own, but also the lives of Aunt Millie, Wes, Alec, Tony, Hector, Mason, the D'Amicos who'd hired me last month for the swimsuit campaign, Tai, and anyone else related to them.

Mind made up, I laid it out for Warren in the only way I could find some semblance of sanity and still look myself in the mirror tomorrow. "Warren, I won't say anything, and I won't press charges, but I do have some demands."

Warren held my other hand and nodded. Kathleen continued to cry.

Slowly, I dished out the things I felt were fair. "He will go into rehab for his drinking. I don't care if it's a private, no-name place and he takes a leave of absence due to a family emergency. Make some shit up. Whatever it is, he needs help. He'll also need anger-management sessions with a qualified professional."

"Done," he answered without hesitation.

"And I want a handwritten letter saying that he will get that help, signed by him, with the original given to me. The letter will state he will do these things or I will take this to the press, regardless of whether any statute of limitation has passed. I will share that letter with the press, detailing his commitment to get help. Do you understand?"

Warren tipped his head and kissed the top of my hand.

"Mia...I'm sorry. Sweet girl, I'm so sorry. Thank you, thank you for being kind."

"One last thing... The money."

"Anything you want, it's yours. Millions, whatever."

I choked on that. He was willing to give me millions of dollars to keep his son out of trouble and save his project. Then again, when a person had the kind of money Warren Shipley had, millions were probably a drop in the bucket. It made me sick to think he'd try to buy me off, but I knew his heart. His only goal was to help me, ease the pain in any way he could. Money was the normal way for someone who was raised with a silver spoon in his mouth.

"Not a dime. I will not take a cent. There will be no settlement or hush money exchanged. I'm not a whore. I'm a woman he defiled. He should be going to jail for what he did to me, Warren, but because of you and what you're trying to do to help the world, the less fortunate, I'm backing down. I'm going against everything I believe in to make sure that nothing happens to stop this program moving forward. Don't make me regret it."

A couple of tears rolled down his face, and he rubbed them away hastily. I patted his cheek, and his eyes said he understood. That he knew exactly where I was coming from, what I was sacrificing, and that he'd respect the severity of it. He moved to take his leave. Kathleen folded me in her arms in that motherly way I adored and cried all over my shirt while clutching me tightly. My back burned at the raw spots. Stoically, like a warrior fresh from battle, I gritted my teeth and hugged her through the pain. She needed it as much as I did.

★ ★ ★ ★

For the few days after my release, I stayed in New York being pampered by Mason, Tai, Rachel, and Kathleen. Warren kept his distance, though he sent me flowers twice a day. It took all of those days for Mason and Tai to get over their anger. Interestingly enough, the two of them hit it off famously, joking like old buddies, ribbing one another about sports teams and the differences between the mainland and the islands.

Eventually, I talked Tai into going back home to his family and his girlfriend. Amy was incredibly supportive, sending me texts and funny messages to lift my spirits. She was a kind soul, and I loved that Tai had her waiting at home. On the last day with Tai, we sat on the balcony of the Four Seasons, enjoying the view.

"Pretty amazing, huh?" I gestured with my foot to the view of the New York skyline.

Tai shrugged. "I prefer the expansive ocean and palm trees to massive structures and lights, but I can appreciate the appeal for some. Too busy, too crazy, too much of everything for me."

I took in what he said. Too much of everything. Boy, was he right about that.

I adjusted my foot, crossing one ankle over the other. Tai's gaze zeroed in on my completely healed tattoo. He smiled so wide this time, and it wasn't his normal sexy grin. It was a full-blown, all-teeth-and-gums smile. His giant hand covered my ankle and pulled it into his lap. I swiveled on my chair so he could inspect it.

"Trust the journey, eh?" His eyes went from studying the words to mine.

AUDREY CARLAN

"Yep."

His finger traced the lettering and then the dandelion and each petal with the small letter inscribed. His thumb stopped over the small T in one of the petals. The heat from that one digit burned into my skin and traveled up my leg to land in the place that was very familiar with Tai. As a matter of fact, I'm pretty sure my pussy has written "Ode to Tai" poems and love letters, wishing he'd come back since I'd left him. Tai, on the other hand, did not have that same passion in his gaze he'd once had. I figured that look was now owned by a pixie of a blonde waiting for him back in Hawaii.

"What do these letters mean?" he asked.

I thought about playing it cool and saying *what letters*, but Tai had never lied or given me anything but the truth, and I'd treat him with the same respect.

Bringing my foot up closer, I pointed at each letter. "These correspond to a man who affected my life in a manner I want to remember. It reminds me that each experience was meant to be, and that for a time, I felt truly loved." Tears pricked at my eyes, but I sucked in a breath, held them back, and swallowed noisily.

Tai traced the single T. "For me?"

Unable to speak, the moment filling me with such emotion, I simply nodded.

Tai leaned down and kissed the letter. "I like that, girlie. A piece of me is with you always."

With that, I leaned to my left and kissed the single tattoo on the ball of his right shoulder, the one that meant friendship in Samoan. The one he got to represent me and our time together. He patted my head as I leaned against him. "You have to go home," I reminded him.

"Much is there for me," he said soundly.

"I know. I love you, Tai. Thank you for coming."

"Never doubt that you're loved, girlie. Family is what you make it, and I'll always be there for you."

Tai left that night. Took the first flight he could back to Oahu. With it, he took another piece of my heart and solidified the belief that he really would be there if I needed him.

★ ★ ★ ★

I spent the next few days in Boston with Mason and Rachel. Mason acted like I'd just survived the plague and needed to be doted on as if I was completely broken. I wasn't, but I totally took advantage anyway. Being with Mason and seeing his brothers and baseball buds again was great. And once again, it proved the reach of these men in my life. I had people. Many people I could count on in a situation. Ones who would lift me up, protect me, fight for me and, most of all, love me.

As I packed my bag, I found my stationery and notepad. I wasn't with Warren and Kathleen but decided they deserved something to commemorate our time. I found an envelope in the desk drawer and scrawled the address to the McMansion on the front. I didn't really have a return address because I wasn't at the studio apartment in California so I simply wrote Mia Saunders on the back fold.

Warren & Kathleen,

I'm sorry for how things ended. I know that you'd never wish what happened to me onto anyone, and I do not blame you. Thank you for sending me the details about Aaron's rehabilitation. Hearing he's getting help makes what happened somehow a bit easier to deal with. My fondest wish is that he finds the peace he needs.

Christine Benoit told me that the first shipment of goods to the UK was planned for next month. Thrilled does not begin to express my happiness over hearing the news. Knowing that so many deserving people are going to get the help they need to live long and happy lives makes it all worth it.

I want you both to know that the time I shared with the two of you was truly lovely. Seeing your relationship progress into something long-lasting is inspiring.

Thank you for letting me be a part of your life.

~ Mia

I folded up the letter and put it in the envelope and asked Rachel to mail it for me. This time I didn't escape while they were sleeping and allowed the two of them to take me to the airport. It was the least I could do after they'd come to my rescue and taken care of me the past week and a half.

We said our good-byes and promised to keep in touch as usual. So far, it had been very easy to keep in touch with the new friends I'd made. Maybe because I didn't have any other friends besides Maddy and Ginelle back home.

When I pushed the airplane seat back, I thought about the past month. From matchmaking, to sexting and wicked hot dreams, to covert business deals, and helping third-world countries, Canadian nymphos, and being attacked, it had been one helluva month. Through it all, I learned three things that wouldn't stop burning through my mind.

First, Wes was my goddamned kryptonite, and I needed to be careful to protect myself if I was going to make it through another six months. Second, never judge a book by its cover, even when they come in drop-dead-sexy suits with political stature and unlimited assets. And third, friends are the family you choose, and I had the best friends and family on the planet.

Yep, life was strange, but I was living it to the fullest. Taking each day as it came and experiencing as much as possible. Accepting the good, the bad, and even the ugly in stride because it was all part of the process. Just like my tattoo said, I had to *trust the journey.*

And my journey was taking me to a mocha-skinned hip-hop artist named Anton Santiago to make a music video. They say white men can't jump. Well, this white chick can't dance. July should prove interesting.

THE END

EXCERPT FROM CALENDAR GIRL: JULY
CHAPTER ONE

Blond. Blue-eyed. Tall. Goddess. Jesus H. Christ. The universe was laughing at me as I stood stock-still and looked the modelesque woman up and down. She looked like she could be Rachel's ungodly perfect sister, and I thought Rachel was stunning. Nope. Totally wrong.

The woman stood next to a shiny black Porsche Boxster, jittering around as if incredibly anxious. Her fingers tapped a solid beat against the sign she held up with my name on it. A not-so-subtle shift from one sky-high stiletto to the other only added to the fierceness rolling off her in waves. Then again, that could've been the Miami heat. Good Lord, it was sweltering, yet this woman was perfectly put together, as if she'd walked right out of a rock video. Skinny jeans so tight I could see the nice curve of her booty. Her tank top had me drooling, complete with a monogram across a set of large tits that said *Hug Me and Die*. There were at least ten necklaces of varying beads, lengths, and sizes wrapped around the smooth column of her neck. She had kick-ass rock-star hair pulled back into a complex system of twists and loose pieces that looked rocker-chic.

After I inspected her for what felt like minutes, she fixed her steel-blue gaze on me. A puff of air left her lungs as she tossed the cardboard in the car window and sauntered over. She scanned me from my flowing black locks, over my sundress, and to the simple flats I wore on two big feet. "This will never do." She shook her head with exasperation. "Come on, time is money," came the flippant retort over her shoulder. The trunk popped open, and I tossed my suitcase in.

"I'm Mia, by the way." I held out my hand as she slid on a pair of ultra-cool aviators, turned her head, and looked at me over the top of them.

"I know who you are. I'm the one that chose you." Her tone held a twinge of distaste as she started the car and hit the gas, not even waiting for me to get the seatbelt fastened. My body jolted forward, and I braced on the smooth leather dash.

"Did I do something to piss you off?" I readjusted the belt and watched her profile.

Her breath came out in a long, slow exhale before she shook her head. "No," she groaned. "I'm sorry. Anton pissed me off. I was in the middle of something big when he told me to come get you because *he* needed our driver so *he* could fuck a couple groupies in the back of the Escalade."

I cringed. Great, sounded like my new boss for the month was a slimy douche. *Not another one.* "That sucks."

She took a quick right turn onto the freeway. "Can we start over?" Her voice now held sincerity and apology. "I'm Heather Renee, by the way, personal assistant to Anton Santiago. Hottest hip-hop artist in the nation."

"Is that right?" Wow. I hadn't realized he was that big-time. I didn't usually listen to much hip-hop. More of an alternative and rock chick.

Heather nodded. "Yep, every album he's done has gone platinum. He's the "It" boy in Hip Hop, and good grief does he know it." She grinned. "Anton wants to meet you right away, but you can't wear that." Her gaze moved down to the plain green sundress I wore. It highlighted my eyes and made my hair look phenomenal. Plus, it was comfortable to travel in.

"Why not?" I tugged at the hem of the dress, suddenly feeling self-conscious.

"Anton is expecting a bombshell model with curves that don't quit." Once more her eyes ran over my outfit. "You've got the curves going for you, but that dress is too Sandra Bullock girl next door. You'll need to wear one of the outfits I bought for you. At the house, you've got a closet full of clothes waiting. Wear them. He'll expect you to look like eye candy at all times."

Scowling, I focused my attention outside as the Porsche cruised Ocean Drive. The art deco buildings overlooking the Atlantic slid by over an enormous stretch of land.

"So there's water on both sides?" I noticed when we had passed over one of the main bridges.

Heather made a hand gesture. "Biscayne Bay Lagoon and the Atlantic sit on both sides of the strip. As you can see"—she pointed up and over to sets of tall buildings—"most of these are hotels, like the Colony Hotel and other iconic landmarks. Then you have the folks"—her eyebrows waggled—"that can afford to live here, like Anton."

Scanning each building as the Porsche jetted down the road, the wind blowing through the windows ruffling my hair, I noted myriad rich colors in palettes I didn't often see. In Vegas, everything seemed brown or terracotta-colored. In LA, you had everything from brilliant white to a variety of muted tones that fit with the California vibe. Here though, colors seemed to burst out in pale sunny oranges, blues, and pinks mixed with white.

"See all these places?" She pointed out the businesses such as the Colony Hotel and Boulevard Hotel with a whisk of her hand into the flowing wind. I nodded and stretched over her form to see better. "They all light up in neon colors at night.

Kind of like in Vegas."

Vegas. I was sure my eyes widened as a steady thud picked up in my chest. A pang of need suddenly coiled around my heart. I needed to call Maddy and Ginelle. Man, Gin would be so pissed when I told her what happened in Washington, DC. Maybe I could get away with never bringing it up? That idea certainly had some serious merit. "That's so cool. I'm originally from Vegas, so it will be nice to see the buildings lit up." I sat back in my seat and enjoyed the breeze, allowing the tension I'd picked up from DC and Boston, when I had to leave Rachel and Mason behind, to dissipate.

Fumbling, I pulled out my phone and turned it on. Several pings rang out. I scanned them, a message from Rachel telling me to text when I'd arrived. A message from Tai asking if the new client was a gentleman or if he needed to get on a plane again. And a text from Ginelle. *Oh, snap.* This was not good.

My stomach felt like a pit the size of the Grand Canyon, a never-ending cavern of dread filling the wide open space.

To: Mia Saunders
From: Skank-a-lot-a-Puss
You were attacked? In the hospital? Why the fuck did I have to hear about it in a text from Tai's brother! If you aren't already dead I'm so going to kill you!

Sucking in a breath between my teeth I typed out a reply.

To: Skank-a-lot-a-Puss
From: Mia Saunders
Just a little mishap. No big deal. Totally fine. Don't worry about me. I'll call you later when I get settled with the Latin

Lov-ah.

To: Mia Saunders
From: Skank-a-lot-a-Puss
Latin Lov-ah? No shit? He's like the biggest thing in hip hop and habanero hot!

To: Skank-a-lot-a-Puss
From: Mia Saunders
I heard he's douchey.

To: Mia Saunders
From: Skank-a-lot-a-Puss
That man can douche me any time...preferably with his tongue!

To: Skank-a-lot-a-Puss
From: Mia Saunders
You're twisted!

To: Mia Saunders
From: Skank-a-lot-a-Puss
I'd like to be the rice and beans on the side of his entre. The churro to end his meal. The flaming flan he blows on and licks clean.

To: Skank-a-lot-a-Puss
From: Mia Saunders
Stop! Crazy whore. Jeez. You make me look like a fucking saint.

To: Mia Saunders
From: Skank-a-lot-a-Puss
At least I know if I'm going to hell you'll be right there giving me a lift!

I laughed out loud as Heather said, "Work?" while gesturing toward my phone. I hit a button and put it on silent before sliding it into my purse.

"Sorry. Best friend. Checking in." I sighed and flicked my hair over one shoulder. The heat was getting to me. Leaning over, I adjusted the air vent to blast me with icy cold goodness. Ah, better. Obviously Heather wasn't worried about wasting the cool air by also having the windows down.

"You close?" Her lips pursed together as she turned into an underground parking garage.

My brows furrowed. What part of "best friend" had she not heard? "Yep. Close as you can get. Known one another forever."

She huffed and slammed the car into park. "You're lucky. I don't have any friends." Her words jolted through me like an electric shock.

"What do you mean? Everyone has friends."

Heather shook her head. "Not me. Too much work to do to cultivate relationships. Anton has to be the best. Even if I'm just his PA, I need to rock the house. Besides, my education is in business management. One day maybe I'll be making the decisions for an artist. If I want my dreams to come true, I have to work hard."

"Guess so." I shrugged and followed her as she walked briskly toward an elevator, passing a line of seriously impressive luxury cars.

"Damn," I whispered under my breath, taking in the Mercedes, Range Rover, Escalade, BMW, Bentley, Ferrari, and several other European cars I didn't get to check out. What I did see—the items that stopped me in my tracks, had me glued to the concrete—were the six hottest sex on wheels I'd ever seen.

BMW HP2 Sport—white with blue rims and an 1170

engine. I might have wet myself at that point. Then there was an MV Agusta F4 1000, the only bike in the world to have a radial valved engine. I twisted around, let go of the handle on my suitcase, and traced the third bike's sexy as fuck seat. The Icon Sheene all black with shiny chrome. I caressed it the way a lover would, with one finger tip, tracing its rounded curves and bold edge design. This bike cost over a hundred and fifty thousand dollars! *Fuck me. No, really, I need to fuck on this bike.*

Air, I needed air! I gasped and crouched down, still not capable of taking my eyes off the pretty. *Sweet baby, come to Mama.* I could happily live in this garage, just staring at the bikes of my dreams.

"Um, hello? Earth to Mia? What the hell are you doing?"

Her voice came through, but I didn't answer. It was like a pesky mosquito that no matter how many times you swatted it away it kept coming back.

I slowly stood, sucked in a replenishing breath, and scanned down the line once more. An orange-and-black sick tricked out KTM Super Duke was hanging out at the back of the line. Probably the most affordable of the lot, definitely on my list of amazing bikes I might one day be able to afford. "Whose bikes are these?" I asked, my voice having dropped an octave, in awe of the pure hot sex on two wheels.

"Anton's. This is his building. His music studio is here, dance club, gym, and of course, the penthouse is his home. The rest of his team each have an apartment in the building as well. You've even got your own loft apartment we use for visiting celebrities or folks who are working on one of his albums.

"Does he ride the bikes?"

She grinned. "Bike enthusiast, huh?"

"You could say that." I had to force the words out, even

though I hadn't yet ripped my gaze from the line of man-made beauty.

"Maybe he'll take you for a ride."

That got my attention. "A ride."

She nodded, her smile so pretty it could be on advertisements selling products across the globe.

"Fuck that. I don't ride bitch, honey. I drive."

Continue reading Mia's journey in:

July: Calendar Girl
(Available Now in eBook)

or

Calendar Girl: Volume Three

ALSO BY AUDREY CARLAN

The Calendar Girl Series

January (Book 1)	July (Book 7)
February (Book 2)	August (Book 8)
March (Book 3)	September (Book 9)
April (Book 4)	October (Book 10)
May (Book 5)	November (Book 11)
June (Book 6)	December (Book 12)

The Falling Series

Angel Falling
London Falling
Justice Falling

The Trinity Trilogy

Body (Book 1)
Mind (Book 2)
Soul (Book 3)

Lotus House Series

Resisting Roots (Book 1)
Sacred Serenity (Book 2)

ACKNOWLEDGEMENTS

To my editor **Ekatarina Sayanova** with **Red Quill Editing, LLC**, I am beyond happy that I found you. It's hard to find an editor that just suits you. You suit me. (www.redquillediting.net)

To my personal assistant **Heather White**, can you believe we're at the point where print copies are being made of each bundle? Must be all those wicked awesome teasers, and extra hard pimping you were doing. Love you girlie.

To **Sarah Saunders**, for always being there for me. I love your face.

To **Jeananna Goodall** - I love the way you experience my stories. The emails, texts, and feedback I get from you always make my day.

To **Ginelle Blanch** - You are such a goddess at finding my quirky errors. Thank you for being you. Because you're pretty damn great!

To **Anita Shofner** - You will rid the world of bad tenses and comma errors one book at a time. For this, I have no doubt! You Anita have a gift. Thank you for sharing it with me and making my work just that much better!

To **Christine Benoit** - I am beyond thrilled that I have an expert to go to for my French. Thank you for being a vital resource in making sure my Alec Dubois's language comes out as beautiful as I intend it to. Thank you.

To the **Audrey's Angels**, together we change the world.

One book at a time. BESOS-4-LIFE lovely ladies.

To all the **Audrey Carlan Wicked Hot Readers**...you make me smile every day. Thank you for your support.

And last, but most definitely not least, my publisher **Waterhouse Press**. You're the *extra* in extraordinary. I couldn't be happier you found me and gave me a home to call my very own. Mad love.

ABOUT AUDREY CARLAN

Audrey Carlan is a #1 New York Times, USA Today, and Wall Street Journal bestselling author. She writes wicked hot love stories that are designed to give the reader a romantic experience that's sexy, sweet, and so hot your ereader might melt. Some of her works include the wildly successful Calendar Girl Serial, Falling Series, and the Trinity Trilogy.

She lives in the California Valley where she enjoys her two children and the love of her life. When she's not writing, you can find her teaching yoga, sipping wine with her "soul sisters" or with her nose stuck in a wicked hot romance novel.

Any and all feedback is greatly appreciated and feeds the soul. You can contact Audrey below:

E-mail: carlan.audrey@gmail.com
Facebook: facebook.com/AudreyCarlan
Website: www.audreycarlan.com